SUNRISE

"COLONEL O'NEILL," Teal'c said, half turned back the way they'd come. "Men are approaching. If we wish to meet with Rhionna Channon we must evade them. I do not believe Pastor Channon would permit us to talk with his daughter."

"He's right," Sam said. "I got the distinct impression that she's *persona non grata* among the Elect — especially with that guy, Camus."

"Which is probably a good sign," Daniel chimed in, hands still deep in his pockets. "Maybe she really does have some useful information."

"I think it's worth a shot," Sam agreed. She glanced over at O'Neill. "Sir?"

He was studying the map, memorizing it, then scrunched up the paper in his fist. "Okay, we meet with her and see what she has to say. But that's all. We are not — repeat, *not* — gonna get dragged into another mercy mission."

STARGÅTE
SG·1.

SUNRISE

J. FRANCES CRANE

FANDEMONIUM BOOKS

An original publication of Fandemonium Ltd, produced under license from MGM Consumer Products.

Fandemonium Books, PO Box 795A, Surbiton, Surrey KT5 8YB, United Kingdom

Visit our website: www.stargatenovels.com

STARGÅTE

SG·1

METRO-GOLDWYN-MAYER Presents
RICHARD DEAN ANDERSON
in
STARGATE SG-1™
MICHAEL SHANKS AMANDA TAPPING CHRISTOPHER JUDGE
DON S. DAVIS
Executive Producers BRAD WRIGHT   MICHAEL GREENBURG
RICHARD DEAN ANDERSON
Developed for Television by BRAD WRIGHT & JONATHAN GLASSNER

WWW.MGM.COM

ISBN: 978-1-905586-51-6   Printed in the USA

For Rona, Bill, and Susan.
LH

For Jessica and Ben, with love.
SM

Author's note: *Sunrise* is set in season four of STARGATE SG-1, soon after the episode 'Beneath the Surface'.

CHAPTER ONE

Dr Maol Caluim's Journal
Acarsaid Dorch Research Outpost
Year Three
Entry #276WB
Our moods are lighter today. Finally, we have a break-
through! Yesterday's simulation was a success, two-way com-
munication was established and we were able to contact the
remote device via its embedded server. Despite the doubts of
so many, we believe we have created a patch that will allow
us to deploy the shield as originally designed — with luck, we
will be in time. Now, all that remains is to test the fix on the
live system, which means we must return to Ierna. If we do
not, all our work will be for naught. The work of a generation
will be for naught.

We must persuade the Elect to listen to us, in that there is
no choice. Lann tells me that an ice storm has raged here all
week, but so caught up was I in the testing that I hadn't even
noticed. He predicts that it will pass overnight and in the
morning we can attempt, once more, to communicate with
the new authorities in the shelter. All our hopes rest on their
acquiescence.

I have not spoken with the others about our return home.
Though none of us utter the words, we all know that we have
been exiled here and that to return will not be a simple ven-
ture. The memories of our leaving are fresh, even three years
on. How can we forget the rage of the people and the tears on
our children's faces? But surely, when we show the Elect what
we have achieved, they will listen to us. They must listen. To
turn from us now would be madness.

Even the wildest zealot must realize that the so called Sciath Dé is our last hope. Without it, our homes — all of Ierna — will perish. Surely they pray for our success as well as for their own deliverance? I cannot conceive that they would embrace this disaster when we are so close to salvation.

I hope that in my entry tomorrow I can speak of our triumph. I hope the self appointed 'Pastor' will listen to reason. I hope we are not already too late.

One way or another, the end draws near.

~~~

Dr Maol Caluim's Journal
Acarsaid Dorch Research Outpost
Year Three
Entry #277WB
Today Lann Dyric opened the Sungate and returned to Ierna. He carried word of our success, proof that we can deploy Sciath Dé and defend our world from the wrath of their Lord. With him he carries the hopes of our world. Though I do not worship their god, I find myself casting my prayers into the stars this night as we wait for Lann to return with word of our fate. Of our world's fate.

~~~

Dr Maol Caluim's Journal
Acarsaid Dorch Research Outpost
Year Three
Entry #278WB
It has been five days and we have received no word from Lann. We cannot decide if this is good news or bad. We can do nothing but wait.

~~~

Dr Maol Caluim's Journal
Acarsaid Dorch Research Outpost
Year Three
Entry #279WB
No entry found.

"There were no more entries after that, General." Dr. Daniel Jackson closed his note book and sat back in his chair, the laptop in the center of the briefing room table showing screeds of text in a language incomprehensible to General George Hammond. He squinted at the jittery data and then skimmed through the translation in front of him.

"You said it was some sort of beta site you found. Perhaps they left to return to their home planet?" Around the briefing room table, SG-1 cast glances at each other, communicating volumes in an unspoken language in which, George knew, he would never be fluent. But four years in this command had taught him a few things, one of them being the ability to read the mood of each of his teams when they returned from a mission. Judging from the apprehension on the faces of the SGC's flagship team, Hammond was certain that whatever they had discovered on P4X-66Q, it was bigger than a few garbled journal entries. "Colonel O'Neill?"

"They didn't leave, sir."

"So what happened?"

Daniel cleared his throat. "Well, first things first, General. The settlement we found wasn't just a beta site. It appeared to be a research outpost of some sort. The language of the text looks like a progression from Irish-Gaelic, but the journal entries were..." He frowned and glanced around at the team. "They were very old, sir. Perhaps two hundred years. And they weren't exactly intact."

"But you managed to translate them?"

"For the most part. The writer, Dr Maol Caluim, talks about their home planet of Ierna — she even gives a gate address — and describes some sort of catastrophe unfolding there. It appears they were working on a way to prevent it from happening."

"The shield."

"Yes, sir. She refers to the project as *Sciath Dé* — God's shield... Or, perhaps, Shield of the Gods, or Shield *from* the Gods."

The phrase hung there, taking on a meaning that would have seemed absurd to George Hammond just four short years ago. The Gods. Only one race he knew was arrogant enough to assume such a moniker.

For the first time throughout the debriefing, Teal'c spoke, voicing Hammond's own thoughts. "General Hammond, it appears these scientists were working on a way to defend themselves against the Goa'uld."

"So what is this shield? Some sort of armor?" He had asked the question of Jackson, but Major Samantha Carter answered instead.

"No, sir. It may be on a slightly bigger scale than that."

"How much bigger, Major?"

"Well, sir, from what I can calculate from Dr Caluim's numbers..." She paused and shook her head with an incredulous smile. "Sir, I think it was planetary."

It took a moment for her words to sink in. "A planetary shield." The notion was astounding; a shield that could protect an entire planet, that could fend off an attack by the System Lords. Hammond sat forward in his chair, considering the enormous implications of such a defense, but the faces before him were less enthusiastic than he'd have anticipated, given the nature of their discovery. "Were they unsuccessful?"

"We're not exactly sure," replied Jackson with a frown.

"Well, Carter did find an energy signature that she got excited about," said O'Neill. He turned to his second in command. "Show the general what Santa left for you, Carter." The major clicked open the small metal case that sat on the table before her. From within, she pulled a flat black box with wires trailing from one end.

"Now I know what you're thinking, sir," continued O'Neill, casting a meaningful glare at his team. "You're thinking 'It's a Playstation.' And that's ok, because that's exactly what it looks like."

"Maybe it does, Colonel, but I wouldn't know a Playstation from a Game Box." He paused for a beat. "So how about you tell me what it *is*."

"Gameboy, sir. Or Xbox."

"Colonel, you're trying my patience."

"Only trying?" O'Neill cleared his throat. "Carter thinks it might be the reason behind all this hoo-ha."

"This little thing is their planetary shield?" Hammond couldn't keep the skepticism from his voice.

"Not exactly," said Carter. "According to the journal, the shield had failed to deploy properly... And I think this could be the key to making it work."

Still, Hammond could see doubt in their eyes. "People, the way I see it, you've just discovered a potential way to protect not only Earth from a Goa'uld attack, but every planet in the Protected Planets Treaty. Why aren't you demanding to go search for this thing?"

"Good question," Jackson said, throwing a pointed look at O'Neill over the rims of his glasses. Hammond got the distinct feeling they'd already had this discussion.

O'Neill tapped his pen irritably against the desk. "Show him, Daniel."

Picking up his camcorder, Daniel flipped open the viewscreen. "That box wasn't the only thing we found on the planet, General. Take a look." He hit play and handed the camera to Hammond.

A grainy image appeared on the tiny screen, the camera sweeping across a snowy landscape bitten through by harsh black rocks. In the near distance squatted a handful of prefabricated aluminum cabins. The scene changed, cutting to what Hammond assumed was the interior of one of those cabins. The image was dark, but he could make out Major Carter kneeling behind what looked like a tall computer stack, one of many that lined the walls of the long room. In the center of the room there was a round table, upon which sat monitors and keyboards.

"You sure you can get the power back up, Carter?" Colonel O'Neill's voice came from somewhere off-screen. "This place is trashed."

"Almost there, sir." In the next moment the stacks behind which Carter was working came to life, and the overhead lights flickered on, illuminating an alarming sight. The entire place had been destroyed. Monitors smashed, torn papers strewn everywhere. The camera zoomed in on one of the stacks which sparked and fizzed, a lethargic protest at the sudden restoration of power; it was clear that this destruction had been no accident.

The scene changed again, a different room, another cabin, this time with a bed and lockers lining the walls. The camera panned round, taking in a nightstand with a book and a pair of spectacles sitting on top, overalls hanging on hooks on the wall, yellow, ragged and moldering. "Looks like no one's been home for a while," said Daniel.

"Yeah." O'Neill's voice again. "But where'd they all go? And why does this place feel like a damned cemetery?" The colonel walked into view, facing the camera. "Ok, kids. This place is giving me the creeps — six hours and we're outta here."

Another cut, and this time they were outside, the sun's harsh reflection turning the snow vibrant white, the image bouncing with the rhythm of Daniel's footsteps. Up ahead stood O'Neill, staring down into a deep gouge in the landscape. "Daniel, get over here."

And then came the grimmest sight of all. A human skeleton lay half buried in snow, its skull punctured with two round holes; George Hammond knew bullet wounds when he saw them.

"Oh my God." Major Carter's voice echoed his own shock.

Hands appeared once more, Daniel's and Teal'c's, clearing away the snow that covered the rest of the skeleton. The sunlight glinted on a small object wedged into the packed snow and Daniel pulled it free, a flat metal disc with a holographic image of a sharp eyed woman of middle years. Next to the picture was printed a name. Dr M Caluim.

Then the camera drew back as Daniel stood, taking in a sickening scene. Strewn around him lay bones and skulls, the detritus of a massacre.

O'Neill spoke again, his voice leaden. "I guess now we know where everyone went." The viewscreen cut to black.

"It was a grave, sir," said Daniel from the other end of the table. "A mass grave."

"Not even a grave," O'Neill chipped in. "These folks haven't been buried; they've just been left to rot."

Daniel's mouth tightened. "And we found ID tags on all of the human remains."

Hammond frowned and was silent a moment, trying to comprehend what he had just witnessed. "Do we have any idea why this happened?"

O'Neill shrugged. "The only thing we know for certain is that it wasn't the Goa'uld. Those wounds were the result of good, old-fashioned bullets." His gaze dropped to the black box at the center of the table. "But I'd bet a few bucks that it's got something to do with that. And not because it plays PGA Tour."

"Well, it's a mystery easily solved. We have a gate address, don't we?"

"All due respect, General," O'Neill said, "I think we're looking at a dead end. Literally. Whatever this shield was, whatever it was meant to do, it was important enough to kill over. Going after it is too big of a risk."

"Too big of a risk?" Hammond stared at him, surprise mingling with a queasy unease. This was not the Jack O'Neill he knew; this was someone else talking.

"Are you serious, Jack?" Jackson jumped in before Hammond could continue. "This shield could protect Earth from a Goa'uld attack!"

"*Could*, Daniel. But probably won't." O'Neill leaned back in his seat, all but putting his boots up on the table. If it was designed to convey nonchalance, it failed. He looked like a coiled spring. "We've been through this," he said, flicking his fingers toward the device with a dismissive gesture. "And you said it yourself; this thing is two hundred years old. Whatever it was designed to fix is long gone."

"You don't know that."

"Two hundred years, Daniel! Call it an educated guess."

"I have never heard of this *Sciath Dé*, nor any device known as a 'Shield of the Gods'," Teal'c volunteered, eyeing both O'Neill and Daniel. "However, if such a technology were to exist, it would be worth risking much to recover."

Fingertips drumming on the desk, O'Neill scowled. Anxious, very anxious.

Hammond glanced at Major Carter who was carefully keeping her gaze fixed on the alien device and looking at none of her team mates. That in itself was unusual. "Major," he said, "what's your opinion?"

She started, almost as if she'd been daydreaming. Impossible, of course. Or would have been, if SG-1 hadn't just returned to duty after having their minds altered by the so-called memory-stamp on P3R-118. Dr. Fraiser had been less than thrilled when she'd passed them fit for duty, and her confidential report was still sitting on his desk with its stark advice fresh in his mind:

It is the recommendation of the CMO that, once deployed to the field, all members of SG-1 be kept under close psychological observation for an initial period of ninety days, in order to ensure early identification of potential fractures in ego integrity resulting from the memory stamp.

"Sorry, sir," Carter said. "I was… Um, I think I agree with

the colonel."

"Oh, of course," Daniel snapped. "Of course you agree with the colonel."

She stared at him. "What does that mean?"

He shook his head, brow furrowed. "Nothing. Sorry. I wasn't — " Then, taking a breath, Daniel leaned forward. "General, think about it. *Sciath Dé* — 'Shield of the Gods'. If it means what we think it means…"

"*If*," O'Neill cut in. "You can't even get the name straight. Shield *of* the Gods, or Shield *from* the Gods? Big difference. For all we know it's some snakehead device designed to screw with anyone who touches it."

"Daniel," Carter said, "whatever it is, this device is pretty old. It may never have worked. In fact, the way it was just left on the planet implies that neither it nor the shield were ever even deployed."

"Does it?" Daniel shuffled the papers in front of him, stabbing his fingers at a line of text. "Or does it imply that whoever killed these people didn't *want* the shield to work?"

"Who cares?" O'Neill flung up his arms, letting his chair drop forward with a thump. "If it didn't work then, whoever they were, they all died two hundred years ago! So either way, putting our asses on the line to chase this thing down is a colossal waste of time."

"Okay, first, that is a huge assumption. Second, if their planet is facing a catastrophe then maybe we can — "

"Oh, here we go…"

" — maybe we can help them."

O'Neill looked at him, flat and angry. "Why?"

"Why…?" Daniel blinked. "Because we can?"

"No. We can't. We can't save every goddamn people we stumble across, Daniel!"

"Why not?"

"Because…" He ran out of words. "Damn it, Daniel, you know why not."

The room sank into a chilly silence. George eyed them both, took in their taut, angry faces, and with a troubled sensation realized that he didn't recognize either man. "I don't know what I'm seeing here, SG-1," he said, "but I sure as hell don't want to see it again in my briefing room."

At least Dr. Jackson had the good grace to look sheepish. "Sorry, General."

But O'Neill remained as bullish as ever. "You're not seriously going to send us after a bunch of two hundred year old refugees from who the hell knows what kind of disaster?"

"No." Hammond rested his hands on the table, caught the glint of triumph in the colonel's eyes and promptly squashed it. "But I agree with Dr. Jackson that the opportunity presented by this shield is worth investigation, despite the passage of years. Major Carter has successfully restored Ancient technology that is tens of thousands of years old, Colonel, and I have every faith that she will be able to fix this 'Shield of the Gods' should you discover the device."

O'Neill looked like he might respond, but Hammond quashed his rebellion with a look not even Jack O'Neill could defy. "Yes, sir."

"General," Carter said, looking somewhat alarmed, "you understand that there's no guarantee that I'll be able to — "

"We'll cross that bridge when we come to it," he said, offering a small smile. He hadn't intended to place such a weight of expectation on her shoulders, but he didn't doubt she could handle it. At least, he wouldn't have doubted it before she came back unsure of her own name... Dismissing thoughts of Fraiser's report, he rose to his feet. "SG-1, the mission's a go. We'll send a MALP through to Ierna in three hours."

The team stood, still tense and ill at ease. "Yes, sir."

As Daniel gathered his papers and closed down his laptop, Carter headed for the door with Teal'c close behind. Across the table, Hammond met Jack's eye. "A word, Colonel," he said, nodding toward his office.

With a glance at Daniel, O'Neill preceded Hammond
into the office and stood in front of the desk while the general closed the door. Taking a seat, Hammond waited until
Daniel had left the briefing room before he said, "What the
hell was that, Colonel?"

"Sir?"

"Don't play the fool with me, Jack. What the hell's going
on between you and Dr. Jackson?"

O'Neill's gaze slid sideways, evasive. "Nothing, just a dis-
agreement."

On the desk Fraiser's report sat waiting, silent as a time
bomb. Hammond placed his hand on the manila folder.
"Take a seat, Jack."

He did so, perching uncomfortably in the edge of the chair.
"Look, sir, I'm sorry. It won't happen again."

"No," Hammond agreed, "it won't." He let out a breath and
leaned back. "Off the record, Jack, your first mission since
P3R-118... What's your assessment?"

His face turned blank, unreadable. "Fine, sir."

"Fine?"

"What d'you want me to say? There were no problems, it
went fine."

"It didn't look fine just now."

"Come on, that's just Daniel being Daniel. We always go
to the mattresses over stuff like this." He hesitated. "Don't
we?"

"Dr. Fraiser thinks — "

"I know what Fraiser thinks."

Hammond laced his fingers over his belly. "Need I remind
you that, if she had her way, you'd all be benched and talking to Dr. McKenzie?"

"No, sir. And I appreciate what you did about that." He
scrubbed a hand through his hair. "Look — okay, I admit the
whole memory stamp thing was... disconcerting. We were all
a little freaked out for a while, but that was weeks ago."

A whole three weeks ago, to be precise. "And now?"

"And now we're fine."

"Major Carter seemed distracted in the briefing."

"She's fine."

"You know that?"

He took a breath, considered, then leaned forward with his arms braced on his knees and his face serious. "Sir, if I thought my team was compromised in *any way* do you think I'd send them out there? If I thought any of them weren't mission-ready I'd tell you. You know that."

"Then why the opposition to the mission, Jack?"

"I..." He shook his head, as if he genuinely couldn't explain himself. "It just feels like a wild goose chase, I guess."

"You said it was too big of a risk."

Jack frowned. "I meant too big of a risk for some trashed technology, that's all. But you're right; we should probably check it out."

"I could always send SG-2, if you think—"

"No. No, we're good to go."

Hammond met and held his gaze, trying to assess the truth behind those inscrutable eyes. Yes, he trusted O'Neill to make the right call for his team. But listening to Jack argue against taking a risk for potentially the most useful piece of defensive technology they'd yet stumbled across rang discordant alarm bells in his head. On the other hand, was he about to rule the colonel unfit for duty based on one—and not the first—squabble with Dr. Jackson? It was pretty far from probable cause. All the same, he couldn't shake the feeling that SG-1 weren't quite themselves.

"Truth is, we need to get out there," O'Neill said, fingers clasping together so tight Hammond could see his knuckles whiten. "If—and I'm not saying there are—but if there were any lingering effects from the stamp, the best way to get rid of them is to get back to doing what we do. Get back to being SG-1, not Jonah and Karlan and—" He looked up. "This is how we deal with crap, sir. We just get back on the horse."

And God knew the memory stamp wasn't the worst thing SG-1 had dealt with over the past four years. They'd dug themselves out of some pretty dark places. Hammond figured they'd probably earned a little latitude, but he was only willing to go so far.

"Okay," he said at last, "you can make the call on this, Jack. But don't give me a reason to doubt that you made the right one."

"Thank you." O'Neill's relief was restrained, but evident. "And I won't, sir."

"I mean it, Jack." He tapped the closed report on his desk. "Any sign that SG-1 is adversely affected by the stamp and I want to know about it—and by SG-1 I mean you too. Do I make myself clear?"

"Crystal, sir."

Hammond nodded a dismissal. "Get back to work, Colonel. Your team has a mission to prep."

CHAPTER TWO

SILVER-BLUE light rippled through the room, the frisson of static and ozone stirring the hairs at the back of Jack O'Neill's neck. But for once his attention was not on the open Stargate at the top of the ramp. Instead it was stuck firmly in Hammond's office, going over and over their last conversation.

It wasn't that he'd lied to his CO. Not exactly.

It was just that there were some things best kept to yourself, some things that you needed to work out in your own time, and not under the spotlight of the head-shrinks who thought they knew best but really knew nothing about it at all. How could they, locked away in their neon-lit offices far, far behind the line?

No, those guys didn't have a clue. But Jack did. He knew what it was like to find yourself in pieces. This wasn't the first time he'd felt that jarring sensation in his mind, as if he'd been broken and reassembled by inexpert hands, all the fracture lines showing and tiny fragments missing; important fragments that no one but he could see. He'd been there before, done that before, and worn the t-shirt out.

So he figured he knew the drill, knew how to get his head back together. You just kept moving. One foot in front of another, one mission after another, until you started to recognize yourself in the mirror again.

That's how it worked.

That's how it usually worked.

But this time... This time he didn't even own all the pieces in his head, he was trying to make fragments fit that had no damn right being there in the first place. He had memories he couldn't be sure were his own, and he had memories he knew were his own, but that he wished he could forget. And when he looked in the mirror, he could still see Jonah.

Not that he was telling Hammond that. Or Fraiser. Or, God forbid, McKenzie.

That last thing he wanted was to 'talk about it'.

And neither did his team, no matter what Fraiser thought. They just needed to get back to doing what they did best; going out and saving the world.

He risked a glance at Daniel as they stood side by side at the foot of the ramp, his short hair looking too much like Karlan's. Daniel didn't look back, his gaze fixed on the event horizon settling into place after the MALP lumbered through the gate.

Jack had a bad feeling about this mission, he'd had it since the moment they set foot on that godforsaken research outpost and found the bodies in the snow. It felt wrong, it stank. His gut twisted into an uneasy knot and he wanted to pull the plug right now. Only... Did he?

Hammond had called him on it, and maybe he was right.

Maybe his doubts weren't his at all; maybe they were Jonah's. Jonah, who'd been happy to shuffle along in the shadows without causing trouble, accepting the bullshit they were being fed, until Daniel and Carter had forced him to start thinking. Or maybe it was some post-traumatic crap that would have him pinned down on McKenzie's couch before he could spit? Either way, he was ignoring that voice. This was SG-1. Taking risks was what they did. They stepped into the unknown and, if necessary, kicked ass when they got there. Nothing had changed that, not really. They had never really been those other people.

On his right he sensed Carter shifting her weapon, impatient. He hated it too, this waiting. Especially now, when he wanted to be moving. He didn't look at Carter. Jonah would have, but he wasn't Jonah. And she wasn't Thera. And that was that.

"O'Neill," Teal'c said, from the far side of Carter. "We should proceed with caution. The bodies on P4X-66Q were killed by projectile weapons. If there are any surviving inhabitant of this world it is likely that they will also possess such weapons."

"I hear you," he said, hands already on his P90.

"We can't automatically assume that they're hostile," Daniel said, looking away from the wormhole at last. "That shouldn't be our default position."

"It's not," Jack snapped, without meaning to. Then, conscious of Hammond in the control room, he said, "Doesn't mean we shouldn't keep our eyes open."

"SG-1." The voice was Harriman's. "MALP telemetry checks out."

Glancing over his shoulder, Jack saw Hammond watching, hands behind his back. Solid as a rock. Their eyes met and, after a heartbeat, the general said, "You have a go, SG-1. God's speed."

Without looking to left or right, Jack started up the ramp. He could feel his team fall in beside him, footsteps ringing out through the gate room. This was what they did, this felt right. And then the tug of the wormhole tore him apart and pieced him back together in a wild, disorienting ride that was both familiar and endlessly strange.

When his boots hit the stone step on the other side of the gate, he had a fleeting moment of confusion, as if all the pieces hadn't quite been put back right, and then he was out and dazzled by an opalescent glare.

"Bright," Carter said at his side.

Jack grunted his agreement and tugged on his shades, taking a step down. He could see the MALP parked a couple yards from the gate, and beyond it rose a stately building of white stone that glistened against a bright white sky. The gate itself was in some kind of grassy courtyard, surrounded on all sides by a colonnade.

"Interesting," Daniel said. "It looks like a cloister, maybe. A place of worship."

"Or of ambush." Teal'c's staff weapon hissed open as he raised it. "O'Neill — there."

Jack turned, his own weapon coming up as a half dozen armed men emerged from the shadows of the cloister. Their wild-eyed panic was clear, but they were disciplined enough to hold their line. That, Jack figured, was a good sign.

"Looks like someone survived," Daniel observed, casting half a glance at Jack. "So much for two hundred year old refugees…"

Jack ignored him and, to his right, he heard Carter unsafe her weapon. His fingers itched to do the same but, conscious of Jonah's fears, he made himself lift his hands away from the gun and say, "Hi, how's it going?"

From between the soldiers another man appeared, shorter and more fleshy. His balding head gleamed with a sheen of sweat but his voice was even, despite the alarm in his eyes. "I am Ennis Channon, Pastor of the Ark. In the name of the Elect, I demand to know who you are." His gaze shifted between Jack and Daniel, looking for a leader. "And what you want here."

"We're explorers," Daniel said, taking Jack's silence as a cue to speak; always wise to keep people guessing about who was the boss. "My name is Daniel Jackson, this is Colonel O'Neill, Major Carter, and Teal'c. We only want to talk to you."

"You have come from *Acarsaid Dorch*?"

Jack recognized the name and the naked fear in the man's eyes. "No," he said. "But we've been there."

Behind them the wormhole abruptly closed, leaving silence in its wake. He could hear the rapid breathing of the soldiers, taste their fear. It was a good bet they'd never seen the Stargate open before.

"We come from a planet called Earth," Daniel said. "We're explorers."

The stranger frowned, his brow creasing. "Then the Sungate reaches places other than *Acarsaid Dorch*?"

"Oh yeah," Jack said. "A whole bunch of other great destinations."

"That's information we can share with you," Daniel said. "Other gate addresses, friendly worlds."

"*Trade* with you," Jack amended, taking another step down from the gate. A ripple of tension flowed through the soldiers, but they didn't back up. "That's information we can trade with you."

"Sir?" Carter's warning came from behind him and, when he looked, she was gesturing with her weapon toward a line of soldiers filtering through the shadows of a cloister to the left of the Stargate. Reinforcements.

He didn't move, but he did let his hands come to rest on his P90. The DHD was behind the line of soldiers, trailing with some kind of flowering creeper that covered the dial; it probably hadn't been used in decades.

"We can have nothing you need," the man — Ennis — said. "We have nothing to spare for trade."

"Actually," Daniel said, "what we're interested in is information. We're looking for something called God's Shield — *Sciath Dé*?"

Ennis Channon's face hardened, his lips compressing into a tight line. "I know nothing of any such thing."

"We found a reference to it at *Acarsaid Dorch*," Daniel persisted. "I think it's meant to be located somewhere called the place of last hope…?"

"I know nothing of such things," Ennis repeated, but he looked distinctly nervous. Behind him, the reinforcements spilled out through the pillars and lined up. There was no talking in the ranks, but Jack could see the looks that darted between them. "I think it would be best," Ennis continued, "if you present yourselves to the Elect. They can — "

"Father!" The strident voice bounced off the courtyard

walls, cutting through the silence in the same way the figure of a slender young woman cut through the ranks of drab soldiers. Dark, unkempt curls fell across eyes that were spitting fire. "You said you would meet —"

"Rhionna, you are not permitted here! Get back to the house."

"I will not. You said you'd meet to —" And then she noticed Jack, her eyes widening as she took in the whole of SG-1 and the soldiers fanned out around them. "What is this?"

Ennis's face grew dark. "They are travelers — they have come through the Sungate."

"Through the Sungate?"

Unlike Ennis, she was scruffily dressed in bright, mismatched clothes and looked like a woman who meant business. Jack decided he liked her. "Hey," he said, raising his hand in greeting. "How's it going?"

She frowned. "How is what going?"

"Life." He smiled. "I'm Jack O'Neill."

"Rhionna Channon." Her curious gaze slid past him, across the rest of the team, and to the gate. "You really came through the Sungate?"

"Yep. Cool, huh?" At his side, Carter cleared her throat and when he looked round, she was staring at him with thinly disguised exasperation. "What?"

"Have you come from *Acarsaid Dorch*?" Rhionna said, doubt and hope painted in clear strokes across her face.

"No," Jack said. "But we've been there."

"We're looking for information about something called *Sciath Dé*," Daniel chipped in. "Or, maybe, God's Shield?"

Her eyes widened, her whole body seemed to jolt with surprise. Ennis put his hand on her arm. "I told you," he said before she could answer, "there is no such thing here." He turned her to face him. "Rhionna — you understand that you cannot speak of this to anyone. It is your duty."

She looked at him, mutiny in her eyes, but all she said was,

"Yes, Father." There was a brief pause, then, "But there are other things we must speak of."

"Now is hardly the time."

"Then when?"

Ennis cast a quick glance toward Jack, then back to his daughter. "Later. After the chapter, perhaps?"

"I'm not going to the — " Her expression altered, like a fish changing direction mid-flow. "Very well then, after the chapter." She cast a final, speculative look at Jack and then turned on her heel and marched off.

As she did so, one of the newly arrived soldiers stepped forward and spoke in Ennis's ear. He nodded and said, "You are invited to attend the Elect; the council will be able to answer any more questions you have."

"Invited," Jack said, casting an eye over the nervous, armed men. "Guess that's an invitation we just can't refuse."

With a glance back at his team, he headed down the stone steps and led them into the cloistered shadows. In the back of his mind, Jonah counseled caution; Jack ignored him.

As they were led into the building, Daniel gazed around, trying to find clues to the origin of this people in the architecture, but the sleek, unembellished lines of the walls and archways gave away nothing. Apparently this was a culture who favored simplicity over ornamentation. It was pleasant, he supposed, if a little bland.

"Nice place," murmured Jack. "But something tells me no snakehead was responsible for the decor."

His words echoed Daniel's own conclusions, but when they were brought before a set of broad double doors, he began to reconsider.

By his side, Jack tensed. "You see what I'm seeing?"

Daniel most certainly did. The handles of the door were wrought in gold, huge and ostentatious, at odds with the otherwise unadorned surroundings. And when fully closed, as they were now, the emblem they depicted was a stylized sun, its rays spearing out towards the edges of the doors.

"It doesn't necessarily mean what we think it means," said Daniel.

"Oh no? Well, there's one way to clear matters up." Jack turned to their escort. "Hey, Ennis," he called, waving his hand at the doors, "this is... interesting. What is it?"

Ennis frowned. "It is the Sun, of course. The embodiment of our Lord God whose light sustains us."

Jack's eyes narrowed. "And your Lord God's name would be?"

Ennis gave an uncertain smile as if confused by Jack's questioning. "The Lord God needs no name, Colonel O'Neill." Apparently satisfied that he had answered sufficiently, he turned to push open the doors.

"So, a sun god, huh?" muttered Jack to Daniel, as they followed Ennis along a dim corridor. "Now, let me think. Do we happen to know any of those?"

"It doesn't make sense though," replied Daniel, keeping his voice low in turn. "I mean, anthropologically speaking, it's unlikely that Ra had any involvement with these people. The timeline is off by about two thousand years. Besides, if it *was* Ra, then we'd be seeing far more evidence of his presence. And he definitely wouldn't have kept his name secret."

"Yeah, understatement was never his style," conceded Jack. "So what are we looking at here, if not Ra?"

Daniel shrugged. "Their language has roots in Gaelic. Irish, I think. So maybe some Celtic sun deity? The important thing is though, that if it was a Goa'uld, then it doesn't look like he's been around in a long time."

Jack nodded. "All the same, eyes and ears open. I'm not taking anything for granted. Not this time."

Those last words were telling, Daniel knew, but he had no time to ponder them further. They'd reached the end of the corridor, and another set of doors bearing the golden sun emblem towered above them.

"The Elect await you," said Ennis, as the doors swung inward.

Slicker than Exxon Valdez was Jack's initial reaction when Brother Tynan Camus of the Ierna Elect introduced himself. The man was younger than he'd expected, perhaps mid-thirties, with a politician's smirk and a look in his eye that was altogether too self-satisfied. His body language was open, welcoming, and Jack guessed it was an image that probably won him a lot of fans among people easily fooled by charm and good looks. But Jack had had too many dealings with men like Camus, both on- and off-world; men who thought they had whole planets in their pocket. You didn't leave your back open to guys like that, you didn't trust them an inch.

For a moment he saw Administrator Caulder's smiling face, just as plausible as this guy's, just as smooth. He'd known better than to trust that guy too, and yet…

He was glad he'd left Carter and Teal'c outside the door, because there was always the possibility that he and Daniel might not come out again.

The council members, including Channon, sat at a crescent table, Camus lounging at one end. Not the seat of a leader, perhaps, but careful observation told Jack the man wielded more power than any of the others would care to admit.

Though the plain robes of the council members were muted in the somber gray light of the room, the councilors' expressions were more than a little pompous. Jack wondered if such officious posturing was for SG-1's benefit.

"Welcome to Ierna, Colonel O'Neill," said Camus. "I do not need to tell you how your arrival has astonished us."

"Yeah," said Jack. "We should have called ahead. Sorry about that."

"And you say you did not come from *Acarsaid Dorch*?"

"No, we didn't. But we've been there." Jack watched closely to see if Camus's reaction to that news would mirror Channon's. The guy barely blinked.

"A hostile environment. Or so we are told."

"Hostile like you wouldn't believe."

"Jack..." Daniel cautioned, and Jack knew he was right. Antagonizing the folk in charge would get them nowhere, but something about Camus's expression really made him want to rattle the guy's cage.

"We must take your word for it, Colonel," Camus said. "The people of the Ark have not used the Sungate in many generations. Indeed, only the Elect are aware of its function."

"And what else might you be aware of?"

Camus arched an eyebrow, a study in nonchalance, but Jack didn't miss how his jaw tightened. One cage, rattled—check!

Daniel stepped forward and Jack knew what was coming. Daniel the Diplomat, Daniel the Mediator, smoothing whatever feathers Jack might have ruffled. It was his default setting, Jack knew, and it made him wonder all the more about Karlan; he was still carrying bruises from their fight.

Question was, had Karlan been a product of the memory stamp or was he a persona buried deep within the psyche of the man he thought he knew? And what did that say about their relationship? What did it say about Jonah? That question led to answers he couldn't begin to deal with, and to rooms that were best left locked.

"Ah...Jack?" Daniel was watching him with a curious expression and Jack nodded for him to carry on, irritated at his tangential thoughts. It wasn't like him to lose focus, not on a mission. Troubled, he listened as Daniel carried on talking. "We really want to ask about one subject in particular, Brother Camus," he said. "We found some writings–"

"The *Sciath Dé*." Camus's tone was flat, almost bored, but Jack didn't miss the ripple of unease that passed through the rest of the council, a lot of frowning and studying of clasped hands. "Yes, I was informed of your interest in that story."

"Story?" asked Daniel, his eyebrows raised.

Camus smiled and spread his hands, a gesture that raised Jack's hackles, but he kept silent, letting Daniel do his thing. "A myth from the Time Before," said Camus. "Any child from the Ark could tell you the tale, Dr. Jackson."

"Um, with all due respect, Brother Camus, we're not really interested in children's stories." From his pocket he retrieved his camera and set it on the table before the Elect; they regarded it like a mongoose eyeing a cobra. "See for yourselves," Daniel said. "We found records on *Acarsaid Dorch* that said this shield technology is real, that it exists. As representatives of our planet, we're willing to negotiate terms that would allow us access to that technology."

"It is Knowledge you seek!" burst out Channon, as if in outrage.

"Well, yeah," said Daniel with a shrug, clearly as bemused as Jack by the Pastor's reaction.

"Heresy! *And lo, the Damned shall seek to be as God, desiring wisdom which only He may possess, and they shall shun the Light he hath bestowed on the world –*"

"Pastor." Camus didn't raise his voice, but one word was enough to silence Channon mid-sermon. The Pastor reddened and sat back in his seat. "Our visitor's are clearly unfamiliar with the Message," said Camus, and Jack decided that there were far too many capital letters floating around in these sentences.

"The Message?"

"The Message by which we live our lives. God's word on Ierna. We will be happy to share it with you."

"You'll tell us what you know?" asked Jack, with no small amount of cynicism.

"We will tell you what you need to know, Colonel O'Neill," said Camus. He rose, dignified in his flowing robes. "Come, join us in the light and partake of the Message."

Jack flung a look at Daniel who gave a small shrug. "Sounds like we're invited to worship with them."

"And here's me without a Bible…"

It was clear from the moment the hall doors reopened that the meeting with the Elect hadn't gone to plan. The colonel and Daniel were led out by an imposing man in long robes, and from the glower on Colonel O'Neill's face it was obvious they hadn't gotten the answers they wanted. O'Neill didn't slow his pace as he strode past her and Teal'c, merely jerked his head for them to follow.

"They don't know anything, sir?" Sam ventured, falling in next to him. She kept her voice low, aware of the other robed figures who surrounded them as they made their way through the cloisters.

"Oh, they know something," the colonel muttered. "They're just not telling."

"About the shield?"

"About the shield, and about those damn bodies we found in that grave."

"Daniel Jackson," said Teal'c, "did you not estimate that the bodies are most likely over a century old?"

"At least that," Daniel agreed. "Jack, you can't believe that these people had anything to do with what we found on *Acarsaid Dorch*."

"You're damned right I believe it."

"Then we must confront them," Teal'c said. "This time we must discover the truth before we become entangled with these people."

For a second, just a second, the colonel hesitated, his eyes flicking down. And in that moment Sam saw another man, one who didn't exist anymore, one who had never really existed in the first place. A man who tried not to rock the boat, who accepted, who didn't question or push or challenge.

Not real. He was never real.

Then he squeezed his eyes shut, took a deep breath, gave a slight shake of his head. "Oh we'll discover the truth alright, Teal'c."

Sam didn't know whether to be relieved or alarmed. "So where exactly is it we're going, sir?" she said as they were led through a vast courtyard towards gates that were slowly swinging inward.

"Get your Sunday best on, Carter, we're going to church."

From the outside, the chapel was instantly recognizable as a place of worship, not least because of the streams of sober, well-dressed people pouring through its doors. The architecture, with its reaching spires and pointed arches, reminded Sam of old gothic cathedrals like Reims or Canterbury, but like all the other buildings they had passed on the way here it was devoid of any ornamentation; its five porticos and twin spires were clean and simple. As her gaze traveled up to study the spires, a flash of reflected light high up caught her attention. Squinting against the sunlight, she could make out a honeycomb of faint lines crisscrossing the entire sky.

"We're in some kind of dome," she said, aloud, as realization struck. A vast one, its structure almost fading into opalescent blue. It solved a riddle she'd been puzzling over since they had emerged from the Elect chambers and seen the sun blazing in a cloudless sky: how could the temperature remain so pleasant? "It must cover the whole city."

"The whole city, huh?" The colonel sent her a look; she knew exactly what he was thinking. "Kind of like a shield…?"

Sam shook her head. If this was *Sciath Dé*, why would the Elect have been evasive about something that was in plain sight? "This looks more like a biosphere, sir. I don't think it has any military applications."

"You are correct, Major Carter." She jumped at the voice, and turned to find Tynan Camus at her elbow. The colonel clearly disliked him, and it wasn't hard to guess why. The guy was altogether too smooth.

"What's its purpose?" she asked. "The dome, I mean."

He gestured around him with a sweep of his arm. "Do you not protect yourselves from the elements? The purpose of the Ark is that we might enjoy the beauty of the Lord's bounty."

"An umbrella?" the colonel said from behind.

Sam peered up. "I'm thinking more along the lines of a parasol." Then, to Camus, she said, "The sun's pretty hot, huh?"

He looked confused. "It is the Sun. Is that not its nature?"

"Well, actually, you'd be surprised by the variation in stellar — " Colonel O'Neill cleared his throat and, with a flash of irritation, Sam broke off. For an instant, it seemed, she was standing before Brenna, being cut dead as she tried to explain her ideas. But she shook it off, not sure if the memory was even real or some lingering impression from the memory stamp, and offered a tight smile to Tynan. "Yeah, suns are generally pretty hot."

"Inside the Ark," he said, "we are protected from the heat and the harmful effects of the Sun. It allows our crops to grow, and the beauty you see here to flourish."

"A climate controlled environment. Impressive." Tynan inclined his head, though Sam didn't for a second believe it was through genuine humility. "I'd be interested in finding out more about your technology," she added.

His smile didn't falter, but his eyes narrowed a fraction. "Come," he said, neatly sidestepping her enquiry. "The Message is about to start. I am confident you will enjoy today's chapter."

They were shown into pews near the front of the packed Chapel. Curious looks were thrown their way, but people smiled and nodded in greeting, and Sam didn't pick up any threatening vibes. On the contrary, the air thrummed with

a sense of anticipation and eventually all eyes turned to the
altar — or more specifically the object that was hanging
behind the altar. The huge screen looked out of place, incongruous in a house of worship, and it was then that she recalled
seeing similar blank screens during their walk through the
city, across the sides of buildings, taking the place of bill-
boards. The people of the Ark clearly loved their TV.

"I wanted something similar for my den," whispered
Colonel O'Neill in her ear, "but it wouldn't fit through my
front door."

Tynan Camus had left them and gone to take up a seat
among the rest of the Elect, who were seated to the side of
the altar like a group of middle-aged choristers. The steady
buzz of excited conversation died down as Pastor Channon
stood and walked to the center.

"My people," he said, spreading his arms wide. "Here we
gather to celebrate the Message of our Lord. To rejoice in the
knowledge that we are saved, that we are one with God, that
He has chosen us and blessed us. Here we gather to celebrate
a new chapter, the embodiment of His Word. "

Sam sneaked a look around her at the wide eyes and
broad smiles on the faces of every member of the congregation. They were waiting for something, she realized, eager
for it to begin.

"And the Lord bestowed His Light on the world," continued
Channon, "that his children might see the glory that is the
coming dawn. And they shall rejoice… in the Sunrise."

On Channon's last word, the lights dimmed and the screen
sparked into life, while music poured from speakers positioned at the four corners of the church. A hush descended
on the congregation as every person drank in the images
that scrolled across the screen, images of smiling faces with
perfect smiles and incongruously perfect hair. The music
drew to a close over a credit that proclaimed the title of what
they were about to watch — *Sunrise*. The title faded and as

she watched the events unfolding on the screen before her, a deep feeling of unease settled over Sam. Surely this Message, that the people of the Ark had gathered to celebrate with such fervor, couldn't be –

"A soap opera?" The colonel's disbelief matched her own. "That's what we're here to watch? That's what they think we want to see? Days of Our goddamned Lives?"

Daniel leaned in. "It does seem to have a religious theme." He was fidgeting, searching his pockets for something. "Maybe this is how they interpret their scriptures. Using the performing arts as a medium to express religious texts is not unheard of in — Damn it, they still have my camera."

"Daniel, it's daytime TV."

"Yes, but a fascinating manifestation of religious observance, don't you think?" He sighed, irritated. "Sam, can I borrow your camcorder? I have to get this."

"It's not what we came here for, Daniel," the colonel growled. "This is a waste of time."

Sam agreed wholeheartedly, but leaving was impossible without creating a disturbance in a crowd who obviously took *Sunrise* very seriously indeed. So she handed Daniel her camera and together they sat through what felt like hours of the sort of overwrought melodrama that normally had her reaching for the remote. The show was filled with trite moralizing, references to the punishment of sinners, and smug posturing that the people of the Ark were amongst God's chosen people. And the congregation were hooked. Worryingly, though, there were times when Sam felt herself being drawn in too, swept along by an asinine story that didn't require thought. It was almost hypnotic.

The final scene ended on a cliff-hanger and Sam had to shake off a creeping curiosity about what happened next. It was insidious, this *Sunrise*, she thought. As the end credits rolled, accompanied by the same nondescript melody that had played at the start, the crowd broke into excited chatter and filtered from their pews towards the doors.

Ennis Channon and Tynan Camus approached the team.

"And what did you make of *Sunrise*, my friends?" asked Ennis, his smile broad.

The colonel opened his mouth to reply but, perhaps prudently, Daniel spoke first. "It certainly taught us a lot about your people, Pastor Channon."

"It is a wondrous thing, is it not? And we have Brother Camus to thank for that. He oversees the production of each new chapter."

"Wow, I've never met a TV producer before," said the colonel.

Camus bowed his head once more in that pseudo-humble gesture. "I am merely God's tool in this realm."

"Yeah," said the colonel, "*tool* is certainly the word that springs to mind."

Daniel cleared his throat. "I have to say, though, we're still curious."

"You wish to learn more of the Ark, Dr. Jackson?" asked Tynan.

Ennis glanced nervously between the two men. "There is very little else to learn–"

Tynan raised his hand, cutting Ennis off. "No, Pastor. I wouldn't want our guests to leave thinking that we have not done our utmost to satisfy their... curiosity. Why don't you take them to the library?"

"The library?" Ennis looked doubtful.

"Yes!" cried Daniel, obviously sniffing a breakthrough. "I'd love to see your library."

"Perhaps then you will see that your pursuit of fables is futile," Camus smiled. "And while you are there, Colonel O'Neill, might I request the pleasure of Major Carter's company? She expressed an interest in our dome and I'd be happy to discuss the subject with her."

Sam fought to keep her expression neutral, trying to figure out Camus's game. Had she asked too many questions? Was there something in the library he didn't want her to see? Or was she collateral to ensure the colonel didn't cause any trouble? Whatever the reason there was no mistaking the tension now humming between their little group.

Colonel O'Neill's gaze flicked from Sam to Tynan to the armed guards positioned discreetly by the wall. When it caught hers once more, she gave an almost imperceptible nod; she'd be fine.

"Teal'c, with Carter," he said. "We won't be long." But as he and Daniel followed Ennis from the church, Sam couldn't help but remember the last time SG-1 had split up on an off-world mission. And how, when they met again, they'd been different people entirely.

The more Jack saw of the city, the creepier it got. Not in a Halloween Special kinda way — there were no monsters in the shadows or gothic towers swathed in London fog — but there was definitely something creepy in the empty plazas and the echo of his footsteps bouncing from tall, silent buildings.

"Is it me," he said to Daniel, "or is this all a bit *Twilight Zone*?"

Daniel was squinting up at the bright sky. "It's not you," he said. Then, to Ennis, "There are no birds."

The Pastor was walking ahead of them, apparently pissed at being taken away from his bizarro soap-opera worshipping. But when Daniel spoke, he turned to glance over his shoulder and said, "No what?"

"Birds?" Daniel mimed a shadow-puppet bird with his hands. "You know, animals that fly?"

Ennis shook his head and kept on walking. "I know of no such thing."

Daniel lifted his eyebrows and glanced at Jack.

"Curiouser and curiouser."

Away from the Chapel — or whatever it was Ennis had

called it — the streets were empty. But on the walls of the buildings, and occasionally erected on large pylons in the deserted plazas, there were large television screens. And they were all on, showing more of the same crap they'd been forced to watch in the church.

"This has to be the first culture we've ever met that worships a daytime soap," Jack said, glancing up at one of the huge screens as they walked past.

Daniel gave a sarcastic bark of laughter. "Really? Not including our own culture you mean?"

"Funny."

"Anyway, you're missing the point. *Sunrise* is just the vehicle for the Message, it's not worshipped in and of itself. It's a tool."

"Yeah, a propaganda tool."

"Or a proselytizing tool; it's just a matter of perspective."

"*It's my honor to serve*," Jack said and cut Daniel a flat look. "Call me cynical, but I don't like being told what to think by the folks in charge."

Ahead of them Ennis lifted his arm and pointed. "The library is in there."

At first Jack thought he was gesturing toward the gleaming white building right in front of them, but when Ennis walked past its broad-stepped entrance he realized that the Pastor meant another, shabbier building skulking in its shadow. Unlike the rest of the city the library was gray and blocky, narrowing from a broad base to a spindly tower that reached toward the sky. The lower levels were windowless and the casements further up were thin, suspicious slits that squinted like narrowed eyes. It was decidedly unwelcoming.

"Has this always been your library?" asked Daniel, his tone dubious. "Its architecture is different from the rest of the city."

Ennis smiled and spread his hands. "I believe so," he said. "Certainly as long as I remember."

Daniel nodded, studying the library as they walked around to the entrance. He trailed a finger along its gray concrete wall, as he almost always did when encountering something new — as if he had to touch it in order to understand it. Jack might have done the same, but he needed no such contact this time. He could tell just by looking that the building was utilitarian and prefabricated; the library had 'military' stamped all over it.

As they turned the corner, they came to a narrow doorway, around which the now familiar stylized image of the sun had been painted. He shared a look with Daniel, who merely shrugged; Ra wasn't the only sun god out there, but still… Jack's hands suddenly felt a lot more comfortable resting on his weapon, and he braced himself for trouble as Ennis pushed open the heavy door.

There was a soft creak, then…nothing.

"The Archivist is waiting for us upstairs," Ennis said and disappeared inside.

Gesturing for Daniel to go first, Jack took one quick look behind him then ducked inside the building and followed.

He found himself in a narrow corridor and snatched off his sunglasses so he could see properly. Definitely military, he thought, noticing a gun rack bolted to the wall. It was empty, but for a couple of coats hanging from its corners.

Ennis led them through in silence and, at the end of the corridor, a set of doors slid open to reveal an elevator. Jack stopped dead, an adrenaline pulse making his heart race. It took a moment to figure out why.

"This way, Colonel. We have much to show you. As Major Carter has correctly surmised, the source of our city's power lies far beneath the planet's surface…"

And then doors closing. Hands holding him down. A fierce pain, suffocating darkness. A hammer blow to the mind and everything shatters. Then…nothing. Then Jonah.

"Jack?" Daniel was peering at him through Karlan's eyes.

"What?"

"You stopped."

At the door of the elevator, Ennis stood with his hands folded. From somewhere, Jack could hear the tinny drone of the *Sunrise* theme tune. "The library is on the twentieth floor," Ennis offered, by way of explanation.

Goosebumps pricked Jack's skin and he shook his head to get rid of them, gesturing for Daniel to go first. Stepping into the elevator he toggled his radio; as he'd suspected, the bunker was shielded. The squawk of static made Ennis jump. Jack didn't apologize, just turned to face the closing doors and curled his fingers around the grip of his weapon.

To his disgust, the increasingly familiar faces of the *Sunrise* cast beamed out their Message on a thin strip of screen above the doors. There was no escaping the bastards.

With a smooth acceleration the elevator began to rise, and Jack felt an irrational relief that it was going up instead of down. After a few moments it slowed and the doors opened onto a bright, rectangular room that Jack figured took up one whole floor in the spindly tower that topped the building.

Windows along one side let in evening sunlight that painted long stripes across a tiled floor, strip-lights overhead casting a whiter, baleful glare. Shelves lined the walls, and in front of them stood a desk stacked with a neat pile of papers. At the far end of the room, crammed between the shelves, there was another door, which opened to admit a short, wiry man of middle years. His hair was graying and pulled back from a pasty face, his clothes as sober and unremarkable as Ennis's. If he'd lived on Earth, the guy would have had his very own pocket protector.

"Pastor Channon," the archivist said with a smile, closing the door behind him. "Well met."

"Well met, Professor." Ennis turned to Daniel. "Allow me to introduce you, Daniel Jackson, to our archivist — Professor Liam Kermit."

The pause dangled. Daniel seemed determined not to look at Jack, but in the end he couldn't help himself.

Neither could Jack. "Kermit?"

"Ah, of Gaelic origin," Daniel said, fixing Jack with a pointed glare. "It means 'without envy' — a variant of Dermot, actually."

"Without envy?" Jack permitted himself a smile. "So — what you're saying is that Kermit's *not* green?"

The archivist — Kermit — darted a perplexed look between them and said, "Please, there is no need for formality. You may call me Liam."

With an exasperated roll of his eyes, Daniel turned away from Jack. "Sorry — uh, Liam. I'm Daniel Jackson, this is Jack O'Neill."

"I know." He smoothed a hand over his hair. "I understand you wish to browse our archive?"

"Yes. I'd love to. Um, specifically we're looking for any texts that might reference the *Sciath Dé* — or maybe a shield, Shield of the Gods?"

The archivist frowned, glancing at Ennis for clarification. "I'm not sure I understand…"

"I told them," Ennis said, with an unmistakable air of warning, "that they would not find any answers here. *Sciath Dé* is no more than a children's fable."

Jack cut him a look, but Ennis's face was unreadable.

"Could I just have a peek?" Daniel asked, taking half a step toward the shelves. "Maybe start with some of your older material?"

Kermit — that name would never get old! — hesitated. "Ennis is correct, you will not find the information you seek here."

Here? Was he imagining things or had there been a slight emphasis on that last word? He slung a look at Daniel, but if he'd heard it too he was keeping quiet.

"Nevertheless," Daniel pressed, "I'd appreciate the opportunity to see some of your older texts. I'm an historian too — I study the past."

"The past," Liam said, uncertain. "Ierna's past?"

"I hope so." Daniel smiled his winning smile. "I'm sure you have much to teach me."

The archivist swallowed, his Adam's apple quivering. "Why would you think so?"

"Because..." Daniel gestured around. "You're the archivist, the keeper of Ierna's history."

Liam nodded. "Yes, of course. Indeed, we have every edition going back over one hundred and fifty years. You are welcome to examine them." He turned toward the shelves, Daniel following. Jack took another look at Ennis, noted a sharpness in the man's eyes, and stayed put. "This," Liam said, pulling a box from one of the shelves, "is our oldest collection."

Placing the box on the desk he opened the lid. There was no dust, everything was spotless. Reaching in, he pulled out a somewhat faded copy of what looked like a newspaper or magazine. "Edition one," he said. "The year forty-eight. Signed by — "

"The year forty-eight?" Daniel interrupted.

Jack caught his glance and knew what he was thinking. The year forty-eight since what, exactly?

"Yes," Kermit said, laying the paper down and smoothing his hand over it. Jack could make out a man's face on the cover, teeth gleaming in a perfect smile. "One hundred and fifty-two years ago; the day *Sunrise* began."

"And I thought *The Simpsons* had a long run..."

Daniel bent closer, brow creasing. "The magazine is about *Sunrise*?" He looked up at Kermit. "About the, uh, show?"

"Yes, and about those who play in it." Liam gave Daniel a long, serious look. "What else did you expect to find here?"

Somehow, it sounded like a genuine question.

It was difficult to feel under threat among a crowd of people drinking wine and snacking on *canapés*, and Tynan

Camus had been his usual slick and charming self ever since
Colonel O'Neill and Daniel had left. Nevertheless, Sam har-
bored no illusions that she was anything but a hostage. She
was just glad that Camus hadn't objected to Teal'c tagging
along; if anything smelly hit the fan she'd rather not have
to deal with it alone.

After the service — if that was what you could call it — Camus had brought them to a hall next door, where some sort of
post-event gathering was taking place. Now their host hovered nearby, watching their every move while he exchanged
pleasantries with members of the crowd. Sam recognized
some of the faces, people who'd sat near SG-1 during the
showing of *Sunrise*, absorbed in the melodrama unfolding
on the screen. Their enthusiasm hadn't wavered, *Sunrise* was
still the only subject on everyone's lips; apparently, today's
episode had been particularly powerful in conveying its
Message to God's Chosen People. Lines from the show were
being bandied about in the same manner in which an evan-
gelical preacher would wield Bible quotations. For the people
of the Ark, *Sunrise* was their scripture and their doctrine; no
part of it was questioned or derided. Tynan Camus seemed
all too satisfied with the situation.

"How can they buy something so clichéd and trite?" Sam
muttered.

"I have often considered the same question with regard
to the people of Earth, Major Carter," said Teal'c, at her
side. "The Tau'ri are apt to become obsessed by the most
trivial of television shows. It has always been beyond my
comprehension." He followed the progress of a waiter carrying a tray of food, then snagged a canapé with a solemn
nod to the man. "Although I acknowledge that *Survivor*
has me intrigued."

Sam blinked and declined to comment. "But this *Sunrise*
is so pervasive," she said, gesturing to the various screens
on the wall, which even now showed the soap on an end-

less loop. "I mean, do they even have a choice whether or not to watch it?"

Teal'c didn't have the chance to answer. A hush fell across the crowd in a wave, traveling gradually forward from the direction of the door. After a few seconds the throng parted to reveal the cause. Rhionna Channon came striding towards them, apparently heedless of the speculative glances cast her way or the low gossiping murmurs that rose in her wake. She was dressed rather more elegantly than she had been that morning, but in her deep red gown she still she managed to stand out against the bland shades favored by the other denizens of the Ark.

From the corner of her eye Sam caught a flash of movement and turned to see Tynan Camus approach with some haste, his gaze fixed on the Pastor's daughter. They both reached Sam and Teal'c at the same time.

"Rhionna," he said, his smile fixed, though fewer teeth were showing now. "You are a little late for the chapter."

Rhionna smiled back, but made no effort to hide her disdain. "Oh, I'd say I'm right on time, Tynan." She plucked a glass of wine from the tray of a passing waiter. "I've come for the catering rather than your little exercise in indoctrination. And to speak more with our visitors of course. I'm curious to hear what they make of our home. Tell me, Major Carter, Teal'c, do you force-feed your people tales of vengeful gods? Are they kept glutted and lazy and unable to think for themselves?"

Tynan turned towards Sam and Teal'c, shrugging in a way that made Sam want to break both his shoulders. "You must excuse Sister Channon's disrespectful manner of speaking," he said. "She shames her father with her refusal to acknowledge the truth of the Message. Indeed, one can only guess where she was taught such heresy."

"I'd call the ability to think for myself more inherent than learned."

When Tynan glanced back at Rhionna, Sam was startled to see, for the first time, genuine emotion flicker across his face. And it looked like ice cold hatred. "Yes," he said, "I'm sure you were concerned with learning... other talents, during your time spent outside the Ark."

"Your taunts are becoming rather dull, Tynan. And as for my other talents, let me assure you that you will never be made to endure them." Much to Sam's amusement, color blazed high on Camus's cheeks — but whether it was anger or embarrassment, she couldn't tell. Either way, it seemed that Rhionna was less blasé than her tone suggested; Sam didn't miss how her hands had clenched into fists at Camus's insult. "As for my time outside the Ark," she said, "I'm surprised you would raise such a subject before our guests. They might discover something you would rather they did not know."

"There is no shame, Sister Channon, in submitting to the Lord's will. The Elect have no secrets."

Rhionna didn't answer, though she looked as if she was chewing on a choice reply. Instead of voicing it, she took a long swallow of wine.

The entire exchange intrigued Sam. What, exactly, existed outside the Ark? She wished Camus would go so she could question Rhionna more closely, especially as she felt pretty sure that the woman was bursting with answers. And for a moment Sam thought she might get her wish, because Camus's attention darted over their heads and to the door.

"Why are they here so early?" he muttered, his mask of composure well shaken now. Sam, Teal'c, and Rhionna followed his line of sight to see two glamorous people enter the room amid a wave of excited chatter from the crowd. They were, unmistakably, the male and female leads from *Sunrise*. With an impatient gesture, the woman beckoned Camus over.

"It would be respectful to go see what she wants, don't you think?" said Rhionna, with a half grin and a raised eyebrow. "They are the great and wonderful players after all." Camus's lips thinned and his stare snapped from Rhionna to Sam and Teal'c. "Don't worry," she said. "I shall entertain our guests, Brother Camus."

After a moment's hesitation, he heaved an exasperated sigh. "Remember, Rhionna," he hissed, "I have ears. Everywhere." Then he spun on his heel and left. For a few seconds, Rhionna watched his retreat before turning back to grab Sam's hand. "I can help you find what you seek," she said, her eyes like flint, all pretence at indifference gone. "But you must help me in return."

"How?"

Rhionna shook her head, shooting a look after Camus. "If you would learn the truth, leave now. I can buy you a few minutes." Then she too disappeared into the throng.

Sam and Teal'c didn't wait. Skirting the crowd they headed for the exit, Sam sparing only one backward glance to see Rhionna engaged in a heated discussion with Camus and the two actors. It wasn't until they'd both reached the empty courtyard that she opened her hand to look at the piece of paper Rhionna had pressed into her palm. On one side was written a handful of words in bold even strokes.

AND THE LIGHT OF THE SUN SHALL SCOUR EVIL FROM THE LAND — *Sunrise, Chapter Three, Year One.*

But it was the words on the other side that provoked a sudden thrill of adventure. She stuffed the note into her pocket. "We've got to find the Colonel and Daniel. Now."

CHAPTER THREE

DANIEL reached the bottom of the box and paused for a moment, staring at the empty plastic container. By its side, on the desk, the magazines sat in a neat pile, being fussed over by their archivist.

And if that wasn't a misnomer he didn't know what was.

He took in a slow breath, held it for a beat, then let it out carefully. Patience wasn't exactly his strong suit, not when it came to history — or, more pertinently, to the destruction of the very fabric of history. "Tell me," he said, lifting his gaze from the box and running his eyes over the shelves in the so called library, "are these magazines all that are kept here?"

Liam blinked at him, eyes twitching. He was hiding something. "We also keep copies of each chapter, of course."

"What about other books?" Daniel pressed. "Ah, stories? Fables? Accounts of things that happened before…" He floundered for a moment.

"Before the Flood?" Liam offered.

"Yes!" He stood up straight, almost knocking over the stack of magazines in his eagerness. "Exactly. Before the flood."

"There is nothing," Ennis cut in. "It was a time of sin that has been long scoured away."

"But there must be something," Daniel protested. "Some records or — "

"I said there is nothing!" There was no mistaking the anger in Ennis's voice, nor the edge of threat. His hands were clasped before him, twisted tight together, and in the light of the fading sun Daniel saw sweat beading on the man's wide forehead. "Such matters," Ennis said in a more collected tone, "are only for the Elect."

"The Elect." Jack shifted where he stood, his attention

switching from Daniel to Ennis. "And who put them in charge? I'm gonna take a wild guess that the Elect weren't actually elected."

"We," Ennis replied, chin lifting, "are elected by God to lead our people. Our seats are handed down through generations."

"Right." Jack eyed him for a moment, but didn't say anymore.

A hereditary council then. Daniel had difficulty picturing Rhionna Channon taking on the role of Pastor some day.

Jack took a step toward the table and thumbed a copy of the magazine. Liam sucked a breath between his teeth and his hand twitched towards Jack's arm, but he didn't dare stop him. "Let me get this straight." Jack's comment was directed at Daniel. "This is a library of *TV Guides*?"

Letting out a controlled sigh, Daniel looked at him over the rim of his glasses. "Pretty much, yeah."

"Bread and circuses," Jack muttered, dropping the magazine back onto the desk. Liam reached for it, smoothing his hands over the cover. "We're not gonna find — "

"*Colonel O'Neill.*" Sam's voice crackled from Jack's radio, making both Ennis and Liam start. "*Do you copy, sir?*"

Jack toggled his radio with obvious relief. Clearly, this high up, the signal could get through. "What's up, Carter?"

There was a pause, and then, "Any luck at the library, sir?"

"It's a bust. How's the après-church party?"

"Interesting, sir. Teal'c and I are headed your way, ETA about twelve minutes. I'll give you a sit-rep then."

Jack shared a look with Daniel. "We'll meet you outside. O'Neill out." He shifted his stance toward Ennis as suspicion crawled across the man's face. Sam hadn't said much, which probably meant she had something to tell them — something she didn't want Ennis Channon to hear. "Apparently Carter and Teal'c want to see the sights too."

"Your words are strange," Ennis said. There was a meaningful pause, and then, "The Sungate is not far; I can have you escorted there if you wish to depart."

Daniel cleared his throat. "What Jack's trying to say, Pastor, is that we'd like to look around some more — if that's okay with you. If the shield we're looking for did once exist here, we might be able to retrieve some of the technology and that could help both our peoples."

"Look around you," Ennis said. "My people are not in need of assistance."

"But mine are," Daniel persisted. "And if we can make it work, the shield could help us defend ourselves against a terrible enemy. We found a device on–"

"Daniel…" There was a warning note in Jack's voice, but Daniel ignored it. You had to throw a little bait to catch a fish. Jack should know that.

Ennis's eyes turned sharp with fear. "Device? What device?"

"We think it's a fix, a way of making the shield work."

"And you have it with you? You have brought it here?"

"No," Jack lied, before Daniel could answer. "No, it's still back on *Acarsaid Dorch*, where we found it."

Liam had been replacing his magazines into the plastic box with a reverence Daniel recognized, but at the mention of *Acarsaid Dorch* his hand stuttered like a CD skipping mid-track, and his breathing hitched in a half-swallowed gasp. Interesting.

"You are a stranger here," Ennis said into the silence that followed, "and so cannot know that speaking of the Other Place is forbidden to any but the Elect. It was a place of apostasy, and memory of what occurred there has been burned from the lips and minds of our people."

Jack fixed him with an appraising look. "Has it?"

Ennis said nothing, his expression closed and defensive. Trust Jack to push it too far. Silence mushroomed between them until, with an intake of breath, Ennis said, "I must bring this matter before the Elect. You will remain until I do so."

"Sure. Why not?" To Daniel's ears, Jack's reply sounded more like 'The Hell we will!' But Ennis seemed satisfied and bowed his head.

"I shall take my leave," he said, clearly trying to hide his anxiety, but the half-strangled voice and sheen of sweat on his face gave him away. "I must return to the Chapel before the Elect depart. Professor Kermit will see to your needs until I send men to escort you back to the Council chamber."

"Oh, I bet he will." Jack offered a crocodile smile and waited, stock still, until the elevator doors shut behind Ennis. Then turned to Daniel, the smile falling away. "We're outta here. Now."

He lifted his eyebrows. "Now?"

"Kermit, where're the stairs?"

Liam looked up, blinking. "Stairs? Through that door, but there are a great many and I should really — "

"Daniel — now."

Refusing to jump like a raw recruit, he turned to the archivist. "Ah, we appreciate you showing us your records," he said. "And if you do come across anything — you know, maybe something old tucked away somewhere — anything that mentions the *Sciath Dé*, please contact us."

Liam's expression tightened again, and he didn't answer, just watched. His teeth were clamped together hard enough to make a muscle jump in his jaw. And as Daniel turned to follow Jack out the door, he could feel Liam's eyes on his back, boring into him until he stepped into the musty corridor and let the heavy door swing shut behind him. The staircase was situated at the end of the hallway, beneath a window dusty in the fading daylight. Jack was already heading down.

Daniel hurried after him. "And we're taking the stairs because...?"

"Because Carter and Teal'c have some intel, and I wanna

be out of here before Caulder's goons show up."

There was silence. Daniel hesitated, then said it anyway. "Ennis."

"What?"

Jack didn't look around, but Daniel could see the tense set of his shoulders. He almost wished he'd kept his mouth shut. "It's Ennis's goons, you said, 'Caulder.'"

Administrator Caulder, a man so blinkered by the need for survival that he'd enslaved half his population to keep the other half safe. Even at the end, after they'd shattered the lies and broken through to the world above, Caulder hadn't understood what he'd done wrong.

I was protecting my people — our civilization. Would you do different?

"Just keep walking," Jack said, not commenting on his slip of the tongue. "The sooner we get out of here the better, I don't trust any of these bastards."

"No," Daniel sighed. "You never do."

It was a strange sunset, Sam thought, as she and Teal'c made their way through the empty streets. The light was so diffuse that half the sky gleamed a misty orange, but there was no cloud strata within the dome to make it spectacular, nothing but a gentle fade from white to apricot to nightfall. There was something sterile about it, something that made Sam want to take a deep breath of wild, clean air. It reminded her too much of a different domed city, holding out against the ice. And she wondered what this city was hiding from — and what secrets it kept.

"Major Carter." Teal'c stopped dead, poised like a cat on the hunt. "Movement ahead."

Following the direction of his gaze, she saw it too. A flicker of a shadow in one of the side streets, close to an ugly gray building. She eased her zat out of its holster and, with a glance at Teal'c, moved into the shadows. Teal'c did the same, his steady presence behind her feeling like a solid wall. She'd missed him, she realized, during the weeks she'd been Thera. She'd missed this sturdy counterpoint to Daniel's bright passion and the colonel's mercurial temper. Perhaps that was why the team had flown apart in the power plant, because Teal'c hadn't been there to anchor them.

Daylight was fading fast now, the speed of the sunset suggesting they were located close to the equator of the planet. Holding up a fist, she signaled Teal'c to stay back while she approached the corner of the street. She flattened herself against the wall, waited and listened. In the distance, she could hear the jangle of *Sunrise* music coming from one of the many screens, and, underlying that, the thump-thump of booted feet. Military, without a doubt, just like the building in front of her, with its slit windows and bunker-style ground floor. Sounded like Tynan Camus had figured out they'd gone AWOL.

Then, around the corner, she heard what might have been the whisper of fabric moving, the slightest scuff of a boot. Time to make her move.

Zat held in both hands, she snapped from cover, feet braced and finger tight on the trigger.

"Damnit Carter!" The colonel's P90 swung away from her, just as she lifted her own weapon.

"Sorry, sir."

Behind him, Daniel said, "A little jumpy, guys?"

"Enemy territory," the colonel snapped.

"You don't know that."

"Daniel…"

"Colonel O'Neill is correct," Teal'c said, rounding the corner to join them. "There is much we do not understand about this world; we must proceed with caution."

Daniel held up his hands in defeat. "So, what did you find out?"

"Well, for a start," Sam said, "I spoke with Rhionna

Channon — Ennis's daughter. She certainly has no love for the Elect, and she says she needs our help."

"Here we go." The colonel angrily kicked his boot against the wall. "This is always how it starts."

"Ah, because this is why we do the job?" Daniel's brow beetled, his hands plunged into his pockets. In the fading light, the lenses of his glasses gleamed bronze. "What kind of help?"

Sam shook her head. "She didn't say."

"Okay, first," the colonel said, prowling back toward them, "this is not why we do the job. We're not the Intergalactic Red Cross! Second — "

"Oh, don't give me that crap about standing orders!" Daniel said. "Weapons technology isn't the only reason — "

"*Defense* technology," the colonel said, "is the *only* reason we came here. We're here for the shield. That's it."

"But if they're asking for our help…"

"I didn't hear anyone asking."

Daniel shook his head, and Sam took advantage of the pause to jump in. "Actually, sir, Rhionna also implied that she knows something about the shield." She dug into her pocket and pulled out the scrawled map the woman had pressed into her hand. "The note says to meet her here, after dark."

The colonel scowled at the paper and after a long moment snatched it from Sam's hand. "And if we help her, she'll tell us what she knows."

"That was the implication, sir."

He looked up from the map, met her eyes through the dusky light. "You trust her?"

Which meant it was her call, her responsibility. She held his gaze. "Yes sir, I think I do."

"Colonel O'Neill," Teal'c said, half turned back the way they'd come. "Men are approaching. If we wish to meet with Rhionna Channon we must evade them. I do not believe Pastor Channon would permit us to talk with his daughter."

"He's right," Sam said. "I got the distinct impression that she's *persona non grata* among the Elect — especially with that guy, Camus."

"Which is probably a good sign," Daniel chimed in, hands still deep in his pockets. "Maybe she really does have some useful information."

"I think it's worth a shot," Sam agreed. She glanced over at O'Neill. "Sir?"

He was studying the map, memorizing it, then scrunched up the paper in his fist. "Okay, we meet with her and see what she has to say. But that's all. We are not — repeat, *not* — gonna get dragged into another mercy mission."

Sam just nodded. Daniel scowled, but wisely held his tongue.

"The men are coming from the direction of the Chapel," Teal'c said, choosing to ignore the tension. "I suggest we head in the opposite direction."

In silence they moved out. Teal'c taking point and the colonel covering their six, they melted into the shadows of the empty city.

The ritual of dinner on Third Night had long been a pretence of normalcy on the part of Rhionna Channon and her father. Their conflicts, both personal and political, were left outside for the duration of the meal, and by some unspoken agreement, their relationship returned to the happy, settled state they had known before. Before she had started questioning the Ark and its purpose. Before she had begun to see the world as it truly was. Before she had been to the Cove.

During their dinners together, for just a few hours, it was as if nothing had changed. Her father was just her father, and her love for him was untainted by the new truths to which her eyes had been opened.

Tonight, though, that fragile peace had been shattered, and it was because the strangers had come. Rhionna toyed with her food, now as cold as the atmosphere in the room. At the other end of the table her father had finished his meal, though he looked to have enjoyed it no more than she, and she guessed that he had forced every bite down his throat just to prove a point. All is as it was, his actions said, all will remain as it was. The strangers will learn nothing and they will leave. Our lives will continue on as they have always done.

But Rhionna could not let the strangers leave having learned nothing. Every instinct told her that those four people had not only the power to help her, they had the courage too. She remembered the sullen challenge in the eye of their leader, Colonel O'Neill, and the hopeful questioning of the one who had introduced himself as Daniel Jackson. It was a tenuous optimism, but one she clung to. Change had to come for Ierna's people. Of that, at least, she was certain.

"Is the food not to your liking, Rhionna? I can have something else prepared if you wish." Her father smiled, though the expression was brittle. It was clear that he had no intention of acknowledging the tension in the room. Things unspoken. It was the way of the Ark, and Ennis Channon was a loyal follower.

"It's not the food that isn't to my liking, Father."

He looked away and took a sip of his wine before saying, "I have no wish to listen to your complaints tonight, girl."

She gave a gasp of laughter. "Complaints? You make me sound like a surly child! This is more than a temper tantrum."

"Well, that's certainly what it sounded like this evening." Her father finally let some of his anger show through.

Rhionna sighed and sat back. The scene she had caused at the chapter had been unfortunate, the public argument with Tynan Camus and the players doing her cause more harm than good — the people of the Ark already considered her something of an oddity — but it had been a necessary diversion to allow Major Carter and Teal'c to escape. She could only hope that the tactic had worked, that the strangers would meet with her as she had requested in her note. "I have apologized for that. It was ill-judged."

"Your behavior embarrasses me, Rhionna. It embarrasses the Elect."

"Damn the Elect!"

Ennis jerked to his feet. His wine glass clattered across the table, leaving a trail of red droplets in its wake. "Your words are blasphemy, girl!"

"Why? Are the Elect divine now? Have they finally achieved the state to which they have aspired for so long?"

"There is but one God."

"Oh, Father, spare me the platitudes."

Ennis took a breath and resumed his seat. "If you would ever come to hear the Message you would not think them platitudes. Why do you persist in opposing God's will?"

"I have no wish to discuss theology with you this evening, Father," she said, weary of the tired argument. "Sometimes I think that even you do not believe half the things you say."

"It is the Message. It is our law."

"It needn't be."

"There is no other way."

"Because no one has looked for it!"

Her father shook his head. "Rhionna, my child, I fear for you. I fear for what's to become of you. Not as your Pastor, but as your father. I don't know why you continue along such a dangerous path. You must see the futility of it. Why are you so intent on saving those who are beyond salvation?"

"Because I don't believe that they are. And you may call it heresy. I call it humanity. I don't understand how you can turn from the truth."

He looked down at the table and drew his finger through a droplet of spilled wine. "Do you still spend your time there? Outside?"

"It's best that I don't answer that."

He nodded; apparently her response was answer enough. "And are you still…do you still…?" He faltered, then said with a sneer, "The Seawolf. Do you spend your time with him?"

The pain was unexpected and powerful. Rhionna swallowed against the sudden constriction in her throat. "No. No, not now." It was all she could trust herself to say, but it seemed to appease her father.

"I believe Brother Camus would yet have you, you know," he said. "You will be Pastor one day, Rhionna. It would be an advantageous marriage."

Whenever her father raised this subject, a favorite of his, Rhionna was always vocal in enumerating the reasons why such an idea was repellent to her, but tonight she hadn't the strength. There were greater battles to fight. She just wished that she could count her father as an ally. "The strangers… They can help us. They know about *Sciath Dé*. Perhaps this is the chance we have waited for."

"I have awaited nothing." His eyes narrowed and he said, "Did you have anything to do with their escape?"

Rhionna toyed with denial, but decided she did not care if her father knew her role in this. "I want them to know the truth."

He brought his fist down on the table, sending the upturned glass crashing to the floor. "Rhionna!"

"Please, Father! Please let them help us."

For a moment he said nothing, simply stared at the shards of crystal on the floor, and in those few seconds hope was bright. Had she, at last, managed to persuade him that the truth could not be hidden? But then he raised his eyes to meet her and all she saw was resignation.

"This is the way of the Message, child. The Sun is our Lord and our Judge. There is no way to change that."

And with her father's words, Rhionna knew that her course was now set. The meeting with the visitors would change everything, and there would be no turning back.

CHAPTER FOUR

THE NIGHT had grown dark, and when Teal'c looked up he could see no stars through the dome that shielded this city from what lay beyond.

He did not speculate as to what that might be, but his instinct — what O'Neill would call his 'gut' — told him that it was dangerous. Too much was hidden in this place, too many lies told in the guise of truth, for him to believe that all was well on the world of Ierna. And so he kept his guard raised, his attention ranging out beyond the whispered discussions between his team, and into the city at large. Even from this distance he could see the white flicker of the screens that projected the Message onto the vast sides of towering buildings, he could hear the distant hubbub of a city, and beneath it all he could detect the tramp of booted feet. Teal'c did not doubt that they were being hunted by the men who served the Elect.

But they did not come close to the place Rhionna Channon had selected as a meeting point, which made him at once thankful and suspicious. Daughter of the Pastor, her loyalties remained unclear despite her protestations. The Jaffa on Chulak had an expression for such situations — bait your trap with Satta-cakes, not gruel. He would be vigilant.

They awaited her in a deserted plaza beneath a vast, empty tower. At the center of the space a flat rectangular structure, about as high as his waist, sloped down toward a circular area surrounded by a low wall. Once, perhaps, it had been a fountain trickling into a pool but now both were dry and dusty. O'Neill sat on the edge of the slope, swinging his legs to mark his boredom, however the tight grip he maintained on his weapon belied his feigned indifference. Major Carter had her back to them all, covering the other entrance to the square. And Daniel Jackson was studying the footage he had taken on his camera, his face ghostly in the light shining up from the screen.

"…really, it's quite remarkable," he was saying, gaze intent and brow creased. "We're looking at a culture that apparently dates its existence from a hundred and fifty years ago."

"Yes, apparently," O'Neill said. His eyes were hidden beneath his cap, shadowed in darkness. Teal'c did not need to see his face to hear the cynicism in his voice. Neither did Daniel Jackson.

"I'm not saying they sprang into being a century and a half ago," he said, his tone skirting irritation. "But there's clearly been a significant loss of knowledge about their own history. And a retrograde step of that magnitude is almost always the result of some kind of societal cataclysm — war, plague, disaster. Huge population loss."

"Collective amnesia?" O'Neill had stopped swinging his legs and sat very still. "Wouldn't be the first time."

After a silence Daniel said, "There are plenty of reasons why people forget their own past, Jack. Almost none of them involve memory stamps."

"Yeah, and almost all of them involve some smart-ass in a suit rewriting history to make himself the good guy."

Daniel Jackson switched off his camera. The small light disappeared and left him in the shadows. "That's a fair point — history, as they say, is written by the victors."

"Question is, who's the enemy?"

"That's what we're here to find out, isn't it?" Daniel Jackson stood up and stretched. "That's why we're meeting Rhionna."

"Is it?" O'Neill didn't move. "Is that why we're here, Daniel? Because I thought it was to get hold of the shield."

"They're not mutually exclusive aims."

"Daniel's right, sir," said Major Carter. "Rhionna may be

able to help us find out more about the shield."

"Sure," O'Neill said. "At a price."

"You don't know that, sir."

"Oh, I think it's a good bet." He jumped down from the fountain, his boots drumming a dull boom from the bottom of the empty pool. "There's always a price."

"Now you just sound cynical," Daniel Jackson said.

"Yes," O'Neill agreed. "That's because I *am* cynical!"

"It may be a price worth paying, sir." Major Carter had half turned from her post. Teal'c could see the gleam of her eyes in the dark. "If that shield really could help defend Earth from attack by the Goa'uld…"

"A price worth paying." It was a muted echo. "And what if the shield turns out to be a crock, then what? What if all that happens is us ending up saving some other screwed-up world from itself while we get— Then what? You still think that's a price worth paying, Major?"

She was silent a moment. "Yes, sir," she said. "I think it is."

O'Neill didn't answer, just muttered something indecipherable under his breath.

"Come on, Jack," Daniel Jackson said, "you've never made this just about the standing orders before."

"Yeah, well P3R-118 changed my mind."

In the silence that followed Major Carter turned back to her watch, but Daniel Jackson was not so wise. "That's just one place."

"They were in our heads, Daniel! They were screwing around with our minds. And what did we get out of it? Nada. Zilch." He slammed his fist against his chest. "Nothing but a pain in the goddamn ass."

"We saved those people from slavery," Major Carter said, her back still turned. "That counts for something."

"Not enough," O'Neill growled. "And, just so we're clear, this time we're here for the shield. And that's all. Got it?"

"Well, you can't just…"

The rest of Daniel Jackson's protest faded from Teal'c's ears as he saw a shape detach itself from one of the buildings in the darkness beyond the plaza. "O'Neill." He raised his weapon and dropped into a defensive crouch. "Someone approaches."

"Carter?" Teal'c heard the snap as O'Neill unsafed his weapon.

"Nothing this side, sir." Her voice was tense, but calm.

Then, from the shadows, stepped the slender figure of Rhionna Channon, her hands raised. "It's me."

"Are you alone?" Teal'c peered into the darkness but could see no other movement.

"Entirely," she said, stopping some distance away. "I'm sorry to have kept you waiting for so long. I was obliged to dine with my father tonight. He would have become suspicious had I not attended."

Keeping her covered, Teal'c rose. Behind him, he sensed O'Neill moving forward. "I guess they're already wondering where we are."

"Yes," she said. "The Elect Guard have been deployed to search. We must leave this place before sun-up."

"Must we?" O'Neill stepped forward, his weapon leveled. "And where *must* we go?"

At his side, Daniel Jackson sighed. "Jack…"

"*Daniel*." He shifted his weapon, using it to indicate Rhionna Channon. "I've got a better idea. We stay right here and you tell us what you know about the shield."

The woman lowered her hands. No longer dressed in the gown in which she had attended the chapter, she was once more attired as if for hard work. "I cannot tell you all you wish to know," she said, her gaze holding O'Neill's. "However, I will take you to a woman who can."

"Bring her here."

"Impossible."

"Why?"

She hesitated. "You must trust me, Colonel O'Neill. The Elect will tell you nothing of *Sciath Dé* — it terrifies them. But I can. I can help you, but you must come with me — you must trust me."

"And why should I do that?"

Folding her arms across her chest, Rhionna Channon appeared as intransigent as O'Neill. "Because, if you want to find God's Shield, you have no choice."

The city after nightfall was just plain weird, and Jack couldn't help thinking back to Daniel's talk of war, plague, and disaster. There was definitely something post-apocalyptic about the dark, empty skyscrapers that loomed along the outskirts while the city's tiny heart flickered with the plasma-glare of 180" screens hanging from the sides of buildings.

Rhionna kept them far away from the light as she led them through the city, and Jack was grateful — if only because he was spared from having to watch more of the god awful soap being pumped out into the streets.

"You'd think they'd get bored," Carter murmured.

"Beggars can't be choosers," Daniel said. He was a couple of steps in front, head turning from side to side as he tried to take it all in at once. "If this is the only entertainment they can get, the only culture permitted…"

"It is the only culture they want," Rhionna said, glancing back at them. There was anger in her dark eyes, a flare of frustration. "They are like animals at the trough, eating only what they are given, without question."

"But you question," Daniel said. "What makes you different?"

Her expression sharpened and she looked away. "What I have seen," she said with a frown. "What I will show you."

It was the truth, Jack thought, but not the whole truth. There was something she wasn't telling them.

Up ahead, a knot of people suddenly appeared around a corner. Rhionna stopped dead, breathing something under her breath. It was difficult to make out details, but Jack knew a soldier when he saw one and instantly raised his weapon. Teal'c and Carter did the same, only Daniel lifted empty hands. "Daniel," Jack hissed, jerking his head in a get-behind-me motion.

Daniel ignored him, of course. "Who are they?" he said to Rhionna.

"The Elect Guard. Stay here." Over her shoulder she glanced at Jack. "Lower your weapon."

"I don't think so."

The soldiers had also stopped, taking up a defensive posture as one man detached himself from the group.

"Captain Tanner," Rhionna said, walking toward him.

"Brother Camus thought you would have some hand in this business," the captain said. He spoke quietly, more anxious than angry. "Would that I had not discovered you."

"Then look with blind eyes, Captain," she said. "I am taking them to the Badlands."

Badlands? Jack exchanged a look with Daniel who just shrugged.

The soldier spared them a glance. "Tonight? Rhionna — they staked three in the Burn just yesterday. Three found in the tunnels. It's not safe."

"This is my only chance to show them."

"But to what end?"

"To..." She hesitated. "They need information. Does not the Message teach that we should help those in need?"

With a snort, Tanner said, "I had not thought you paid so much attention to the Message, Rhionna."

"Only when it is in my interest to do so." Reaching out, she touched the man's arm. "They seek *Sciath Dé*. If they can find it..."

The captain looked from her face back toward SG-1. "You

have no reason to trust them; did they not come from the Other Place?"

"Tanner, you know we must question all we are told. Everything we know of the Other Place is told to us through the Message. How can we trust it?"

He looked down at his boots, thinking. At Jack's side, Carter mouthed 'Other Place?' When Tanner spoke again, it was in a voice so low that Jack could barely hear him. "Very well, this night my eyes are blind to you and my men will keep their silence. But go quick, Rhionna Channon. The Elect fear these strangers."

"I know," she said. "And that is why we should trust them." She squeezed his arm. "My thanks, Captain Tanner, to you and your men. I know what you risk."

Then she turned back to Jack and beckoned them forward. "We must hurry. This way." With that, she disappeared around a corner.

Carter broke into a jog to follow, Daniel and Teal'c on her heels. Jack brought up the rear, casting a glance at the soldier watching them with serious eyes. Neither spoke, but in the gloom Jack saw an honest face and gave the man a nod. Tanner did the same, then spun on his heel and returned to his men.

Clearly there was much more going on in the Ark than met the eye.

And Jack hated that.

Gripping his weapon more tightly, he followed his team. As he rounded the corner, he saw Rhionna crouching in the middle of the road, staring at the pavement.

Jack drew closer. "What's going on?"

Tension in her face, Carter shot him a look. "Secret passage."

"Not secret," Rhionna said, grunting with effort as she lifted a heavy metal plate from the road. "But hidden from these *òinseach*."

The foreign word held enough bile not to need translation. And, anyway, Daniel didn't seem to be paying attention. His gaze was fixed on the gaping black hole Rhionna had just opened up. "Down there?" he said with a rasp in his voice.

Jack felt something thump hard in his chest, a beat of alien panic. Jonah's panic. Carter shuffled her feet, fingers turning white where she grasped her weapon. And Daniel glanced up at the night sky as if drawing strength.

He remembered, like half a half-forgotten scent, his first day in the mines. Except he'd never been in the mines and it wasn't really his memory.

Other memories were, though; memories of unremitting labor and lightless, stifling heat. The tasteless slop, the constant hunger, the hopelessness —

"What's down there?" Carter's voice broke into his thoughts.

Rhionna looked up, the distant light of a dozen television screens catching in her eyes. "They are service tunnels — engineers use them to maintain the city's water and sewage systems."

"No boiler rooms, then?" Jack said, mostly for the benefit of his team.

Daniel's mouth curled toward a bitter smile, but Carter's gaze remained locked on the metal ladder leading down into the dark.

Rhionna frowned. "Boiler rooms?"

"Never mind." Jack took a breath and pushed the memories aside — over the years he'd grown accustomed to locking certain thoughts into little dark rooms, and this was no different. "You wanna tell us where we're going?"

He met Rhionna's gaze, taking the measure of her. She stood up, unfazed by his scrutiny. "Outside the Ark. This is the only way to leave. You will have to trust me, Jack O'Neill."

"I guess I will." He flung a look at Teal'c, who nodded — it wasn't exactly approval, more like agreement, but it was welcome; Teal'c's instincts were always on the money.

"There is light in the tunnel," Rhionna said, without waiting for more of an answer. She swung onto the ladder, slipping down fast and sure, and Jack was reminded of a firefighter.

"I'll take point," he said, stepping onto the ladder and testing his weight on the iron rungs; they felt solid. "Teal'c, cover our six."

With that, he started to climb down and tried not to imagine the crushing weight of a mile of ice above his head.

Sam had never in her whole life felt claustrophobic. Yet, as she reached the bottom of the ladder and blackness pressed in around her, her breaths came short and sharp. She grabbed her weapon, the weight in her hands familiar and comforting, but the clamor of the power plant still echoed in her mind and incipient panic clawed at her chest.

Then light flared, a magnesium-bright lantern held aloft by Rhionna. Sam forced the tension in her shoulders to ease and in the bone-white glare saw Daniel squinting and turning away. He looked strange with his short hair, less like Daniel and more like Karlan.

She didn't like it down here, in the depths.

"I don't like it down here." Daniel's words were all but drowned by the scrape of metal on stone that ricocheted down the tunnel. Teal'c had shut the manhole cover.

Sam took a breath and let it out slowly.

"This way." Rhionna turned to lead them out into a wider space.

Sam followed, aware of the colonel falling in beside her. She didn't look at him, afraid that in this place she might see another man looking back. To distract herself from the confusion of memories, she focused on understanding exactly where they were.

The tunnel was rough-hewn, but with enough conformity

to suggest that it had been excavated mechanically rather than by hand. The stone was gray and dry, cut on a gentle downward slope, and through the center of the tunnel ran three large pipes supported at intervals by struts. Her footsteps scuffed on the stone, but all was not silent and, in the distance, Sam could hear the hum and clank of machinery.

She tried not to hear the steam-hiss of boilers.

"We'll go down here," their guide said, stopping before what looked like a cage. It took a moment for Sam to interpret the shadows well enough to realize it was an elevator. Of sorts. Rhionna rattled open the door and stepped inside, lifting her lamp high. "It's not far once we get down."

"How deep does it go?" Daniel asked as they all piled in.

"Almost to sea-level."

The ride down was teeth-rattling and very fast; Sam had to brace herself against the side of the cage to keep her balance. Daniel's eyes were wide, but the colonel just grinned.

"Cool," he said, as they juddered to a halt.

"Indeed." Even Teal'c had cracked a small smile.

They followed Rhionna through another long tunnel, at the end of which, finally, crouched a heavy, barred door. It looked like an airlock and Sam couldn't help wondering what it was designed to keep out.

Rhionna slung the lamp's handle over a peg on the wall, its light dancing wildly in the tunnel. From her pocket she fished a scarlet bandana, tied it low across her brow, then she tugged out a pair of makeshift sunglasses. "You have sunwear?" she asked, gesturing toward SG-1. "I noticed that you wore it when you first arrived here."

The colonel pulled out his shades. "Bright out there?"

"Fierce," she said. "Dawn has broken and we are beyond the dome. Cover what you can."

Despite her unease, Sam's interest was piqued. "The dome acts as a UV filter?"

Rhionna's quick gaze fixed on her, assessing. "If you mean

it protects the people inside from sun damage, then yes, that is what it does." She turned toward the door and began to spin the wheel that kept it locked. "The Ark protects them from many harsh realities."

The first thing Sam noticed as the door swung open was the stark light. The second was a dry wash of heat, permeated by an unbearable stench. She put her hand to her nose. "God, what's that?"

"Come, in a moment you will understand." Rhionna picked up a rock from outside, wedging it into the doorway to keep the door from closing behind them. Then she slipped on her sunglasses, hiding her bright, intelligent eyes. "My father would have his people bend their knee in worship to the Sun, but they are ignorant of their god's ferocious nature. And he is happy to keep them so."

"Interesting," Daniel said, pulling a hat out of his vest, apparently oblivious to the smell. "Maybe Ra wasn't the only ferocious sun god around these parts."

"Perhaps." Teal'c watched Rhionna as she walked away. "But the Goa'uld wear many guises. We must proceed with caution."

"Always," the colonel agreed, donning his own glasses and tugging down the brim of his cap.

Sam couldn't see his eyes through the reflective lenses, only her own distorted mirror image. The flash of Thera looking back at her was disconcerting and she turned away, slipping on her own sunglasses. "We're probably looking at UV levels way above those we're used to on Earth — we should take care to minimize our exposure," she said. "That includes you, Teal'c."

He eyed her hat, then Daniel's, and said, "My symbiote will protect me against any damage caused by the sun's radiation."

The colonel bit back a grin, heading out after Rhionna. "He's just too cool for school, Carter."

"Whereas I," Daniel said, settling his ubiquitous boonie onto his head, "never was."

With a smile, Sam followed Daniel through the entrance of the tunnel. She was squinting even before she reached the spot where Rhionna stood, gazing out.

"Holy crap," breathed the colonel, as he came to stand at her side.

Sam couldn't have put it better herself.

They were on an island, a hillside of scrubby grass sloping down toward a wide and glittering ocean. Above and behind them the opalescent glaze of the city's dome was perched atop high walls, and beyond it a copper-blue sky went on forever, devoid of a single cloud. Heat shimmered up from the ground, despite the sun's low angle, and everything was bathed in milky shades of indigo. Sam could already feel her lips drying out. She took a sip from her canteen, then looked again.

But it wasn't the sparkling water or the picture-perfect sky that drew her attention, it was something else entirely. Crouched between the foot of the hill and the sea, huddled beneath the punishing sun, sprawled a vast and ugly shanty town. Sheets of rusty iron, canvas, plastic—*anything*—had been used to construct the makeshift shelters that spread out along the coast in both directions. Even from this distance Sam could see people swarming through the narrow streets, making the most, she assumed, of the morning's relative cool. Noise drifted up on the hot wind, and with it the stench of poverty and despair.

"Okay," Daniel said, his tone balanced between disbelief and outrage, "I wasn't expecting that."

"Kinda spoils the view," Jack agreed, turning his gaze on Rhionna. "Wanna explain?"

"These," she replied, "are the Badlands. And here you will find the history my father hides from his people; here, you will find the information that you seek." She pulled off her glasses, eyes hard as diamonds in the sunlight. "For a price, of course."

CHAPTER FIVE

SORCHA Caratauc had been birthed with her toes in the sea, so the saying went.

Her mother had died of fever before she was five, and the rat-holes and alleys of the Badlands had become her child-hood home. There she'd scavenged for water and food, found shade beneath the rotting timbers of the docks, and learned to catch fish with her hands.

There too she'd learned to listen — to the women around the pumps, and to the old men telling tales they'd gleaned from other old men, long dead. She'd learned of the Time Before, a mythical place when a man could walk across oceans of grass, when bellies were full, and when ships had taken to the air like the birds.

When her friends had stopped believing in such tales, Sorcha had not. Each night, she'd crept closer to the old men, until one day she'd met the steady eye of Eoin Madoc and he had opened to her a new world.

"It's writing," he'd whispered that night, in the secret light of a flickering lantern. "It's words, put down upon a page. Its stories and remembrances, eh? More'n a man can keep right in his head."

The scratched marks across the paper had seemed to creep and crawl, and she had to slam down her hand to keep them still. "How does it work?"

He had shown her, that night and every night, until the creeping, crawling words gave up their secrets. Sorcha had always been a fast learner.

Less than a year later, the soldiers came from the Ark. Madoc was taken away, his shack trampled into the dust. They got one book, and Sorcha had watched from behind the sullen crowd as Eoin Madoc was pulled away. His glance had caught hers but once, the glint in his eye telling her what she already knew.

They got one book; the others were still safe. And now they were hers.

She never saw Madoc alive again. But she saw his body, staked out beneath the Burn, lips and skin blistered by the sun. Purified, so said the young man upon the hill, his white face like a ghost's against the black robes that proclaimed him Pastor. Purified by the fire of the Lord, his sins burned away — the sins of learning and of gathering forbidden Knowledge. That was why he had suffered and died. That was why everyone in the Badlands suffered and died, blemished by the mark of God, because sin was in their very bones and the Lord chose to punish them with every sunrise.

So said Pastor Ennis Channon.

But Sorcha's anger burned fiercer even than the sun. And that day she swore vengeance against the milk-skinned pastor of the Ark — and against the cruel God he worshipped.

And so her work began. Though Madoc was gone, Sorcha had his books and she rebuilt his shack over the secret place where they were hidden. It became her home — and hers alone. What use had she for men and brats when she had writing and books? Besides, it was a dangerous knowledge, too dangerous to share with any who might seek to share her bed.

And soon it became her obsession.

She found words all through the Badlands, peeking out from the walls and roofs of the flotsam city — *bargain, emergency, sale, sanitation, cargo, re-hydration*. Hundreds of disembodied words, floating through the city, hinting at what once had been, before the waters had come. Sorcha gathered them all, piecing together the fragmented story of her people.

And then, one day, when she was still no more than a girl, though thought herself full grown, she traveled with the Seachrání to the Cove.

There, for the second time in her life, a new world opened.

There, she first learned of the Sungate, of *Acarsaid Dorch*, of *Sciath Dé* — and of what truly happened to those who had tried to save Ierna.

Now, with her creaky bones and sun-leathered skin, the proof of a lifetime's obsession had appeared before her in the flesh. She cocked her head and squinted at the four strangers standing brazen in the morning glare.

"They came through the Sungate, Sorcha." Rhionna Channon spoke in a low voice, but her excitement was obvious. "And not from *Acarsaid Dorch*, though they have been there. It must also lead to other worlds."

"Many other worlds," said one of the strangers, a man. He had removed his sunwear and squinted at her through the brightness. "My name's Daniel Jackson," he said. "This is Jack O'Neill, Sam Carter, and Teal'c. We're explorers."

"We're looking for something called *Sciath Dé*," the one named as O'Neill said. He did not look like an explorer.

"You are soldiers," Sorcha said, eying the weapons across their chests.

O'Neill inclined his head. "Yes, we are."

Honest, at least.

Rhionna turned an eye to the burning sky. "We should talk inside."

"Aye, for many reasons," Sorcha agreed. She stepped back and gestured with her arm for the strangers to enter.

It was crowded, with them all inside, and late enough in the morning for the air to quickly stifle. She folded her legs beneath her to sit and watched as the others struggled to emulate her. Their limbs were stiff as they lowered themselves to the floor, and they appeared awkward and uncomfortable.

"Rhionna," she said. "Fetch water."

With a nod, Rhionna did as she was bid and handed a cup to the woman called Carter. Carter had taken off her sunwear and beneath it her skin was fair and soft as the skin of those in the Ark. She did not even sip the water and failed to mask her distaste. Neither did she pass on the cup, as courtesy dictated, until the one named Daniel Jackson coughed and held out his hand. He was sharp, Sorcha noted and wondered if he read books.

"There is no fresh water in the Badlands," Rhionna said as she too sat, crossing her legs. "It has to be carried down from the pumps at the desalination plant. As a result, there is much sickness here."

O'Neill made a show of drinking, but Sorcha expected he did not let the liquid touch his lips. The one named Teal'c, with skin the color of tarred wood, drank a mouthful and passed the cup to her with a gracious nod. "My thanks, Sorcha Caratauc," he said.

"You are my guests." Her gaze moved across them. "Many say the Sungate is a myth, a legend no more real than flying boats."

"Many legends," Daniel Jackson said, "have their origins in truth."

"So I've always believed, though few would agree." She rubbed her hands across her face, swiping at the sweat. "Have you come to help us?"

A look passed between Daniel Jackson and O'Neill. He had not removed his sunwear, his face inscrutable beneath the shade across his eyes. "We're looking for the shield," he said. "Do you know anything about it?"

"I do."

There was a pause, then he said, "And can you tell us anything about it?"

"I can. Whether I will, however, is less certain."

A smile darted across Daniel Jackson's lips. The woman, Carter, shifted. "If we can help you," she said, "we will. It's just —"

"We can't make any promises," O'Neill cut in. He was

used to having the last word, Sorcha decided. Probably the leader of the group. Shame. She liked the other one, Daniel Jackson, better.

"We think *Sciath Dé* might be able to help both our peoples," Jackson said. "It could protect us all from the Goa'uld."

"I do not know the word Goa'uld." She smiled; she liked new words, new knowledge. "Explain."

It was Teal'c who answered, and with feeling. "They are a parasitic life form," he said, "who inhabit a human body and rule as tyrants over their people in the guise of false gods."

Sorcha snorted a laugh. "Does that not describe your father, Rhionna?"

"Tynan Camus is the only god in the Ark," she replied through tight lips. "At least, in his own mind."

"Then your father is his High Priest?" Sorcha smiled to soften the words, and Rhionna did not deny their truth.

"Tynan Camus is no Goa'uld," Teal'c said, a note of chastisement in his voice. "If he were, all upon this world would suffer beneath his tyranny."

Sorcha spread a hand before her. "Do we not suffer?"

"But you are free," Teal'c said. "A free people may end their suffering if they choose."

O'Neill cleared his throat. "The point is, this shield thing can protect us against the Goa'uld. It can protect all of us."

"Um, also," Daniel Jackson said, rummaging in the bag he carried upon his back. "We found this…"

"For crying out loud, Daniel!" O'Neill growled the words, anger in his voice and in the tight set of his jaw.

"We have to trust someone," Daniel Jackson said, and in his hands he held something black and square that looked alien to Sorcha's eyes. "We found this," he explained, "at *Acarsaid Dorch*. We think it could help fix the shield — make it work."

Sorcha felt her heart race, blood pounding like waves in her ears. Across the room, Rhionna sucked air through her teeth. Sorcha closed her fingers into fists, endeavoring to hide the thudding of her heart from the strangers. With a careful nod, she said, "You have brought us a gift, Daniel Jackson. We would be fools to ignore that."

"Then you'll help us?"

Sorcha inclined her head. "Yes. O'Neill is correct. Finding *Sciath Dé* will protect all of us from our enemies, by whichever name we know them." Across the shack she caught Rhionna's eye. "Finding it is more important than anything else."

"Sorcha!" A head appeared around the canvas door, a midday scarf protecting his face; it was Maor, one of her runners. When the lad saw the strangers in her shack his voice faded, but she encouraged him to continue with a brief nod. In a quieter voice, half a glance lingering on Rhionna, Maor said, "The Seachrání have been sighted, coming around *Dubh Carraig*. Closing fast."

In the shaded light, Rhionna Channon hissed a curse.

Sunlight ricocheted off the water, and even with her shades it was difficult to look at the sea for long. Besides, the ships were too far off the coast for Sam to see them clearly. From what she could make out, they resembled tall ships of old, majestic and proud. Every so often, their sails would flash in the sunlight, as if they were made of mirrors. It was so bright she had to look away, back up to the cobalt sky. And for an instant she saw something, an ephemeral arc of color — like a translucent rainbow — then another and another, all across the sky. Some kind of aurora, she guessed, photons dancing in a fierce solar wind. She smiled, entranced as always by the beauty of the cosmos, and was about to comment when the colonel spoke.

"Looks like you've got company, Sorcha." He was squinting through his monocular, sunglasses pushed up onto his forehead.

A handful of small boats, fishing dories and dinghies, were

cutting rapidly through the waves, heading for the shore. No, not through the waves, Sam noted, but on top of them, the vessels utilizing some form of hover technology. Sam's curiosity twitched, especially when she saw that the sails were made of the same reflective material that was used on the ships. Solar panels, she was sure. The largest dory sailed in front, crewed by a lone boatman.

Rhionna stepped forward, as if to better make out the figure, and Sam noticed the tense set of her jaw. By her side, her hands had balled into fists.

"Is it him?" asked Sorcha.

"I don't know," replied Rhionna, her voice hoarse. Then a pause. "Yes, I think so."

"Is it who?" asked Colonel O'Neill. "Someone we need to worry about?"

Rhionna shook her head. "He's no one. A scavenger. A beggar. He's not important."

From the expression on her face, Sam suspected that the opposite was true. The colonel apparently shared her sentiments. "That's quite an armada he's got out there, for a beggar."

Rhionna ignored him. "What's he doing here, Sorcha?"

The older woman shrugged. "I have not the slightest idea. But if your friends here are in search of *Sciath Dé* then it is fortunate that he has come, is it not?"

Sam caught the colonel's eye; definitely important then.

"No one wants him here, Sorcha. No one trusts him." Rhionna's sharp words sounded almost like a reprimand.

"Remember what is important, Rhionna," Sorcha replied. "We must all make sacrifices."

Rhionna's jaw clenched. "I'm sorry." Then she turned away without another word and strode back into Sorcha's hut.

"Someone mind telling me who the hell this guy is? And whether or not I'll have to shoot him?"

Sam could hear the thread of impatience running through

the colonel's words. It spoke to a new anxiety within herself that she was reluctant to acknowledge, one that made her want to turn tail and run at even the slightest hint of a threat, one that kept her on edge, constantly suspecting, never trusting. The fallout, she supposed, of having your own mind used as a weapon against you. A P90 was nothing compared to that.

"The Seachrání are no threat to you, O'Neill," said Sorcha. She seemed relaxed enough, and Sam tried to take comfort in that. "They are a people who simply choose to live by their own rules."

"Oh goody," said the colonel, "pirates." He jerked his thumb over his shoulder. "And what about this guy?" The boats were almost at the rickety docks. In the lead vessel, the lone figure seated in its stern was more visible now, but his face was obscured by black goggles and a faded scarf tied around his mouth, a wide brimmed hat pulled low on his head.

"That is Faelan Garret," replied Sorcha. "An intriguing individual." She turned to look in the direction Rhionna had gone. "He is a man who inspires strong reactions in many people."

Sam cast her eye over the shanty town. "It looks like Rhionna's not the only one who isn't exactly pleased to see him." People had gathered there, at the edge of the dilapidated shacks. They clustered in groups, watching the arrival of the newcomers, every nuance of their body language radiating caution.

Sorcha just shrugged. "The Seachrání do not give much of themselves away. Their ways are strange, and people fear that which they do not understand, eh? Fear and fascination mixed in equal measure. They live far from here and allow very few outsiders within their Cove. But they keep us supplied with oil, with water when they can spare it, and with food when they can catch it. Many from the Badlands, I think, would join them, but they are a reclusive band. Too many secrets, perhaps."

"And how does he fit in?" asked the colonel, watching the stranger.

"I suppose you'd call Faelan Garret their leader, though he'd dispute the claim."

"Rhionna doesn't seem to like him," Daniel observed, glancing up at the hut.

Sorcha chuckled. "Dislike isn't quite how I'd describe it. As I said, strong reactions."

"Not so unimportant as she'd have us believe then?"

"Daniel Jackson, the only person who would truly believe Faelan Garret unimportant is Faelan himself. Come, I'll introduce you to him. You could be useful to each other, I think."

She led them down to the quay while Garret's dory glided in to dock, the other boats following. With a graceful leap, he landed on the wooden planking and began mooring his boat, an antiquated looking vessel at odds with the intriguing technology it employed. Sam itched to ask him about it, but she knew this was not the time. Judging by what Sorcha had said, she doubted she would get any answers anyway.

The man turned, his long gray duster flapping round his ankles, then pulled off his hat, glasses and scarf to reveal dark hair that hung over his forehead, and a face which, despite its weather-hardened skin, was younger than Sam had expected. His eyes, though, suggested he had lived three lifetimes, none of them good. It was those eyes that now narrowed as they took in SG-1, becoming guarded and uncertain. Without looking back, he tossed the line of his boat to one of the sailors. The man caught it and finished the task of securing it to the dock.

"*Dia dhuit*, Sorcha," said Faelan, though he didn't look at her, his gaze scanning the team instead. The other Seachráni drew in behind him, their stance far from casual. This was a defense formation, Sam suspected, one they knew by rote, geared for fight or flight.

"*Dia dhuit*, Faelan. *Céad míle fáilte*." Sorcha stepped forward, between Faelan and SG-1, as if providing a barrier, though Sam could not guess whom she was protecting. "Faelan, these people are visitors from another world. They came through the Sungate."

His sharp eyes flicked towards her, disbelief written on his face. "But that's –"

"I always told you it was true."

"They're from *Acarsaid Dorch* then?"

Sorcha laughed. "No, the Sungate opens to other places too. Not just there. Can you imagine, Faelan? Can you conceive of the possibilities?"

"Of course he can't," said a brittle voice. "He can barely conceive of anything beyond himself."

Faelan's jaw tensed, his dark features turning stormy, while Sam and the others spun around to find Rhionna standing behind them. Her arms were crossed and, though her expression was hard to read behind her dark glasses, tension radiated from her.

"Rhionna," said Faelan, dispensing with the warm greeting he had offered Sorcha. "Not seen you in quite a while. Still doing your bit for needy causes, I see. The folk of the Badlands must thank their lucky stars to have the condescension of so… fashionable a patroness." His words were mocking, but Sam thought she could detect something raw beneath them.

"It's not condescension, it's called caring. Not that you'd be familiar with that concept."

"I'm familiar with the concept of a losing battle."

"Ever the defeatist, Faelan."

"Ever the dreamer, Rhionna."

She shrugged, as if conceding the point. "But not so much as I used to be, eh?"

For some reason, that halted him in his tracks, and he didn't reply.

"Must we go through this every time?" The exasperation was not hard to hear in Sorcha's tone, but both Faelan and Rhionna seemed oblivious to anything but each other.

Colonel O'Neill cleared his throat. "Not that this situation is at all awkward or uncomfortable, but is there a chance we could get out of this sun? I'm crisping here."

Faelan glanced at the sky and brushed his hair back from his eyes, before pushing his hat back on. "The Burn will start soon. We should get inside. And I've news you might want to hear."

"A storm?" The worry in Sorcha's voice told Jack this was likely to be more than just a little thunder and lightning.

Faelan nodded, wiping sweat from his forehead with his shirt sleeve. Outside the midday sun scorched everything it touched, and in the stuffy half-light of Sorcha's shack the heat was unbearable, especially with an extra couple of bodies now crowding inside. The Burn could not have been a more fitting name for this time of day. Jack pulled the collar of his t-shirt away from his neck and wished they'd landed on a planet where nudity was acceptable.

"We've endured storms before," said Sorcha. "Why the need for such a dire warning, Faelan?"

"There's never been a storm like this before. The readings from our data buoys are off the scale."

Carter leaned forward, perspiration darkening the ends of her hair. "What readings?" Jack knew it was curiosity that made her ask the question, but Faelan frowned as if she were doubting him. "Salinity, wave height, water temperature. But it's more than that. I can just feel it. I can smell it. It's going to hit fast, and it's going to be big."

"How fast?" asked Jack.

"Three days. Maybe a little longer, but not much." He turned to Sorcha. "You've got to get the people out of the Badlands. Get them to safety."

"But the shelters–"

"A few pits in the hillside aren't going to be good enough. They have to get to higher ground."

With a bark of laughter, Rhionna pushed herself away from the wall. "And where do you propose we take them? You pride yourself on being such a realist, but are you actually listening to yourself?"

Faelan rose to face her.

"Oh, here we go again," muttered Jack.

"You know for a fact that there is more than enough space in the Ark to harbor them."

"Yes, I'm sure that the Elect will just throw the doors wide open when I show up and tell them I've brought some guests for dinner."

Faelan shrugged, but the gesture looked forced and deliberate. "You asked me for a solution, and I gave you one. I only came to pass on fair warning about the storm. What you do now is none of my business."

"None of your –? God, Faelan, how can you be so ignorant? You've shut yourself away in the Cove for so long that you've become blind to the plight of these people."

"Don't you dare, Rhionna," he said in a low voice.

"Um," said Daniel, with half a glance at Jack, "maybe we can help? Perhaps if we spoke to your father. Explained the situation –?"

And this was how it began. Always. "Daniel."

"What? Are we just going to do nothing?"

"Speaking to my father is futile," Rhionna said, before Jack could answer. She offered Daniel a weak smile. "Thank you, though. But I'm afraid that, in my father's eyes, these people are already damned. Besides, he is not the one who wields the power in the Elect."

Jack didn't have to ask to know that she was referring to Camus. He looked at Faelan, who was still glaring at Rhionna. "What about this Cove? Can't you take them there?"

But Faelan just shook his head and looked away.

"Why not?"

"Because these people are not my concern! The Cove is for the Seachtraní."

"So, what?" Daniel snapped, "You're just going to let them die here?"

"It's no business of yours," Faelan retorted. "I've come here to warn them, and that's all I can do."

A sudden silence dropped, hot and stifling. Into it, Rhionna spoke in a low voice full of apprehension. "Because the Cove's not safe either, is it?"

"We'll be fine," he said "The Cove is protected."

Jack doubted it, and he wasn't the only one. Rhionna grabbed hold of Faelan's sleeve, forcing him to turn and face her.

"Faelan, the Cove is crumbling into the sea. It won't survive this kind of storm. Tell me you have somewhere else to go." Beneath a thin veneer of anger, you could hear what almost sounded like a plea.

Faelan took hold of her arm and loosened her grip on him. He didn't let go of her wrist. "We'll be fine, Rhionna. Muirne is helping us."

"You're not serious! That place can barely support those already living there. It will never hold all of the Seachtraní."

There was a moment of silence that spoke volumes. "It will take most of us," said Faelan, though he didn't look Rhionna in the eye.

She pulled away, freeing herself from Faelan's grip with an impatient jerk of her arm. "But not you."

"What is it you want me to tell you, Rhionna?" The man's voice thickened with a weariness familiar to Jack. It was the voice of an old soldier who'd suffered through too many battles and knew when the last stand was about to be fought. It was the voice of a guy with one final bullet in the clip. It didn't belong on someone so young.

"I want you to tell me you'll figure it out."

He shook his head. "Rhionna."

Reluctant as he was to encroach on what was becoming an increasingly private moment, Jack spoke up. "Why don't you bring them here? There's room in the Ark for these folks as well as your own — take the lead, make them let you in."

"The Seachrání are hardly welcome in the Badlands, never mind up there," growled an old man who sat in the corner. Jack was pretty sure the phrase 'sea dog' had been invented to describe him. "They won't open their doors to the likes of us."

"So break them down."

"We don't interfere in business that isn't Seachrání."

Jack's retort died on his tongue. The man's words echoed his own feelings too closely; sometimes you just had to take care of your own.

"Settle down, Pádraig," said Faelan. "We won't be breaking down any doors."

"Why did you even come here, Faelan?" said Rhionna.

"Don't –"

"Your warnings are just words, if you don't take action. O'Neill is right — bring your people here, lead us all into the Ark."

He shook his head.

"Help me help these people, Faelan. You know you could. You won't even try!"

His face hardened and he turned away, snatching his hat up from the bench where he'd sat. "Burn's almost over. We need to get back to the ship." He stalked to the door. A jerk of his head summoned Pádraig to follow.

Daniel scrambled to his feet as the flap shut behind Faelan, grabbing his camcorder from the ground. "I'm going with him."

"I don't think so." Jack looked stubborn beneath his Wiley-X shades.

"Just to the docks. We didn't even ask him about the shield." Daniel slipped his own sunglasses on, plunging the dim shack into even deeper gloom. "This could be our only chance, Jack."

At his side, he saw Teal'c rise. "I shall accompany him, O'Neill."

"Me too." Sam got up too, she looked hot and uncomfortable, and Daniel figured she wanted some fresh air as much as he did. As fresh as you could get in this furnace of a place. "I'd like to check out the technology on their boats, sir. I think they might be using some kind of solar technology which could possibly be transferable to —"

"Okay." Jack held up a hand, cutting her off. "We'll all go."

But as he started to head for the door, Sorcha reached out her hand and clasped his arm. "Wait."

Jack looked down; Daniel didn't even know how he could see her through his sunglasses in the gloomy shack. "What?"

"I would speak with you, Colonel O'Neill. We have matters to discuss."

Jack rubbed at the back of his neck, then with a sigh said, "Sure, why not?" He jerked his head toward Daniel. "Keep in touch."

Fishing his hat out of a pocket, Daniel nodded. "Will do."

He'd just turned to leave when Rhionna moved past him. Sweat stained the bandanna tied about her head, and she pulled her goggles on before he could make eye contact. Her face was set, somewhere between anger and hurt. "I'll show you down to the docks," she said, slipping out into the glare.

Daniel followed in silence. Suspecting that she had other motives for her decision to follow Faelan Garret, he didn't point out that the docks would be hard to miss.

Outside the heat was fierce. The Burn might be over, but it still felt like being caught between a hammer and an anvil. Even through his boots he could feel the scorching earth. "How do they survive in this?" he asked, half to himself and half to Rhionna.

"They don't," she said, not turning around. "Not for long. Life expectancy here is very short — too much disease, most of it caused by the Burn. Everyone has cankers on their skin, many are blind, especially the children. The sunlight damages their eyes, burns away their sight."

"I can feel it," Sam said from behind them. "I can feel my hands burning." She was looking down at her fingers, turning them over in the glare. "You want some sunblock, Daniel?"

At that word, Rhionna turned. "Sunblock?"

Sam pulled a tube of factor 50 from her vest. "It can prevent sun damage to your skin," she told Rhionna, squeezing some into her hand. "It prevents the harmful light reaching it."

Rhionna regarded her. "Your people have great Knowledge, do they not?"

"About some things," Sam said. "That's the kind of thing we could share with your people."

In the distance, down at the water's edge, a commotion had broken out. Faelan was talking in heated tones to Pádraig, who was overseeing the unloading of a mishmash of plastic containers. Impatient to be gone, Faelan was gesturing toward the boats. His comrade remained stalwart, meeting temper with folded arms and a phlegmatic shrug. It reminded Daniel of Jack railing at Teal'c.

Rhionna made a sound, somewhere between a snort and a laugh. "Pádraig is one of the few men who can stand his ground against Faelan."

"You managed pretty well," Daniel said.

"For all the good it did." Rhionna turned away and continued to walk down to the docks.

"Touchy," Sam said, offering Daniel the sun block as they

watched Rhionna pick her way through the shanty town.
Several children darted out of the shade as she passed, hanging onto her hands and following her toward the sea. They
were thin and wiry, their skin dry and damaged.

"I think I might be touchy too, living here," Daniel said.
On impulse he pulled out his camcorder, capturing the children who fled into doorways and under drooping eaves to
avoid the sun. One of them stumbled and fell, turning blind
eyes to the camera as he scrambled upright and disappeared
into the shadows of a shack. Daniel felt his heart constrict,
pumping anger with every beat.

"I know what you mean," Sam agreed with a sigh. Then
she tapped him on the shoulder and started walking again.
"Come on, I want to check out that solar technology before
Faelan leaves."

Trailing along, he kept his camera rolling as they made
their way past the flimsy shacks that made up this flotsam
city. Daniel tried not to think about a storm raging through
the Badlands, with seas rising and the wind screeching like a
banshee. You didn't need much imagination to see the whole
place swept away like so much garbage.

How Jack could pretend it was none of their business he
couldn't fathom, not for a moment. And he'd be damned if
he'd leave these people to their fate, whatever Jack O'Neill
had to say on the matter.

"You don't want to be here," Sorcha said, sitting back on
her heels and watching the man called O'Neill as he ducked
back in to her home. "In this shack," she said, flicking her
wrist to encompass all. "Or on this world."

For the first time since they had met, he pulled the sunwear from his face. The eyes beneath were penetrating, but
gave away little — as guarded by nature as they had been by
the glasses. "In my experience," he said, "sticking your nose
into other people's business never ends well. All we want is

the lowdown on this shield."

"You see how we live — how they live inside the Ark. Do you feel no pity, no outrage?"

"I've seen a lot of things, in a lot of places." His expression hardened. "And paid the price for getting involved."

She spread her hands. "Then we face an impasse, O'Neill. For I know much of the shield, but what incentive do I have to speak of it, if there is no gain for me or my people?"

O'Neill's face twisted and he scrubbed a hand through graying hair. It was strange to see such a shade, for most men of the Badlands were dead long before their hair turned silver, victims of disease or the Burn. "What do you want from us?" he asked, turning away and lifting the door flap to peer outside. "Sure, we could send medicine and food, but the gate's inside the city and I'm betting Ennis isn't going to deliver."

"Pastor Ennis," she spat onto the floor, "would see us all burn, if he had his way."

Where O'Neill had lifted the door flap the sun cut a harsh line into her shack. Sorcha edged away from it. "We don't need your food or medicine; there is plenty within the Ark."

He dropped the flap, and the shack fell back into shadow. "Then go get it. There's got to be thousands of people here. Just go into the city and take what you need."

She barked a dry laugh. "So easy as that?"

"Why not?"

"My people are already defeated, O'Neill. They need someone to show them that the battle is worth fighting. They need a leader."

In the gloom she could make out only half his face. Just enough to see him frown. "Rhionna?"

Sorcha shrugged. "Rhionna has done her best, but the Badlanders can be prejudiced too. Sometimes they see only a woman of rank and privilege who will one day become Pastor, just like her father. When that day comes, she says she will bring change, but even then she shall have the Elect to deal with. She cannot help us on her own."

"And what is it you think we can do to help?"

She looked up at him, searching for the dark glint of his eyes. "Find *Sciath Dé* , and make it work."

He regarded her in silence. From outside she could hear the calls of people at the dock, the clink of rigging on the ships moored there, the thud of skins of whale oil being unloaded. The Seachrání had come to trade, then, as well as warn.

"This shield," O'Neill said at last, "what is it?"

"It is the last hope for our world," she admitted, her heart pattering at the risk she was taking.

"Last hope how?"

"*Sciath Dé* was made in the time Time Before, to protect Ierna from the power of our sun."

A flash of recognition crossed O'Neill's face, swiftly followed by suspicion. "Shield of the Gods," he said, low, as if he spoke to himself. "Let me guess, it was given to you by your 'Lord'?"

Sorcha shook her head. "Pastor Channon will tell you it was made by apostates to thwart the Lord's will." She gave a sour smile. "Since His will is that the damned succumb to the Burn I cannot be sorry for that." Narrowing her eyes, she endeavored to read O'Neill's expression. "But I think you have seen such a thing before?"

"Something like it," he said, evasive now. "You wanna tell me what it looks like? Big column of orange light shooting up into the sky? That kinda thing?"

"*Sciath Dé* failed, Jack O'Neill. No one now living has seen it, few even believe in its existence."

"And what about the Goa'uld? You believe in them?"

"I know nothing of your enemies," Sorcha said, spreading her hands to show the truth. "All I know is that the seas rose and all of Ierna was lost. All but the Ark and the fanatics who stole our refuge for themselves."

O'Neill's shoulders rose and fell, as though he were sighing in resignation. "That's why the Ark is half empty then?"

"Those who have," Sorcha said, "fear those who have not. In our faces, they see their own fate and dread it. So we must build a future for ourselves, here beyond the Ark — once *Sciath Dé* can shield us from the sun."

"And what makes you think we can help you?"

"Because you have been to *Acarsaid Dorch*, because you have brought from there the Knowledge that we have lost."

O'Neill shook his head. "I'm sorry, we're not here to — "

"Would you turn your back?" Desperation made her angry, but she strove to hide her temper as she scrambled to her feet. Though O'Neill towered over her she was not afraid. Let him kill her if he would, it mattered not; she knew in her bones that, if these strangers did not help, no other chance would come in her lifetime. "Would you return to your world and leave us here, O'Neill, as those in the Ark do? Would you close the gates to us and let us die?"

"There are thousands of you out here," he said, "why don't you storm the Ark? Make them let you in?"

"You have seen their soldiers. Would we fight them with our bare hands?"

"Yes!"

"Folly," she spat. "As you well know, O'Neill."

He glared at her, then turned away. His back was stiff and she could hear him suck in a breath and let it out. "This isn't our fight," he said. "This isn't why we came here."

"You came here to find *Sciath Dé*," Sorcha said. "And that is all that I ask of you now."

Without turning around he said, "I take it you know where it is?"

In silence, she moved to her sleeping pallet. From beneath it she withdraw the small book in which she wrote the truths she had learned. It was her most precious possession, and she had no intention of giving it to this man. Nursing it as she sat, she said to him, "First, you must know of the Cove.

There our secrets are hidden. Rooms upon rooms of secrets, most lost to the sea. But some are still dry and from them I have woven my theories. Faelan thinks those the wild ramblings of an old woman, but he is a child of the sea and takes no interest in past times. But I… I would know more, Jack O'Neill. I would know more of a world where land spread to the far horizon and people roamed it, as the *moil mór* roam the sea."

O'Neill looked back at her, a slight grimace crossing his face as he moved; his knee, she suspected, carried an old wound. "That's what it was like here then, back in the day?"

"Does it sound farfetched? Have you ever seen such vast stretches of land?"

He paused for a moment, and Sorcha realized she was holding her breath. Then, with a curt nod, he said, "Yeah, pretty much every place I've been."

"Oh…" She sighed, grief and joy combined. "Then it is true — the legends of the Time Before are real."

"Do you know what caused it, this flood?"

Sorcha lifted her face to the ceiling. "Ennis believes the Lord sent his Sun to rid the world of sin."

"And what do you believe?"

She smoothed her hand over the cover of her book. "I believe…" Her heart thumped loud in her chest; she had never spoken of this to anyone other than the Seachráni. Speaking of it now put them at risk, but she had waited so long and perhaps it was these very people for whom she had been waiting. Sorcha met his gaze and in a low voice said, "I believe the shield was constructed at the Cove, and that there you will find the answers we seek."

"The Cove."

"You must persuade Faelan to take you there; you and the object you brought from *Acarsaid Dorch*."

O'Neill rubbed a hand across his chin. "I'm sorry. That's not why we — "

A loud rat-tat-tat ricocheted through the Badlands, followed by shouting and a terrified scream. O'Neill was on his feet in an instant. "That was gunfire."

"Soldiers," Sorcha hissed, lifting the heavy stone beneath her hearth and dropping her book into the space below. "Ennis has sent his men."

A slick click drew her eyes to O'Neill's weapon; he held it ready for use. "Stay here," he said, and ducked out beneath the canvas.

Chaos descended on them with the thunder of boots and the sharp report of warning fire, turning the chatter of children into screams of terror. Teal'c readied his staff weapon, crouching into a defensive stance. By his side, Major Carter adopted a similar position. The Seachráni too were arming themselves, withdrawing mean looking blades from the folds of their ragged garments. Such weapons would be ineffectual, of course, against the automatic weapons of the Elect Guard.

Guns raised, the soldiers came to a halt just yards away, disciplined and determined; warriors then, despite the Ark's benign façade. For if there had been any doubt that this was the city's militia, it was dispelled by the man who stalked through their ranks. Tynan Camus stared at them with steely-eyed fury, and in his wake Ennis Channon cowered, milk-faced.

"You would disobey the will of the Elect, Rhionna Channon?" Tynan's voice was calm, as it always was, but there was an edge to it that signaled danger.

"You brought an army here just because I disobeyed you?"

"I brought an army here to deal with these... Seawolves." He spat the last word. "They are a pollution. A danger not only to our way of life, but to these people to whom you so desperately wish to provide salvation."

"How dare you! How dare you feign sympathy for their plight when you would have them washed into the sea if you could." Rhionna's face was rigid with anger, while the Seachrání, poised and ready for battle, awaited the command of their leader. Teal'c did not dare to lower his weapon; the air crackled with tension, and he knew blood would be shed unless matters were diffused quickly. As always, Daniel Jackson was the one to take the task of arbitration upon himself.

"There's no need for violence. The Seachrání haven't come here with hostile intentions, Brother Camus. They only came to warn these people that a storm's headed this way." His voice was calm and reassuring, but neither side moved. "In fact, Tynan, your coming here today may prove useful. We need to find a safe place for these people during the storm, and Rhionna tells us that the Ark has plenty of space..."

Tynan let out a bark of laughter. "You expect us to shelter these... sinners? The Ark is a sanctuary for those chosen by God. It is a hallowed place. I would not sully it with the stench of these wretched creatures."

This provoked a torrent of angry shouts from the Seachrání and the crowd who had gathered nearby to watch the drama unfold.

"Please!" called Daniel, raising his hands, palms outward. "Please listen." He moved towards the nearest member of the Seachrání, the bull-faced man Faelan had called Pádraig. His second in command, Teal'c supposed.

"Daniel..." Major Carter's caution was low but firm, her P90 still held tight to her shoulder.

"It's ok, Sam." He turned to the man with a placating gesture. "Lower your weapons and we can discuss this with the Pastor. Ennis — surely you won't hurt these people. They've done no harm and they need your help. After all," he added, nodding towards Faelan, "this man is already your daughter's friend."

Immediately, Teal'c knew it was the wrong thing to say.

Tynan Camus's expression turned to one of cold contempt while Ennis, who had been pensive and wary, suddenly turned thunderous.

"Friend?" he snarled.

"Father, please!"

But Rhionna Channon's plea went unheard. "This Seawolf scum defiled my daughter! He turned her away from the Light and cast her into shadow. He stole her from me, Dr. Jackson. And he will Burn for it! Seize him!" As soon as the order was given, the soldiers moved. Major Carter cried out a warning, but there were too many of them for one P90 and a staff weapon. The Seachrání raised their blades to fight, despite the odds, and Teal'c admired their tenacity. Then Faelan Garret charged with a yell.

From the corner of his eye, Teal'c saw a blur of dark hair as Rhionna Channon ran forward. "Faelan! No!" Then all was motion, all was madness, and with a flash of steel Faelan made his move. "Stop where you are or I'll cut her damn throat!"

Everything slammed to a halt, teetering on a knife edge.

"You would not," hissed Ennis, his eyes wide, gaze fixed like everyone else's on the man who held a blade to his daughter's jugular. In Faelan's arms Rhionna Channon moved not a muscle.

"Believe me, Pastor, I would."

"Faelan, what are you doing?" Rhionna's voice contained the barest tremor; she was afraid but seeking to conceal it. "This is lunacy."

"Always had a bit of madness about me, wouldn't you say?" he muttered in her ear, before turning back to Ennis. "Tell your men to back off, Pastor."

"You are a fool," Tynan Camus said, "if you think to threaten us with the life of one woman who has already fallen into darkness."

Faelan pulled her head backward, exposing more of her throat. "What say you, Pastor? Will you see her die here, now?"

Ennis Channon appeared frozen. But as Tynan opened his mouth to speak once more, the Pastor grabbed his arm and said, "In the name of the Lord, Tynan, she is my daughter."

"Is she?"

That question remained unanswered, but after a pause Ennis Channon gestured to the soldiers to lower their guns.

"You will answer for this," Tynan said, icy beneath the beating sun. "You will answer before the Council."

Ennis did not reply, and Teal'c kept his staff weapon leveled at the soldiers, in case any of them chose to act against the Pastor.

"Now you, Faelan." Major Carter had her P90 aimed at Faelan. "Lower the knife and let her go. I have a shot, Garret, and I swear I'll take it."

But Faelan only grinned, and it was then that Teal'c saw the reason why.

"Uh, Sam…" Stock still and looking more than a little chagrined, Daniel Jackson stood off to one side, the fierce sunlight reflecting like fire upon the blade that Pádraig held to his throat.

The old woman ignored his order to stay in her shack — no surprise there. Tugging a thin veil across her eyes, she scurried after him as Jack stalked through the rat's nest of alleyways and toward the sounds of commotion.

He could hear shouting — a man's voice raised in desperation, his words lost in a thick accent that Jack found difficult to penetrate. He had no difficulty, however, making out Daniel's placating tones.

"It's okay, everyone just…calm down."

Jack slowed at a corner where the wall of a shack — it might once have been the side of a packing crate — stuck out awkwardly into the alley and provided enough cover for him to peer around.

Behind him, Sorcha moved on silent feet; nimble for an old bird. He waved her back and put his finger to his lips. She ignored his order with a toss of her head and crowded close, peering with him around the corner.

Jack muttered a curse. Through the narrow gap between the shacks, he could make out the glitter of the sea, the ragged dock. Standing to one side, half obscured by the makeshift structures, was Faelan. With one arm, he held Rhionna pinned against his chest, the free hand pressed a knife to her throat. His second in command stood next to him — and he had Daniel. Opposite stood Sam and Teal'c, weapons raised, and behind them Ennis's soldiers were arrayed in attack formation. It was simply a question of who killed whom first.

"Crap."

Sorcha grunted her agreement. "Now," she said, "things are more complicated."

"Ya think?" Jack tried to draw a bead, but couldn't get a clear shot at the guy holding Daniel. Besides, firing first would be like throwing a spark into a tinder box.

"Back off!" Faelan shouted. "Y'hear me? I'll cut her throat, and don't think I won't!"

Jack didn't miss the tremor in that knife-hand, but wasn't convinced the man was lying. Faelan looked desperate enough to do anything as he backed toward his boat.

"Listen to him, Father! He means it!" Rhionna's fingers clutched at her captor's arm, pulling it back from her throat.

His only choice, Jack decided, was to circle around behind them. He figured he had two, maybe three, minutes before Faelan reached the boat and got away. But it was going to be tight, and there was every chance the whole thing would blow up in his face — with Carter, Daniel, and Teal'c the sitting ducks in the middle. Lowering his gun, Jack pulled back around the corner.

"Don't follow," he ordered Sorcha. "I mean it."

Despite the sun, she lifted the ragged gauze from her face and pinned him with a beady eye. "Once Faelan has gone, he'll not be back. Not for a long time."

He drew his Beretta and chambered a round. "Exactly why he's not gonna be taking Daniel with him."

The old woman put her hand on the gun. "Do you think you can end this with violence?"

"Can you think of a better way?"

She jerked her head toward the docks. "There are many ships, and you seem like a resourceful man. Travel with the Seachráni to the Cove and you will have an opportunity to free your friend without risking the lives of so many."

"And while we're at it we can find your shield?"

Her lined face was impassive. "Perhaps fate has conspired to join our interests together, Jack O'Neill."

"Convenient," he said with a sigh. "You know, if it wasn't crazy, I might think you'd planned this all along."

Sorcha said nothing. She didn't have to. She knew he had no choice.

There was a chance, Sam knew, that she could take aim and fire before the man holding Daniel had time to inflict a fatal wound with his knife. There was a chance that Teal'c could dispatch any of the soldiers who might decide to take matters into their own hands. And there was an above-average chance that Faelan was bluffing and that he had no intention of hurting Rhionna. In fact Sam was more certain of that than of anything else.

But Sam Carter didn't deal in chances. She dealt in fact and hard evidence, and the evidence told her that, with one P90 and a staff weapon against two warring factions, the odds were not in their favor. She didn't take the shot. Nor did she lower her gun.

"You're making a mistake, Faelan. Tell your men to stand down and release your hostages."

"Not a chance."

Ennis Channon strode forward, jowly face white with fear and rage. "I swear I shall send you to perdition, Garret!"

Faelan barked a hard laugh and looked around him. "Your kind sent us all there long ago, Pastor." He started moving backwards, dragging Rhionna with him, and Pádraig followed suit, leading Daniel back towards the boats. Their knives sat snug against their hostages' necks.

Once they were in the boats Sam knew it would be almost impossible to stop them. She sensed the Elect troops grow restless behind her, a tinderbox ready to ignite — with Rhionna, Daniel, and who knew how many innocent people, caught in the conflagration. "Hold your men back, Camus," she said, without taking her eyes off the retreating Seachrání. "We'll settle this without bullets if we can."

"Do not presume to give orders to the Elect," Tynan growled. "Men, open — "

"Unless you wish to feel the burn of a staff blast, Tynan Camus," said Teal'c in smooth tones, "you should heed Major Carter's words."

There was silence, save perhaps the sound of Tynan's teeth grinding, but none of the soldiers made a move.

Sam took slow steps forward, keeping Pádraig in the gun's sight, but the Seachrání held the advantage and she knew she couldn't take the shot. If the colonel was anywhere near, perhaps he could —

Movement behind and to the left of the Seachrání caught her attention, and she slid a furtive glance in that direction. In the near distance, Colonel O'Neill was in a crouch, trying to keep to the cover of the rocks littering the coastline, making his way towards one of the Seachrání longboats. There was a burst of static in her earpiece, and then his low voice. "Stand down, Major. Can't win this one." With a lurch she realized what he was doing. He was choosing his battlefield, letting them take Daniel because he'd be right alongside him, ready to make his move and bring him back.

Major Samantha Carter knew he was right, that the risk of collateral damage was much lower this way. But lately the *major* was at odds with that other part of herself, the part that remembered the burnt iron smell of the furnaces and the heat and grime of a subterranean prison. The part of her that was still Thera.

Still, she wasn't Thera, she was Sam Carter, and Sam Carter followed orders. Grimly, she acknowledged the order with a double tap on her radio and lowered her P90. "Go," she told Faelan.

"What are you doing?" Ennis cried in impotent rage, his gaze darting between Rhionna and the staff weapon Teal'c pointed at him. "Please, my daughter…"

"Let her go," Tynan sneered. "It is for the Lord to judge her now."

"No! Men, stop—"

The hiss of the staff weapon opening cut him off. "I advise silence," Teal'c said.

"Wise move, Miss," said Faelan, backing towards the boats. But there was a tremor in his voice, and the hand that held the knife shook. Sam wondered if the situation had spiraled out of his control.

Ignoring him, she looked at Daniel. "I'm sorry. We'll bring you back."

Daniel gave a reassuring smile. "It's okay," he said, as Pádraig pulled him backwards into the boat. "You did the right thing."

Sam wasn't so sure, but there was nothing she could do except stand powerless on the dock, watching as her friend was shoved into Faelan's dory and the motley flotilla sped off toward the larger vessels that squatted in the sunlight far out to sea.

And then, behind her, Tynan ordered, "Seize the strangers."

CHAPTER SIX

WHITE steps gleamed beneath the noontide glare, and Pastor Ennis Channon climbed them slowly. It was a mark of respect for the Chambers of the Elect, yes, but also a useful moment of self-reflection. Time to compose himself before his audience.

Rhionna was gone, taken by the black-handed villain who had first defiled her. His grief and anger would have been less if he could believe that she had not gone willingly. But he knew his daughter too well; she stood in sin, she had turned from the light of the Sun long ago and rejected the duty for which God had granted her life. Ennis prayed every day for her soul, but he feared that prayer would not be enough. The Elect would demand more.

At the top of the steps, he paused to catch his breath and looked up at the glistening pillars that flanked the entrance to the Chambers. Beyond them hovered darkness, a reminder to those without that the business of the Elect was no business of *theirs*. Pride ran her fingers the length of Ennis's spine, and he stood straighter in his robes of state; from the first time he had come here, his father's death still raw in his heart, he had felt that pride like rock beneath his feet.

He, Ennis Channon, was Pastor of the Ark.

He was Elect, and the glory of the Lord was his promise.

Now, he had to do his duty.

Lifting his hood to cover his head, he stepped into the shadows and walked the familiar path, blind until his eyes adjusted to the dim light. Above the circular audience chamber dust danced in ribbons of brightness that filtered through a hundred narrow slits in the vaulted ceiling. In the shadows beneath the Elect sat in session, their faces obscured by cowled robes.

"Well met, Pastor Channon," said Sister Eilís Nevin, one of

the council elders. "Though this day brings us no joy."

Ennis stopped before the table and bowed his head in polite greeting. "Well met, Sister Nevin. Council."

Nevin sat at the apex of the crescent table, directly before Ennis. Only her narrow jaw and tight-pressed lips were visible beneath her hood. Her expression was enough to reveal her anger, but her brittle voice left no doubt of her fury.

"You have erred, Pastor," she said. "The strangers from the Sungate should never have been allowed to leave the Ark."

Ennis felt a stir of unease. "It was never my intention to — "

"Your intention is irrelevant, only the fact is pertinent. These heretics from the Sungate are dangerous. All the more so as they now are in the hands of the Seawolves."

"Only one was taken by the wolves," Ennis reminded her. "Two are in our custody and the fourth — "

"Roams free in the Badlands." Nevin's lip curled in disgust. "What heresy will he spread there? What discontent will he rouse?"

From the end of the table Tynan Camus spoke, leaning back with feigned nonchalance. His voice was smooth and plausible. "What do we care that these heretics spread their lies among the damned?" Tynan said. "Our walls are strong, and if they choose to wallow in dirt and sin, it is of no concern to us. The Lord punishes them daily; the Burn will take care of their lies." His mouth curved into a smile, and his eyes moved from Nevin to fix firmly on Ennis. "Of course, there is no question that any of those who have rejected the Ark should be permitted to return to its shelter. Leaving is evidence enough that the Lord has not elected them for salvation."

Ennis swallowed. "My daughter — "

"Has been granted grace enough by virtue of her birth!" Tynan pointed a finger, long and elegant. "It is clear to all, Pastor, that she is not among the saved. She was permitted to return once, though all could see the stain of sin upon her flesh. But this? To lead these heretics beyond the Ark? It is too much, even for Rhionna Channon."

"Tynan speaks true," Nevin said, her voice less passionate but no less harsh. "You have no choice, Pastor. These Seawolves may attempt blackmail, but you must cast off your daughter; she is dead to you now."

Rhionna's angry face rose before his eyes, fierce and determined. Beautiful, like her mother. His wife dwelled in the presence of the Lord now, but how could he bear that their daughter would never join her? "Rhionna is no heretic, it is only misplaced compassion that motivates her. If she did lead the strangers out —"

"If?" Tynan sneered, leaning back in his chair.

"It was not done through any disrespect to our Lord," Ennis protested. "Her concerns are only with the people of the Badlands."

"With sinners." Tynan folded his hands upon the table. "Yes, we all know how *personally* she concerns herself with those who endure the Lord's just punishment."

"Intentions matter not, Pastor Channon," Nevin reminded him. "These strangers are more dangerous then even you know, and the deed is done. Tynan is right. None of them may return to the Ark — including your daughter. The Knowledge they carry is too dangerous."

Reeling, Ennis said, "What Knowledge? They came here to seek Knowledge, and we know there is none to find!"

There was a shuffling among the Elect, a low muttering, and then Tynan produced a silver box and placed it on the table. "Do you know what this is?"

Ennis peered at the object, suppressing a shudder. "The one called Daniel Jackson brought it, did he not?"

"He did. It is a camera for the capture of moving images."

"So small?" For a moment, his concern was wiped away by amazement.

Tynan nodded. "Pick it up and press the button on the top."

Doing as instructed, Ennis watched in amazement as the small black screen on the back of the device flickered to life and showed the faces of the strangers. He thought they must be players until he realized that the recording did not proclaim the Message but instead documented their activities — he saw a colorless landscape covered in strange, white sand, pierced by black rocks. He assumed it must be somewhere outside the Ark, for the strangers wore many garments that appeared like sunwear. But then he saw that their clothing was so thick that they would boil beneath the Sun. Was this, then, another world? A world where the Sun was weak and the air cold?

The image changed to that of Jack O'Neill looking down at something in the ground.

Daniel, get over here.

His voice sounded like a tinny rattle. The view changed again, and Ennis started at the sight of human remains, half buried beneath the white sand. He saw a skull, pierced as if by a bullet.

Oh, my God.

Major Carter's voice. Then gloved hands pushed back the strange sand and the focus shifted so that Ennis could read the writing on a tag lost in the skeleton's ribs.

It made the hairs on the back of his neck bristle.

Dr. Maol Caluim.

He all but threw the camera back onto the table. "What is this?"

"*Acarsaid Dorch.*" Tynan's voice was harsh as stone.

"But..." Ennis shook his head in confusion, disturbing his hood until he had to tug it back on. "The Lord struck down the heretics on *Acarsaid Dorch*, how is it that there are any remains?"

"The Lord," Nevin said, picking up the camera and switching it off, "uses many tools to achieve His ends. Their heresy was ended by righteous hands and God's just punishment was delivered to our sinful world. That is all that matters. However..."

Here she paused, and Tynan, still lounging in his chair, continued. "However, the strangers bring Knowledge of Caluim's heresy. They talk of *Sciath Dé*, of bringing it to life in defiance of God's will." His voice lowered, losing its smooth edge. Ennis felt his dread and shared it; the image of Caluim's skull, vivid against *Acarsaid Dorch's* sin-black soil, turned his stomach. "And now that Knowledge will pass to the cursed Seachráni, to the Seawolves who scorn God's people and live in defiance of His teaching."

"They will seek to subvert the will of the Lord," Nevin agreed. "For generations the Ark has sheltered the pure from His wrath and now we must stand, as our forefathers once stood, in defense of His chosen people. *Sciath Dé* must never be activated, and those who seek to try are the enemies of God."

"Will you stand with us, Pastor Ennis?" Tynan said, reclining still but tense, as if he might leap from his chair at any moment. "Will you cast off the daughter who has brought heresy back into our world? Will you stand with the Elect in defense of our Lord?" He paused, the silence slight and meaningful. "Or will you stand with *them*, with the heretics and defilers, who would tear down the Ark and hand our world back to the damned?"

To that question, there could be only one answer. He lifted his chin, shoulders straight. "I stand in God's Light. I stand with the Elect."

Tynan smiled, and it looked like triumph.

As prisons went, it wasn't the worst Sam had been in. It even had cable — whether you wanted it or not. *Sunrise* played on a large TV screen attached to one wall, and to her consternation, during the hours they had been held here, she'd found herself caught up by its meandering plotline and melodramatic dialogue. More than once, she'd had to force herself to look away. Teal'c sat on the floor, legs crossed and eyes closed, and at times like this, when there was nothing to do but wait and worry, Sam envied him his *kelnoreem*.

With even her watch confiscated, along with their weapons and radios, there was no way to tell how long they had been held. However, Sam had counted five episodes of *Sunrise*, each of which were at least an hour long. By now, Daniel and the colonel could be anywhere. She just hoped Ennis's men had some way of tracking the Seachrání, otherwise looking for a couple of ships in that limitless ocean would be close to pointless. On the other hand, if the soldiers did find them, would they just end up in jail like she and Teal'c, facing torture by soap opera? When it came right down to it, Sam wasn't sure which scenario she should hope for.

The opening credits for yet another episode of *Sunrise* rolled across the screen, and Sam fought the urge to scream. Instead she got up and, despite the futility, walked over to examine the featureless cell door once more. Of course, just like the last twenty times she'd checked, it was still sealed by some kind of internal electronic mechanism; there would be no escape this way.

She'd just turned away when the door hissed open behind her. Teal'c was on his feet in an instant, and when Pastor Channon stepped into the cell seconds later Sam briefly considered rushing him. But the two armed guards flanking him changed her mind.

"What's going on, Channon?" she demanded. "Have you found Daniel and Rhionna yet?"

His fleshy face creased with worry, and for a moment she glimpsed a father's anguish. But then his lips tightened and anger swallowed his concern. "It is your other friend who interests me most, Major Carter. Where is Colonel O'Neill?"

She shrugged and made a show of looking around. "Well, he's not in here."

"I think you fail to understand the gravity of this situation. Sorcha Caratauc has already failed to answer my questions and will pay the price, so I would suggest that you show more cooperation."

So they'd taken Sorcha too. She felt a surge of revulsion. "What have you done to her? She's an old woman."

"A troublesome old woman," Channon snapped, "and a corrupter of young minds. Save your pity, Major Carter. You know nothing of this world or its sins."

"I think I know enough — like how half the population live in poverty while you — "

"*That* is the Lord's will."

"Oh, come on, you think I haven't seen this same exact thing on a dozen other planets? Call it God or necessity, it's always the same — the rich get richer and the poor get screwed."

"Enough!" His face flushed red with anger. "I will not hear your heresy. Tell me now where Colonel O'Neill is hiding or face the consequences." The demand contained a note of desperation, and Sam reminded herself that his daughter was also missing.

Getting hold of her own anger, she tried to imagine what Daniel would do in this situation. Reason, look for common ground. "Pastor, listen," she said, striving for calm, "we have technology that could help you find your daughter. If you'll let us return through the Star — Sungate we can bring back a device that would let us locate — "

He took a step back, horror-struck. "You speak of Knowledge?"

Confused, she said, "It's a machine. We call it a UAV."

"You would bring Knowledge here from *Acarsaid Dorch*?"

"No. It's our technology. It's not from there."

Ennis shook his head, sweat beading on his brow. He

swiped at it. "You have broken the law, Major Carter. You have left the Ark and consorted with criminals. Because of you, my daughter is now in the hands of the Seawolves. Do you propose that I just set you free to contaminate the Ark with your heresy?"

"Pastor Channon," said Teal'c, "I believe the Seachráni acted out of fear. Had you not demonstrated such force, they would have left in peace. I do not believe they will harm your daughter."

Channon made a noise of disgust. "They have already harmed her! The Seachráni are brutes. Savages! Their purpose is to sow seeds of unrest and cause disorder wherever they go. It is the sole reason they come to the Badlands."

"You're wrong, Pastor," said Sam. "They came to warn the people there. To warn you. You have to–"

"The storm?" He waved a dismissive hand, but Sam could see a thread of fear in his eyes. "Storms do not concern us in the Ark."

"And what of those outside the Ark?" said Teal'c.

For a moment he clamped his jaw shut, then said, as if by rote, "If it is God's will that they be punished, then who am I to question Him?"

"But what about Rhionna?" Sam said.

Ennis didn't reply, his face rigid.

"You can't believe she deserves to be punished," Sam pressed. "She was kidnapped. So was Daniel." She took a step closer and might have put a hand on his arm if he hadn't looked so brittle. "Let us out of here, let us help you with the search and rescue."

His brow creased as she spoke, his eyes flitting away to fix on the screen behind her. The *Sunrise* music swelled into the room. "There will be no search and rescue."

At first, she doubted she'd heard him right. "You mean you haven't started looking for them? Five hours and you haven't even started looking for them?"

"We have not the means. There is no need for ships in the Ark."

"But the people of the Badlands, they have boats. They're small, of course, but surely–"

"We have no need of ships, Major Carter, because anyone who turns their back on the Lord and puts themselves in the hands of the Seachrání is already damned. The Elect have passed their judgment on the matter."

Silence fell as the meaning of his words sank in. No search, no rescue, and as far as Ennis was concerned, his daughter was lost to him. He wouldn't even try to find her — or Daniel.

"You can't mean that," Sam said, incredulous. "Let me speak to the Elect. Let me tell them–"

"I said the judgment has been passed!" he cried. "There will be no reversal. Now I will ask you again. Where is Colonel O'Neill?"

But Sam could only shake her head in dismay.

Channon took a breath and when he spoke again his voice was calmer. "Very well. You will remain here and face the consequences of your lack of cooperation. But trust me, Major Carter, I *will* find O'Neill. I will not allow him to spread blasphemous lies about *Sciath Dé*."

He turned to leave, but before he reached the door Teal'c spoke again. "Your daughter, Pastor Channon. How is it you can so readily abandon a child of your blood?"

Channon stopped, but didn't look around. "If God chooses to smite the wicked," he whispered, "then who am I to question His will?"

Then the door hissed open and, flanked by his guards, he was gone.

It was the stench that got to him first, that and the heat and the need for a breath of clean air. So he moved before he should, taking a chance that the dusky light would be enough to mask any untoward movement in the little boat.

He'd slipped underneath the tarp just as everything kicked off back on the docks, and had spent the best part of the day sweltering beneath the heavy fabric that covered the stern of the boat. He'd probably lost a couple of pounds in sweat, and only surreptitious swallows from his canteen had kept him going in the devastating heat. Not that he hadn't endured worse. Jack O'Neill had suffered his fair share of stifling hell holes — some figurative, others more literal — and, by comparison, bivouacking under a stinking tarp for a few hours was a walk in the park.

He could have done without the stench, though. Whatever these people used to waterproof their gear reeked of dead fish.

It was that, in the end, which provoked him to risk lifting a corner of the tarp before night had truly fallen. The sun was a golden dazzle on the horizon and he had to blink until his eyes adjusted enough to let him assess the situation.

It didn't come as a surprise.

Twenty minutes out from the docks, shouting had started. The language was obscure, but the meaning had been clear; they were docking with one of the ships. He'd heard the clank of chains and a few moments later the whine of winches — and then they'd taken flight. Slowly. The longboat had swung side-to-side in the davits and then been manhandled onto the deck.

That had been the most dangerous time, and his hands had been tight on his weapon as he waited, every moment, for the tarp to be whisked away and the stowaway revealed. It hadn't happened. Clearly, something else was going down. More shouting, then the hum of servos far above him.

And then the ship had started moving. *Really* moving. Jack knew a thing or two about speed, and he'd never felt that kind of acceleration on anything that wasn't airborne.

Now, peering out from beneath the tarp, he realized why. The damn boat was flying! Not in the air, not really, but damn close. He felt the familiar pump of flyboy adrenaline and suppressed a smile. Shuffling to the other side of the longboat, he lifted another corner of the tarp and this time found himself looking out across the deck of a large ship. Patches of it gleamed in the golden light, but others were dull and rusted and the whole thing looked too damn old to be traveling so fast. A couple of low cabins ran the length of the foredeck, with heavy doors shut tight against both sun and sea. They might once have been painted red, but the peeling remnants were a dull brown and dotted the steel surface like a scabrous pox. Only a few thick-glassed windows protruded along the length of the cabins, misty with salt-spray, and Jack doubted anyone inside would be able to see through.

He shifted again, his knee protesting, and made the decision to move out. He needed more information and, frankly, he needed to get away from the dead-fish stink. Glancing up and down the deck, he slid out from beneath the tarp, slipped over the side of the longboat, and dropped into a crouch on the deck below.

His knee was unimpressed and he bit back a curse. Moving silently, he darted between the cabins and stopped with his back pressed against the wall of one, his gun leveled at the door of the other. It didn't open, and he heard no alarm sounding — which didn't mean it hadn't gone off.

He paused a moment and took stock of his position. The deck was about fifty feet wide and surrounded by a high, curved shield made of what looked like scratched plastic — a windshield, he guessed, given their velocity. Without it, no one would be able to come on deck while the ship was in motion. Clever, but it was the sight looming above him that really caught his eye.

Sails were the best description, though these were no canvas sheets. A half dozen vast metallic solar cells positioned so that they caught the dying rays of the sun, and they glittered so bright in the twilight that he had to shield his eyes.

Carter would have been fascinated. He wondered briefly where she was, then pushed the resulting coil of anxiety out of his mind. With luck, she and Teal'c had hightailed it back to the gate and were, even now, debriefing Hammond on the whole mess and planning to return with a platoon of marines at their backs. Daniel, on the other hand...

Keeping low beneath the windows, Jack made his way along the side of the superstructure until he reached its end. In front of him rose the mast, its massive trunk rooted into the deck. Behind it a shambles of cargo stretched back across the rest of the deck. Crates, barrels, and bundles of tarp-covered goods lay in a haphazard pile, as if flung there in careless haste. A heist, Jack wondered, or an evacuation?

In the distance, something glinted, drawing his attention to the sea. Sails gleamed on a dozen other ships of various sizes, all keeping pace with the sleek, predatory ship that flew out ahead of the Seachráni fleet. No prizes for guessing who captained that one — or where Daniel and the woman were being held.

On the upside, Faelan's ship was close enough; Jack toggled his radio and murmured, "Daniel, do you copy?" The only reply was a hiss of static. Not that he'd really expected anything else, but still... "Daniel, do you — ?"

A door slammed. He heard voices, indistinct beneath the rush of the wind but getting closer. Jack ran across the deck, launched himself up and over a tarp-covered bale and wiggled into the gap between that and a wooden crate. He stilled, evening out his breathing, and noted the words, in very faded print, on the side of the crate.

Emergency Re-hydration Salts.

English, not the gobbledygook the Seachráni chose to converse in.

He had no time to ponder it, however. Two men swung around the side of the cabin. Like Faelan's, their skin was tanned dark, and they wore tatty but sturdy clothes, with wide-brimmed hats pushed back on their heads now that the sun had almost set. They were talking, loud so as to be heard over the wind, but Jack couldn't understand a word of their language. He watched instead, taking note as they opened a hatch at the base of the mast and began to haul on a number of huge levers. Above them, one of the sails began to move, folding in on itself like a shutter.

Immediately, the ship began to slow, the rush of wind diminishing, and the voices of the men grew louder. Jack still couldn't understand what they were saying, but their mood was clear enough; they were pissed. He heard Faelan's name mentioned a number of times, with much shaking of heads.

Far above, another sail began to furl. The ship slowed further.

Then a third man, little more than a lanky kid, appeared from around the cabin, less tanned than the others and with the look of the Badlands about him. When he spoke it was without the Seachráni lilt, and Jack caught every word.

"We're to keep moving on reserves," he said, hands buried in deep pockets and a scarf tied low over his forehead. "Captain said we're to keep traveling 'til sunup, then unfurl."

One of the other men grunted and spat on the deck. "Aye, with no thought for the crew."

"T'ain't the captain's fault," the kid said, squinting up at the sails. "He got orders, is all."

"Ain't blaming the captain, am I? We all know what's going on. We all heard what Faelan Garret done, stealing the Pastor's daughter again. Bloody *dùr*, what's he thinkin'?"

The other man snorted a laugh. "He ain't thinkin' with his head, right enough."

"Aye," said the first. "Well, the Cove isn't needing a leader that's thinking with his bleedin' *slat*. Not now, not with what's comin'."

"Garret'll see us right," said the other man. "He's never failed us before."

Conversation ground to a halt, all three men chasing their own thoughts. Then one of the Seachráni slapped the kid on the shoulder. "Get back to your supper, Geran. No point in blatherin' on, eh?"

The boy nodded and turned away, but before he left he looked back and said, "Storm's not gonna be so bad, eh?"

Jack felt his stomach twist. He'd seen that same look on the faces of men in his own command; kids themselves too, looking for certainty where none existed. Looking for hope.

"Sure, it won't," the older man said, casting a glance at his dour friend who just contemplated the sail levers in silence. "No worse'n we've seen before."

It was a lie. But the kid nodded, determined to believe, and walked away with his hands still buried deep in his pockets.

The other man slammed down hard on the remaining lever, and the final sail began to furl. "*Mac an donais,*" he growled.

Jack didn't need to speak their language to know it was a curse.

CHAPTER SEVEN

THE SHIP was old, patched and ramshackle, as if repairs were done on the hop with whatever materials could be scavenged. From what Daniel had gathered before he and Rhionna were escorted down into the brig, the rest of the Seachráni fleet was in a similar condition. The dazzling sails they'd sighted in the distance had offered a small glimpse of a technology that would have Sam as excited as a kid at Christmas, but beneath that technological dazzle the fleet was battered and worn. A strange hybrid. How advanced had this society been before disaster struck, how far had it fallen?

Old though the vessel was, no ominous creak or groan rose from its metal bones. Only the faint but constant vibration of the planks beneath him and an almost inaudible hum gave any indication that they were moving at all. But moving they were, and fast.

"They must look after their boats well," he said to Rhionna, who sat against the bulkhead, head tilted back and eyes closed. He thought she might be asleep, then decided he didn't care if he woke her. They'd been stuck down here too long and he itched with the inactivity. He wanted to know, to find, to ask, and Rhionna was the only one around. Besides, he suspected that she had more answers than she was letting on.

"Ships, not boats," she muttered, not opening her eyes.

"Hmm?"

Rhionna shook her head and sighed. "Doesn't matter." She looked around the small cell. "Yeah, they take care of them. The ships are their lives. They couldn't survive without them."

"You've been on one before?"

She smiled at that. "A few times. I've even been in this

brig before." She frowned then and looked away, as if mired in a memory. Daniel hesitated, remembering her reaction to Faelan back at the docks, and his to her — what was the story there? After a brief, silent debate on whether to push the matter or not, he decided to proceed with care.

"How is it they do it? Survive, I mean. What are they?"

"Scavengers mostly. Sometimes hunters."

"Ah…hunters of what?"

"Anything they can find." She smiled when she said it, but the expression had a hard edge, as if she were trying to provoke him, or scare him. It didn't quite work.

"Why don't they live with the others? In the Badlands?"

"Would you want to live there?"

Daniel shrugged his concession to the point. "Then where are they taking us?"

"You ask me a lot of questions, Dr. Jackson. What makes you think I have the answers?"

"Because you've been on this ship before. You know the Seachráni."

But Rhionna just laughed and pushed herself to her feet, wincing a little as she unfolded limbs that had been in the same position for too long. "The more someone knows of the Seachráni, the more questions they have. They are a very guarded people, Dr. Jackson."

"It's Daniel, and I suspect they're not the only ones who are guarded." That earned him a sharp look, but he was undaunted. "You don't believe they will harm us."

"I believe they are scared and desperate. Those are powerful motivators."

"Yes, they are, but I also know that you tried to protect them back at the Badlands. You wouldn't have done that without reason."

Rather than reply, Rhionna crossed over to lean against the door and stare through the bars, evidently having decided that the conversation was over. Daniel thought it was time to try a different tack, no matter how personal it might be.

"This Faelan..." Her shoulders tensed at the mention of the name. "He's their leader. Can't you talk to him? Reason with him to take us back to the docks?"

"He won't listen to me."

Daniel remembered the looks that had passed between them and said, "Oh, I think he will."

She rounded on him, anger flashing. "If you are so observant, Daniel, so intuitive, then surely you saw how much attention Faelan pays to my opinion. He's stubborn and foolhardy, and the Seachráni won't move a muscle without him. He *is* their leader, and they are loyal to a fault. If he wants to take us to the Cove, then that's where we're going. There is nothing I could say to him that would make any difference. If anything it would only make matters worse."

"Worse than us dying along with his people when the storm hits this Cove of his?" She flinched at that, but he persisted. "Can't you reason with him?"

She turned away, leaning on the cell door, gazing out through the bars once more. "I don't think there's anyone alive who'd know how to reason with Faelan Garret."

"But you knew him."

Rhionna shook her head and said quietly, "Not nearly so well as I thought."

The ninth episode of *Sunrise* crawled to a close. Outside, Sam calculated, it had to be dark. They had most likely missed their scheduled report by hours, which meant SG-1 were officially overdue. She could picture General Hammond, grim-faced in the control room, arms crossed, glaring at the empty Stargate. That gave her some comfort, although she couldn't imagine what he might do to help. One thing was certain though — he wouldn't let Ennis spin him a line, not after enduring weeks of Caulder's barefaced lies. And he wouldn't give up. Not ever.

But the truth was, when it came right down to it, SG-1 were

on their own. They had to take care of themselves — and each other.

She glanced across at Teal'c. He'd not said a word since Ennis had left, withdrawing into meditation. Preparing. He'd be rested when the time came for action. And that time would come, she'd make sure of it.

The *Sunrise* theme started again, a jangle of sound that scratched across her nerves like fingernails across a chalkboard. It was a peculiar kind of torture, at once soporific and enervating. Deliberately, she refused to cup her hands over her ears, refused to pace the cell — she refused to acknowledge that it was having any effect. Instead, she fixed her eyes on the screen and let them blur until all she saw were swimming colors and —

And that's when she noticed it; a brief dimming of the image. Then again. She looked up at the lights, unsure if she'd been imagining it, and felt a little surge of anticipation as their white, featureless glare flickered.

Teal'c opened his eyes. "Their power supply does not appear to be reliable."

"No." Sam scrambled to her feet. "It doesn't." The lights flickered again. "When it's dark out, there must be a surge in demand. All those lights. Their grid can't handle it." Circling the cell, she wound up at the door and pressed her hand against the smooth metal. The subtle hum of the electronic lock tingled against her palm. She glanced at the TV. "And if more people are home, tuning in…"

The lights dipped and, for half a second, the cell was lit only by the screen. Beneath her palm something clicked off and on again. Sam caught her breath.

"Major Carter?" Teal'c was on his feet, scrutinizing her.

She lifted her hand from the door, flexing her fingers. "Teal'c," she smiled. "I have a plan."

Without daylight for reference, time lost meaning, and the journey seemed endless. Daniel dozed in fits and starts, unsure if Rhionna slept at all. At one point, he tugged out the device they'd brought from *Acarsaid Dorch* and, in the gloomy light, tried for the umpteenth time to make sense of it. But its use was no clearer here than it had been back at the SGC and he quickly gave up, stuffing it back into his vest before any of the Seachrání noticed. Sam wouldn't thank him if he lost it and, until he understood his current situation, he planned to keep his powder dry. Jack, he thought, would be proud of his circumspection — even if he was pissed that Daniel had managed to get himself captured.

Time meandered on, listless and without definition. The monotony was broken only by the stern-faced man who brought them food, the same man who'd grabbed him back at the docks, Faelan's second in command.

Rhionna darted to her feet when he approached the cell. "Pádraig," she said, in a greeting that was far from friendly.

Pádraig's frown deepened, as if the acknowledgment troubled him. "Stand back from the door, Rhionna," he said, not looking at her. "Both of you."

"Why is he doing this, Pádraig?" she asked, ignoring his instruction.

"'Twas little choice you gave him. Now stand back from the door."

"*I* gave him little choice?" She barked an incredulous laugh. "Did I put the knife to my own throat and drag myself onboard this ship?"

"Sure, it was your father, was it not, who brought his armed guard and had them waving their guns at innocent folks? Now stand back from the bloody door if you want this meal, or else starve."

She set her jaw and complied. "That wasn't my doing, and don't tell me you think it was. Don't tell me *he* thinks it was."

Pádraig looked uncertain and busied himself with unlocking the door. "And how is it you'd explain these folks then?" he

said, nodding at Daniel. "Where'd they come from if not the
Ark? They've got the look of Channon's people about them."

"I can vouch for what Rhionna says," said Daniel. "We're
not from the Ark. In fact, we're from somewhere much further away. And I can assure you that Rhionna knew nothing
about her father's actions. She took us to the docks to help
the people of the Badlands."

Pádraig smirked. "And how might you be able to help those
poor souls?" he asked, and shook his head when it was clear
Daniel had no answer. "Ah, it makes no difference. The deed
is done and here you are."

"Here we are," Daniel agreed. "Um...so, what do you intend
to do with us now?"

"The decision isn't mine," replied Pádraig, and there was a
disapproval in his voice that, as Daniel suspected, was aimed
neither at himself nor at Rhionna. Pádraig set the tray on the
floor, then turned to leave.

"Let me speak to him," said Rhionna, the words coming in
a rush as if she had to force them from her mouth.

Pádraig paused in the doorway and turned back. "And
what would you be hoping to speak to him about?"

"I want to make him see sense. This will not end well for
any of us. Surely you can understand that."

"I can, and don't you think I've told him as much?" The
man's manner had changed somewhat, and Daniel thought
there was even a trace of amity in the way he spoke to Rhionna,
a glimpse perhaps of an old camaraderie. "You know how
the boy is."

"Then perhaps if I can-"

"I'll not have any of that old business rearing its head
again, Rhionna," he said, sharply. "It caused more trouble
than you'll ever know."

Daniel was tempted to ask what business he meant, curious about the history between the two peoples of the planet,
but he sensed there was a far more human story beneath it all,

one that was none of his concern, so he held his tongue.

"I only want to resolve this situation, Pádraig," Rhionna said. "Let me speak to him. Please."

His only reply was to leave the cell, locking the door behind him. "Eat your food," he recommended from outside. "We'll be at the Cove in a couple of hours."

"Pádraig!" cried Rhionna through the bars, but the clang of the hatch told them that he was already gone.

Like anywhere else in the universe, nighttime on Ierna was when folks came out to play. Under clear and balmy skies the crew of the Seachráni ship spilled from the cabins and onto the deck, some bringing food and drink, others trying their luck at the usual games of chance. The ship cruised along at a leisurely speed and sound traveled easily without the buffeting wind to snatch it away. Conversation seemed animated, but most of it was spoken in the Seachráni language and Jack could only guess at the meaning. Faelan's name cropped up a lot, however, accompanied by much shaking of heads and grumbling under the breath. Kidnap, it seemed, wasn't these guys' usual MO and they were pissed. Which was good news for Daniel, if not for Faelan Garret.

The atmosphere wasn't exactly mutinous, but Jack was beginning to wonder exactly what kind of position Garret really held with these people. The old woman, Sorcha, had spoken of him as a leader, but Jack knew a leader when he saw one and Garret wasn't it. He had charisma, no doubt, but no steel in his spine. People wanted to follow him, but he didn't want to lead. He refused the burden of command. That made him weak and his people afraid. *That* made him resort to kidnap instead of standing his ground.

And Jack had no patience for that kind of cowardice.

Hunkering lower, he squirmed to get comfortable between the crate and the tarp-covered bale. He had just enough room to stretch his aching knee, and could prop his back against the tarp. Ignoring the dead-fish aroma of the ship, he pulled a power bar out of his vest and began to eat. He still had a few swallows of water left in his canteen which would be enough for now. Tough luck if wasn't, though, because he was going nowhere with the whole damn crew taking their R&R right on his doorstep. As hiding places went, he'd had better.

When he'd finished eating, he drank a mouthful of water and tucked the canteen back into his vest. His P90 rested comfortably against his chest and he held it there as he settled back against a bale, closed his eyes and let himself slip into a light soldier's sleep.

George Hammond supposed that the handsome features and plausible smile of the man on the screen before him might be considered attractive, but he remembered Administrator Caulder's smooth platitudes all too well and he wasn't in the mood to play nice. Not this time. Besides, there was a sharpness in the man's eyes, even filtered through the camera of the MALP, that instantly set Hammond on edge. No, Tynan Camus was a man to watch like a snake in the grass, and George Hammond didn't intend to give him an inch.

"They have broken our laws, General Hammond," Camus said, with a regretful spread of his hands. "We must deal with them as our law dictates."

George took in the two armed guards who flanked the man. "And what exactly does your law dictate?"

"They will be brought before our council of the Elect tomorrow and a decision will made as to their fate."

"Their fate? Now listen here, if my team have transgressed your law I can assure you, sir, it was done by accident and —"

"Hardly by accident, General Hammond. They left the city when it was expressly forbidden for them to do so. They have consorted with known criminals whose declared intent is to destabilize our government. The facts are clear. There is no need for prevarication."

He wouldn't put it past Jack to have done any of those things, of course, but that was hardly the point. "I appreciate what you're saying, Brother Camus, and I assure you that we will conduct our own investigation and take necessary steps if we find that our team have breached any —"

"Unacceptable. The Lord demands that justice be done and His punishment meted out to those who transgress; and there is only one punishment for their heresy."

Hammond felt a cold fist grasp his heart, but he kept his face impassive. "And that would be?"

"The Burn."

Whatever the devil that was, it didn't sound good. "I'm sorry, Brother Camus, but that is not acceptable."

Camus spread his hands again. "Acceptable or not, it is how matters stand." Then he smiled, a practiced baring of white teeth. "And I advise you not to send anyone through the Sungate against my instructions." He gestured to the men on either side of him. "As you can see, General, we are not without defensive capabilities."

Hammond frowned, realizing that one avenue of rescue had just been cut off. Fighting your way through a gate was all but impossible without a huge amount of firepower and all the attendant collateral damage. He wasn't at that point. Yet. Folding his hands behind his back, he said, "I have no wish to use any force or aggression, but you must understand that I cannot wash my hands of the matter. I assure you that SG-1 would not knowingly break your laws. If you would let me send people through to better determine the circumstances behind this–"

"There will be no further discussion on this matter. I will not allow any more of your heretical people to set foot in the Ark."

Biting back a sigh of frustration, Hammond said, "Then at least let me speak to Colonel O'Neill."

Camus paused, as if considering his request, then said, "I

will allow you to speak with Major Carter for a short time."

It seemed a strange compromise, and for a second George considered pushing the matter and demanding that he speak to the colonel. But then he wondered whether Camus was willing let Major Carter talk to him because she was a woman; perhaps he underestimated her ability to provide a full and accurate report? If that was the case, then they might manipulate his prejudice to their advantage. "Agreed," he said, and without another word Camus disappeared from the screen gesturing for his men to follow.

Sometime later Samantha Carter appeared in his place. Before she spoke, her gaze slid to the side, telling him that Camus's heavies were just off-screen. He was relieved to note that she looked unharmed. "Major Carter, are you ok?"

"I'm fine, sir. Just a little anxious to get out of here."

"And the others?"

She gave another sideways glance and Hammond could hear a low voice in the background; was Camus restricting what she could and couldn't say? What did the man have to hide?

"To my knowledge, the others are fine, sir."

To her knowledge.

"Can you give me a SITREP, Major?"

"Sir, Pastor Channon's daughter asked for our help and led us to a settlement outside the Ark. There was a skirmish, and we were caught in the middle."

"Brother Camus says that you broke the law."

She gave a chagrined grimace. "Yes, sir. We were aware that leaving the Ark was probably prohibited."

"Yet you went ahead anyway."

Carter shrugged. "She asked for our help, sir."

And it really was as simple as that. SG-1's MO; help those who cannot help themselves. It wasn't the first time they'd taken such rash action and he suspected — in fact, hoped — it wouldn't be the last. But though this version of events seemed to make sense, Hammond couldn't help thinking there was something she wasn't saying. But unlike Tynan Camus, she clearly had something she *wanted* to say.

"So how do you suggest we proceed, Major?"

"Nothing much we can do about it at present, sir. I think we just have to ride this one out."

Definitely something she wasn't saying.

"Brother Camus has refused permission for anyone else to visit Ierna. However, SG-3 are on standby." And she would know exactly what that meant; the Marine Combat Unit was the SGC's primary search and rescue team.

But Major Carter was already shaking her head. "I wouldn't advise it, sir. They'd have a hostile reception, and there's a pretty big storm headed this way. I'm not sure how hard it's going to hit, but it wouldn't be a good idea to send any SGC personnel through right now."

Her gaze flicked to the side once more. Hammond frowned. "Then I suppose we do as you say and ride this one out?"

"Don't worry about us, General. We'll be fine. Everything's under control." She leaned forward, her eyes narrowed, a slight smile on her lips. "You should just focus on something else for now. Like Thera and Tor coming home real soon."

George took a moment before he answered. "Yes, I'm looking forward to that," he said carefully. "And I hope they'll be bringing Jonah and Karlan with them?"

The major hesitated, then said, "I'm sure they'll do everything possible to make that happen, sir."

A grim smile spread across Hammond's face, and he was glad there was no visual on the MALP. As usual, SG-1 had it under control — more or less. "I'm very much looking forward to her arrival, Major," he said. "And I hope her journey isn't too difficult."

"I'm confident it'll be trouble-free, sir."

He nodded and ended the transmission, uttering a silent prayer that Sam Carter's confidence was not misplaced.

CHAPTER EIGHT

THEY'D picked up speed again, accompanied by a clanging from above and more pronounced vibrations that thrummed through the hull.

"We're almost there," said Rhionna with certainty.

"How many times have you made this journey?"

"Enough."

"So is the Cove — ?"

His question was cut off by the clatter of the hatch and the thud of boots descending the ladder. Pádraig's face appeared at the bars of the brig and an instant later the door swung open. "Come on," he said to Daniel, but when Rhionna got to her feet he added, "No, child, not you. Only him." She backed away into the darkness of the cell, silent, but radiating anger.

The deck above was alive with activity, the Seachráni taking advantage of the remaining dark before temperatures soared. Daniel saw that a thin line of purple had appeared on the horizon; dawn promised to be beautiful, a harsh lie considering how savage the day would be. Right now, however, night chill still hung in the air, cooled further by the cloud of spray that flew past the massive glass screen at the bow and swirled across the deck. In seconds, Daniel's hair and clothes were coated in a fine film of moisture.

"This way," said Pádraig, heading aforeships. Looks of both curiosity and distrust were flung at Daniel as he followed, but the Seachráni's attention to their work never faltered. Then he spotted the man who walked among them, throwing out instructions with quiet authority. Faelan glanced up and gestured towards the bow as he saw them.

"I'll leave you to it," said Pádraig, and retreated.

"I owe you an apology, I think, Daniel Jackson," said Faelan. It was not the conversation opener Daniel had expected.

"Um, you do? I mean, yes, you do, but I'm surprised to hear you say so."

Faelan ran a hand over his face and into his hair, wiping away a layer of spray. "You were caught in the middle of something that was none of your concern. It's regrettable how it all unfolded, but Pádraig was only following my lead."

"And by 'your lead' you mean taking Pastor Channon's daughter hostage?"

Faelan's expression was inscrutable. "Desperate situations call for desperate measures. How else was I supposed to get my people out of there?"

"You could have tried reasoning with Tynan Camus, or the Pastor. My team was there. We've dealt with situations like this before."

Faelan leaned back on the ship's railing and regarded Daniel carefully. "You strike me as a man who relies on words to solve his problems, Daniel Jackson, but I don't think you're a fool. Don't tell me you think we could've talked our way out of trouble back there."

To push the point would've been to lie, so instead Daniel settled back on the railing beside him and said, "I'm surprised you've taken time to talk to me now."

"Pádraig said you were quite insistent."

"I'd say Rhionna was more insistent. Why didn't you speak to her?"

Faelan's eyes flashed and he turned away, looking aft, towards the rising sun. "Rhionna isn't — I can't..." He shook his head, as if hoping the rest of the sentence would fall into place, then with a sigh he said, "Speaking with her would only create more problems than it'd solve."

"Old business, huh?" said Daniel. But not old enough that it didn't matter, it seemed.

Faelan didn't reply, looking lost in thought as he stared

at the horizon, but then his eyes took on a keener aspect and he walked away, brow furrowed in harsh lines. Daniel followed his gaze, but could see only daylight beginning to burn the sky.

"It's getting closer," he muttered, and by his tone, Daniel knew he was talking about the storm.

"How long?"

"Two days. Probably less."

"Faelan, we have to get out of here. We have to get your people to safety." But Daniel's words fell on deaf ears; Faelan was already calling for Pádraig to take him back down to the brig. "What are you going to do with us?" demanded Daniel, as the first mate appeared and took his arm.

Faelan stared at him with an expression that gave nothing away.

Desperate situations call for desperate measures, thought Daniel, but refused to believe that this was a man who would act rashly without reason. He could only hope that there would be no need to dispose of two hostages.

"I'll decide that once we get to the Cove," said Faelan.

"And how long will that take?"

Even as Daniel asked the question, Faelan's gaze drifted to a point over his shoulder and a rare smile lifted the corners of his mouth. "Not long, Daniel Jackson. Not long at all."

When Daniel turned to look, the sight that greeted him made his breath stop.

A mournful wail startled Jack awake.

Before the sound faded he was in a low crouch, finger tight on the trigger, and for a disorienting moment he felt lost.

Fog sat heavy over the ship, damp and cold. He could taste its tang on his lips, grateful for the moisture after so much sun and heat. It wouldn't last long, though, because a white glare already rose on the horizon. Backlit by daybreak, figures moved about in the mist. Words were shouted and the foghorn blared again, echoed a moment later by another. Then another.

Taking advantage of the cover, Jack crept out of his hiding place. The motion of the ship had changed, now it rocked from side to side instead of pushing steadily ahead. He was no sailor, but he had the definite impression that they were stopping.

Keeping low, he made his way toward the bow. The horn sounded again, and he realized it wasn't coming from the ship at all, but from somewhere out in the fog. He peered ahead, straining his eyes and trying to make out shapes in the haze. Then a door slammed open, right in front of him.

Jack froze.

Light flooded from the cabin, a warm flickering glow, and a woman stepped out onto the deck. Like all the Seachráni, she wore a wide-brimmed hat, pushed back to hang from a cord around her neck, and a coat down below her knees. She coughed and pulled the coat tight around her, muttering something in her language. Jack loosely interpreted it as 'Goddamn, it's cold'.

She heaved the door shut, the clang resonating through the fog, then, head down and no more than two meters away, she stalked past him and aft.

Silently, Jack moved on.

"*Sé bhur mbeatha!*" The cry came from above — a lookout, Jack guessed. It sounded like a hail and, after a moment, he heard a reply. Squinting, he tried again to discern details. As he did so, a breeze stirred his hair and the mist eddied. He glimpsed a light, close but high up. Then another, then —

"Whoa..."

Out of the mist loomed a vast monolith — no, several. Lights peppered the surface, blinking as the fog eddied. He glimpsed walkways, gunmetal-gray and bolted in haphazard chaos to other structures still lost in the haze. They were so close Jack thought they were going to smash into the thing until he realized they were sailing through it — under a bridge that dripped with rusty moisture — and close enough for him to figure out exactly what he was seeing.

It was a city. A drowned city, and they were drifting past the derelict remains of its skyscrapers. It could have been Chicago under a hundred meters of water. And below... Jack O'Neill wasn't easily creeped out, but the idea of a whole city down there beneath the black water made him shiver.

Looking up as they passed beneath the bridge, he heard other shouts — greetings, excited sounds of welcome — and he wondered how long this ship and its crew had been away. Then they were past the bridge and he realized where this place got its name — lights glittered through the fog on all sides, a weird and freaked-out fishing village welcoming the fleet into the safety of its cove.

Only these were no fishermen, and there was no dry land to be seen. He could smell the rot and decay in the air, could feel the precarious sway of these damaged structures, and remembered Rhionna's fear about the coming storm; it looked like the whole damn place would come crashing down in a stiff breeze.

The foghorn blared again, and behind him he sensed movement. They were getting ready to dock. Up ahead he could see the longboat, its shape recognizable even if no details were visible. Moving quickly, he ducked behind it. Hidden from the crew by its bulk, he risked standing up and watching through the transparent shielding as the ship drew closer to a platform — more of a dock, really — that had been built out over the water from one of the buildings. People had gathered there, amid excited chatter and sharp barks as ropes were thrown and secured. Further up, in another berth, Jack recognized the slim, fast ship he'd previously identified as Faelan's. It hadn't docked yet, and Jack figured he had only a few minutes to get himself down onto the dock and across to the other ship in time to stand a chance of seeing Daniel being brought ashore. If he missed him...

Well, there was no way in hell he could search this vast, moldering city before the storm struck. And one thing was for sure, the coming storm was going to rip this place apart. Jack O'Neill would be damned if he let Daniel go down with the city.

Dawn was heralded by a chaotic chorus of gunfire and cries. Ennis Channon picked his way through the Badlands. All around him the Elect Guard demonstrated the true power of the Lord to the heathens who huddled in this savage wasteland. Some of the hovels burned, lighting his path like the flames of the Sun, while above, on giant screens, the Message was spread. In less than an hour, the Lord would cast his punishing fire across this landscape; it was essential that their work be done by then, their goal achieved. Colonel Jack O'Neill had to be found.

A tall figure fell into step beside him. "This place reeks," said Tynan Camus, his elegant face twisted in disgust. "These people are little more than animals."

"They are worse than animals," replied Ennis. "Animals have no soul to stain. These heathens are marked for eternity."

Tynan raised an eyebrow. "Quite."

Ennis ignored the note of mockery in his tone. "Has there been any sign of him?"

"No," said Tynan, with a bored sigh. "The man has disappeared. We have demonstrated the penalties incurred for harboring a fugitive, and the people are frightened enough, yet not one has cracked and given us his whereabouts. I think it's safe to assume they don't know where he is. In all honesty, I'm not sure I even care where he is."

"Your meaning?"

"He is a stranger to this planet, Pastor. He knows nothing of its caprice. Let him fall into the sea, or be incinerated by the Burn. What does it matter to us?"

"He spreads heresy."

"Then let him spread it. As if these illiterates could even make sense of anything he might say."

"I was under the impression that you shared Sister Nevin's conviction that the strangers must be ground under the heels of our boots."

Tynan snorted and looked down at his feet as they walked. "Not if it means that my boots must be muddied by the filth of the Badlands. I am reluctant to even guess what I might be stepping in. It was my recommendation to lock the doors and let God do the rest."

"I am well aware of your recommendation, Brother Camus," ground out Ennis.

The look Tynan slanted at him was almost amused. "Do you object to our decision with regard to your daughter, Pastor?"

Ennis took a breath. "You know that I do not."

"Yet you still insist on this little excursion."

"You saw what they found on *Acarsaid Dorch.* They seek *Sciath Dé.*"

"Whomever they speak to will assure them that they seek a myth."

Both men came to a standstill and their gazes locked. It seemed as though Tynan was daring Ennis to contradict him. So be it. "Perhaps not so much of a myth after all."

Tynan grinned, and in the light of the low-burning fires, his smirk glinted like a blade. "Be very careful, Ennis."

"I would suggest that we all must be careful, Tynan. That is why we are here." He looked over his shoulder at the dark squat of Sorcha Caratauc's shack. "Come."

Inside, the guards had misunderstood his order to search the place and were in the process of tearing the room apart. Papers flew, notes and drawings were scattered on the ground, boxes were upended and their contents strewn everywhere.

"Enough!" cried Ennis. The men froze in their ransacking. "I ordered a systematic search, not a demolition."

Brushing past him into the shack, Tynan laughed. "What does it matter what happens to the crone's collection of refuse." A loose page fluttered by, and he plucked it from the air. "Tell me that this excursion is not on account of these worthless scribblings, Pastor."

"Perhaps you should look and see exactly what she has been scribbling about."

The smirk still on his face, Tynan scanned the page he held. Finally his amusement faded and his eyes narrowed. Then he pursed his lips. "The woman has been detained?"

"She has."

"Very well, then. Have her nonsense burned and let the Lord take care of her heresy."

Anger flashed through Ennis at the young man's dismissive tone, at the smug grin he wore while handing out his judgments, at his refusal, and that of the Elect, to acknowledge what was right in front of their faces. "Do you not understand?" Conscious of the soldiers close by he lowered his voice, struggling to contain his fears. "She has Knowledge. Who else may know what she knows? Do you not see that we face the gravest threat to our way of life that we have ever known?"

Tynan grabbed his arm, fingers biting deep and his cool tone belying the anger in his eyes. "This nonsense matters not, Pastor. The Lord has sent a storm to wash away this vile place and the strangers with it, if you would but let His justice be done." He stood back, lips curling into another sneer. "You are the Pastor, Ennis Channon, the security of the Ark falls to you — unless you feel the burden is too heavy?"

The threat was not subtle, and it stopped Ennis cold. With dignity, he straightened to his full height, still a head shorter than Tynan Camus. "It is no burden. It is my duty and my honor."

Tynan gave an insincere nod. "Then do your duty — punish the heretics in your custody, and let those who have chosen to live beyond the Light face the Lord's justice. If you do not…" He left it hanging, but Ennis did not doubt his meaning; Tynan Camus would be Pastor if he could.

At his feet, a rising breeze sent the papers flapping through the dirt. The stench of the place suddenly became overwhelming. This woman, this old crone of a heretic, living amid refuse and disease, had poisoned his daughter's mind against him. Had driven Rhionna into the arms of the Seawolf and ruined every hope he had nursed for her future.

And now, just as his forebears had predicted, men bringing Knowledge from *Acarsaid Dorch* would destroy them all.

The world was changing. Everything that had once been order was turning into chaos. And he knew not whether it was the Lord's will that Rhionna should perish with the godless, but as he watched Tynan Camus pick his careful steps through the filth-ridden alleyways of the Badlands, he wondered who it was that bore the greater sin.

There was no doubt that this was a homecoming. He'd seen it a dozen times on a dozen airfields: proud parents, crying wives, and bemused, awestruck kids. Felt it too, that disorienting clash of realities, stepping out of a war zone and into Sara's arms, Charlie's wet kisses like a candle in the darkness he couldn't leave behind. Nothing beat coming home.

Even if home was a half drowned city that felt like it could come down around his ears at any moment. Clearly the Cove was more than a bandits' hideout, it was a community. Of sorts. As he pushed through the crowd, glancing up from beneath the wide-brimmed hat he'd lifted from a careless sailor, Jack saw poverty and hardship in the chiseled faces of these people. A community, maybe, but not a thriving one. Like the folk in the Badlands, this was a people living on the edge.

He kept his weapon ready, figuring it was mostly hidden by the long coat he now wore. He'd felt a pang of guilt when he'd taken it from the deck of the ship — these were poor people, and he supposed a replacement would be hard to find — but that had soon passed. Getting caught wasn't an option, and if the coming storm was as ferocious as Faelan believed, then the coat's previous owner would soon have more than a missing garment to worry about.

The mist was less dense here — either that or the rising sun was already burning it away — but it was still enough to allow his feeble disguise to work. Head down, he pushed through the crowd until he was at the far end of the docks where another throng had gathered. Some kind of walkway was being lowered into place as he arrived, accompanied by much shouting and the rattle of a chain being left to run. It landed with a clang that echoed against the walls of the surrounding buildings.

Jack worked his way forward, close enough to see, but not so close that Daniel might notice him and react. Before long Faelan made his entrance, all swagger and confidence — an assurance belied by the tension in his face. At the shouts of welcome, Faelan raised his hand in greeting. He seemed respected here, less surly than he'd appeared in the Badlands; a man coming home to his people. Grudgingly, Jack found himself impressed.

The feeling lasted approximately ten seconds, then Rhionna walked down the ramp, Daniel on her heels. Faelan's second in command trailed them both, a wicked looking knife tucked into his belt and one meaty hand resting on Rhionna's shoulder, as if he expected her to run.

Like she had anywhere to go.

Behind them followed other sailors, shouting out to friends and family, and Daniel's group soon disappeared among the throng of people. Keeping his distance, Jack tailed them. Faelan, it seemed, was leader enough to make the crowd part for him, and it was easy for Jack to stalk along in his wake without being noticed.

But the crowd thinned as soon as they left the pier behind, and Jack suddenly found himself exposed. He fell back, clinging to the tattered edges of the welcoming committee at the docks, and watched as Faelan led his prisoners up a short ladder and from there onto a narrow bridge about twelve feet up. Their footsteps clanged on the metal walkway, and Jack darted across the open space and scrambled up the ladder behind them, slowing at the top to watch as Faelan climbed a second ladder and disappeared inside one of the towers. Daniel had stopped to look back at Rhionna, earning himself a shove from Faelan's lackey, which motivated him to climb the ladder himself and vanish into the darkness of the building. He wasn't injured at least — that would make things easier getting out.

Walking as quietly as the makeshift bridge allowed, Jack followed, pausing at the base of the ladder to check the lay of the land. There was only one way out of this death trap, and that was by boat — he hoped to hell he'd be able to work out how to sail one. It couldn't be harder than an F-16, right?

Cautiously continuing to climb, he could hear voices from inside the tower, women and kids, but none close, and he could smell cooking fish and smoke. Something rattled and whined, the noise masking other sounds for a moment, then it faded. With care, he unholstered his nine-millimeter and let the P90 hang at his chest. He wasn't about to wave a submachinegun at a roomful of women and kids.

On a silent count of three, he slipped into the room.

No one seemed to notice. His eyes adjusted fast, and he saw a large space that might once have been some kind of office, but had deteriorated into a shanty long ago. Most of the windows had been boarded up, which explained the gloom. Hanging from the ceiling were pieces of tarp, carving out territory, and low-hanging lamps that gave off a warm glow and enough smoke to turn the walls black. He touched the wall behind him and his fingers came away covered in an oily black grease. Rubbing his fingers together, he sniffed, grimaced; like everything else in the goddamn place the black gunk stank of dead fish. Then, looking closer, he saw that next to the mark his fingers had left on the wall words had been scratched into the soot — *An Dóchas Deireanach*. And again, in larger letters above. And, now that he was looking for them, the damn words were scrawled everywhere.

If Daniel were with him, Jack might have asked for a translation. Or not. Except, Daniel wasn't with him. People moved about the camp, children shouted and parents scolded, but there was no sign of Daniel. Or Faelan.

A mechanical rattle clanked through the room, making Jack start. It was the same noise he'd heard before, and this time he found what was causing the racket. An elevator. Loosely speaking.

The elevator shaft was close to the door — which once had been a window — and in the light trickling in from outside Jack could see a kind of cage hanging in the place of a real elevator car. It reminded him of the deathtrap in the tunnels Rhionna used to leave the city, only this looked even more unreliable. But at least it proved that there was power in the city — of sorts.

No one paid attention to the elevator, so Jack assumed it rattled up and down all day. Banking on that assumption, he ducked his head and crossed the room to take a ride. It stood to reason that Faelan wouldn't conduct his business down here, at the waterline, with these poor and dirty people within earshot. Much better to be upstairs, safer, dryer, and far from the stink of dead fish.

Bad guys were the same, the galaxy over.

With some trepidation, Jack stepped into the rickety cage. There was no door, no Muzak — and, thankfully, no *Sunrise*. There was only a lever, which he yanked down. With a clunk and a shudder, the elevator began to trundle upward. He guessed he'd gone up maybe five floors — none of which had been inhabited — before the elevator ground to a halt, the cage facing a long, windowless corridor. More lamps dangled from crude fittings, their oily smoke thick on the ceiling.

It was quiet here, not silent, but quieter than below. What doors remained were closed, but most rooms just gaped doorless, letting in mist-filtered sunlight. Down the corridor hummed voices, and so Jack walked quietly until, at the far end, he caught sight of Faelan's second. He also caught the briefest glimpse of a BDU jacket as Daniel was shoved into a room. That one came equipped with a door, which promptly crashed shut. Then the meathead guard turned and walked away. Directly toward Jack.

There was no time to hide. All he could do was keep his head down and his Beretta tight to his side, hoping that shadow and distraction would do the rest.

They met halfway down the corridor. Jack held his breath, finger on the trigger. They passed each other like the proverbial ships in the night. A few seconds later, he heard the elevator clank onto its downward journey.

Letting out a slow breath, Jack glanced over his shoulder. The corridor was empty. Now or never.

The door to Daniel's room didn't look sturdy, he could break the lock with a kick. It would be noisy, but there was nothing to be done about that, and besides, Jack was fitter, better fed, and better trained than any of these people. He and Daniel would be gone in ten seconds flat, lost in the darkness of the crumbling tower, then out and looking for a ride home.

Piece of cake.

He leveled the gun, adjusted his balance. One swift kick made the door burst open, and Jack sailed after it into the room.

Where he stopped dead.

Faelan sprawled in a low chair, Rhionna sitting opposite with Daniel by her side. He was staring at Jack wide-eyed, a steaming mug arrested halfway to his lips. After a moment he raised a hand in greeting. "Hi, Jack."

CHAPTER NINE

"HI, JACK."

Daniel hoped the levity in his tone would defuse the knife-edge tension in the small room. In other circumstances, he might have been amused at the look of confusion on Jack's face as he stood in the doorway, dressed in a strange hat and ragged coat, gun in hand and the Beretta drooping with surprise.

From the corner of his eye, he noticed Faelan's sudden alertness, how his hand stole to the knife at his belt as soon as Jack had burst into the room. Thankfully the man had more sense than to react with open aggression; he probably knew he stood no chance against Jack's gun.

"Daniel," said Jack, his tone wary, his eyes never leaving Faelan. "You okay?"

"Yeah, I'm fine. We were just having a chat."

Faelan's jaw tensed and he aimed a pointed stare at the handgun.

"A chat," said Jack, deadpan.

"Yeah. Uh, why don't you join us?"

Jack looked over at him, then glanced around the room. He nodded at Rhionna, who gave a tentative smile in return, her eyes flicking between him and Faelan. "I'd given more thought to getting our asses out of here," said Jack.

"I guess that's an option. How did you get here anyway?"

"Does that matter?"

"It matters to me." It was Faelan who had spoken this time, glowering at Jack. "How did you get into the Cove?"

"I hitched a ride. You really should be careful who you let aboard your ships."

"Jack, I have this under control," said Daniel. "In fact..."

He set his mug down on the table and picked up the item he'd been perusing when Jack made his dramatic entrance; an electronic tablet which he activated by pressing the screen. "Faelan's given me some information that I think may be of use to us. About the shield. This is a data module that was discovered in one of the laboratories here. It's written in the same derivation of Gaelic we found on *Acarsaid Dorch*, but dates further back. Faelan tells me there are more of them here, up in the laboratories."

"Awful pally now, isn't he?" said Jack, but he edged into the room all the same, weapon now at his side. But not holstered. Yet.

Faelan also relaxed, his hand easing away from the knife. Next to him him, Daniel heard Rhionna's relieved sigh.

Jack nodded at the writing that scrolled across the tablet. "So what does it mean?"

"It means nothing," Faelan said. "It's just a story from before the Flood. A myth."

"Like the Sungate?" Rhionna said pointedly.

Faelan ignored her, glared out the window at the fragile towers of his dying city.

"The Elect know something of the shield," Rhionna said. "I know they do — and they fear it. Talk of the shield is forbidden inside the Ark."

"In my experience," Jack said, "it's always the important stuff they don't let you talk about. What's it say, Daniel?"

Daniel looked up from the tablet. "This by itself? Not much, but if I could take a look at the rest of the material, I might be able to make some sense of it." He glanced down at the device, at the tantalizing hints of a lost past — and at the truth he was keeping from Jack. But it was no good, he couldn't do it. He couldn't lie. With a sigh, he put the device down and said, "Actually, there's more. According to this the shield — "

" — is a really big sunshade?" Jack swiped the hat off his

head and flung it onto the floor. "Yeah, I know."

"You know that?" Daniel blinked. "How do you know that?"

"I have my sources, why?"

Daniel shrugged. "I don't know, I just... So you're not here to find the shield?"

Jack was tugging off his coat, avoiding his gaze. "I came here to find *you*, Daniel. Before hurricane season starts." He dropped the coat and readjusted his vest, at last looking up and meeting Daniel's eyes. "No one gets left behind, remember? It's an SG-1 thing."

"Yeah," Daniel nodded, hiding a smile. "I remember." And he did, he did remember. This was who they were, this was what they did. Then another thought struck him. "We still have to find the shield. If we can make it work, there's a good chance the planet would start cooling enough for sea levels to begin to fall."

"And for kids to grow up without going blind? Yeah, I get it." He holstered the Beretta. "So, what do we do?"

Daniel grinned. Yeah, this was what they did. This was who they were. He smiled expectantly at Faelan, who still appeared distrustful. But the look shared between the man and Rhionna seemed to be filled, however briefly, with something like hope. "Faelan," Daniel said, choosing his words with care, "if I'm right, I might be able to uncover technology that will help your people. All of them, including those in the Badlands. To dismiss these records as myth is myopic. Imprudent at best. Surely you're wiser than that."

"Don't patronize me, Jackson," said Faelan, but his glance flicked over Daniel's shoulder again, to where Rhionna stood by the window. Daniel thought he saw a question there, some silent communication. Rhionna gave a small nod, and Faelan sighed. "We don't have much time," he said, rising and heading for the door. "The storm is building, and we need to start the evacuation. Come now. You have until tomorrow to find out if what you seek is truly here. After that, it will be too late—the

Cove will take her secrets to the deep."

As they left the room, Jack's eyes strayed upwards scanning the ubiquitous graffiti that was daubed on practically every surface. Their host followed his gaze.

"*An Dóchas Deireanach*," he quoted. "A misplaced conviction, eh? It continues to amuse us even now." His mouth curled into a wry grin, then he set off up the corridor, Rhionna by his side.

Jack arched a look of query at Daniel. "The Last Hope," he translated, with a shrug. "The original name of this place apparently."

"How apt," Jack said sourly, stalking after Faelan.

Daniel was left to follow — and to pray that the conviction wasn't so misplaced after all.

Sam woke with a jolt as the cell door flew open and a bundle of rags and bones were thrown inside.

"Heretic!" Ennis Channon filled the doorway. Scrunched in his hand was a wad of paper, his knuckles white around the yellowing parchment. "Filthy defiler of the innocent! Did you think you could undermine the Lord's will?"

Sam jumped to her feet as the bundle of rags resolved itself into Sorcha Caratauc, her face ominously bruised as she scrambled upright. All gristle and bone, she stood defiant before her accuser.

"They're only words, Ennis Channon," she said. "Is your Lord so feeble that mere words can undermine His will?"

Edging forward, Sam placed herself between Channon and the skinny old woman. No doubt Sorcha could handle herself, but Ennis was furious and Sam wasn't taking any chances. She held up her hands, placating. "Look, Ennis, I'm sure — "

"You," he spat, jabbing the papers at her. "You dare come here with the very dust of *Acarsaid Dorch* on your feet? You seek to raise an abomination against our Lord! I'll hear no word from you."

Across the cell, Teal'c shifted onto the balls of his feet and cast a glance at Sam. She knew what he was thinking; there is one of him, and two of us. Three, including Sorcha.

There were no guards.

"This vile heresy is over," Ennis continued, still shaking the papers and making them rustle like leaves in a fall storm. "It is all destroyed, burned in that pit you call a home." He must have seen shock on Sorcha's face because he smiled, a malicious curl of his lips. "Yes, it is all gone — turned to ash. As you will be. You will never corrupt another innocent soul."

"Innocent you call it?" Sorcha laughed, a dry rattle in her throat. "It is ignorance you peddle, Pastor."

"Ignorance of sin."

"Of Knowledge!"

Teal'c's fingers flexed, and Sam recognized the question in the slight lift of his eyebrow. But it was broad daylight, and someone had to know Ennis was there — someone outside, perhaps close enough to hear a struggle. They'd only have one shot at this, and their odds were much better after dark.

"Knowledge." Ennis spat the word. "It was Knowledge that brought the Lord's wrath upon us! It was Knowledge that befouled the Garden, that turned rank what once was beautiful. Did not the Lord send his great flood to wash away Knowledge and return us to innocence? And yet you seek to bring it back, to defy His will! Your sin is foul indeed, Sorcha Caratauc, and must be cleansed."

"Kill me if you will," Sorcha said. "But Knowledge cannot be so easily destroyed. Do you think that my death will change what is true? Do you think it will return your daughter to ignorance?"

His jaw clenched, as if holding back bile, and his eyes flashed murder. But all he said was, "I have no daughter."

Sorcha was silent. Teal'c was balanced to pounce, like a hunting cat. Sam held her breath.

"They have forced you to this?" Sorcha said at last. "A strange kind of god who demands a father disown his beloved daughter. The same god who condemns the children for the sins of their fathers — the children, and their children's children — who lets them burn beneath his Sun and damns them even as they are birthed!"

"Silence, heretic!" Breath hissed through his locked teeth, and the papers he held fell to the floor. "Only the Lord can judge you for your sins against Him, Sorcha Caratauc. Therefore, it is the will of the Elect that you be given over to His mercy; at Sunrise tomorrow you shall be taken from the Ark to a place of judgment, there to be staked out, flesh bared to the purifying fire of His Sun. By His will shall your heresies be burned away and your soul cast into the damnation it deserves."

Sorcha said nothing, merely spat her contempt at his feet.

The evacuation of the Cove had begun. In the gray predawn light, a steady stream of people wound their way along the docks and onto the ships, while Jack O'Neill watched from his perch on what might have been a balcony once, but was now just a jagged, jutting jaw of granite propped up by unstable scaffolding. He'd seen operations like this before, of course, but here there was something missing.

In his experience, with a mass migration of people, there was always an undercurrent of barely checked panic, a desperation to escape whatever disaster was on their heels. The Seachráni did not panic, and any desperation was buried under a bone-hard shell of stoicism. Survival for them was not just instinct; it was habit, honed throughout their lives. They didn't know how *not* to do it.

There was another characteristic of the Seachráni, however, that Jack found especially noteworthy: their strength as a unit. He had witnessed it on the ship, the devotion they had to one another and the bond that glued them together. It came from shared experience — hard experience — and it couldn't be forced. Recently Jack had worried that it could be broken beyond repair. One thing he did know for sure; such a bond required one element that kept the parts of the whole together and stopped it from flying apart at the first gust of an ill wind. Down on the docks, that element walked among his people.

Faelan Garret was a conundrum to Jack. More bitter and hardened than any jaded veteran Jack had known, with a hair-trigger temper, the man was a liability; Jack still hadn't entirely ruled out shooting him so that he and Daniel could get the hell out of here. But an irritating inner voice insisted that this guy was so much more than what he claimed to be. Jack hated the wasted potential and hated even more that he found himself unable to dismiss it as someone else's problem.

He watched the captain make his way through the crowd, confident and assured, betraying none of the fears or doubts that might be brewing in his chest. With just a touch or a smile, he sowed encouragement.

"No matter what he thinks, he *is* their leader," said Jack to the man who had appeared at his elbow.

"I won't be arguing with you," said Pádraig, scratching a thumb across the gray stubble of his beard.

"Why is he so reluctant to accept that fact?"

"Faelan does what needs to be done. Doesn't matter what he tells himself."

"Sorry, Pádraig, but that sounds like bullshit to me."

Pádraig's brow drew down, landing him the look of a man waiting to see whether a right hook might be called for. "And what would you be meaning by that?"

"The way I see it, there's a lot that needs to be done on this planet beyond running and hiding."

Pádraig faced him fully. "Now you listen to me, Jack O'Neill. I've known Faelan Garret since he first came wailing from his mother's belly. His da was my brother in all but blood. That boy is Seachtraní in his very marrow, and whatever he does, he does for his people."

"And what about those other people back at the Badlands?"

Pádraig just turned back to glower down at the docks.

"Yeah, I get it," said Jack. "Not your problem."

"We take care of ours, O'Neill. We stand firm against the wind until it blows us over. It's the way it's always been."

Jack bit back a sigh of frustration at the old sailor's mulishness. "Y'know, sometimes desperate times call for desperate measures."

But Pádraig just gave a chuckle like the rasp of a match. "Times are always desperate, O'Neill."

"Don't try and tell me you've faced something as big as this before."

For a moment, Pádraig was silent, watching the activity below. After a while, he said, "Every Seachrání must face his final storm one day, O'Neill. Maybe this is ours."

"And you plan to go down with your ship, is that it?"

But Pádraig didn't answer, just turned and strode back into the lamp-lit building.

Jack watched him go until the rattle of scaffolding against the ledge drew his attention. Peering over the edge, he saw Faelan swinging his way upwards on nimble hands and feet.

"Jackson is still in the library?" asked the captain, as he pulled himself onto the balcony.

"Yeah. Once Daniel has his nose in a book, he makes a terrible conversationalist. Rhionna's helping him with the translations. I got bored and thought I'd take a look around. Hope that's okay."

Faelan shrugged. Apparently they weren't prisoners anymore. "Do you think he'll find what he's looking for?"

"If anyone can sniff out a needle in a haystack, Daniel can. Though, in general, it has to be a really old needle. With weird writing on it. He loves weird writing."

The captain glanced over Jack's shoulder and into the building beyond. "What did Pádraig have to say to you?" he asked with a jerk of his chin.

"Oh, nothing much. We were just shooting the breeze."

Faelan didn't look convinced, but said nothing more.

"Where are you taking them?" asked Jack, scanning the docks again. The ships were filling rapidly, and men and women swarmed across the yards and lines, readying them for the voyage. On the quay, a few of the more hardened Seachrání remained, showing no intention to board.

"Somewhere I hope is safer than here."

"And what about us?" he asked, hoping that his take on the guy wasn't wrong, and that he wasn't going to leave him, Daniel and Rhionna here for the storm to get them.

"I'll make sure you get back to the Ark."

"You realize that's not what you're supposed to do with hostages?"

"That was a poor decision I made, Colonel. And not the first one either. I apologize for it."

Jack nodded. "Sometimes we all make decisions we regret."

A pained, fleeting expression crossed Faelan's face; Jack suspected it had little to do with what had happened in the Badlands.

"So you're not coming back here then," he guessed.

"What makes you say that?"

"I just figured…" Jack trailed off, something Pádraig had said scratching at the edges of his thoughts. He looked down again at the people still standing on the quay.

"You'll need a ship. I'll bring one back," said Faelan.

There was a question that needed to be asked there, Jack knew, but it wasn't the right time, so instead he nodded in the direction of the harbor. "Can I come with you?"

Faelan looked surprised. "You want to join us on the voyage?"

"Not especially, but considering these buildings aren't much steadier than those boats — sorry, ships — then I figure I might as well stick to you like glue and make sure you keep your word about getting us home." It wasn't the truth; he had no doubt that Faelan would keep his promise. But there was that voice again, telling him that he just needed a little more time to talk this guy out of his bitter shell and persuade him that he could, in fact, make a difference.

Apparently, Faelan wasn't convinced by his explanation. He folded his arms across his chest and said, "What is it you hope to achieve here, O'Neill?"

"Maybe nothing. Humor me all the same, huh?"

After a brief pause, Faelan sighed in resignation. A flick of his head invited Jack to follow him down the scaffold. Feeling his way from pole to pole, trying in vain to keep pace with Faelan and not betray the ache in his knee, Jack questioned the wisdom of his plan.

Perhaps there was no hope for these people. Perhaps memories were influencing his actions, memories of bread rations and fear, and days colored by the furnace's glare, when the only respite was a head resting on his shoulder. Perhaps this time, there was no hidden door to escape through.

But perhaps, if there was a door, then Captain Faelan Garret would be the one to open it.

CHAPTER TEN

FAELAN'S vessel, the *Fánaí na Mara*, set sail upon a too-calm sea. The sun had burned away the fog and now shone like vengeance on the mirror-flat surface. Even through sunglasses the glare was blinding. It was like nothing Jack had ever seen before, and from the look on Faelan's face when they left the Cove, neither had he. The air felt heavy, expectant, and smelled of scorched metal. But if that hadn't told him something big was coming, then the fat clot of black clouds squatting far off on the horizon certainly did.

"They aren't moving," Faelan had muttered, almost to himself. "Why aren't they moving?" The words, which turned those clouds into sentient creatures priming themselves to attack, had sent cold fingers walking up Jack's spine.

Now he sat in Faelan's cabin, waiting out the Burn, which was harsher and lasted longer this far out to sea. The captain himself was off dealing with whatever matters needed to be dealt with on a ship like this. Eventually the door opened and Jack's host entered, shucking off his coat and removing his hat and sun-visor.

"So you gonna tell me where we're headed?" said Jack, impatient beyond the point of small talk.

Faelan ignored him. "Thirsty?" he asked, rubbing a hand over unkempt hair.

Though he didn't appreciate how the man avoided his question, Jack couldn't deny the rasp in his throat and nodded. Faelan pulled a metal canteen and two cups from a chest on the floor. He filled both cups, handing one to Jack, who took a sip and pursed his lips in appreciation. It was just water, but cleaner and less bitter than the stuff he'd drunk back at Sorcha's shack. He had to resist gulping it back.

"We have more efficient desalination plants at the Cove," explained Faelan. "What water we can spare we take to the people of the Badlands, but it's never enough."

"For a man of no consequence, you seem to put great effort into helping people."

Faelan sat back, drank. "You seem fixated on my word choice, Colonel."

"I'm just wondering why bother? You seem convinced this planet is going to hell in a handbasket. Surely a few barrels of water won't make that much of a difference."

"We have resources to spare. We'd be Seawolves indeed, eh, not to share what we can, when we can?"

Jack thought of the empty buildings he'd seen within the Ark, and shook his head. "So what else do you share? Food?"

"Sometimes. Mostly we give them fuel."

"Oil," said Jack, remembering the barrels being unloaded on the shore. "So you drill. Is that where we're going?"

"We don't drill. Those deposits were depleted long ago. No, Colonel, we hunt for our oil."

"Hunt?"

"Yes. Do you have *moil mór* on your planet?"

Jack shrugged, perplexed.

"Oil fish," explained Faelan. "We hunt them for fuel, for meat, for their hides."

Jack drew back in disgust. "I'm on a whaling ship? And I was thinking you people were some kind of hippies."

"You're shocked," said Faelan. "Your world doesn't utilize animals for such purposes then?"

"No! Well, yeah, but we're… selective. Jeez, next you'll be telling me you cook dolphin stew."

"No, of course not," replied Faelan. "Dolphin meat tastes disgusting." He laughed at Jack's expression and said, "Why is the idea so appalling, Colonel? You've already told me that your people hunt and farm."

"Yeah, but the whale thing is definitely frowned upon, on

account of them being almost extinct. Or something."

At that, Faelan threw his head back and laughed out loud, before glancing at the grimy face of the clock on the wall. Then he stood and opened the hatch of a porthole. "Burn's over," he said with a small grin. "Come with me, Colonel. There's a sight outside that may interest you."

They donned their protective gear and headed above deck, where Jack was greeted with a view that could only be called awe-inspiring. As far as the eye could see, the ocean churned with whales, dipping in and out of the water, tails flipping, sending liquid gems into the air to be caught by the sunlight. He'd watched enough Discovery Channel to recognize blue and sperm, but there were other species that he couldn't name, blowing great plumes like a thousand fountains.

"Wow," he said. "It's where motivational posters come to die."

"We hunt to live, Colonel O'Neill," said Faelan. "These are our natural resources. Without them…" He shrugged, but his meaning was clear. Faelan and his people were engaged in a constant struggle for survival. Their environment was harsh and unforgiving, and the odds were stacked against them. Yet here they were, defiant and resolute, and Jack didn't doubt that was down to their reluctant leader.

"So how else do you take care of your people, Faelan? What else do you do to survive?"

The captain's smile faded. "You'll see soon enough, Colonel."

"I could have overpowered him with ease." Teal'c sat cross legged and ramrod-straight, his eyes closed. Sam had assumed he was meditating, but apparently not.

She sighed and let her head knock back against the wall. "I know, but there had to be other guards outside and it's broad daylight. Besides, if we can get out of here without force I'd prefer to do it that way."

"You were unable to do so last night." His eyes opened to slide her a look.

She shrugged, acknowledging the truth. "Because by the time I got back from speaking with General Hammond it was too late; there wasn't another power dip significant enough to release the locking mechanism. I guess it only happens at times of peak usage." She fished out her DoD pass and waggled it in his direction. "Tonight I'll be ready."

"And where will you go, when you escape this place?" The voice belonged to Sorcha, who sat with her knees pulled up to her chest. Ennis's threat of execution had done little to dull the shrewd gleam in her eyes. "Will you return to your world and leave us to our fate?"

Uneasy with the question, Sam straightened. "Colonel O'Neill and Daniel have to be my priority. I'm sorry. It's not that we want to abandon you, but I have to give General Hammond a full report on what's going on here so that we can figure out how to get our people back."

"Your people come first." Sorcha gave a sharp nod. "Yes, that is as it should be. But what if I were to tell you that I can help you find your people?"

Sam shared a quick look with Teal'c.

"You have already told us," he said to Sorcha, "that Colonel O'Neill and Daniel Jackson are in the place called the Cove — a place inaccessible without a boat. We do not have a boat."

"True enough, and by the looks of you there's no seawater in your veins."

Teal'c inclined his head. "Indeed, there is not."

"But…" Sorcha glanced up at the ceiling, and Sam wondered if she was looking for a video surveillance camera. More quietly, Sorcha continued. "I have a device, given to me by Faelan some years ago." She smiled, a flash of crooked teeth. "Well, given to Rhionna in truth, but given into my care. A device through which I can talk to the Seachráni at the Cove."

"A radio?" Sam scrabbled across the floor to Sorcha. "You have a radio? Where?"

"Radio," Sorcha repeated, as if tasting the word for the first time. "Radio... Yes, if that is what you call such things."

"Where is it? At your home? Ennis said it was burned to the ground."

Sorcha smiled again. "Ennis is a fool, and I am not. Did you think I would leave all my precious Knowledge under nothing but canvas? This is not the first time the men of the Ark have tried to destroy my work, but they are fools and do not know what they see." Her bony hand reached out and touched Sam's wrist. "Come with me, come back to the Badlands, and talk with your friends."

"It is unlikely," Teal'c said, "that their captors would permit them access to this radio."

"Captors," Sorcha said with a shake of her head. "Faelan Garret is a stubborn fool, no doubt, but he did what he did to save his life, not to take another's. Your friend Daniel Jackson is safe, I'll vouch for that, and for Jack O'Neill too if he didn't tip himself into the drink or burn upon the deck."

Neither of which was likely, Sam knew; if anyone could take care of himself it was the colonel. But she'd seen the knife pressed to Daniel's throat, seen the desperation in Faelan's eyes, and she knew what fear could do to good men. Whatever Sorcha thought, she had no doubt that Faelan Garret would pitch both Daniel and the colonel overboard if he thought they posed a threat to his people. However, even a slim chance to speak to them was hard to pass up. "If we go with you," she said, "it'll be difficult to get back to the gate."

"If you return to your world," Sorcha countered, "it will be impossible to return to the Badlands, impossible to find your friends — or the shield you seek. Would you leave Ierna without the means of protecting your world against its foes?"

Sam shook her head. "We have other technologies..." But she trailed off, imagining the debate with Hammond. No one got left behind, sure. But Tynan Camus had made it clear that the Elect would resist. How many men would it take to fight a way through the Ark and out into the Badlands? More than Hammond would be willing — or permitted — to deploy. And then what? Faelan's people could be anywhere in that vast ocean, and the storm was closing in fast.

"If you speak the truth," Teal'c said to Sorcha, "then it is likely that our best chance of retrieving O'Neill and Daniel Jackson lies in your hands."

"I speak the truth," Sorcha promised. "I pledge my life to that. Come with me, speak with your friends — find out what they have discovered at the place of Last Hope. Then choose your path."

"Discovered?" Sam echoed. "You believe the shield is there, then? At the Cove."

"I am certain of it," Sorcha said with a firm nod, fixing Sam with an unbreakable gaze.

It made her uncomfortable, reminded her too much of Brenna's fixed stare as the lies had fallen from the woman's lips. A hot burst of anger flared in her chest, and Sam took a swift breath to cool it. Different place, different person. Move on.

"Okay," she said, when the silence had grown long. "We'll go with you and speak to our friends. And after that?"

Sorcha smiled. "After that, Samantha Carter, you can decide what path best serves the interest of your people. And mine."

For a while, Jack was left alone with nothing to do but lean on the railing and watch the play of the whales. Then, as the sun continued its downward arc, even they disappeared. Impatient, he pushed away, determined to find Faelan, only to see the man striding toward him.

"At the risk of sounding like a five year old on a trip to Disneyland, are we nearly there yet?"

To Jack's immense relief, Faelan nodded. "The crew are preparing to boats to go ashore. Are you still keen to see how my people live? I warn you, Colonel. It is not a pleasant sight."

Though Faelan's eyes were hidden behind the sun visor, Jack could see the tight set of his jaw. He also heard the brittle edge to his voice. How much worse than the Badlands could this other place be? And why did it seem to matter so much more to this man?

Doubting he'd get a straight answer, Jack simply said, "I think I can handle it."

Faelan regarded him for a few more seconds, the visor's black plastic reflecting nothing but Jack's own image. Then the captain nodded for Jack to follow.

Once in the longboat they headed for a jagged strip of dark gray in the near distance. Land.

Progress was swift, and they quickly approached the shore. It was completely different from what Jack had expected. This wasn't the ramshackle wooden quays of the Badlands or the decaying spires of the Cove, but rather a sleek marina with purpose-built piers glinting in the light of the setting sun. And it was empty, entirely empty, apart from the vessels docked along each pier; fishing boats past their sell-by date that looked likely to break apart the first large wave they encountered. The tiny crafts bobbed in their berths, lonely and cheerless. The place was steeped in a feeling of civilization forgotten; a lost land ready to tip over the edge of the world. Unease prickled along Jack's spine.

Beyond the marina rose a series of low, rocky peaks. When Jack surveyed the terrain he noticed a glimmer of reflected sunlight at the summit of one of the hills. There was a building up there.

"Is that where we're headed?" he asked one of the crew as he climbed ashore, but the woman barely glanced at him as she walked past.

"I don't think they like me very much," he said, when he

caught up with Faelan.

The Seachrání captain shook his head. "Not at all, Colonel. They're intrigued by you. They can't understand why you would bring your people to a world like this. They don't know what you hope to achieve."

It was a good point, but one Jack couldn't really answer. "Maybe they just don't understand hope very well."

Faelan gave a grunt of derisive laughter. "They understand the futility of it."

"And why would that be?" The question was stupid, Jack realized; all he had to do was look around him to see why these people had so little hope. But rather than hand him the obvious answer, Faelan rubbed the back of his neck and turned away. At that point Jack knew there was another story here.

Just then, a shout from up ahead drew his attention. The cause of the commotion was behind them, though. Turning around, Jack saw a vane of dust moving towards them; vehicles were headed their way. Jack shifted his balance forward onto the balls of his feet, ready to move, the only visible concession he made to his instinctive apprehension.

The approaching vehicle turned out to be something resembling a bus; old, but sturdy, and designed for all terrains. Engine chugging into silence the bus stopped, and its driver stepped out, an older woman wearing the vital sunvisor, with a scarf wrapped round her head.

"*Cead míle fáilte*, Finn," she called, words of welcome that Jack had heard uttered in the Badlands. She strode towards them and, to Jack's astonishment, grasped the Seachrání captain in a tight embrace, which Faelan returned. After a moment, she drew away from him and smoothed her hand across his cheek. "*A leanbh, fáilte, fáilte,*" she said, her voice softer now, obvious affection in every word. "Too long it's been, boy."

Faelan only nodded, looking abashed.

The woman turned to the rest of the crew, embracing others in turn, exchanging fond greetings. The closeness between them only served to make Jack feel like more of a stranger, outnumbered and on his own.

Then, as the crew turned to the task of loading supplies onto the bus, the woman's gaze landed on him and her lips thinned. "You've brought me a guest, Finn? And you haven't yet introduced him?" Her words were friendly, but it was impossible to miss the suspicion that laced them. Jack couldn't say he blamed her.

"Muirne Connaught, this is Colonel Jack O'Neill," offered Faelan.

"From the Ark?" asked Muirne, extending hand in greeting despite her obvious apprehension. Her head tilted as she took in Jack's clothing.

"From Earth," replied Jack.

Muirne turned sharply to face Faelan, who nodded in confirmation. "He came through the Sungate, along with three others. Sorcha was right."

"If she was right about the Sungate, Finn, then what of her other claims?"

Faelan only shrugged.

"You mean the shield?" said Jack. Muirne's eyebrows rose with surprise.

"It's why he's here," said Faelan. "He and his team are chasing old children's tales."

"Don't be so dismissive of that which you don't understand, Faelan Garret," said Muirne, in stern tones. "If not for Sorcha Caratauc's children's stories we would not have a refuge here."

Faelan set his jaw. "Reason enough to distrust everything she says on the matter," he muttered, but Muirne ignored him.

"Well," she said, "it's hardly hospitable having a guest stand about in this heat. Let us go to the *Tearmann*. I'll send more transports down for the others."

The journey up into the hills was dusty and bumpy, and the noise from the bus's engine made small talk impossible. Which suited Jack just fine. Muirne handled the wheel deftly, but even her skill couldn't make the trip comfortable. He was grateful when they finally rumbled to a halt inside a walled compound. As they disembarked, he realized that there was something familiar about the surrounding buildings.

"This is the Ark," he said to Faelan, while Muirne dealt out commands to both the Seachráni and those who had approached from inside. Jack looked up and saw the familiar glimmer of a dome far above. "This is exactly like the Ark."

"Not exactly," replied Faelan, pulling off his hat and visor and shedding his coat. Though the sun's rays were filtered, the temperature inside the dome was stifling.

"Okay, so your AC's not as efficient but —"

"Look around you, Colonel. These people are hungry. They're sick and they're poor. Do they resemble anyone you'd see in the Ark?"

Jack glanced at the faces of the men and women who bustled around them, some unloading supplies with brisk efficiency, some boarding other vehicles to make a second trip down to the marina. Faelan was right; they all had that same pinched look he'd seen among the Seachráni, the people of the Badlands, and a dozen other places he didn't want to remember; it was the look of those who knew deep, bone-gnawing hunger.

And yet there was something else about them too, a keenness, an intelligence. There was none of the broken despair of the Badlands, or the addled complacency of those within the Ark, nor the bitter cynicism of the Seachráni. They laughed, they spoke frequently, and in rapid sentences. There was a vibrancy here that Jack hadn't encountered anywhere else on the planet. But for some reason Faelan couldn't see it.

He turned to say as much, but found that the man had

already marched off to help the others.

"My apologies, Colonel," said Muirne, appearing at his shoulder. "His tongue sometimes forgets what good manners are."

Jack shrugged off the apology and followed Muirne. The woman seemed keen to talk, and he figured she'd be more likely to give him an answer than Faelan. "So what is this place?" he asked looking around. Though it resembled the Ark, on closer inspection it was easy to spot how different it actually was. The buildings looked older, most of them in disrepair, and there were no ornamental gardens or parks. The most notable difference was the lack of giant screens with their endless loops of *Sunrise*. Jack decided that he liked it a hell of a lot better this way.

"I think it was a prototype of sorts," Muirne was saying. "As far as I know, they built it before the Ark."

"They?"

"The men of Knowledge, those who were cast out." She smiled. "Ennis Channon and his ilk, I believe, call them heretics, though their only heresy was wanting to help their people survive the Great Flood."

We are helping our people survive an ice age...

Jack squeezed his eyes shut. "We found them," he said. In his mind, he saw the open grave, the skulls with holes in them. "I think we found them on *Acarsaid Dorch*. They'd been killed." He stopped dead in the street. "Wait! Are you telling me they were killed because they were trying to prevent this flood?"

Muirne shrugged. "Ours is a dark and bloody past, Colonel O'Neill, but I'm not a gatherer of stories. Speak to Sorcha Caratauc if you wish to know more. I only know that they built this place as a refuge, the first of several, with the Ark being the last and the greatest. A shelter for all against the coming floods, a place of refuge until... Well, then we return to children's stories, hmm?"

"If this is a refuge, then why's it empty? There are thousands of people in the Badlands who could come here. Why doesn't Faelan bring them?" As far as he could tell the vast spaces and empty buildings could shelter countless more people.

Muirne's gaze drifted back to where Faelan stacked barrels and crates with his men. "It was his intention to do just that. He had a plan..." She sighed, a sad sound. "He was so consumed by the idea back then, so sure it would work. Hardly more than a boy he was, though I doubt I'll ever see him as anything else. Back then he still had that drive. He still had dreams." She paused, as if considering how much to say. Jack kept silent, curious despite himself to hear the story. It was hard for him to imagine the cynical Seachráni as an idealistic youngster.

"There was a girl, you see," continued Muirne. "I think there often is in such cases. She gave him hope."

"Rhionna Channon," said Jack.

Muirne looked at him in surprise. "You know her."

"She, uh... She sailed with us to the Cove." Considering the woman's affection for Faelan, Jack decided not to divulge the full details.

"She came back? She is with him again?" In contrast to the wary reception Rhionna had received among the Seachráni, this woman seemed to almost welcome the news.

"Maybe you'd better ask Faelan about that."

Muirne rolled her eyes. "For all the response I'd get. He's tight-lipped, is our Finn. Even with me." She shook her head. "It was Rhionna who told him about the *Tearmann* and the other places like it. She learned about them from Sorcha. I suppose you'd say it was Rhionna's idea in the first place. We were living at the Cove then. Cramped and overcrowded." Her smile held something nostalgic. "It was home of a sort, but not a place to raise children."

"You're Seachráni then."

"We all are, Colonel, though many of us no longer take to the water."

"So it was Faelan who brought you here?"

She nodded. "He wanted to create a real sanctuary here, a place of safety, where his people could be happy. I think he hoped for too much though. He worked too hard trying to bring it to pass and for a while it seemed that his plan would bear fruit. But then…"

"Then?"

Muirne fixed him with a shrewd gaze. "A storm. Bad it was, but not the worst we've weathered. This place is over two hundred years old, Colonel O'Neill, and these buildings were derelict all that time. That night, two of them collapsed when a section of the dome caved in; three families died here, buried beneath the rubble, and Faelan has carried them with him all the years since."

This was a burden Jack understood all too well. And he understood how hard it was to let go. "Wasn't his fault."

Muirne shrugged. "At night we still must burn oil lamps, and the dome does nothing to keep out the heat. Our crops wilt beneath the sun, and we are always hungry. Like Faelan said, Colonel, look around you. This is not the future he dreamed for his people."

"At least he tried," said Jack, watching the hive of activity in the compound. "Y'know, some might say that he even succeeded."

Going by Muirne's smile, she was pleased that Jack got it. "Yes, some might say that. Not Faelan though. He only sees where he failed. He only remembers those people who died. He doesn't see the gratitude of those whose lives are better because of his actions."

"Those people," asked Jack, "would they call him their leader?"

Her eyes narrowed in contemplation. "Would you?"

Jack shook his head. "He's too angry."

"Sometimes a leader needs to be angry. Sometimes they need that fire."

With a purse of his lips, Jack conceded the point, but then said, "He's bitter though. That's never a good thing."

"He's young. He needs someone to temper that. When he met Rhionna, I thought…" She let the sentence trail off. "I'm still proud of him, Colonel O'Neill. Never doubt that."

An earlier suspicion of Jack's solidified at those words. "What mother wouldn't be?" he observed.

Muirne's answering smile was confirmation enough. Then she glanced over his shoulder and her smile widened. Jack turned to find Faelan walking towards them, wiping his face with a rag. His eyes narrowed and shifted between Muirne and Jack, as if he knew he'd been the subject of their conversation.

"You'll stay for the evening meal," said Muirne.

Faelan shook his head. "I can't, it's not safe to delay much longer. Which is part of the reason I've come. To warn you –"

"About the storm."

"You already know?"

Grinning, Muirne patted her son's cheek. "Remember who it is you're talking to, boy. You think I haven't tasted it in the air for a week now? You think I can't see what sits on the horizon? We've already closed off the unstable sections. We'll be fine."

Faelan nodded and looked down at the rag he twisted in his hands. Then he cleared his throat. "There's another thing. The people I brought with me. There are families among them, children. They can't stay at the Cove any longer."

"There is room for them here," said Muirne, clasping his shoulder.

His throat worked as he swallowed — gratitude or shame? — but when he spoke his voice was steady and matter of fact. "Keep them safe."

"Always."

"If…" He heaved a breath. "If the storm is as bad as we think, I might never be able to come back here."

Muirne shook her head. "I'll see you again, *leanbh*. I'll see you again." She placed her hands on either side of his face, her eyes bright now. "Ah, Finn, my warrior boy. What burdens you have on your shoulders, eh? Won't you let someone share them for a while?"

But Faelan drew back. "*Slán, máthair*," he said, his voice breaking on the last word.

"*Slán*, my boy. Goodbye, and go well." But she spoke to her son's retreating back, and Jack had no choice but to follow Faelan back to his ship.

CHAPTER ELEVEN

THE LIGHTS flickered, but the electronic lock didn't move. Cursing under her breath, Sam kept her ID card poised in the slim crack between the door and the frame. Her back ached, her shoulders were stiff, and she waited for a chance that might not even come any time soon.

A low rumble filtered down into their windowless cell, and Sorcha lifted her head. "It comes," she said. "No more than a day."

"The storm?" Sam glanced up at the ceiling as if she could see through it to the sky above.

"I can feel it. If we were outside, I could smell it."

Teal'c hovered at Sam's side, ready to rush the door. "Sorcha Caratauc," he said, "do you believe this storm will overwhelm the place you call the Cove?"

She sniffed, pulling her arms closer to her chest. "I'm no Seachráni, I have not their weather-lore. If Faelan says the Cove will stand, then it will stand."

"But he didn't," Sam said, blinking her eyes back into focus on the lock. Any minute now the lights would flicker and the lock would disengage... "It was pretty clear he thought the Cove was in danger, even if he didn't say as much."

Sorcha grunted. "Perhaps."

"Which means Daniel and Jonah are in danger."

There was a pause, enough time for her stomach to clench and a flush of angry heat to color her face. Then Teal'c said, "Major Carter?"

Through gritted teeth she growled, "I'm fine. Slip of the tongue."

Another roll of thunder filled the room, not the sharp crack of a storm overhead, but the low snarl of a distant and menacing beast. Again, the lights flickered but the bolt did not move. Sam spat another curse. *Come on, come on...* She needed to get out of this place, needed to move. To *do* something.

Behind her, the theme of *Sunrise* began to swell. Again. The music scraped across her skin, jangling claws snatching at the breath in her lungs. "Come on!"

In the distant height of his lodging, the topmost apartment in the Chapel, Ennis Channon did not watch the replay of the most recent chapter of *Sunrise*.

Instead he stood at the window, looking out through the opalescent protection of the Ark toward a dark horizon, Smudged by the dome, he could still see the crouching clouds menacing the sunset. He could still see the flash of white light, hear the distant thunder.

A storm was coming.

Fear churned in the pit of his stomach, an anxiety even his devotion to the Lord could not quell. For though his daughter was already lost to him, he could not help but think of her out there, amid the violence of the storm. His fingers clenched, and he imagined them around the neck of the Seachráni scum who had stolen his child and corrupted her soul, turned her against the light of the Sun and cast her into this black and vicious storm.

But in truth, her blood was not solely on the hands of Faelan Garret. Even now, within the *Sunrise* building, Tynan Camus was at work on a new chapter of the Message, indifferent to the Rhionna's plight, damning her without mercy, though she was guilty of nothing except misguided compassion.

As lightning tore across the sky, Ennis could not help but question the god who could call such a punishment just.

The lights dipped, distant thunder growled, and Major Carter's hiss of triumph cut through the momentary darkness.

"Got it." She was crouched before the door, one hand pressed flat to its surface, jamming the slender ID card between the bolt and the frame. "Teal'c, get this open."

Only when he moved to stand behind her, surveying the narrow crack, did he understood the flaw in her plan; the door opened inward, and there was no handle, nothing on which to obtain purchase. The lock might have been deactivated, but the pressure Major Carter exerted to stop it from reengaging kept the door firmly closed. He ran his fingers down its edge, nails slipping as he tried to pull it open. Had O'Neill been present, he would have voiced an appropriate expletive.

"Damn it," Carter hissed, when she realized the problem. "We need some kind of lever."

Teal'c's gaze strayed to the wall-mounted television on the far side of the cell. The now familiar voices droned above a background of syrupy music, and he lifted an eyebrow in sudden anticipation. "Sorcha Caratauc," he said, marching across the room, "step away from the screen."

One hand either side of the television, he tested the weight and then yanked at the device with a sudden movement. A spark of protesting electronics flew up, metal ground against stone, and the screen blinked to black. The cell fell into silence, bar the fizzing of torn cables, a silence which he shattered by dropping the screen to the floor.

"Umph," Sorcha grunted. "Would that more screens suffered the same fate."

Bracing one foot against its back, Teal'c wrapped both hands around a strut of the metal bracket that had fastened the television to the wall. He pulled and it came away, a shard of plastic casing clinging to one end.

Major Carter grinned at him over her shoulder. "Nice."

Knowing that the disturbance might well have triggered an alarm, Teal'c dropped to his knees, cheek pressed against the cool floor, and slid the twisted metal bracket beneath the door, then turned it so that the bent end caught. "Keep the card in place," he told Major Carter.

It was the work of a moment. The door gave, the locking mechanism came free of the frame, and Major Carter rocked back onto her heels and dropped her arm. "Good work," she whispered, rising into a low crouch as she peered out of the cell. "Clear," she said, glancing back at him.

With a nod, he moved to take point. Behind him, Major Carter said, "Sorcha, stay close. If we meet any resistance, just keep out of the way. Teal'c and I can handle it."

The old woman snorted. "I've taken care of myself these fifty years or more, girl." Nonetheless she did as Major Carter had bidden as Teal'c shoved open the door and stepped into the corridor outside.

Featureless, it reminded him of the utilitarian hallways of Stargate Command. To his left and right were other cell doors, all locked. Ahead, the corridor ended in a turn. If there were guards, he assumed that they would have taken up post there. Signalling Sorcha Caratauc and Major Carter to stay back, he flattened himself to the wall and made his way to peer around the corner.

Two men stood guard, shoulders propped against the wall on opposite sides of a staircase that led up to daylight. Like slovenly bookends, these were not men used to fighting. They were soft, and though they were armed and he was not, Teal'c felt no misgivings as he crept up behind them on cat-silent feet. A hand on each neck, he crunched their heads together before either made a sound. Limp-limbed they fell at his feet and he crouched to pull their weapons from the leg holsters.

"Ouch," Major Carter observed, coming up behind him.

He turned, offering her one of the alien handguns. "Indeed."

"You could have killed them," Sorcha said, and Teal'c was unsure if she was accusing or merely commenting.

He stood, shoving the gun into his belt. "I could have," he agreed, meeting her ice-chip gaze. It was the old woman who looked away first.

Walking past them, Major Carter led the way up the stairs and cracked open the doors to the outside. "That's the Chambers," she said, nodding across the street. "The gate must be around here somewhere."

He knew the path of her thoughts. "If we leave now, it is unlikely we will be able to return in time to save Colonel —"

"We're not leaving," she said. "I was just pointing it out, is all." She squinted through the narrow gap at the buildings around them, bright against a darkening sky. "I know where we are; the tunnel Rhionna showed us isn't far."

In the distance thunder rumbled again, louder now. "Then let us leave," Sorcha Caratauc said. "The storm is closing, and we have little time."

With Major Carter on point and Teal'c bringing up the rear, they crept through the deepening shadows toward the bright city lights — and from there, into the tunnels beneath.

He stands with his face pressed to the curve of the Ark, the world beyond misted and vague. But he can see her, she is vivid in scarlet beyond the safety of the dome. He can see her hair, free and blowing in the wind, dark curls like her mother's against a blackening sky.

He reaches for her, but his hand touches the smooth warmth of the dome, and when he calls her name no sound leaves his lips.

She turns and the devil is there, a blade held to her neck and a leer on his fiendish face. "I claim her," he says, stepping backward, taking her with him, and Ennis can already see a vibrant streak of blood against her ivory throat. "She's mine now."

But it is not Garret's face that he wears.

He hammers against the dome, he shouts for her and to her — Only death awaits you outside, only fire and damnation await you in sin! Return, return to the Sun! But she cannot hear because, though his throat is raw, it makes no sound.

He is silent, helpless. And she is fading, fading into the darkness and —

"Pastor Channon?"

Jerking awake, he peered with bleary eyes at the man standing in the doorway to his bedchamber. A guard's uniform, silhouetted by the light from outside. Fumbling, Ennis switched on the light by his bed. "What the devil is this?"

"My apologies, sir. Brother Camus instructed me to wake you immediately. There is a situation."

Throwing off the sheet, he stood up and did his best to feel dignified in his rumpled nightshirt. "What situation, soldier?"

The man shuffled his feet. "The prisoners, sir. They've gone."

"Gone?"

"From the cell."

Ennis blinked. "Impossible. How?"

The guard shrugged. "We don't know how they got out. They overpowered the guards at the entrance, however. We think they're heading for the Badlands."

"Of course they are," he snarled, snatching up a night robe and flinging it on. "Where else would they go?"

"The Council has been summoned," the guard said, in lieu of a reply. "Immediately. Brother Camus —"

"The Council?" He felt a chill, a swift dread running from top to toe. "Now?"

The guard said nothing, his gaze averted. Ennis didn't blame him; there would be an accounting for this and, as Pastor, the security of the Ark fell on his shoulders. He took a breath, calming himself, and walked to the window. Outside it was dark, the gathering storm swamped by the night. But it was still there, bearing down on the heathens beyond the protection of the Ark.

Bearing down on Rhionna.

"Send all the men into the Badlands," he said. "I want them found. Do what must be done to discover them; spare none who stand in your way. I want them back in their cell by dawn."

There was a pause, then, "Yes, sir."

"And you…" He could see the guard reflected in the glass window, his face studiously impassive; this was Camus's man, and Ennis could feel his scorn. "You go to the cells, find out everything you can. I want to know what devilry was involved in their escape."

The guard nodded. "I shall tell Brother Camus that you are on your way."

Ennis didn't answer, just waited for the man to leave. If Tynan Camus thought he could use this to undermine him, to snatch his birthright from him, then he was mistaken. The outsiders would be found, their heresy quashed, and Ennis Channon would remain Pastor of the Ark — as his father had been before him, and his before him, back until the Great Flood itself.

He pressed a hand to the glass, hard and cool. Outside the Ark, clouds blew across the night sky, hiding the stars.

Much to Sam's relief, night had fallen by the time they made their way out of the maintenance tunnel. As Rhionna had done, she wedged a rock into the doorway to keep it open then straightened up to look around. The air was balmy and the sky above starless, thickened by cloud. Sorcha was heading straight down the hill toward the Badlands, and Sam had no intention of losing her in the dark.

"Wait up," she called, hurrying after the woman.

Glancing back over her shoulder, Sorcha waved a bony hand toward the horizon. "There. Do you see? We must hurry."

The distant flash of sheet lightning left no doubt of what was approaching.

"The storm," Teal'c said from close behind her.

"Will it have reached the Cove yet?"

Sorcha shrugged. "Let us hope not. But hurry. You will know for sure when we communicate with your friends. Let us hope that the storm does not render the blue star ineffectual."

"The blue star?"

"If not for the clouds, it would be visible by now," Sorcha said, looking at the sky. "But it is there. A bright star that appears with regularity. Without it the device would not work."

"A satellite," Sam guessed, casting a glance at Teal'c. "A communication satellite."

"Satellite?" Sorcha repeated, taking care with each syllable. Tasting the word. "You must tell me more as we walk. Come, there is not much time."

They scrambled down the scrubby hillside and into the noisome alleyways of the Badlands. Sorcha lifted an eyebrow at Sam's assertion that, in the past, her people might have possessed space technology, but she did not speak up until Sam was finished.

"There are those," she said, "who would scoff at such a notion. But they do not know all that I know about the Time Before; perhaps you are right Samantha Carter." She paused. "It would be a wonderful thing if you were."

The Badlands were not as dark as Sam had expected, nor as crowded. In fact, the place seemed deserted. Although warm light leaked from behind canvas and between the wooden planks of crude shacks, they met no one as they crossed the shantytown. And there was another light abroad in the streets, an all-encompassing white glow, which emanated from a block of huge screens that rose up at the heart of the settlement. Even from a distance, Sam could hear the saccharine music.

Sorcha grunted when she saw the direction of Sam's gaze. "The Elect seek to proselytize, even here among the damned. They bring us food to dull our hunger and *Sunrise* to dull our minds; prison walls could not be so effective." She poked a finger into Teal'c's arm. "We need more of your sort, eh? To smash the screens upon the ground and wake the people up."

Teal'c looked over at the massive screens, their light a glint in his eyes. "You speak of revolution, Sorcha Caratauc."

"A man such as you could lead us."

He shook his head, and when he spoke there was a weight in his voice that Sam well understood. "None can lead those who do not wish to follow."

He wasn't talking about Sorcha's people. At least, not only. "A revolution isn't born in a day," she reminded him, "it takes time for ideas to filter through a population."

Teal'c inclined his head. "Perhaps. But time is not on our side."

Sorcha's penetrating gaze cut between them, but all she said was, "You speak true. The blue star is overhead. We must hurry."

Her tatty clothes flapped as she hurried through the rabbit warren of alleyways. With a final glance at Teal'c, Sam followed, staying close and keeping one hand on the butt of the alien weapon. She wished it was a Beretta.

At length Sorcha slowed, coming to a halt before a heap of refuse. It took Sam a moment to realize that it was, in fact, the remains of Sorcha's home. The whole thing had been destroyed, burned and trampled into the dirt. Whatever kind of communication device she'd been hiding, it couldn't have survived this assault. Sam swallowed a mouthful of bitter disappointment. "I'm sorry," she said, touching the woman's shoulder. And she *was* sorry, but her mind was swamped by her own problems and a dreadful realization: *we can't contact Daniel and the Colonel.*

"Ennis's men have done this," Sorcha said with a sniff. She crouched and picked up a scrap of burned paper, turning it over and letting it crumble between her fingers. "I am not surprised."

"You're not?" Sam clenched her jaw. "But you said—"

Sorcha rose, picking her way through the debris with her eyes fixed on the ground. In the bland light of the vast screens the wreckage looked colorless, a trampled mess of dirt. With the toe of her sandal, Sorcha turned over an old piece of board, beneath it the blackened remains of her hearth lay scattered. She crouched again, tested its heat with her finger, then swept away the rest of the soot and ash and began digging into the dirt.

Curious, Sam stepped closer. Something beneath her boots crunched, but Sorcha didn't look up from the hearth where her excavation had begun outlining a stone square, a large metal ring in its center. She grasped it tight, then looked up at Sam. Her lined face was bright and wary. "Take care that we are unwatched," she said.

Teal'c moved to join them, walking backward with his gaze turned out into the city. "I see no one."

"Me neither," said Sam.

Sorcha grunted. "Some are at the screens, others sleep while it is cool."

"Good for us, then."

She heaved on the iron ring and, with a rasp of stone on stone, the square opened up to reveal a lightless hole. A grin cut across Sorcha's leathery face. "Be quick," she said. "There is a ladder. All that we need lies below."

The Chambers were lit by lamplight, casting the hallowed hall into shadow deeper than usual.

As he entered, Ennis smoothed his hands over his robes and composed his features. He would not allow Tynan Camus to blame him for this disaster and refused to be cowed.

The rest of the Elect were already assembled; he suspected he'd been the last to be alerted. Petty gamesmanship, which only was to be expected of Tynan Camus. "Sister Nevin," Ennis said, bowing slightly as he came to stand before them. "Council."

"Pastor Channon." Nevin's thin face was frosty. "This situation grows increasingly intolerable. What have you to say on the matter?"

"Only this." He cast a look at Tynan, who lounged in his usual position at the end of the table. "As we speak, our guards are moving into the Badlands to root out the outsiders and their accomplice."

Nevin lifted an eyebrow. "Accomplice?"

"Sorcha Caratauc."

Nevin grimaced. "Ah, the old crone."

"The old crone," Tynan interrupted, waving a languid hand, "can read. We found books in her hovel, scribblings about *Sciath Dé*."

A gasp of shock went up from the other council members.

"*Sciath Dé*?" Nevin's eyes were like ice. "Is this true, Pastor?"

"Her writings have been destroyed," he said. His palms were clammy. "They have been burned."

"Why did you not seek to bring this to the Council? If she has Knowledge…"

Ennis flung a look at Tynan. "Brother Camus and I believed—"

"She is like a prattling child who knows nothing of what she speaks," Tynan said. "If she has lured these outsiders with fairytales and nonsense, why should we care? *Sciath Dé* is anathema to the Lord's will; He will not permit its existence." He met Ennis's gaze. "Will He?"

"No, but—"

"Then I see no reason for this panic." Tynan yawned. "The matter is in the Lord's hands and to be dragged from one's bed at such an hour, for such a reason, is most unreasonable."

Nevin frowned. "The Council of the Elect is not called at

your convenience, Brother Camus. These are grave matters; heresy can never be ignored, for fear it will spread like disease among the ignorant."

Tynan sat up, adopting a more reverential tone. "You misunderstand. I meant no disrespect to the Council, Sister Nevin. But, if I may, I would like to make one further point." When Nevin didn't stop him, Tynan continued. He waved a hand towards the Chamber doors. "Two centuries ago, the Lord punished our world for its sin — he sent the Great Flood to drown the heathens, the sinners, and those who rejected his Light. But sin has returned. I have seen it with my own eyes. I have walked in the filth of the Badlands, among people blind to the Light. I have seen how they live, like animals, their souls as black as their feet. And now, Council, I see storm clouds upon the horizon, and in them I see the hand of the Lord."

He rose to his feet, walking around the table to stand before the Council as if *he* were the Pastor! Ennis ground his teeth, but held his silence, finding himself lost in the shadow of the man.

"Two hundred years ago, the Elect brought the righteous into the Ark and saved them from the Lord's vengeance." Tynan spread his hands. "Brothers and Sisters, it is time for us to do so again. It is time to close the doors to sin, to cut off the water and the food, to let the seas rise and the Sun burn. It is time to let those beyond His protection suffer the Lord's wrath. *For I will execute vengeance in anger and fury upon the heathen*, sayeth the Lord. And He shall wash away sin and, with it, the heresy brought here from *Acarsaid Dorch*."

In the silence that followed, heightened and fervent, Ennis Channon felt the ground begin to shift like sand beneath his feet.

At least the soldiers at the Ark hadn't taken her MagLite. Stepping off the bottom of the short ladder, Sam swept the small flashlight across room. The place looked like a hoarder's paradise, racks of shelves holding piles of papers and books. Actual books!

"Wow," she breathed, moving deeper into the chamber. Behind her, she heard other footsteps on the ladder. "Where did you find all this stuff?"

"Here and there," Sorcha said. There was a rattle, a hiss, and yellow lamplight bloomed. Sorcha hung the lamp onto a hook in the low ceiling. "The collection was begun by another man, Eoin Madoc. He taught me to read and to question, to learn of the Time Before."

"The Time Before," Sam repeated, turning her attention back to the books. She picked one up, studying the alien words on the front. If only Daniel were here! Flashlight wedged under her chin, she flicked through the pages. They were thin and old, water damaged, but nonetheless her breath caught. Alien as it was, she recognized the book for what it was — she'd seen hundreds of them. She looked at Sorcha. "It's an instruction manual."

Sorcha blinked at her, uncomprehending.

"It tells you how to operate a machine — a technology."

"Ah!" The woman nodded, smiling. "Yes, yes. This I know — in the Time Before there was great Knowledge, great machines, but now the Elect hoard it like misers, doling out only what they deem necessary. And here," she said, moving into a shadowy corner, "here is all I have learned about *Sciath Dé*; many writings, many arguments I think." Carrying a large pile of papers, topped by a notebook, Sorcha returned into the halo of light beneath the lamp. She sat down on the floor, placing the papers next to her, and offered the book to Sam. "Look inside. It is all laid down as I have found it."

Curious, and not a little in awe of Sorcha's tenacity, Sam opened the book. It had a hard cover, mildewed in places, and its lined pages were filled with precise handwriting. "This is your work?" Sam said, looking up.

Sorcha's pride was evident. "I have spent many years gathering evidence about *Sciath Dé*, but I have more questions than answers. The truth lies at the Cove; it was there, I believe, that the shield was constructed. But the Seachráni..." She shook her head. "They have no need for Knowledge, they say it has no worth in this world. It is of the Time Before and cannot help us."

"But you think otherwise?" She flicked through the pages as she spoke, wishing she could understand the language. Wishing Daniel were with her.

"I think otherwise," Sorcha confirmed. "The Elect tell us that Knowledge brought ruin to our world, but I say that Knowledge can save our world. We were not always as we are now, clinging to the shore and burning beneath the Sun. Once we understood the world better than we do now. We were greater than we are now. And I do not see why we cannot be so again, I do not see why we should fear Knowledge."

Sam turned the book over in her hands. "In my experience," she said, "it's not the knowledge that's dangerous, but the people who wield it. Something happened to your world, Sorcha. A disaster. Maybe it *was* technology — knowledge — that caused it, maybe it wasn't, but you're right, knowledge could help your people too. And, perhaps, ours. If we can find the shield it could protect us all from — "

"Yes," Sorcha nodded, taking the book and clutching it tight. "The shield is the answer — and that we must seek at the Cove."

"Talking of which — "

"Major Carter." Teal'c called down through the trapdoor, his voice low but not urgent.

Scrambling to her feet, she moved to the foot of the ladder. "Teal'c, it's amazing down here, she's collected a whole archive."

"I shall remain here," he said. "It is not possible to close and disguise this doorway from below. We must remain undetected."

"Right." Sam curbed her enthusiasm, returning to the practical. "Good idea."

Sorcha pushed close to her, craning her neck to see Teal'c. "And you must find shelter before dawn," she said. "You cannot withstand the Burn."

"I shall find shelter," he confirmed, addressing the words to Sam. "And remain within eyesight of the door."

She nodded. "Any sign of trouble…"

His hand touched the weapon in his belt. "I shall be vigilant."

With that, let the stone hatch drop into place. Dust sifted down beneath its weight, settling in Sam's hair. She sucked in stale air and tried not to think about being trapped underground in the suffocating, endless dark.

"Come." Sorcha touched her arm. "We must try to contact your friends while we can; the answers we both seek are at the Cove."

Shaking off her claustrophobia, Sam nodded. A distraction was exactly what she needed.

The device itself evidently was a satellite phone, or had been. Judging from the tangle of wires it had been substantially jerry-rigged over the years, which didn't come as a surprise. "How is it powered?" she asked, sitting down on the floor next to the device.

"There is a panel above," Sorcha said. "It converts the Sun's heat into power."

"Right, solar technology of course." Smiling, Sam picked up the handset, which looked to her like an early cell phone. There was a keypad, but she didn't recognize any of the symbols. "You touch these buttons?"

Sorcha took the handset from her with a proprietorial air. "It is delicate," she said. "The sequence must be offered in the correct order." Saying no more, she began to dial.

It was somewhat surreal, sitting in this secret underground chamber, surrounded by user manuals for long-lost technology, watching Sorcha dial a phone number with the same reverence Sam had seen in the eyes of Jaffa kneeling before their false gods.

Silence followed, and Sam found herself counting the seconds; to Sorcha, she supposed, this wait had to almost seem magical. Then the phone crackled, and there was a hiss of communication — a data burst, Sam thought — and a tinny voice said, "*Dia dhuit*, Sorcha Caratauc."

"*Go mbeannaí Dia dhuit*," she answered, and then continued to speak in the same fluid language. Sam recognized only a few words — Faelan, O'Neill, and Daniel Jackson — and then the line went dead.

"What happened?"

Sorcha's brow pinched into a frown. "O'Neill is not there," she said. "He has left the Cove with Faelan Garret."

"What?" Sam felt a lurch of unease. "Why?"

"To evacuate the Cove and warn those at the *Tearmann* of the storm to come." Judging by the shake of her head, Sorcha didn't think it was a great idea.

Sam concurred. "What about Daniel?" she asked, shoving away her concern for the Colonel. "Is he okay?"

"Yes, he is at work in the archives of the Cove. A vast and wonderful place, Samantha." Sorcha waved a hand around them. "This is nothing to it, nothing at all."

Daniel having his nose in a book, with a deadly storm on the way, didn't sound like such a great idea either. He'd be up to his knees in water before he even looked up. "And the weather?" Sam pressed. "Has the storm reached them?"

"No," Sorcha said. "But it is closing in; they are preparing."

"Damnit," she hissed. "I need to speak to Daniel."

"He is being fetched." Sorcha folded her arms across her chest.

"Fetched?"

"To the radio." She turned her gaze back to the phone. "When he is ready, it will alert us."

Sam schooled herself to patience. "Right," she said, glaring at the hotchpotch of failing technology. "I guess we wait for him to call."

She just hoped Daniel hadn't found a particularly riveting book; waiting never was her strong suit.

CHAPTER TWELVE

FEW THINGS could distract Daniel Jackson from his research once he was in the zone. Strong coffee was one, wind slamming into the side of the building and making the whole structure sway like a drunk was another.

He lifted his head from the files scattered across the old desk and glanced out the window. The horizon was definitely skewed, tipped to the right at an unlikely angle. "Okay, so that's not looking good," he decided.

"What isn't?"

Rhionna's voice just about made him jump out of his skin; he'd been so lost in his work that he'd forgotten she was still there, sitting silently in the shadows. He blinked at her, taking in the tanned face and pinched features; she was pretty, he thought, or would have been if she weren't always scowling. He jerked his head toward the window and the darkening horizon, just as another gust of wind battered the tower. "We're swaying."

Rhionna rose to her feet, her attention shifting to the scene outside. "I know. Faelan thinks these towers were designed that way — designed to move with the seas."

Daniel considered his answer. He was no architect, but in his opinion it was a miracle the towers were still standing at all. "Faelan may be right," he said at length. "That is, these towers would have been built to flex in the wind but…"

Rhionna was at the window now, haloed by gray light and with the storm gathering behind her. He decided she wasn't the type to like her medicine sugarcoated.

He tried to ease a kink from his neck. "Look, I don't know how much of your history you know, but just a cursory look through these records tells me that this place wasn't designed to be up to its ears in water. It's only a matter of time before they fall into the sea, and this storm…"

"Yes. Sorcha has said as much for many years; this place, she says, was built upon dry land. She has read the records, but there are few who believe her. Few among the Seachráni — and that includes Faelan. Children's stories, he says."

"But it's all right here," Daniel protested, waving a hand at the files spread before him. "He could read it for himself."

Rhionna shrugged. "He knows what Sorcha has discovered — and I've argued with him until my jaw aches. But Faelan Garret is stubborn as rock and cannot see the use for such Knowledge. And in truth, perhaps he's right. Whatever the people were doing here, they failed. They could not prevent the Great Flood. What use is there in picking over the bones of their failure? We must live in the present, not the past."

"Sure," Daniel agreed. "But sometimes the past has a lot to teach. You can't know who you are until you know who you were, you can't set a course for the future unless you know where you came from." He waved a hand around the mildewed room. "If we can find out what caused the flood, maybe it can be reversed?"

Her eyes narrowed. "We know what caused the flood, Daniel. It was the Sun."

"Yes, I mean — Wait." A thought occurred to him, striking hard. Outside, the wind slammed into the tower and he barely noticed. "The sun caused it? You mean the sun deity, right?"

Rhionna looked away, uncomfortable. "So my father believes."

"But you don't, do you?"

"I —"

"You've read these papers, you and Sorcha. You knew all along what the shield was meant to do. You knew it couldn't protect us from the Goa'uld."

"You asked about *Sciath Dé*," she said, still not looking at him. "We told you how to find it."

"Yes, but you knew what *Sciath Dé* was," he said, sitting back in his chair. "And you knew from the start that it wasn't what we were looking for. You lied to us, Rhionna."

She flashed him a look, more anger than guilt. "And would you have helped us if I hadn't? If I'd told you there was nothing here for your people, would you have helped mine?"

"Yes," he said, then remembered Jack's reluctance and added, "probably."

She held his look, then turned away to stare out the window. "I couldn't risk that. When I realized what you were — where you had come from and what you had found — I couldn't risk letting you leave. My world is dying, Daniel. *Sciath Dé* may be the only thing that can save us."

He watched her, stiff-backed and proud, and found that he couldn't blame her despite the black storm bearing down on them. He might die here, and still he couldn't blame her. "Look, Rhionna, I understand why you —"

He was interrupted by a clatter of feet as a young Seachráni boy flew, helter-skelter, into the room. "Rhionna," he said, "Sorcha Carataud wishes you to contact her on the speaker. The blue star has only minutes and she said to bring *him*."

Him, Daniel supposed, was himself. He got to his feet. "The speaker?"

Rhionna was already walking as she replied. "A remnant of Knowledge Faelan discovered here some years ago — it allows Sorcha to talk to us from the Badlands. Perhaps she has news of your friends."

"Yes." A beat of adrenaline pumped. "That would be good."

It would be very good indeed.

There were soldiers in the Badlands. Although he could not see them, Teal'c could hear the barked orders floating over the rag-and-bone city. From his position, concealed beneath a heap of canvas several meters from the remains of Sorcha Caratauc's home, he listened and anticipated their approach.

In light of their escape it was likely that this would be the first place to be revisited. But he had gone to great pains to hide the secret doorway beneath the remains of the hearth and did not think the Elect Guard would think it anything but a patch of ash and scorched earth. Nevertheless, discovery was a risk and he was prepared.

The gun he had taken from the prison guard was primitive, akin to the the Tauri's less sophisticated firearms. He would have felt more at ease with his staff weapon or a *zat'ni'katel*, but it was futile to wish for something he did not have. He would make do; the gun and his own martial skills would be enough.

Time moved on slowly. At a point he judged to be close to midnight, the white glow of the giant screens blinked off and the texture of the darkness changed. Now it was lit only by yellow lamplight. Occasionally lightning flashed inside the clouds, and for a moment they would glow like a nebula. In the distance thunder rumbled.

But the soldiers did not come. Their shouts grew no closer, despite the streets now filling with people returning from the screens. Teal'c watched as they made their way through the darkness, chattering in a dialect and accent he found difficult to understand. They appeared content, however; he detected no anger or restlessness in their talk. Sorcha Caratauc was right, this was not a people poised to revolt, despite the iniquity of their lives.

Had he not seen as much complaisance among the Jaffa, he might have condemned them for it, but his own people were no less complicit in their own enslavement. He understood their reluctance to risk the little they had in exchange for an uncertain future. He understood, even if he did not share that fear. For what was death compared to a life of slavery?

Once the Badlanders had disappeared into their shacks

the streets grew quiet. Then the lamplight died too, and there were few stars left to light the sky. But still the soldiers did not come. He could no longer hear them, and far above, on the parched hillside, a slow caterpillar of light weaved its way upward. The soldiers were retreating to the Ark. They must have been recalled before accomplishing their purpose. Teal'c could not help but wonder why.

Out to sea, thunder rumbled again, ominous in the ever-darkening night. A drop of rain splashed onto Teal'c's upturned face, fat and heavy, and the wind scuttled about his ankles. On the crest of the hill the Ark shone bright, a glittering city beneath its dome.

This, as the clouds finally swallowed the stars, was the only light left in the world.

The phone rang, making Sam jump. Its shrill bleep wouldn't have been out of place at home, and it sounded incongruous enough to put her on edge.

Sorcha snatched the device up, held it to her ear, and after a moment nodded and muttered something Sam couldn't understand. Then she handed over the phone.

Careful not to disturb the delicate wiring, Sam took it. "Hello?"

"*Sam?*"

The wave of relief she felt at hearing Daniel's voice was enormous. She grinned. "Daniel, thank God. Are you okay?"

"*Yeah. You? Where's Teal'c?*"

"He's okay, he's standing guard. We're at Sorcha's place — under it, actually. Where are — ?"

"*Sam, listen. I know what the shield is, and it's not what we thought.*"

"What?" She glanced over at Sorcha who was watching her with sharp eyes. "What do you mean?"

"*It protects the planet from the sun, not from the Goa'uld. And they knew that all along. Sorcha lied to us.*"

Her jaw tightened. "From the sun?"

Apparently Daniel understood the direction of her thoughts. "*It's not Goa'uld, Sam. It's not like P3X-513. This is definitely Iernan technology.*"

His assertion did little to mollify her. Functioning or not, the shield's very existence had led to an imbalance on this planet, where men and women had assumed a power to which they had no right, just like Jonas.

"Have you found it?" she asked.

"*No. Sam—I don't even know where to start looking. I think this was some kind of research—*" His voice dropped out for a moment, then continued. "*—is stuffed with files I can translate, but can't understand.*"

"Say again, Daniel. I didn't hear all that."

"*It was a research laboratory, I think, and—*" Again, his voice dropped out.

"I'm losing the connection," she said to Sorcha, resisting the temptation to start walking around in hope of a better reception. She knew exactly what was happening; the satellite was moving out of range.

"*—need you to figure out what they were doing here.*"

"Daniel," she said, urgent now. "Listen, forget the shield. You have to get out of there. The storm is going to be really bad. You can't stay."

"*—know that.*" Daniel's voice was scratchy and distorted. "*—can still help these people, Sam.*"

"No, you have to get out of there. Now."

"*If we can activate the shield—*"

"Tell the colonel you have to get out of there."

"*—can't just abandon—*"

Static drowned his words, and after a couple of moments Sam lowered the phone.

"The storm interferes with the star." Sorcha glanced up at the ceiling. "It will be a matter of luck whether or not we can speak to the Cove again."

Sam squeezed the bridge of her nose in frustration.

Sorcha sat forward, her gaze intent. "What did your friend say? Did he speak of *Sciath Dé*?"

"He said it's not what we thought." She paused, considering how much to tell her. "He said you lied."

Sorcha didn't deny it, simply folded her hands into her lap. "You told Ennis Channon that you could make *Sciath Dé* work; he will never permit that. Would you have gone against his wishes if you'd not believed it to be in your interest? Would you have ever left the Ark?"

"Maybe." She put the phone down and scrambled to her feet, anger rising. "We'll never know, will we? You lied to us, you used us."

Sorcha said nothing.

Straightening her shoulders, Sam took a breath. "You should have trusted us, Sorcha."

"I did not have that luxury," she said. "Only *Sciath Dé* can save my people, and you are our best hope of discovering it. Would you not do as much to save your people?"

Sam turned away, stomping toward the ladder. Part of her wanted to just walk away, to turn her back on Sorcha and her half-truths. Lies had stung them before, and that wound still smarted. Now Daniel and the colonel were in mortal danger yet again. But her foot stopped on the lowest rung of the ladder. Daniel's scratchy pleas rang like her conscience in Sam's ears.

We can still help these people. We can't just abandon them.

"Because of you," she said into the silence, "my friends are out there, in the path of that storm. They might die." Despite the stuffy heat, the truth chilled her bones. "They might die out there, trying to save your people." She turned her head, studying the old woman half lost in the shadows. "You owed us the truth. We had the right to choose whether to risk our lives for you."

Sorcha rose and stepped into the light. Thin as she was, she seemed to fill the room. "What's done is done, Samantha. But you can choose now: will you help us find *Sciath Dé*, or will you leave and let us burn?"

All things considered, there was only one answer Sam could give.

CHAPTER THIRTEEN

THE STORM was on them now, rain thrown against the window by furious gusts, wind wailing through the decaying tower.

Daniel read on.

An Dóchas Deireanach.

The words were written all over the Cove, painted or scratched into the walls. An ironic twist, Faelan had said — the Last Hope. That's what they'd called this place, back when the seas were rising and they'd been working on the shield. It was all in the documents, the mounting urgency clear in every word.

The Southern Archipelago lost.

Bràigh Mhàrr dam breached, the plains flooding. Refugees. Saline contamination.

Disease. Disaster. Death.

Most of the papers were typed — or printed, probably. Remnants of the Ierna version of PCs dotted the room, similar to those he'd found back at the *Acarsaid Dorch* outpost.

But the later documents were mostly handwritten and on poorer quality paper, which made Daniel suspect power outages. Or supply problems. Both, probably. He guessed this was what it would be like at the end of the world, civilization retreating in increments. From print to ink to scrawls on the wall, and from there a short step to illiteracy.

Two hundred years. Six generations. And a civilization destroyed in a cosmic blink of an eye.

He shivered and kept on reading, searching for something that would pinpoint the shield. His biggest fear, and not an unlikely scenario, was that the device was already drowned somewhere in the bowels of the city. Then again, with flooding being such a risk, wouldn't they have kept their Last Hope at the top of the tower? On the roof?

It would help if he knew exactly what he was looking for. He soon learned that *Sciath Dé* was not the project's original title — it seemed to be a colloquialism, he'd seen it mentioned a couple of times as 'the so-called Shield of the Gods', but its real name was the more prosaic 'global deflector'; he envisaged a giant parasol popping up from the roof of the tower.

The problem was, while he could translate the documents readily enough, he wasn't entirely sure what the translations meant. There were schematics and graphs and data tables, none of which made a hell of a lot of sense to him; he needed Sam. She, of course, was probably knee-deep in her own schematics and graphs and data tables and unable to translate a word.

In short, a profoundly frustrating scenario.

A sharp breeze wormed into the room, ruffling the papers on the desk. He smoothed them down and pulled a new document from the pile. It looked like a memo, hand-written on thin paper. He didn't need to see the date to know that it must have been written close to the end. It was headed: *Relocation of the global deflector interface to an Dóchas Mhaireann.*

A blast of wind screamed into the tower, somewhere a window broke, and a squall whipped into the room. Papers went flying, and Daniel flung his arms over the pages in front of him just as the door slammed shut. The draft subsided, and he heard footsteps.

"Any progress?" Rhionna sounded as weary as he felt, her voice devoid of hope.

He turned around. "Not a lot."

Her gaze scanned the chaos around him, and she said, "Faelan's ship has been sighted; he'll be back within half an hour."

"And then?"

Her shoulders slumped. "Then he'll take you back to the

Badlands, run before the storm. You should be able to…" She trailed off and looked away, blinking.

The wind howled through the silence. "You said 'you'. You said 'he'll take you back'."

She wiped a hand across one cheek. "You have something to go back to, Dr. Jackson. If the Cove falls, if the Badlands are washed away. Then what do I have?"

"Your father?"

It triggered a bitter laugh. "Do you think I could stand it, to live in that dome while the whole world dies around me? To live there, waiting for the power to fail, for the crops to fail? To live there, watching their damn *Sunrise*, pretending everything is like it was, while outside — " She shook her head. Her voice was steadier when she spoke again, hard and heavy. "They called this place the Last Hope, Dr. Jackson. They were right. It was. And now that hope has failed."

Daniel didn't answer, just nudged his glasses along the bridge of his nose and turned back to the memo trapped beneath his hand.

Relocation of the global deflector interface to an Dóchas a Mhaireann.

Following last week's disaster, we now fear that the Uplands will fall by the end of the week. Therefore the interface must be moved as a matter of urgency. We must consider evacuation of the research team, but given the current political situation it is possible that we will not be permitted to enter an Dóchas a Mhaireann, though it was conceived as a shelter for all–

Wait. He stared at the document, blinking at the words — *an Dóchas a Mhaireann.*

That wasn't the name of the place written in Dr. Maol Caluim's journal, it wasn't what was scrawled all over the walls of the Cove. "Rhionna?" he said, still staring at the memo. "What do the Seachráni call this place?"

There was a surprised pause, then she replied, "*An Dóchas Deireanach.*"

"Which means?"

"The place of Last Hope. You know that."

He nodded. "Right. And before the disaster? Do you know what it was called then?"

"No." She frowned, shook her head. "Does it say in those papers?"

He rubbed a hand across his brow, fingers pressing hard to dispel a brewing headache. "Maybe. I don't know. There's something…"

Daniel read on.

"Okay." Sam raked her fingers through her hair. "Okay. I think I'm getting it."

Cross-legged on the floor, Sorcha sat in silence while Sam spread a number of schematics around her. The room was getting stuffy now, and Sam was beginning to think they should risk cracking the hatch, just to get some air. But she was on a roll and didn't want to lose track of all the threads she was holding in her mind.

The shield was nothing like the Ark, that much she did know. Even without Sorcha's explanations — limited as they were by her total lack of scientific understanding — the schematics were clear. In fact, *Sciath Dé* appeared to be an astonishing feat of geo-engineering. The shield itself had already been deployed, probably years before the final disaster, considering that it would have required huge power resources. As far as she could tell it consisted of a sequence of lenses orbiting the planet and designed to deflect varying amounts of solar radiation. The strange translucent rainbows she'd glimpsed in the sky, the bright too-large stars, confirmed that the shield was in place. Theoretically, the angle of the lenses could be adjusted remotely to manage the amount of sunlight that got through, depending on the planet's climatic requirements. Only, it evidently hadn't worked. The lenses weren't deflecting nearly enough radiation and the planet hadn't cooled. Which left two questions — why wasn't it working, and could it be fixed?

The Goa'uld weren't the only threats to Earth's future, and Sam could already see the obvious application of this knowledge at home. Geo-engineering was the future, and this technology could put them a hundred years ahead of themselves — if she could just get it to work. She smiled, the thrill of discovery quickening her blood, and, truth be told, it felt good not to be working on a weapon for once.

"Okay," she said again, "what we need to find is the interface, the computers that control the shield." She looked over at Sorcha. "Do you know where that is?"

The old woman nodded. "At the place of Last Hope."

"Appropriate name." Sam sighed and rocked back on her heels. "I need to get there. If we're going to get this working, I need to get there. Are there any boats?"

"None that can travel so far, nor fast enough to beat this storm." Sorcha frowned. "But your friend has the device from *Acarsaid Dorch*. Can he not do what must be done to make the shield work?"

Sam glanced at the phone. "It's not that simple. Maybe I could talk him through it, but…" She stared at Sorcha again, at the ardent hope in her eyes, and tried to find words to explain. "Look, the device we found at the outpost — at *Acarsaid Dorch* — can't do anything on its own. It's… Think of it as a patch to fix a leaky bucket. It's useless if we can't find the bucket to begin with."

"And this 'bucket' is?"

"Some kind of control room — a bank of computers, machines. Something that can communicate with the shield in the same way your phone" — she waved a hand toward the device — "can communicate with the Cove."

Sorcha frowned. "There are old machines at the Cove — screens that are lifeless, they do not show *Sunrise* or anything else."

"Well, that could be it." Sam nodded. "That could be the control room. But it's pretty old, Sorcha, and I don't know if Daniel will be able to figure out how to install the *Acarsaid Dorch* device. And that's assuming there's power there." She trailed off in a sigh.

And into the silence the phone bleeped. Sorcha stirred. "The link is back. Now, you can speak to your friend. You can tell him what he must do."

"Yeah," Sam said, reaching for the handset. "Sure. Piece of cake."

Despite his best efforts to quell his motion sickness, the voyage back to the Cove severely tested Jack's limits. The sea churned beneath a night sky blackened further by the coming storm. The solar sails, useless in these conditions, had long been furled. The ship crested and fell with every mountainous wave, but the Seachráni barely blinked an eye and went about their duties with as much industry as ever. After a short debate with himself over proving his manly stamina versus retreating from the elements, Jack chose the latter and shut himself in Faelan's cabin. On deck he was only getting under people's feet anyway.

"How can you even stay upright in this?" he asked Faelan, when the drenched captain eventually appeared below to pore over some charts.

Faelan grinned. "This is nothing, Colonel. A light breeze. The sea can do much worse." His humor faded and he said, "You'll find that out soon enough."

"Will we make it back to the Cove?"

"We should, but even if we do…" He didn't need to finish the sentence. If the coming storm was of the magnitude predicted, then it was doubtful that the already fragile structures of the Cove would remain standing.

"You have to get the rest of your people out of there, Faelan," Jack said around a wince.

"We've evacuated as many as we can. The *Tearmann* can take

no more. There are only a few of us left, and there's nowhere else for us to go."

"Oh, I think there is. I think you're just too pigheaded to admit it."

Faelan fixed his attention on the charts. "I don't need to hear this from you, Colonel. I've heard it enough times from Rhionna. I will not plead for refuge at the Ark only to have the door slammed in our faces. Or worse."

"Worse how?"

"You saw how we were treated in the Badlands. Even you and your people will have been judged by now. Do you think Ennis Channon would show us mercy? Do you think he even has that power? There are others who rule from the shadows, Colonel."

This assertion might have sounded like paranoia if Jack had not already assumed as much; there was always a man behind the curtain. And there was no way that Channon, or Camus, or whoever called the shots, would be persuaded to open the doors to a people they despised. It was a truth that could not be avoided.

Still, he could not understand Faelan's conviction that the Cove would withstand the storm. What was more, Jack could not forget his own selfish motivation. He had Daniel to worry about. And Teal'c. And Sam. He had to get back to them and to the gate. "Look, Faelan," he said, trying to reason with the man, "we can't stay at the Cove. It's a miracle the entire place hasn't fallen apart already. How can you think risking death there is better than taking our chances at the Ark?"

Faelan folded up his charts and stowed them in a chest. "Rhionna can take you and Dr Jackson back to the Ark. I'll provide you with a seaworthy vessel."

"But what if the Cove doesn't hold? Why won't you –" Jack broke off, the truth dawning. "You don't care if it holds." It wasn't a question. "You don't expect to make it, do you? Maybe you don't even want to."

Faelan's silence was answer enough.

The knowledge sickened Jack, and for an instant, the cold metal of his P90 triggered a memory of Charlie's room and another gun in his hand and a time when giving up seemed like the only option left. "Why are you so afraid?" he asked Faelan.

The captain spun around, eyes blazing. "Don't you dare."

"Oh, I think it's you who doesn't dare. You don't dare hope, or let other people hope, because it's all or nothing with you. You had big dreams that didn't pan out, and so you just throw in the towel? Is that how this is going to end for you, Faelan? Going down with the proverbial ship? You'll forgive me if I don't call that brave."

Faelan turned back to lean on the table, the muscles in his shoulders bunching in anger. When he spoke his voice was quiet, but passionate. "I had hope once. I told my people I could help them. I asked them to let me lead them. I asked them to trust me."

"They *still* trust you, damnit!"

"Then they're fools."

"They're a hell of a lot smarter than you!" Irritated, Jack scrubbed his palms over three days worth of stubble. He hated this familiar frustration, but was helpless against it. There was always a Faelan. On every planet, in every desperate situation, there was always that one person who had the potential to change the way things worked. Sometimes they understood that duty when it fell to them. But mostly their potential went wasted, through fear, or ignorance, or just plain bullheadedness. And all too recently, he'd been that guy.

Not anymore. Turning a blind eye wasn't part of a colonel's job description, and neither was giving up easily.

Besides, this wasn't just some wiseass airman fresh out of the Academy. For Faelan, his proving ground was on a larger scale, with more at stake. Jack took a steadying breath. "You think you failed them, but I think you'll find a few people back at the *Tearmann* who'd disagree with you. Imagine how many more you could add to their number."

Faelan stood still as a statue, unmoved by the pitch and roll of the ship. Then he said, "I'm tired of fighting."

To that, Jack had no reply.

Something wasn't right.

His nose all but pressed to the wall, Daniel Jackson was tracing his fingers over the scrawled words that showed up everywhere in the Cove.

An Dóchas Deireanach. The Last Hope.

The bitter irony of it was not lost on Rhionna Channon, nor on the Seachráni. But what Daniel Jackson found so interesting about these scribblings, she could not imagine.

"Daniel?" The tinny voice that came through the handset belonged to Major Carter.

"This is Rhionna," she said, "he's just here. Daniel — it's Major Carter."

He turned away from the wall with a startled look, as if he'd forgotten why they were in the room. "Right." He nodded, gathering the wad of papers under his arm, and headed over. "Thanks."

Taking the handset from her, he sat down at the little table in the comms room and spread the papers out in front of him. "Okay," he said into the device, "what have you got?"

Whatever the answer was, it made him frown, and Rhionna paced, trying to pay attention to Daniel while listening out for the arrival of Faelan's ship at the same time. They were going to fight again, and she was bracing herself for it — bracing for the fight, bracing for the fact that this might be the end. Of everything.

Outside the storm blew harder, she could hear the sea thundering far below as it battered the Cove's ancient foundations. Beneath her feet she felt the sway and wondered what it would look like at the end, when it all came crashing down. The Last Hope, swallowed in the end by the waters that had claimed her world.

"No, that's what I'm saying!" The rising pitch of Daniel's voice drew her from her morbid thoughts. "It's not here — there's nothing here like that. There's no control room, there's not even any power. I'm reading by lamplight here." He continued to listen, brow furrowing again as he looked through the papers. Then he nodded. "Yeah — okay. Look, it says here that they moved it at some point, close to the end I think. Maybe they tried to move it here, but they never made it. The thing is, and this might be nothing, but there's something…odd with the name." Another pause. "Last Hope. Yeah, but actually no. That's not what it says. The place of last hope translates as *an Dóchas Deireanach*, it's written all over the walls here, like a slogan. But what it says in the documents, what it actually says, is that they moved it to *an Dóchas a Mhaireann* — which translates as the place of *Lasting* Hope. I wonder if — ?"

"Oh, my God," Rhionna's voice was a whisper, but it still managed to reach him.

He turned and shot her a curious look. "*An Dóchas a Mhaireann*? You've heard of it?"

"Yes," she said, that last hope sinking like a stone. "I know it. Speaking that name is forbidden, I've never heard it said aloud, but I know it."

His eyes were sharp, penetrating. "And do you know where it is?"

She managed a nod. "It might as well be at the bottom of the ocean."

CHAPTER FOURTEEN

FOR ALL the punishment taken by the *Fánaí na Mara* on the journey back to the Cove, it was the final few moments that proved the most treacherous. In just a few hours, the sea level had risen alarmingly, and when Jack saw the gap between the tops of the furious waves and the archway to the Cove's dilapidated buildings he felt certain there was no way in hell anything would get through.

"We'll never make it," he yelled at Faelan over the roar of the storm, and then winced at the God-awful cliché.

But Faelan only grinned, wild and reckless, and spun the ship's wheel with expert hands. "Course we'll make it, Colonel. The *Fánaí* could fit though the eye of a needle if I asked her."

He's actually lost it, thought Jack, trying to quell his panic as the Cove walls raced closer. *He's actually gone completely crazy.*

Then the entire ship was engulfed by shadow. The massive arch loomed overhead, swallowing them like a closing throat. Jack was sure that, if he reached up, he could scrape his fingers along the underside. Shutting his eyes, he waited for the impact and the inevitable screech of metal against metal when the sea crushed them against the towering buildings.

And then all was calm. Calm-*ish*.

Rain still lashed the decks, and the ship still rolled in a way that made him glad he hadn't eaten supper, but as Faelan and the crew guided the *Fánaí na Mara* in to dock, it looked as though the threat of death was no longer imminent.

With the lines barely secured, the captain was already striding down the gangway, but Jack had no intention of letting him go so easily. He matched his gait, catching up with him on the quay.

"Faelan!"

The man whirled around. "Stop, Colonel! Just stop!"

Jack shook his head, wiping away the rain that stung his eyes. "You don't understand the mistake you're making."

"No, it's you who doesn't understand. The *Sciath Dé*, do you know what Ennis Channon and his like call it?" He didn't wait for a response. "They call it Knowledge, and they sneer when they say the word, as if it's something filthy, something corrupt. They let their people fill their heads with banalities, and keep them gorged on words without meaning. And do you know why they do that?"

He paused, expecting an answer this time, but Jack said nothing, merely held his gaze. There was no need to reply, because the reason was obvious.

"*Knowledge*, Colonel O'Neill." His lips drew back, as if in disgust. "Said just like that. They call it sinful, wicked, and damn everyone who pursues it, while they hoard the truth like greedy kings and grow fat on their lies." He threw his arms up, gesturing to the buildings that swayed dangerously around them. "This is my kingdom, Colonel. And if it falls then I fall with it."

Faelan turned away, his shoulders dropping, and when he spoke again, the fire was gone. "I'll send you back in the *Fánaí* with the last of my crew. Good men and women. If anyone can get you home, they will."

With that he left, his footsteps echoing along the wooden dock. Only then Jack realized someone had been calling his name. He turned to find Daniel running towards him.

"You made it back," said Daniel, a grin on his face.

"I made it back. Though I can't say the same for the last three meals I ate. Never let me set foot on a boat again."

"Ship," Daniel murmured absently, looking over Jack's shoulder. "Was that Faelan?"

"Yeah. He's in a mood."

"A mood?" Daniel's eyebrow quirked, and his tone was deadpan.

"Doesn't matter." Jack brushed past him, stalking toward the *Fánaí na Mara,* which was already being prepared for the voyage back to the Ark. "Get your stuff. We gotta get out of here."

"Uh, yeah I know."

"And I don't want to hear about how you haven't found the shield yet–"

"I have found the shield."

"Or how if you just had a bit more time–"

"I don't need any more time."

"Because this whole place is about to come crumbling down around our ears."

"Jack, we have to get back to the Ark."

"So we have to get back to the Ark. Wait. What?"

"I found *Sciath Dé.* It's back at the Ark. We have to get there, and quickly."

"Daniel, are you telling me this entire jaunt was completely pointless? That the shield was back at the Ark the whole time?"

Daniel cleared his throat. "Well, if by pointless you mean accomplishing nothing, then no, because I would never have discovered some key information if it hadn't been for the records here. Not to mention the whole saving me from the Seachráni part. In fact, what I did discover here was that the shield is in, uh, the place where we thought it would be right at the start."

Jack took a breath. "This better be good, Daniel."

"Oh, it is."

A shout came from the deck. Twenty minutes until they sailed.

Jack grinned. "Clock's tickin', Daniel."

When the line went dead, Sam sat back on her heels and stared at the handset. Sorcha shifted, got to her feet and moved toward the bookshelves that lined the walls.

"*An Dóchas a Mhaireann,*" she muttered. "I've never heard the Ark called such a name. Never seen those words written."

Sam rubbed a hand through sweat-tangled hair. Going by the rising heat, the sun had to be up by now, beating down on the dirt roof of the cellar and baking them like a pair of chickens in a clay oven. Shooing away her nascent claustrophobia, she said, "Daniel's rarely wrong about these things, and Rhionna confirmed the name; *Sciath Dé* is in the Ark, Sorcha."

The old woman shook her head and for the first time since they'd met, Sam thought she looked beaten. "Impossible. The Elect believe the existence of *Sciath Dé* to be an affront to the will of their god — by its very nature it seeks to diminish His power, to shield all the world from His wrath instead of only them, the chosen few. Do you think the Elect would ever have permitted it to enter their precious Ark?"

"Well apparently they did, once," Sam said. "People change, Sorcha. Lines harden over time. Maybe things were different then? Less black and white."

Sorcha snorted, dismissive and defeated. "If it is in the Ark, then I tell you it is guarded by the Elect. They would not risk its discovery."

"I'm not so sure." Sam rose, stretching out stiff legs. "I don't think Ennis knew where it was — I don't think he knows much about it at all."

"Ennis Channon is not the sum of the Elect," Sorcha said. "He is simply their tool."

Sam shrugged. "So you just want to give up? Daniel and the Colonel are bringing the patch back here, running ahead of that storm, and you just want to give up on the bucket?"

"No! Do not seek to school me in patience, Samantha Carter. This is the work of my life we are discussing. But this is my world, and I understand how it works. If *Sciath Dé* is in the Ark, then mark me — it is under the protection of the Elect. That is how such things work."

"You're assuming they know what it is," Sam countered. She shook her head, pacing as her mind began to connect the dots. "No. You said it yourself, Sorcha — they hate knowledge, they've done everything they can to destroy it. They killed the scientists at the outpost, just to destroy what they knew!"

"Then they have already destroyed the shield!" Sorcha snapped. "For it is either hidden or destroyed, and either way it is unreachable to us."

With another shake of the head, Sam began to climb the ladder. "I think you're wrong. Either way I *am* going back to the Ark. Stay here if you want, but Téal'c and I are leaving."

Sorcha remained quiet until Sam had reached the top and was pushing at the trapdoor. "Take care," she said, looking up. "It is past sunrise."

Wedging her hat onto her head and fishing out her sunglasses, Sam gave it one last try. "Come with us. What do you have to lose?"

The woman's eyes narrowed in her lined face. "Hope," she replied. "Which is all I've ever had."

Sam studied her in the flickering lamplight. Spare and worn — maybe ten years her senior, but looking a generation older. This was the end, Sam realized, of a lifetime's work, and if it ended in disaster, if the shield had been destroyed... Maybe, in Sorcha's position, she too would want to stay buried in this little hole in the ground, covering her eyes as the last hope for her people sank. Maybe. But that didn't mean it was right. "You can't give up now," she said at last. "Whatever's happened to the shield, Sorcha, you have to see this through to the end. You have to discover the truth."

Sorcha stayed still for a long moment, then, with a curt nod, her decision was made. "Very well."

Bracing herself for the heat and the glare, Sam put her shoulder against the trapdoor. It was heavy and took some effort to lift. When it eventually cracked open she got a face-full of mud instead of dust. "What the — ?"

Something powerful tore the hatch from her grip, whipped it back on its hinge and slammed it into the dirt. Debris hurtled past as Sam clambered out of the cellar, yelling down for Sorcha to stay put. Everywhere she looked she saw devastation.

The storm had hit hard and was laying waste to the flotsam city of the Badlands; the makeshift shelters were strewn like garbage in the wind, and the dock was being thrashed to splinters by the raging sea.

No more than ten feet away, Teal'c lay face down in the mud, a gash across the back of his head, rain washing his blood into the dirt.

"It was the translation," said Daniel, as he and Jack made their way down into Faelan's cabin and the few remaining crew members readied the ship for what might be its last voyage.

"The final hope, or rather, the *lasting* hope… logic would dictate that it's a short leap from that to *last* hope — phonetically speaking — and so when I heard what they called this place, I thought it must be here. But it turns out that it's not just a linguistic quirk. It was Rhionna who pointed it out."

"Daniel, is this going to be one of those times when I wave my hands in the air and make loud noises just so you'll stop talking?"

Daniel frowned. "Possibly."

"Okay, and you say Rhionna knows what the hell you're talking about?"

"Uh, yeah."

"Then why don't we let her tell it to keep my brain from exploding?"

Daniel shrugged. "You can try, but I'm not sure she's coming."

"God, what is it with Romeo and Juliet?"

"What?"

Jack shook his head. "Never mind, let's just — "

Suddenly the noise of the rain grew louder, and Daniel turned to find Rhionna standing in the open doorway.

"You've decided to come back with us?" he asked carefully.

She smiled, a tight expression. "I've decided there's a little more fight left in me." Then she looked around the cabin. "Where's Faelan?"

"I hope you haven't forgotten anything, Daniel," said Jack ignoring her. "It's time to go." His frown at the mention of the Seachráni's name was impossible to miss.

"Where is Faelan?" repeated Rhionna, louder this time, a note of desperation in her voice. "We can't leave without him."

Jack rounded on her. "I don't know where the hell Faelan is. Probably at the top of that tower waiting for it to drop out from under him."

"What?" The word was a frayed at the end, like a broken thread.

Apparently it tweaked whatever sympathy Jack had left in him, because his voice softened when he spoke again. "He's not coming, Rhionna. I'm sorry. I tried."

But Jack was talking to a slamming door. Rhionna had turned on her heel and fled into the rain.

CHAPTER FIFTEEN

HIS LONG robes almost tripped him as Ennis scurried after Sister Nevin. He picked them up, hurrying down the Chapel steps.

Outside, the light was murky and Ennis stumbled to a halt in momentary confusion. Far above the dome the sky was boiling black, blotting out the Sun. The portent of such imagery was not lost on Pastor Channon. With a shiver, he hurried after Nevin.

"Sister!" he called, lungs burning with the effort of running. "Please, I beg a word with you, Sister Nevin."

He knew the older woman had heard him, even though it took a good few steps before she stopped and turned around. The storm-light cast her face in shadows, and Ennis couldn't see her eyes or fathom her mood. "What is there to say, Pastor, that was not said in Council?"

Ennis drew closer, using the scant time to draw a breath and gather his thoughts. He lowered his voice. "Sister Nevin, surely you are not swayed by Tynan Camus's words? We cannot abandon the heathens of the Badlands; it would be utter folly!"

"Brother Tynan speaks of the Lord's Will, Pastor. Was it folly when the Lord brought the Elect to *an Dóchas a Mhaireann* and, in so doing, saved us?"

Ennis winced at the heathen word, its coarse syllables falling from Nevin's cultured lips. But he ignored the deliberate provocation and said, "Without food in their bellies and *Sunrise* to distract their minds, do you think the people of the Badlands will remain content? Do you think they will submit to Tynan's will — "

"It is the Lord's will."

"Tynan does not speak with the Lord's voice!"

Nevin's eyes narrowed. "All of the Elect speak with the Lord's voice, Pastor. It is heresy to say otherwise."

Ennis clamped his jaw shut. Outside, thunder rumbled and rain lashed against the Ark, running down the dome in silver-gleaming waterfalls. "I beg you, Sister Nevin, to see reason. I know the Badlands, I know what they suffer. My daughter —"

"Your daughter!" Nevin spat. "Yes, I fear it is her voice with which you speak, Pastor. A harlot's whisperings."

"They will revolt!" he cried. "They will swarm through the access tunnels, they will take what we refuse to give! They are men, even if they are heathen; they will not sit by idle and wait to starve. Do you not see that?"

Nevin gathered her robe of office around her, tilted her head toward the sky. "It is you who fails to see, Pastor. It is you who fails to see the hand of the Lord." She lifted an arm and pointed to the storm clouds. "Behold! As He has done before, so He will once more wash away those who would threaten the Lasting Hope of the Lord!"

"No," Ennis backed off a step. "No. This is madness, this will destroy us!"

"Have a care, Pastor." Nevin drew closer, eyes glinting in the shadow. "Your lack of faith is troubling, and at times like these we cannot permit any but the most faithful to remain under the protection of the Lord."

"I do not question the Lord —"

"Then do not question His Council." Lightning flashed, and for a moment Nevin's face appeared clear and hard before him. Then the shadows fell again. "Return to your home Ennis Channon, and pray for your daughter's soul. Tomorrow will see a new dawn for the faithful."

With those words, Sister Nevin strode away into the gloomy morning, leaving Ennis alone outside the silent Chapel. Beyond the dome the storm hunched closer, and in his mind's eye he saw Rhionna at its heart, a ragged strip of color brazen against the raging seas.

But he did not pray for her; he could not find the words.

"Teal'c!" Sam slipped and slid through the mud toward him, rolling him onto his side. "Teal'c!"

Sorcha was close behind, ducking low in the howling wind. "Was he shot?" she shouted, looking around for soldiers. "We must get out of sight."

Ignoring her, Sam tapped Teal'c's cheek. "Hey, wake up. Come on."

It took a moment, but at last his eyes fluttered open, blinking against the driving rain. "Major Carter?"

"Teal'c, we gotta move. Can you walk?"

He considered for a moment, then sat up. His wince was barely a flicker, but enough to tell Sam that he had to be in pain; she made a note to check for concussion as soon as they could stop. Teal'c felt the back of his head, examining his bloodied fingers. "I believe I was struck by a piece of flying debris."

"Ennis's men?" Sorcha said.

"They have retreated into the Ark." Teal'c rose to his feet, swayed slightly, then found his balance. "Perhaps they feared the storm?"

"Maybe," Sam said, also rising, shoulders drawn up against the buffeting wind. "Looks like they were right."

"We must find shelter," Teal'c said, his gaze traveling to the trap door over Sorcha's hidden room. "Perhaps — "

"No," Sam said. "We have to get back into the Ark."

Teal'c quirked an eyebrow. "What of O'Neill and Daniel Jackson?"

With a frown, Sam said, "They're on their way."

"I see." His gaze drifted out toward the white-capped, raging sea. "I do not wish to leave this planet without them."

"We won't. We're not going back to leave."

Teal'c looked at her, a question in his eyes.

"The shield interface is in the Ark. Daniel figured it out. It was there all along, we just have to find it."

Rain ran in streams over Teal'c's head and face as his gaze returned to the sea.

"We can't help them, Teal'c," Sam said. "They're on their own. All we can do is try to find the shield so that, when Daniel shows up with the device, we can patch it in."

He released a breath and nodded. "You are correct, Major Carter."

Sorcha's gaze flickered away from Teal'c to Sam. "Come," she said, "there is still much to be done."

Faelan Garret did not consider himself a thinking man. It was not the Seachráni way to debate lofty principles or philosophize on whether or not a deity watched over them from the heavens. If such a being did exist, then at best it was indifferent to the trials of Faelan and his people; it was fitting therefore that the Seachráni returned the sentiment.

There had been an occasion, in his early youth, when he had asked Muirne whether it was true, what the people of the Ark said about the Seachráni — that the Lord had sent the Sun to punish them for their wickedness. Muirne had smiled and hugged him close, as he had hoped she would. "If God exists, then he is within you, my Finn." Thinking back now on his mother's answer, Faelan realized how little comfort there was to be had in her words. For if God was within, then He had been lost long ago, and Faelan was not disposed to go looking for him.

He avoided, as much as he could, quiet moments of solitude. He worked, he moved, he fought. Every day, he fought. There was nothing else to be done if his people were to survive, and there was no point in asking why life was so. Life just *was*.

At night however, in his sleep, his mind was allowed free

rein. And it took full advantage of that freedom, letting loose with dark and twisted dreams that spoke in the voices of those who had died in the *Tearmann* so long ago. Insidious whispers of hopelessness and grief and failure. Above all else, failure.

It had not always been so. Once, there had been a time when he questioned everything, when could see something other than this desperate existence, something richer, better. And he had known without doubt that it was his duty to bring it to pass. Rhionna had come then, with her promises and her hope and her ideals, letting him believe in the worth of such a goal. Infectious, she was; something golden, he'd thought. But even that had proven a lie.

He couldn't have her near him after that, making him believe that their lives could be better, telling him that he was something noble, when in truth he was just one piece of a less than functioning whole. A man, no more and no less than those who stood next to him. *There is nothing other than this*, he'd told her. *There is no more.* And he'd forced himself to endure the look in her eye. What had that been? Anger? Confusion? Disappointment? It didn't matter. She didn't know him truly, and he owed her nothing. Let her think what she would.

Only now she had returned and that look was still there, but it was tempered with something else, with that other hateful idea; hope. And in her eyes, it wasn't a perverse joke.

It was only right that he make her realize how foolish the word was. Surely now, with this final act, he would accomplish that much.

When he reached the roof, the door was jammed, and Faelan wondered if the building had begun to buckle already, leaving everything skewed at odd angles. He put his shoulder to the door and the wind did the rest, throwing it back against the outer wall. Outside, the maelstrom howled in earnest, but Faelan knew that it was only the edges of the storm grazing the Cove so far. What was to come would be much worse. He closed his eyes and let the wind buffet him, let the rain soak him to the skin. He held fast to the parapet, knowing with a certain sense of calm that, if he let go, the force of the storm would just suck him away.

"What are you doing, Faelan?"

He whirled at the voice, though it barely carried over the roar of the hurricane, and when he saw Rhionna making her way towards him, alarm burned in his chest. The building tilted suddenly, and she staggered. His grip on the rail tightened, but this time it was not the storm that lured him.

"Why aren't you on the ship?" he cried, angry that she could confuse matters so, even now. "You have to go! They'll leave without you."

"Then they'll leave without me." She was sodden, her hair plastered to her head, her bright scarf darkened by the rain. "What are you doing, Faelan?"

"You know what I'm doing."

Her eyes flashed, the set of her mouth fixed and determined, but when she spoke her voice was level, as if it she were approaching a wounded animal. "No, Faelan. I won't allow it."

He laughed, desperate and helpless. "You have no say in how I die."

"Maybe not." She was closer now, and he could see how she shivered with cold, her clothes more suited to the heat of the Badlands. "But I have a say in how *I* die. If you stay, then I stay with you."

"No!"

"I won't let you turn coward on me."

"Don't, Rhionna," he growled, but he could not meet her eye. Her words echoed Colonel O'Neill's, and though Pádraig often spoke of a noble Seachráni death, Faelan considered that perhaps there was cowardice in such an end after all.

Rhionna grabbed his arm and pulled him round to face

her fully, letting her anger show. "Why are you so afraid to hope? You never were before."

"It's not about fear!" he lied. "It's about facing the truth! It's about accepting what can and can't be done, and knowing when it's time to stop fighting. Your father was right all along! We're all damned. And if this is Divine Judgment, then who am I to claim otherwise?"

His words only riled her further. "You're Faelan Garret," she cried. "Since when do you believe what my father says? He and his kind have long claimed the sky will fall on anyone who doesn't bow down to God's Will."

"Look up, Rhionna! The sky *is* falling."

She shook her head, refusing to concede. "Don't use God as your reason for giving up. I won't accept such a pitiful excuse."

And there it was again; that disappointment in her eyes. Once more he was letting her down and didn't know how to stop himself. Seething with frustration, he wiped the raindrops from his face as though they were tears. "You have no choice."

"There's always a choice! I won't stand by and watch my world drown."

He faltered at that, and for a moment he wanted to ask what she meant, whether this was about something other than ideals, but there was no time. A shudder coursed through the building beneath them.

She snatched at him as she fell forward, grabbing hold of the sodden fabric of his shirt. "Faelan, please!"

"No, Rhionna."

"I won't let you do this, Faelan. I won't…" Her voice broke and she pressed her lips together, jaw set.

Through the water on her face, Faelan couldn't tell if she wept. All he knew was that he felt a sting in his own eyes. He clutched her shoulders. "What is it you want from me?"

"What *I* want? God, Faelan, you know what I want." She

let her hands fall to curl round his forearms. "You know what I want. But that's nothing — *nothing* — to what your people want."

"You don't know what you're talking about." The wind whipped at them both, flinging his hair into his eyes, the needles of rain cutting into his hands, his neck, his face. "My people want nothing I can give them."

"They want a leader, Faelan!"

"I called myself their leader before and people died!"

"And people *lived.*" She was crying now, the rain doing nothing to disguise it. She reached out and brushed his hair from his eyes. "People lived, Faelan. Because of you and what you did."

Such determination she had, such faith as he didn't deserve. "I can't save everyone, Rhionna."

She smiled, and there was sadness in the expression, but still that look of hope, the one that made his heart turn traitor. "I'm not asking you to. Why do you always dwell on what can't be done, Faelan, when there is so much you *can* do?"

People lived.

Too much of what she said resonated within him. Her words fed that voice that spoke from the depths of his soul.

There is more than this, it said. *Of course there is more.*

She was closer now, her hand still on his cheek, and when the building shook again he barely noticed the movement.

God is within you.

"Choose, Faelan," she said. "Please choose."

Closing his eyes, he dropped his forehead against hers. "Infectious, you are," he whispered. "Golden." And by the time he kissed her, his choice had already been made.

CHAPTER SIXTEEN

SAM KNEW they were in trouble as soon as she saw the rainwater sluicing down the bone-dry hillside, turning dust into a mudslide that threatened to swamp the landward side of the Badlands.

Rocky outcrops to the east were dotted with crouched, desperate figures who had scrambled up from the disintegrating shanty and clung to the hillside, and to each other, in the face of the storm.

"These people need shelter!" Teal'c bellowed through the wind, bracing himself against its force.

She couldn't argue with that. "Sorcha, can we take them into the tunnels?"

But the brittle old woman shook her head. "The three of us might slip past the soldiers' notice, yes. But with these poor wretches upon our heels? Impossible."

"We can't leave them out here!"

Gray hair plastered to her head, Sorcha's eyes flashed. She grabbed Sam's shirt in her fist, yanking her face close to her own. "These are *my* people, Samantha Carter. Do not tell me what I can or cannot do!" She paused, snatched a breath. "If some are washed away in this storm, then so be it. They will not be the first. But if we fail to activate *Sciath Dé* then neither will they be the last. Do you not understand? We *must* succeed."

"Whatever the cost?"

"The cost of failure will be higher." She released her hold on Sam and turned to squint up the mountainside. "Follow, I know a route that will avoid the mudslip."

Exchanging a look with Teal'c, Sam followed. Sorcha had a point, and she suspected that the colonel would have agreed — in principle, if not in practice. She understood about the mission objective, but it was hard to ignore the shivering, frightened people — men, women, and children — clinging to the very edges of survival. Ahead she saw a woman, crouched with two small children clutched to her skinny body, trying to shelter them from the pitiless storm with a ragged sheet of canvas. It was pathetic, and despite her years of training, despite everything she had seen in a brutal galaxy, Sam felt her throat close. She couldn't walk by.

While Sorcha powered ahead on wiry legs, Sam slowed. She sensed Teal'c at her shoulder and took his silence as approval. Holding out her hand to the woman she said, "Come on, follow us. We'll take you to safety."

A moment's hesitation, then Sam saw her words spread like a ripple on a pond across all those desperate faces that peered at them through the rain. The woman rose to her feet, picking up the smaller child. The older one seemed lost until Teal'c reached down and swung the scrap of a boy onto his hip.

His gaze met Sam's. "We must hurry."

When they started walking again, the people of the Badlands followed.

Inside the Ark, Ennis Channon could hear the mighty doors to the service tunnels swing shut. The noise reverberated through his feet, clanging against the walls of empty buildings and echoing through the city.

They were alone now, while outside the storm raged. Some of the Ark's inhabitants had come to watch the spectacle, standing atop the wall, close to the edge of the dome, and looking out at the inky clouds and at the rain slanting sideways in the wind.

Ennis asked himself what it would feel like to be unprotected in so much water. To feel it on your skin, soaking

your clothes. Rainstorms were not unheard of outside, but
they were not common. He had seen five in his lifetime,
three of which had occurred in the past year — each one
more ferocious than the last. Still, he had never experi-
enced the power of such a storm, and as he pressed his
hand against the dome, he felt an uncomfortable desire to
tear apart its protective shield and stand with his face to
the wind and have the rain beat against his skin.

Rhionna, he supposed, knew what such things felt like.
She had gone in search of them her whole life — different
experiences, new adventure, old Knowledge. Now the very
things she had sought would claim that life.

At the sound of a soldier's step he turned to see the first
of his men climbing out of the service tunnel. Others followed, all wet from the rain. The commander acknowledged him and walked over, stopping with a salute.

"Pastor Channon," he said. "The tunnels have been
closed, all services discontinued. The Ark is secure."

Breathing in the strange, tangy scent of rain and mud,
Ennis nodded. "Tell me, Commander," he said. "What
does the rain feel like?"

"Cold, sir," came the reply, with a slight, curious crease
of the brow. "And wet."

"And the Sun does not burn today?"

The soldier shook his head. "No, sir."

"Its light cannot penetrate the clouds," Ennis said, considering the notion. "The clouds stand between the Sun
and the people. They...shield them."

The commander looked at him but did not answer.
Behind the man's shoulder one of the public screens came
to life. *Sunrise* began to play and everyone turned to look,
even the commander. It was much too early for a new chapter to air; Tynan Camus, it seemed, had been busy.

Ennis observed as the people of the Ark drifted away
from watching the storm, gathering in excited groups

beneath the screen or rushing home for a private viewing. He looked at their faces, alight with pleasure and devoid of anything else, and for the first time in his life saw them as Rhionna had always seen them.

Glutted and lazy and unable to think for themselves.

The last of the soldiers returned from sealing the tunnels, dropped the heavy hatch and, catching sight of the screen, joined the other spectators. Alone, Ennis returned his gaze to the rain and let his wandering thoughts drift back to the fate of the Seachráni. And to Rhionna, lost among them.

The fall of the Cove came and went without the drama Jack had anticipated. When it happened, the *Fánaí na Mara* was already far enough away that the Cove had become simply a small cluster of lights at the edge of the world, there one second and gone the next. They didn't witness any cataclysmic explosion; just a surge of water beneath them some minutes later, barely noticeable compared to the already towering waves. If the Cove made a sound as it was swallowed by the sea, no one heard it over the roar of the storm. Hardly impressive at all.

Of course, the true impact of the Cove's collapse had nothing to do with spectacle. The man standing aft was proof of that.

Faelan watched the destruction of his home without comment or expression, though Jack didn't miss how his hand curled into Rhionna's at the final moment. The crew, few though they were, had paused in their labors to watch their old life wink out of existence, silent and motionless as if there were no storm trying to pound each of them from the deck. Faelan allowed them those moments, but when he spun around his face was steely and the orders he threw out were not those of a man with a death wish; Jack even thought he caught a grin on the captain's lips.

What had happened between him and Rhionna, Jack didn't want to know. All he cared about was that Faelan Garret had turned into a man with a corner to fight.

The game was most definitely on.

The weight of the child he carried was insignificant; Teal'c could feel the boy's bones through his skin, thin fingers gripping his jacket, and a tiny face buried at his neck to hide from the wind and the rain.

Teal'c had carried his own son thus, though Rya'c had been strong and vigorous his whole life, a solid weight of muscle and energy. It offended him that this child, this nameless boy, should have been starved to skin and bone while the people of the Ark grew fat and lazy. This planet offended him deeply. It was time for it to change.

Ahead, Sorcha Caratauc had turned to watch their shabby parade, fists on her hips and her lips pressed tight. She too had been worn down to her bones, but in her flinty expression Teal'c saw evidence that more than her flesh had been gnarled by the suffering of her people. There was no pity there, only anger and determination.

"This will not serve us," she snapped as soon as Teal'c was close enough to hear. "Bringing these people is folly. If we fail—"

"We shall not fail." Even as he spoke, a fist of wind pummeled his back and he stumbled forward. The child gripped tighter, and he gentled his hand against the boy's wet hair while struggling to regain his balance. At the foot of the hill devastation spread out like a blanket. What had once been the Badlands was little more than a refuse heap, swamped by mudslides and battered by a raging sea. Wave upon wave crashed against the shore, tearing at the docks, flooding the streets. The boom-crash of its fury was the roar of a wounded beast, and Teal'c felt a twist of fear; this was an enemy that no weapon could stay.

Not far behind him, Major Carter fought her way up the hill. She still clutched the hand of the child's mother, whose hand in turn held that of another child. The ragged procession struggled against the force of the wind and behind them followed the survivors of the Badlands, scrambling up toward the Ark, desperate for hope. Once more Teal'c told himself what he had told Sorcha: we shall not fail.

"Teal'c!" Major Carter called, waving with her free hand toward the sea. "I thought I saw something. A ship."

He turned his gaze back to the ocean. Among the lashing rain and the waves breaking out to sea, it was difficult to distinguish anything.

"There," Major Carter said, coming to stand with him and pointing.

He followed the line of her gaze and after a moment saw a silver flash, quickly swallowed by the rolling sea. But then it was back, dipping up and down, and he realized Major Carter was correct. "It is a ship," he confirmed.

"Faelan's. Has to be." She sucked a breath through her teeth. "I hope Daniel brought some Dramamine."

Sorcha Caratauc's sinewy hand grabbed his arm. Supporting herself, she pushed forward to look. "Seachráni, yes," she nodded. "But not Faelan. Nothing would make him abandon the Cove. Not even *Sciath Dé*."

Major Carter swiped rain water from her eyes. "Whoever it is, they'll have a hell of a time docking."

Teal'c's gaze fell on the waterfront where the dock had once stood. Now there was nothing left but crashing waves.

Grunting, Sorcha Caratauc turned back toward the tunnels. "They're Seachráni," she said. "They'll get ashore. Even without Faelan Garret at the helm."

"Then we had better find shelter and await their arrival," Teal'c said, shifting the shivering child on his hip.

Major Carter nodded. "It's not far now."

She was correct. Above the next rise of the hill Teal'c could see the arch of the concrete tunnel. Without further comment, he resumed the climb. Sorcha trailed a few steps behind, seeking shelter from the fury of the storm in his bulk. And so it was that Teal'c crested the rise first, stepping down toward the tunnel through which they'd left the Ark. There he stopped, a hard knot of fury freezing him in his tracks.

"Crap," Major Carter observed behind him.

His thought precisely.

"They've locked the doors. They've sealed themselves in, the bastards."

Teal'c looked back at the frightened, desperate people following them, then at Major Carter. "We shall find a way."

She nodded, eyes alight with fury. "Damn right we shall."

It was past dawn when the lookout called landfall near the Badlands. According to Faelan at least. As far as Jack was concerned you couldn't possibly tell day from night in the roiling black of the storm. The same principle applied to the deck and hull of the *Fánaí na Mara*, as the ship stomped and swayed with no proper regard for which way was up. Jack couldn't wait to put his feet on solid ground.

With land sighted, Faelan ordered the engines powered down, which gave Jack a chance to venture on deck for a little recon.

While he still pondered the prospect of heading into the Badlands blindly, the captain clambered down the rigging, slinging his binoculars around his neck. Faelan dropped the last few feet to the deck and hardly missed a beat as he strode towards the helm. Jack followed him, considerably less sure-footed.

"How are we going to get your boats into the docks?" he yelled above the storm's wail.

"We're not," Faelan shouted back.

"What the hell does that mean?"

"Look at this sea, Colonel. Surely even someone like you can see that a dory or longboat would be crushed in seconds."

"Hey! What do you mean, someone like me?"

Grinning at Jack's insulted pride, Faelan beckoned over a crewman, with whom he exchanged a few words in their own tongue. Despite the language barrier, it was hard to misinterpret the curse that the other man muttered before he walked off. "Besides," Faelan continued to Jack, "we have another problem."

"Oh yeah?" A wave slammed over the side of the ship, knocking Jack hard into the side of one of the cabins. He swallowed a mouthful of seawater, coughed, and spat. "Sonofabitch!"

While he struggled to regain his feet, Faelan looked as if he'd barely moved. *Smug bastard.*

"We can't take the boats into the dock because there are no docks," Faelan explained. "Sea's already took them."

"Then how the hell do we get over there? And don't say swim." But Faelan didn't need to say a word; the *Fánaí na Mara's* engines roared into life once more.

"Oh, you have got to be kidding me," said Jack.

The Seachráni captain's grin broadened, "I suggest you get below, Colonel. And hold on to something that's tied down tight."

"Storm doors," Sorcha snarled, the wind snatching her words away. "We should have moved faster."

Sam didn't miss the accusation, but was unrepentant. All around them the people of the Badlands were gathering, crouched against the storm, pressing up to the scant shelter of the doorway. She couldn't have left them behind.

Running her hands over the heavy door, she muttered, "If we just had some C4." It would be a piece of cake to blow the tunnel right open if she had more to hand than the peashooter she'd snatched from their prison guard. Still, there *had* to be a way.

"Major Carter!" Teal'c was standing lookout on the low rise they'd climbed, his attention turned out to sea. She knew what he was watching for and scrambled up to join him, Sorcha following in recriminating silence.

"Holy…" Sam breathed as she joined Teal'c to stare down at the ravaged Badlands. The Seachráni ship was close now, clearly visible despite the rain and driving spray. It was huge, long and sleek, with a couple of tall masts and tightly furled sails, and it barreled across the waves with a speed she'd rarely seen on water. "It must use some kind of aerodynamic levitation technology to diminish the hydrodynamic drag."

"The docks are gone," Sorcha said. "They will have to anchor and come ashore in longboats."

"In those seas?" Sam shook her head. "That's impossible."

Sorcha pushed wet hair from her eyes. "Watch," she said. "There is a reason the Seachráni are called Seawolves."

She did watch, trying not to think about the fact that the colonel and Daniel were probably aboard, trying not to imagine what it would be like to make land in a tiny longboat in thirty-foot seas. But Sorcha was right, the Seachráni knew what they were doing. All she could do was put faith in their skills.

Except, the ship wasn't slowing. If anything it was speeding up, making a graceful turn as it aligned itself with the sideways sweep of the waves that sliced across the Badlands. And still it didn't slow.

"They're not stopping," she said aloud, glancing at Teal'c.

He lifted an eyebrow. "Indeed."

"Oh my God," she said, realization dawning, "they're going to beach the ship!"

"Impossible!" Sorcha clenched her fists. "Madness."

Madness maybe, but true. Sam figured the ship was surfing the waves, using them to give it more lift and to keep the keel from snagging for a little longer. Although she didn't understand how a ship that tall, with a corresponding draft, could hope to get anywhere close to shore. But it definitely wasn't slowing, in fact it seemed to increase its speed as it rode the breakers, and for a second she thought it was flying. Then it struck ground, the screech of rending metal drowning out the roar of the storm as the hull tore across the jagged rocks and impaled itself on the debris of the Badlands.

For a moment it stopped, at rest, and then with a slow, inevitable grace it toppled and crunched onto its side.

"Huh," Sorcha grunted. "Perhaps Faelan is at the helm after all."

Daniel's first thought when he came to was that the ceiling looked different; it took him a few seconds to realize that he was actually flat on his back and staring up at the bulkhead. There was no sound save the ringing in his ears, and the violent pitch and roll of the ship was notably absent. Apart from the buffeting by the storm, the vessel had come to a total standstill — and apparently on its side.

He tried to lever himself up, but found his elbow sinking into something soft.

"Ow! Watch it!"

"Sorry," he mumbled, as Jack dug Daniel's elbow from his stomach and sat up. "What happened? Did we crash?"

There'd been little warning before the ship's sudden burst of speed, apart from Jack tearing into the cabin and yelling for Daniel to grab on to something. That had been followed by a gut-whipping lurch, and then they'd both been thrown backward, sliding up against the bulkhead as the ship accelerated. But the worst of it came in the last few moments, as they were tossed around the cabin like dice in a cup.

"Faelan and his harebrained scheme to get us on dry land is what happened," growled Jack, rolling his neck until it clicked. "I think we've run aground."

Daniel pushed himself to his feet, attempting to figure out how they were going to get through a door that was now located halfway up the wall. Suddenly that same door flew open and a head poked through. "Need a hand?" asked Faelan.

"I need Tylenol and a chiropractor thanks to you," muttered Jack, but he grasped Faelan's outstretched arm all the same and let himself be pulled up through the door. Moments later Daniel followed suit.

They clambered down the sloping deck, trying in vain to hide from the worst of the storm, and found themselves in a disaster zone. It was the Badlands, but they were devastated beyond recognition, torn up by the vicious wind and sea until nothing but fragments was left. In the middle of it all, like a defeated leviathan, sat the *Fánaí na Mara*. Faelan wandered through the wreckage, heedless of the debris that the wind hurled at his head. Daniel and the others tagged along.

"Who could survive this?" whispered Daniel, thinking of the people they'd left here just days before. By the look on his face, Faelan was asking himself the same question.

"They did survive," said Jack, picking up on Faelan's questioning glance. "There's no bodies," he added. "They couldn't have been here when this happened."

True enough. Despite the devastation, there was no sign of any human casualties; by all appearances, the Badlands had been abandoned. Shielding his eyes from the lash of the storm, Daniel scanned the bleak landscape.

"Then where –?" began Faelan.

"I think someone's trying to get our attention, Captain." The Seachráni who had spoken pointed toward the nearby mountain. High on the ridge, a light blinked on and off.

The tiny figures that had spilled from the beached ship now moved toward them, up the hill and away from the teeth of the storm. They had seen his signal. Satisfied, Teal'c tucked Major Carter's flashlight back into his pocket.

Through the rain it was difficult to distinguish one man

from another, but he kept his eyes fixed on the group until, halfway up the hill, two of the amorphous shapes resolved into Colonel O'Neill and Daniel Jackson.

Permitting himself a small smile of relief, he turned to where Major Carter was once more studying the storm doors. "O'Neill and Daniel Jackson are among the Seachráni," he called down.

She spun around in a flash, a broad grin lighting her face. "Thank God."

Teal'c kept his thoughts about divine involvement to himself, and merely said, "Let us hope that O'Neill still carries his C4."

"You got that right." Squinting up at the Ark, whose vast walls rose high above them, she said, "If we can't get in this way, we may have to knock on the front door."

Sorcha Caratauc, squatting with her back to the tunnel wall, cast a baleful glance at the major. "You're a fool if you think they will ever open their door, to you or to anyone else. *Sciath Dé* is the only hope for my people."

"Your people," Major Carter said, and Teal'c recognized the bite in her words, "will die if they don't find shelter. The shield — even if we get it working — can't protect them from this storm. Or from the sea, or from the flooding. You have to understand, it's a long term project."

"Do not lecture me about perspective, Samantha Carter. Have I not devoted my life to this cause?" Sorcha Caratauc shifted, drawing her ragged clothes about her. "This is not the first storm we have endured. These are not the first people I have seen die. *Sciath Dé* is all that matters."

Teal'c met Major Carter's eyes and shrugged; it was futile to argue with such single-minded resolve. Sorcha Caratauc, in her own way, was as blind as the leaders of the Ark.

"What? No beer?"

The voice propelled Teal'c around to the sight of the colonel cresting the hill. "O'Neill," he said, glad to see his old friend.

"Teal'c." O'Neill's gaze moved to the major. "Carter. Good you see you're all in one piece."

"You too, sir." Her smile lingered, then she said, "Where's Daniel?"

O'Neill jerked his head back over his shoulder. "Rabble rousing with the pirates."

"Pirates?"

"Rum, parrots, pieces of eight. You wouldn't believe it."

She swallowed a smile. "No, sir."

Sauntering toward the tunnel, O'Neill took in the shivering refugees and the decidedly closed storm doors. "Hit a dead end here, Carter?"

"Actually, yes." She bumped her fist against the door. "Ennis locked us out. We were hoping you'd have the key, sir."

Only the glitter in his eyes betrayed O'Neill's amusement. "Shoo these people to a safe distance, Carter. It's time to get out of the rain."

CHAPTER SEVENTEEN

"PASTOR Channon?"

The hesitant voice came from further down the city wall, and Ennis realized he was not alone in watching the progress of the storm. Walking toward him, stoop-shouldered and vague against the gray skies beyond the Ark, was their chief Archivist. He gestured toward the storm. "I did not expect to see you here, Pastor, when a new chapter of *Sunrise* is on the screens."

"Nor I you," Ennis said. They stopped some distance apart, and he found himself wary. There was something unspoken between them. "What brings you from the Library, Liam?"

"I come here sometimes," he said.

"I rarely do," Ennis confessed. "But…" Above them the dome was momentarily lit by a flash amid the clouds, a distant rumble of thunder following.

Liam's eyes were flinty. "I heard that your daughter was outside."

"I have no —" He stopped himself, unable to tell the lie again. Water ran in sheets down the dome, hammered against it by the relentless gale. In a low voice he said, "Yes. My daughter is outside, among the condemned."

A pause stretched, seemingly endless, then Liam asked in a conversational tone, "Did you know, Pastor, that the word Ark has two meanings? One, as we are aware, means a place of refuge. More spiritually, however, it means the inmost heaven — the dwelling place of divine truth."

The subtle emphasis on that last word was hard to miss. "Truth," Ennis said, taking a step closer, "is often more complex than it appears."

Liam smiled. "Truth is always simple, Pastor. The complexity comes in the telling of it."

"Especially," Ennis added, "when the truth is unpalatable."

"Indeed."

Another pause filled with thunder and a flash of lightning, one atop the other. The archivist glanced out at the storm. "I am glad," he said, "to be inside the Ark. But there are those who would benefit from being brought within." He smiled again, his meaning clear. "Within the Ark of Divine Truth, of course."

Ennis let his own gaze stray toward the people gathered before the screens, faces upturned. The players' earnest expressions suddenly looked like beautiful lies, and he realized that no word of truth had ever passed their lips. *Sunrise* was a thing of artifice, not truth. And somehow Rhionna, his child, had seen that — she had seen that to which he had been blind. "You spoke to her," he said, suddenly understanding. "You spoke to Rhionna of this, of truth and what lies beyond our walls."

Less sanguine but not afraid, Liam lifted his chin. Quietly he said, "There are truths hidden here, truths I have not seen save in the footprints they left upon the Library — words that once held meaning and now do not. What is a 'scientist' and why are they condemned? What is a 'satellite' and what danger does it pose? And what is the 'Sungate'?"

"Knowledge," Ennis said. "They are words of Knowledge."

"Truths denied to us, like the truth of the condemned and the world outside."

Hearing the accusation in his tone, Ennis asked, "What would you have me do? I am but one man."

"Tell us the truth." Liam's arm swept into a circle, encompassing the men and women enrapt in *Sunrise*. "Tell us the truth of what lies outside and of the Time Before."

"But I do not know it!"

"Then find it out!" Liam seized his shoulder, fingers biting. "Do you think Tynan Camus does not know the truth?"

Above them the studio building loomed, the word *Sunrise* emblazoned across its façade. Once Ennis had regarded this place as hallowed ground, now its golden gleam appeared sickly and oppressive.

"You can find it out," Liam said. "And if you speak it, the people must listen; you are their Pastor."

"And what if they do? What then?"

Liam only shrugged. "To that I have no answer."

The smoke cleared quickly, beaten down by the unrelenting rain. Daniel shook his head, waiting for his hearing to return to normal; he didn't think he'd ever get used to the force of a C4 blast.

With Jack leading the way, the long file of refugees snaked past the remnants of the tunnel doors, half starved, thirsty, and eager for shelter. Soaked and battered though they were, Daniel sensed that they were far from dispirited. A new energy was being created here, as they marched deeper into the tunnel. A sense of purpose that he hadn't anticipated. He wasn't imagining the looks sent in the direction of Faelan and Rhionna; expectant looks, from a people awaiting guidance. He only hoped they weren't expecting too much; they still had to find their way into the Ark, which wasn't going to be easy. The plan for now was simply to distribute water and what little rations they'd brought with them.

Easier said than done, as it turned out.

"The bastards have turned off the pump." In vain, Faelan spun the metal valve that controlled the Badlands' water; the outlet pipe remained dry.

"Okay." Jack shrugged. "So we go to plan B." To the best of Daniel's knowledge, plan B hadn't existed until about thirty seconds ago. Not that Jack was fazed by this minor inconvenience. "Carter and I go topside and get this water back on. Then we take it from there."

But Faelan shook his head, striding towards the blackened

and buckled remains of the storm doors and staring out into the maelstrom beyond. "We don't have time for that. This isn't the worst of it, Colonel. Something's coming. Something big, and when it hits, it'll hit hard. This tunnel will be no protection at all." He cursed and slapped the wall. "Do they think they can play God here? Do they think they can hand out judgment and decide who is damned and who is worthy to enter their bloody Ark?"

Rhionna stepped up and placed her hand on his arm, but said nothing. It appeared she didn't need to.

"I'm not giving up, if that's what you think," he said, so softly that Daniel barely heard the words.

She smiled. "That's not what I think."

He nodded, as if satisfied by her faith in him, then looked over at Jack. "Colonel, we need a new plan, and we have about five minutes to come up with it."

As Jack, Sam, Faelan and Rhionna discussed their options, and Teal'c handed out rations, Daniel dug in his pack for his camera — now was the ideal time to document just how harshly these people were treated by the Elect. It extended beyond benign indifference now; this was an active attempt at genocide. He spooled through his existing footage, trying to find the end of the timeline, more sickened than ever by the images he'd captured. Given what he knew of human cruelty, the question might be naïve, but still he found himself asking how any decent person could see such suffering and turn a blind eye?

Then he hit the 'pause' button, the spark of an idea suddenly kindling in his mind.

"Uh, guys?" The others stopped what they were doing and turned to him. "I think I might have a solution."

The tunnel was narrow and smelled bad, and Sam really didn't want to know what kind of things populated the puddle of water they were crawling through. Good job it was dark.

"I'm gonna take a guess," the colonel grunted behind her. "This isn't exactly the front door."

Rhionna's voice drifted back to them from the darkness ahead. "It's not exactly the back door, either. But sometimes I come this way if I really don't want to be seen. It won't be locked, the soldiers don't know about it."

"Can't imagine why not."

Puddle or no, Sam had to smile; it felt good to have Colonel O'Neill back. Not Jonah, but the colonel with his dark humor and unwavering moral compass. Yeah, it felt right. "How are your knees, sir?"

"Terrible. Thanks for asking, Carter."

"Not far now," Rhionna promised them softly. Then a beam of light appeared, all but blinding Sam as it sliced across her face.

"Hey!" she protested, screwing her eyes shut against dancing red blobs.

"Sorry," Rhionna whispered, lowering the flashlight. "I just need to find the — There it is, we're here."

Struggling to get her feet under her in the confined space, Sam crouched and peered up at the ceiling of the tunnel. Above them the underside of a manhole punched a black circle. The colonel crowded in at her side, solid and familiar, and behind him Sorcha's pinched face appeared. Clearly she was no more happy with the plan now than she'd been when Daniel first suggested it.

It was a risk, Sam had to admit. Daniel's backpack, containing the *Acarsaid Dorch* device, felt heavy across her shoulder; a lot was riding on the success of this mission.

"We just push this up and climb out in the middle of the street?" O'Neill said, shifting to get a better look. "If anyone's up there, it'll be like shooting fish in a barrel. Literally."

"It's in one of the disused parts of the city," Rhionna assured him. "We won't be seen."

Sam readied her P90. O'Neill cast her a look. "You and

Sorcha stay back. Carter and I'll check what's going on top-side."

Squeezing past him, Rhionna grabbed Sorcha's arm and pulled her away into the shadows. A couple of muttered words in Sorcha's native language drifted through the narrow tunnel, then a sharp retort from Rhionna. Sam hid a grin and turned to face O'Neill.

"Here goes, Major," he said, bracing his hands against the cover. "On three. Three."

He lifted it an inch, enough for her to get an ant's-eye view of a deserted street. Moving around him in an awkward three-sixty, she checked out the limited visual. "I'm not seeing anything."

"Good." His voice was tight with the strain of holding the metal cover, but he lifted it another inch and said. "Now?"

"Still clear."

"Okay, go." With a grunt, he pushed the cover off to one side.

Sam scrambled out, rolled to her feet. Vaguely grateful that she'd managed to persuade Daniel to trade his P90 for the prison guard's popgun, she spot-welded the weapon to her cheek and turned a careful circle.

"Clear," she said, straightening though not relaxing. Sentry-like buildings surrounded her, pristine and silent. It was eerie. And the light was different from last time she'd been in the Ark. The glistening opalescence was gone. In its place, a storm-dark sky painted everything in shifting shades of menace.

O'Neill was next, pushing himself up without much effort. Behind him came Rhionna, who stopped at the rim of the manhole to give Sorcha a hand. The old woman didn't seem to need much help. Or appreciate the offer.

"Over here," O'Neill said, before anyone else could speak. He herded them into the doorway of a building. Eyes roving across the blind, black windows, he asked, "Which way?"

"The *Sunrise* building is not far." A strand of Rhionna's

hair had slipped from under her headscarf. She tucked it away without apparent concern, oblivious to the danger that might be hiding behind those dark windows. "I will take you."

Sorcha spat on the ground, mumbling a curse. "Foolish nonsense," she said. "There will be time for that once we have found *Sciath Dé*!"

"Didn't we have this discussion already?" Colonel O'Neill's gaze still scanned the street. "You know what the plan is."

"Aye, foolish is what it is."

"We don't even know where to start looking for the shield," Sam explained, for what felt like the hundredth time. "Once the people from the Badlands are safe we can —"

"Save it, Carter." O'Neill turned to glare at Sorcha. "We're doing you a *favor*, lady. Remember that."

Her eyes narrowed. "A favor."

"Yeah. We've got enough troubles of our own. We don't need yours too."

Lips pressed tight, eyes hard as granite, Sorcha said nothing and tried to stare him down instead. But she was no match for Jack O'Neill on a bad day — and this had been a very, very bad day.

"Carter, take point," he said, never interrupting the staring contest. "Rhionna, show her the way." With his handgun, he gestured for Sorcha to follow. "Ladies first."

Sam didn't wait to hear her answer, and she headed out into the empty streets.

Teal'c kept within the shadows and watched with no little admiration as Faelan Garrett addressed the people of the Badlands. Flashes of lightning illuminated faces hardened by suffering, but now raptly attentive and suffused with burgeoning hope. What Faelan Garret said, Teal'c did not know; his language was unfamiliar. But the meaning was clear. He rallied these people to arms, one hand jabbing repeatedly up toward the city above.

"*Kalach shal tek*," Teal'c vowed quietly, fist to his heart.

"Victory or death?" A dry smile was audible in Daniel Jackson's voice. "I'm hoping for a more peaceful solution."

"As am I." Teal'c turned to see him leaning against the tunnel wall some distance away, also watching Faelan. What little light there was reflected on the lenses of his spectacles and masked his eyes. "But you place great faith in humanity, Daniel Jackson."

"Too much, maybe?" Another fork of lightning rent the sky and for a split-second his earnest face flashed pale in the darkness. Daniel Jackson looked very young, even by human standards; unlike many, grief and loss had not tarnished his inherent optimism.

It was a confidence Teal'c respected, but could not share. "Do you believe the people of the Ark will divide their wealth among these *kresh'taa* simply because charity demands it?" he asked. "They have not done so before."

"Because they didn't really know was going on out here."

"If they wished to know, they could have found out," Teal'c insisted. "As Rhionna Channon did."

Hands plunged into his jacket pocket, Daniel Jackson moved closer. "Those people up there, they aren't so different from people at home. Most of the time they're happy to go to work, take the kids to school, watch a little TV at night. And that's okay, you know? Most people just want to live their lives. But sometimes…" He turned to look at Faelan Garrett, at the people he rallied. "Sometimes people have to see what's going on out in the big wide world, and when they do — then they don't want to just sit at home and watch TV. Then they want to *do* something."

"Has Rhionna Channon not already attempted to alert her people to the injustices of her world?"

"Yes, and the Elect have done everything they could to silence her and make sure everyone else is fixated on *Sunrise*."

"And so the people of the Ark are complicit in their own deception." Teal'c shook his head. "I cannot share your faith, Daniel Jackson. Perhaps I have witnessed too much indifference to the suffering of others, but I believe Faelan Garrett and his people must fight for their rightful share of this world. It will not be freely given."

"Maybe," Daniel Jackson admitted. "Maybe you're right. But sometimes I think people just have to see for themselves." He gave a bleak smile. "You know what they say — a picture's worth a thousand words."

Teal'c considered the adage. "But a weapon," he decided, hand resting on the P90 O'Neill had given him, "is more valuable still."

To that, Daniel Jackson made no answer.

CHAPTER EIGHTEEN

FLATTENED against the wall, Jack signaled Carter to keep the others back and peered around the corner and out on the plaza ahead. Given the way the crowd sat like spellbound toddlers before the giant TV screen in the center of the square, his caution was probably unnecessary. Still, he wasn't going to take any chances. The damn TV was loud though, blaring out its melodrama as if in competition with the rumbling storm clouds outside. Glancing up it occurred to him that that was exactly what *Sunrise* was doing — drowning out, quite literally, everything beyond these folks' sweet little snow globe home.

Across the street stood the building from which *Sunrise* was broadcast. Sleek and ostentatiously affluent and difficult to reconcile with the hovels of the Badlands or the drowned city of the Seachráni. Perhaps the whole world had looked like this once, but now the Ark was all that remained; a living museum to a dead culture. Time to change things around a little.

He fell back to where Carter had Rhionna were the old woman were waiting. Sorcha was increasingly sour faced, so he blanked her — no time or energy for another argument — and said, "It's right across the square, Major. If you're lucky you'll catch the ten o'clock tour."

Carter did her best to swallow a smile, but it was in her eyes all the same. "I'll bring you back a t-shirt, sir."

"Extra large. I like 'em roomy."

Rhionna glanced between them with a look of sudden revelation, but before she could say anything stupid Jack cut her off. "You're with me," he said. "We've got a little errand to run."

Her "What do you mean?" clashed with Carter's "Sir?"

Jack pulled his cap down further onto his forehead and drew his Beretta. He missed the weight of the P90 and briefly wished he hadn't given it to Teal'c. He felt kind of naked being so lightly armed. Not that he'd let anyone see that. "Carter, once you've finished in the studio, take Sorcha and go look for the shield."

"And what are you going to do?" An edge of irritated concern laced Carter's voice. Not entirely appropriate for an officer talking to her CO.

He shot her a warning look. "What I'm gonna do," he said, "is pay a visit to the leader of this outfit."

Rhionna's eyes widened. "To my father?"

"Nope." Jack shook his head. "Tynan Camus. No offence, but I think we all know where the real power lies. And when Daniel and Teal'c come banging at the front door, I want to make sure Camus is right where I want him." He lifted his weapon. "On the wrong end of this."

There came a time, Teal'c knew, when all arduous endeavors were reduced to one simple ability, that of putting one foot in front of the other. So it was for the people of the Badlands, from the oldest to the youngest. With all other options removed, it was now a question of stamina — keep going, keep walking, do not stop because, in this storm, with Ierna's earth, sea and air fighting a battle for dominance, to stop would be to die.

They had walked for what felt like hours, but Teal'c knew from his watch that barely forty minutes had passed. The rain stabbed at his head, icy needles that slashed and numbed in equal measure, but he forced away the pain, focusing instead on his feet. One in front of the other, keep going, keep moving, do not stop. Around him, the refugees did the same, each of them pushing themselves onwards without a sound. Even the children had stopped crying.

Their caravan had reached the wall now, a huge and daunting structure, a monument to intimidation and inequality, yet people huddled against it as if seeking the shelter of oppression. Daniel Jackson walked somewhere behind, and Teal'c wondered how his friend was faring.

Faelan Garret led the procession, turning frequently to check on his battered brigade, frequently halting to assist those who stumbled or fell. A determined man, Teal'c thought, an unwilling leader, reluctant to realize the command he might wield. In Teal'c's experience, such men were invariably possessed of more honor than those whose objective was the quest for power. Faelan Garret and Rhionna Channon would make a formidable partnership.

But this partnership would be for naught if the refugees did not survive this apocalyptic weather. Here and now it seemed that sheer determination to survive might not be enough. By Teal'c's side, one of the older men broke to his hands and knees, his head hanging in rain-sodden defeat. When Teal'c bent to help him up, the man weakly shrugged off his aid.

"Leave me. I can go no further." The man's voice was ragged, barely audible above the clamor of the wind. Others shuffled around him, but their steps slowed, their eyes shifting from his hunched form to the long path ahead; his collapse spoke to the part of them that wanted to give in. Teal'c recognized how precarious this moment was. If one fell, they all might.

"You must rise, my friend. You must not succumb."

"I can't," sobbed the man, dragging himself over to slump against the gray stone of the wall. "I can't. What's the point?"

"We do not have much further to go," said Teal'c. "Soon we shall find shelter inside the Ark."

"You fool. You think this plan will come to aught? We will never be permitted inside the Ark. They would rather see us swallowed by the sea than share their luxury. Why should they open their doors to us?"

Teal'c refrained from arguing. It would be enough to get the man back on his feet. "You must rise," he repeated. "Do not give in."

The man threw up his hands, a weak, defeated gesture, and simply closed his eyes.

Teal'c was unsure what else he could say; in truth, he had the same doubts, but refused to heed them. Where no options were left, doubts became futile. As it turned out however, a reply was unnecessary. A hand reached past him and grabbed the man's sodden coat, hauling him to his feet.

"You would die here, Abbán Ó Braoin? You would allow them this victory?" Faelan Garret's face showed no compassion, and Teal'c understood the root of his anger. It was the Seachráni's duty to deliver these people, every last one of them, to safety.

Abbán Ó Braoin gave a weak laugh and rested his head against the wall. "Hardly a victory, Faelan, when they barely realize we exist."

"The Elect know we exist, Abbán, and we shan't let them win. As for the others, they are not our enemy. If they don't know we exist, then we *let* them know. And if we have to ask for their help, we shall ask."

"And what makes you think they will help the likes of us?" said Abbán Ó Braoin, though his voice was harder now, challenging, as if he were genuinely seeking an answer.

"Belief," replied Faelan Garret. "I'll no longer live in fear of believing in others, Abbán. And I'll not accept such cowardice in you either. Now keep walking, if not for your sake then for the sake of the others." He let go of the man's coat. "Believe, Abbán. And walk."

And so they did, into the teeth of the storm.

The wide windows of Tynan Camus's rooms looked out across Sunrise Plaza and toward the city's largest view screen. Halfway through the evening's extended broadcast — he had worked the players hard in order to produce so much in one day, but it had been necessary in order to distract the people from the storm — he was pleased to see the crowd growing, settled in their seats as food sellers plied their wares up and down the aisles. With luck, the worst of the storm would have passed before the chapter ended.

He glanced up at the dome above. It had dulled to a murky gray instead of glowing with its customary brightness. But soon this trial would be over, and once the storm had passed, the land beyond would be washed clean of its blight and the strangers from the Sungate would have perished together with Ennis Channon's troublesome — if comely — daughter.

It was a shame that Rhionna had not been more pliant. Her spirit would have been a challenge, and an alliance between his family and hers would have been expedient. But marriage was certainly not the only way to rise to the position of Pastor. With Rhionna and her Seawolf lover dead, Channon had no heir. Tynan smiled at the thought, smoothing his hands across his velvet robes of office. It was only a matter of time before the position was his.

Behind him, a door opened and soft footsteps approached. Below, in the plaza, the chapter was unfolding, and through the glass window he heard the gasps of the audience as the drama reached its climax. He felt a presence at his shoulder, but did not turn around. There was no need. "What is it, Aidan?"

"Pastor Ennis Channon wishes to speak with you, Brother Camus. He is most insistent."

Tynan did not bother to suppress his sigh. "Tell him I am in the *Sunrise* building and not to be disturbed."

"He appears…agitated. He asks to speak to you about his daughter."

At this, Tynan turned around. Aidan looked worried and refused to meet his gaze. "About his daughter?"

"Yes, Brother."

Could it be that the crab had discovered its claws? The influence of the strangers appeared to be more damaging than Tynan had anticipated. Yet he was not blind to the opportunity this might present. Folding his hands, he thought for a moment. "Tell Pastor Channon that I will meet him in the broadcast room in one hour, to hear what he wishes to say about his disgraced daughter. When you have given him the message, return here immediately."

Aidan bowed and retreated in silence. Tynan smiled to himself. Yes, an opportunity indeed. Rhionna was cast out. To mention her name defied the will of the Elect. It would be a matter of great ease to record the Pastor's heretical words in the broadcast room, and thus to condemn him before the Elect. Channon would soon be the last of his family to bear the noble title of 'Pastor.'

As the door clicked shut, Tynan turned back to the window.

"Nice apartment." The accented voice was close to his ear, and something cold and metallic was pressed to the side of his head. "Shame about the view."

"O'Neill." Tynan let his lip curl. "I thought you were dead."

"Sorry to disappoint. Not." Keeping the gun leveled, O'Neill circled around to stand in front of him. "You and I are going for a little walk."

"Is that so?" Any minute now, Aidan would be back. Tynan offered a smile. "Tell me, how did you elude my men in the Badlands?"

"I took a little ride with some friends."

"Ah, the Seawolves." He wrinkled his nose. "I hope you didn't bring back anything contagious."

"Highly contagious," O'Neill said. "Freedom, justice, and apple pie on Sunday."

Secretly amused by the prospect of Aidan's imminent return and its inevitable consequences, Tynan played along. "Pie?"

Then the door opened and Aidan fell through, inert and face-first on the floor, with blue energy dancing across his limbs. Behind him stood Rhionna Channon, brandishing one of the outsider's weapons, a grim smile on her face. "Hello Tynan," she said, aiming the gun at him. "Surprise."

Fury shredded any fear he might have felt. "You dare to raise arms against the Elect? To return here when even your father has disowned you as a Seawolf whore?"

She never even flinched as she stepped over Aidan's prone body. "We should go now," she advised O'Neill. "I saw my father leave, but everyone else is watching tonight's chapter." Eyes alive with rage, she turned on Tynan and he drew back despite himself. The woman was wild, crazed as the Seachráni. How had he ever desired to bed her? "There is irony in that, is there not, Tynan Camus?" she crowed. "*Sunrise* — your great distraction — will distract your men tonight."

"You will pay with your life for this," he hissed. "All of you."

Gun still raised, O'Neill moved in beside Rhionna. "If I had a dime for every bad guy who told me that..." He glanced at her. "We need to get to the top of the wall, close to the gates."

She nodded. "There is a way, but we must hurry. The worst of the storm will soon be upon them, and they cannot last long against it."

"What do you intend?" Glancing at their sun-coarsened faces, Tynan felt a new beat of fear, a new unease. "What do you intend to do?"

O'Neill smiled, a brief quirk of his lips. "Like I said — freedom, justice and apple pie. Highly contagious." With his weapon, he prodded Tynan to move. "And you're gonna get a front row seat at the show."

Gaining entry to the *Sunrise* building was less difficult than Sam had anticipated. Unlike any other city she'd visited, the streets here were deserted at the best of times, but now, with the Ark's tiny population clustered around the TV screens, she half expected to see tumbleweed blowing past.

At the back of the building, she found a door whose lock was no match for a swift kick. The noise was a calculated risk, but she figured it was worth taking. Sorcha watched her in silence, her wiry frame growing tenser by the moment. Sam waited for a slow count of one hundred. When she didn't hear any sounds of alarm being raised, she gestured for Sorcha to follow her inside.

The power supply seemed to be selective, and on these lower floors the only illumination consisted of filtered daylight that crept out of disused offices. With the tip of her gun she pushed open several doors until she found what she was looking for: a stairwell.

"Rhionna said the studio is on the tenth floor."

"This plan will fail." Trailing Sam like a grumpy shadow, Sorcha continued her doomsaying. "We will be captured and executed and *Sciath Dé* will never be activated; you toy with the fate of this world, Samantha Carter."

"We can't just let those people die out there." Sam looked up the stairwell as high as she could see. Nothing. With a nod, she gestured for Sorcha to follow and began to climb the stairs. "Once they're inside, there'll be plenty of time to figure out how to get the shield working. Trust me."

Sorcha snorted. "Trust is a luxury."

"Maybe, but —" A sound above. Her hand gripped Sorcha's thin arm, squeezing hard to ensure silence. A door closed, the noise bouncing down the stairs until it faded away to nothing. Sam let out a quiet sigh. "Come on, let's just get this done."

Sorcha on her heels, she continued up the staircase.

Ennis Channon crossed Sunrise Plaza as if it were the first time that he had walked beneath the golden sign or stared up at the vast screen. He suddenly felt alien in his own city, and the feeling was profoundly disturbing. Everywhere he looked he saw faces consumed by an appetite he no longer shared.

Did they not understand the emptiness they worshiped — the vacuous content of what he had once considered the Message, but now saw as no more than entertainment? Did they not see that they were being manipulated by the Elect, that they were complicit in their own ignorance? Ennis suspected that he had known this truth for some time but, through cowardice, had chosen to pretend otherwise. Until, for his child, his blood, it was too late. That Rhionna was out there, perhaps already lost to the raging sea, made him sick to his core. Made him brittle with anger.

He stalked past the rows of oblivious faces, all lifted to the screen and ignoring the storm gathering above them. Ignoring the world. He hated their mindless indifference, the lure of *Sunrise's* complaisant hypocrisy — all will be well, all *is* well, do not worry.

It was time to do what he had never dared do before; stand up to Tynan Camus. Stand up to the Elect and speak truth to the people. And if he was banished to the Badlands for his efforts or, worse, to *Acarsaid Dorch*, then so be it. He knew he could live within the Ark no longer. Not without Rhionna — not with the guilt he bore for her exile and death.

Sweeping into the *Sunrise* building, he pushed past the startled guards, torn away from their screens by his arrival. They dared not stop him, and were, he supposed, only too glad to return to their entertainment.

In the elevator, he closed his eyes so that he would not see the strip-screen above the door, but he could not block the players' voices from his mind. While his daughter was dying outside, these players feigned tears over fictitious sorrows and the people of the Ark looked on in avid delight.

The doors slid open, and as he stepped out into the empty

corridor of Floor Ten, his footsteps echoed, empty in an empty world.

It made him want to weep with regret and shame.

The studio was a large square room, big and scruffy with pieces of set piled up against one wall. Distinctly unglamorous. It was also deserted.

Hands resting on her weapon, Sam entered the room, Sorcha by her side. The old woman was peering around the studio, interested despite herself. "This is all?" she said, gazing up at the cardboard sets. "Even the homes in which they live are not real."

"It's called a set," Sam said, scanning the corridor again. "TV is all fake."

"Like the Ark," Sorcha said, and her face creased into a smile for the first time since they'd left the Badlands. "Their whole world is a mere 'set'." She seemed to enjoy the new word. "They live isolated from the reality and distract their minds with another fictitious world built within the first."

"Ironic," Sam admitted, walking further into the room and stepping over a nest of trailing wires that led from a small glass-sided annex to the cluster of lights and cameras in the center of the floor. "Stay there," she said, waving Sorcha back to the studio door. "I'm going to check out that annex. If someone comes, call me."

Sorcha snorted, glancing irritably into the corridor. "If I am to play guardsman while you work, at least give me your weapon so I might defend myself."

Sam's fingers tightened around her gun, an involuntary reaction.

"Ah," Sorcha said with a bitter smile. "You do not trust me."

"It's not that." But it was, and they both knew it. The P90 felt heavy in Sam's hands, a weight between them now.

Saying no more, Sorcha just looked at her with those hard eyes of hers. Judging.

With a sigh, Sam unclipped her weapon and handed it over. Thera would have disapproved, but she wasn't Thera. She'd never been Thera. And trust, Daniel had proven again and again, usually paid dividends.

Sorcha took the weapon with a nod and listened intently as Sam explained how to fire. "Give me five minutes," Sam said when she was done. "And don't pull that trigger unless you've got no choice."

"I will not," Sorcha promised, turning back to the doorway and fixing her gaze on the hallway beyond.

Sam watched her for a moment, then headed across the studio and ducked into the annex. As she'd suspected, it was the studio's equivalent of the SGC's control room and a brief survey of the equipment was enough to show her that the plan was at least possible. *Sunrise* appeared to be recorded digitally — which made sense, given the Ark's limited resources. It also meant that patching in Daniel's camcorder was just a question of finding a way to interface with the Ark's technology. Kinda like making a Mac talk to a PC — if Macs had been invented on Mars and PCs on Venus.

With a sigh she crouched behind the desk to get a closer look. A small monitor was showing the current episode as it played, simply streaming it from the local mainframe out to the screens in the city. Broadcast was really the wrong word. This was more like a wide area network, with all the terminals connected to a central server that —

"Samantha!"

Sam looked up, startled. Sorcha stood in the doorway to the annex and in her hand was the P90. It was pointed right at Sam.

"You should have listened to your instincts," Sorcha said. "In the Badlands we learn to trust none but our kin."

CHAPTER NINETEEN

JACK KEPT his gun leveled at Tynan Camus's back while Rhionna led them up a narrow staircase toward the top of the wall that surrounded the Ark. Seeing it up close, he noted the curvature of the smooth gray stone and realized the thing was a built like a giant sea wall. He wasn't prone to flights of fancy — he didn't always enjoy the path his imagination chose, so he kept it on a tight leash — but it was impossible not to imagine the last days of this world; seas flooding through cities, and terrified people holing up in this final refuge while outside their civilization drowned.

Desperate times threw up all kinds of leaders — some good, most bad. Telling those last survivors that they were special, saved by divine purpose instead of by blind goddamn luck, must have been an easy sell for the predecessors of Tynan Camus. Desperate people believed anything that made sense out of their misery; they were easy to lead. Easy to deceive.

And the Elect had exploited that to the hilt. They'd lived like kings, while outside their world went to hell.

At the top of the staircase Rhionna stopped and waited. The wall opened out to a path about five meters wide, with the Ark's dome rising up on the right and sweeping skyward toward the scudding thunderclouds. Rain streamed down its side in writhing torrents, so heavy Jack couldn't make out where the Badlands had once sprawled. Or maybe, he thought with a sick drop in his gut, they just weren't there anymore.

"How far's the gate?" he asked as he herded Tynan up to the top of the wall. The man's face was pasty, and he glanced out at the storm with unease. Maybe he didn't like heights.

"There." Rhionna pointed at a shoulder of steel that stuck up from the wall a couple hundred meters further along. Doubt clouded her face. "That's the mechanism. It's not been opened for over a hundred and eighty years, though."

"Good job I packed some WD40."

She stared at him, uncomprehending. Into the silence, Camus said, "Are you imbecilic enough to consider opening the gates, Colonel O'Neill?"

Jack fixed him with a look. "I'm imbecilic enough to do just about anything."

"In the middle of this storm and with the seas rising?" Camus snorted. "You would destroy us all!"

"Guess you should have thought of that before you locked half your people out."

Camus's lip curled. "If you mean the creatures in the Badlands, then you are mistaken. It is the Lord who has set them Outside, where the light of the Sun might purge their sins. We cannot interfere with His will."

"Well, as we like to say on Earth" — Jack prodded him into motion with the barrel of his gun — "bullshit."

Camus stumbled forward a step, feet tangling in his heavy robe. He scowled at Jack, but kept walking and turned his attention to Rhionna instead. "Do you think the soldiers will obey you?" he asked. "Do you think they will open the gates at the command of a Seawolf whore?"

She glanced over her shoulder, jaw tight. "No," she said. "Because you're going to give the order."

He laughed, a grating trill of derision. "And why would I do that?"

"Because," Jack said, slowing as they reached the massive gate mechanism, "your flock down there are going to demand it."

Camus stared at him. "This is madness indeed." He jabbed a finger at the people sitting engrossed before the screen. "Do you honestly believe *they* will demand that I open the gates?"

"You might be surprised."

Ice crept into Camus's eyes. "What have you done?"

"Nothing." Jack smiled. "Yet."

"I will never open the gates!" shouted Camus. "I would rather die before I gave that order."

"They are *people*!" Rhionna cried, with a look that reminded Jack all too much of Daniel. "How can you just stand here and let them die out there?"

"Because the Lord decrees it."

"Arrant nonsense!" Rhionna shot back. "You know it is. Don't make the mistake of thinking me as empty-headed as your followers. I have a mind of my own and I have used it. You don't believe the Lord has decreed it any more than I do."

"Perhaps I don't," Camus conceded. "Nevertheless, the Ark was not made for them. It was made for us, and there is not enough room or food to house the Badland beggars. *That* is a fact."

"Then we must all have less — an equal share."

"An equal share?" He flung a hand toward the plaza. "Do you think they will agree to your equal share, Rhionna Channon?"

"They will when they see what the people in the Badlands have suffered."

Camus laughed. "You are a naive fool, like your father. You think they will feel pity for these people? When they see them thronging before the gates, do you think they will feel pity, will wish to share their homes and food?" He glared at Jack. "You know what they will feel, O'Neill. You have seen it, I am sure."

Saying nothing, Jack kept his face deliberately blank. But he knew, he knew exactly what Camus was talking about.

"Fear," Tynan said. "They will feel fear and terror, and they will turn to me — to the Elect — to save them from the hordes outside the gates." He laughed again. "This was your plan? You are a greater fool than I had imagined. Bringing the damned here only strengthens my hand!"

"You're right, that was our plan," Jack said with a shrug. "But not all of our plan." He glanced at his watch and turned to look at the screen in the plaza below. "Watch this. Three, two, one…"

Nothing happened.

Sunrise continued to play out its Technicolor melodrama uninterrupted.

"Impressive," Tynan said. "Very impressive."

Jack ignored him, glancing over at the vast *Sunrise* building with a knot of cold fear in the pit of his stomach. *Carter.*

Something had gone wrong.

Hands raised, Sam stood up. "Sorcha, what are you doing?"

"I cannot allow you to do this." The old woman took a step closer. "You are wasting our best hope of activating *Sciath Dé*."

The P90 sat awkward in her hands, but it was lethal all the same. Sam cursed herself, glad the colonel wasn't around to witness this profound gaffe. How could she have been so stupid? "Look, we don't have time for this," she said. "If we don't get the gates open, they'll all die out there. Faelan. My friends. They're depending on us."

On me.

"You will bring down the soldiers upon us before we can activate the shield," Sorcha protested, edging further into the room. "And then more than the Badlands will be lost. All of Ierna will die."

"But if we tell the people the truth," Sam countered, "if we show them what life is like in the Badlands and beyond, then they'll help us find the controls for the shield and — "

"Truth!" Sorcha spat. "Why should they care about truth while their bellies are full and their minds empty? The truth is before their eyes yet they remain blind!"

"They won't be able to ignore this," Sam said. "They're not bad people, they're just ignorant."

With a derisive grunt, Sorcha advanced further into the room, forcing Sam to take a step back. Claw-like hands jerked the gun up a fraction. "Help me activate the shield, or I shall take the device you stole from *Acarsaid Dorch* and do it myself."

"What about Faelan?" Sam pressed, looking for a weak spot. "Are you just going to let him die out there?"

"*Sciath Dé* is all that matters. More than his life, more than yours. Faelan would understand that." The gun jerked again. "Give me the device."

"No." Rolling onto the balls of her feet, slow and subtle, Sam judged the distance she'd have to cross to reach Sorcha. A low tackle would do it. Chances were the old woman would never get a shot in. "If you want it, you'll to have to come get it."

Sorcha's face hardened and her finger tensed on the trigger. Sam ducked to the right, diving for the scant shelter of the desk. Bullets spewed, and she felt a bright stripe of pain across her arm. She fell awkwardly, hit her left knee, rolled. From the corner of her eye she caught a flash of movement outside the annex window.

"I do not wish to harm you." Sorcha's voice was tight, uninflected. "Give me the device."

On the floor, still covered by the desk, Sam shifted so her back was to the wall. She was dimly aware of the pain in her arm, and through the thunder of her heartbeat she realized two things; there was no way out, and the gunfire undoubtedly had alerted the Elect Guard. It would only be a matter of minutes before they were discovered.

She eyed the desk, trying to calculate its weight. If that tipped over, it might distract Sorcha long enough to overpower her. She was only an old woman, after all. An old woman with a submachine gun — *her* submachine gun. Sorcha moved, her footsteps tentative. "The Guard will be here soon," she said, frustration rising. "Give me the —"

A man rushed into the annex, swinging something solid-looking at Sorcha's head. She cried out — anger and fear — and Sam flung her arms over her head when a burst from the P90 shattered the glass window and showered her in fragments. Someone fell hard, toppling over a chair, and then the only sounds were her own harsh breathing and the monotonous drone of *Sunrise* still oozing from the studio's computer.

CHAPTER TWENTY

THE WALK was over, but standing in the shadow of the great metal doors, bearing the brunt of the planet's climate, Daniel knew that the really hard part hadn't even begun yet.

Never had he been so cold or so tired. Never had so much depended on a single act of compassion from one people to another.

The refugees huddled together, shielding each other as best they could, but the wind and rain were merciless. Behind him, the sea pounded at what was left of the shore, its waves like unrelenting fists. This high up the hill, they were safe from the ocean, but that wouldn't last; he was reluctant to ask Faelan how long it would take for the waters to reach them.

Right now the captain was making his way through the throng of battered people, handing out rations of water, words of encouragement, whatever would hold this fragile band together and keep them standing. Daniel figured that, somewhere along the line, Jack must have made an impression; he almost smiled to see Faelan so committed to SG-1's pledge that no one got left behind.

As if sensing the scrutiny, Faelan turned and caught Daniel's eye. His jerk of the chin was a summons, and Daniel pushed his way towards him. Together, they walked a short distance from the group.

"We can't last out here much longer, Dr. Jackson."

Reluctantly giving voice to his own anxieties, Daniel replied, "Are you worried that they didn't make it?"

Faelan wiped a hand over his face, pushing back his soaked hair in a futile gesture. "I trust in your friends, and I trust in Rhionna." It was an affirmation of sorts, but the doubt was still there.

"And Sorcha?"

"Sorcha Caratauc is single-minded, Daniel, and she does not like this plan."

"The plan doesn't hinge on her. They'll make it with or without her."

"There's still the Elect Guard to contend with. They're slow and lazy, but they are everywhere and they are armed."

"So are Jack and Sam," replied Daniel.

Looking somewhat reassured, Faelan nodded, but anything he might have said was cut off when the huge screens mounted outside the gates sputtered to life. As one, the refugees raised their heads, as if awaiting salvation; in a way, it was an appropriate notion.

Daniel couldn't contain his grin and clapped Faelan on the shoulder. "I knew it. I knew that they'd make it." But his relief was short-lived; in grainy images that spiked and flickered on damaged screens, *Sunrise* began to play. He turned back to Faelan, who was now staring out across the sea. "It doesn't mean anything, Faelan. They can still make it."

"Perhaps they can, Daniel. But the question now is: can we?" He pointed out into the very teeth of the storm, and with sick dread, Daniel realized what he was talking about. Where the horizon used to be, there was now a thick line, a slash of deep gray cutting through the tumultuous seascape.

"It's a wave." Faelan's voice was leaden. "In a little while everything — everyone — that isn't inside the dome will swept into the sea. Rhionna and your friends *must* succeed. If those gates don't open, Daniel, then nothing in Ierna can save us."

Carefully, Sam lowered her arms. Biting off a curse at the pain in her left bicep, she watched her sleeve darkening with blood. Her fingers still moved alright, though, so it probably was just a scratch. It hurt like hell, even so. Clamping her hand over the wound, she got to her feet and cautiously peered over the desk. Sorcha lay sprawled on her back, the gun flung free of her grip. Next to her lay her assailant, curled up and clearly in pain. Though she could hardly believe her eyes, she recognized the long robes and the fleshy face — now pale and clammy — of Pastor Ennis Channon. He'd been shot, at least once, his robes blooming crimson over his chest.

Treading across the broken glass, one eye on the studio door because she expected the Elect Guard to burst through any moment now, Sam snatched up her weapon and clipped it to her vest. Better. Then she turned to Ennis.

He was looking up at her, his breathing fast and shallow. "Rhionna," he whispered. Blood foamed pink on his lips.

Sam darted a glance out into the studio, listened for footsteps. "She's alive," she said. "She's trying to help bring the people of the Badlands inside."

Ennis nodded. "As she always has."

"But the Elect Guard will be here any second so I can't — "

"No." The word was a wheezing sigh.

Sam frowned. "They will have heard the gunfire."

Lifting a heavy hand, Ennis gestured toward the studio door. Sam craned her neck to see. It was closed, Ennis himself must have shut it. Still, it was hardly enough to keep the soldiers out.

Smiling, Ennis bared blood-stained teeth. "No noise," he breathed. "For *Sunrise*."

It took a moment for Sam to get it. "The studio is soundproof. Of course it is. They didn't hear anything?"

Ennis shook his head. "Show them the truth," he said. "Show them."

Behind her, Sorcha stirred. Keeping her good hand on her weapon, Sam crouched before Ennis. He was dying, the wound in his chest pumping out blood with each beat of his heart. She fished out one of the dressings she carried, knowing it would do little good but unable to just sit there and do nothing. Ignoring her own pain, she tore open the packet and pressed the bandage against the wound. "I can contact Rhionna," she said. "Bring her here. She would want to see you before — "

"No." Ennis's hand covered her own where she was holding the dressing against his chest. "She will be Pastor now — let her lead the people. Let her open their eyes to the truth before it is too late."

"But — "

"Please." His face was waxen, lips turning blue. Sam Carter had seen death before and recognized its approach. "Rhionna must be my redemption now," Ennis whispered. "Let her lead them."

With a nod, Sam withdrew her hand. "Then I have a job to do."

Ennis closed his eyes, his breath coming in a wet, wheezing rattle now.

Stepping over Sorcha's prone body, Sam paused to press her fingers to the woman's neck. Her pulse was steady. With no time to do more, she reached for another dressing and using her good hand and her teeth tied it as best she could around the wound in her own arm. Then, hunkering down before the alien computer, she got to work. Outside the storm was worsening, and the people of the Badlands didn't have long.

Daniel and Teal'c didn't have long.

"It has been many years since our last execution within the Ark. But I have long thought that it was time the practice was reintroduced — the people are becoming sloppy in their devotions, their respect for the Elect is faltering." Tynan Camus peered down the length of his nose. "I should thank you, Colonel O'Neill, for providing me with the opportunity to restore one of our old customs. The death of the outlander heretic will demonstrate the power of the Elect most effectively."

Jack didn't bother to reply; smarter men than Camus had tried to goad him into a hasty response, and he was way too seasoned to fall for anything so amateurish. Instead he spoke to Rhionna, whose white face said more about her fears than any words could express. "Keep that on him," he said, nodding toward her gun.

"What do you think's happened?" Her gaze darted to the *Sunrise* building.

"Nothing. Carter's on the case. Just give her a few more minutes." He said it with confidence, partly to quell his own unease. No one was more capable than Carter, no one was more likely to get the job done. Unless...

No point in going there.

A flicker of light caught his eye, and he glanced out through the water-drenched dome. One of the giant screens outside glimmered through the slashing rain. "Watch him," he told Rhionna and trotted over to the far side of the wall for a closer look.

The rain was blowing in horizontal blades, and it was difficult to make out anything through the sheets of water. But in the cold light of the screen he saw movement — a shifting, swaying mass ducking beneath the onslaught of the storm. The screen flickered again, brightness glancing off sodden hair plastered to thin, terrified faces. Faelan's people had arrived, and he could almost feel their desperation pressing against the impassive gates of the Ark.

His hope hardened into anger. Two steps propelled him back to Camus, and he dragged the man across the wall and toward the edge of the dome. "Look!" he shouted, shoving him up close. "Look at them."

Camus's face remained impassive. "Folly, to bring them here. If it's the Lord's will that they perish, perish they shall."

"The *Lord's* will?" Jack yanked him around, jamming his pistol beneath the man's chin and forcing him back hard against the railing. This close, he could see the contempt in Camus's eyes. He could smell it. "It's *your* will, you arrogant son of a —"

"Jack!"

He turned at Rhionna's startled shout. Weapon raised, she was aiming it with a steady hand at the half dozen Elect Guard stalking the length of the wall toward her. Knowing what he'd see, Jack looked the other way and saw another group of soldiers, guns readied, closing in on them.

"Did you really believe you could take me captive without anyone noticing?"

Jack kept his Beretta pressed beneath Camus's chin, forcing his head up. "Don't think I won't enjoy shutting that smart mouth of yours." The barrel of the gun rose a little, fell again, as Camus swallowed hard. "Back off!" Jack hollered at the guards. "Back off *now*!"

"We don't want to hurt anyone," Rhionna called — a point on which Jack didn't exactly agree, but he let it slide. "We just want to show you the truth! We want you to know what the Elect are doing in your name!"

"This woman is depraved!" Camus screamed, glaring at Jack and daring him to do his worst. "The Lord has damned her and all the visitors from *Acarsaid Dorch*! They must be set Outside to face His wrath!"

Sonofabitch was calling his bluff.

"Please," Rhionna shouted as the Guardsmen glanced at each other and took a hesitant step forward. One man broke from their ranks, and Jack recognized the soldier who had let them go on the night they'd left the city. "Captain Tanner," said Rhionna, the zat in her hand shaking. "I don't want to hurt you. Please, you must listen. There are people outside. If we don't open the Ark and let them in —"

The captain shook his head, approaching her slowly. "Rhionna, this is unwise –"

"You hear her madness!" Tynan crowed. "Open the Ark? She is crazed!"

"Enough from you!" shouted Tanner, shocking Tynan into silence.

"There's still time, Tanner!" pleaded Rhionna.

As she spoke lightning flashed overhead, thunder cracked, and all at once the screens went black. From the plaza below rose a fearful gasp, a chatter of uncertainty. Jack turned his head a fraction to see what was happening and felt a sharp crack across his jaw; Tynan Camus was stronger than he looked. Reeling from the blow, Jack staggered back, whirling to keep his weapon trained on the Guardsmen. But without Camus, he was out of cards to play. There were twelve of them and one of him; they could shoot him where he stood. He worked his jaw. "Crap."

"Disarm them," Tynan ordered, retreating behind the line of soldiers. "And secure them in the cells. I shall speak with the Elect about their execution."

"Please, look out there!" Rhionna said, her voice was ragged with grief. Jack could feel it too, jagged in his chest. "There are children and women."

Tanner actually risked a glances, but the storm was so violent that the man couldn't possibly see anything.

"For crying out loud," Jack shouted. "She's telling the truth. There are people out there who —"

His words were drowned out by the *Sunrise* theme, blaring triumphant from the screens as they booted up again. Rhionna visibly sagged, her gun drooping to point uselessly at the floor. "No," she breathed, staring up at their failure. "He'll die out there..."

Jack knew whom she meant, but said nothing. Daniel and Teal'c were out there too.

He raised his weapon, looking for a shot. Camus was hiding behind the soldiers, but Jack was an expert marksman, and if he could just —

A loud hiss of static burst from the screen. The image juddered, pixilated, then froze. A moment later it was gone, replaced by something entirely different. "My name is Faelan Garret," said a familiar voice. "These are my people and this is how we live."

On the screen, the image painted broad across *Sunrise* plaza, was Daniel's raw footage of the Badlands. The shanty town, the blinded children, the poverty and want.

"We are at your gates now," Faelan's voice continued, buffeted by the wind outside but still audible through the microphone. "The storm is upon us, and if you don't let us in, we'll die out here while you live in peace and plenty."

The scene changed, showed a thin, sun-browned boy with a wide smile, showed Daniel's hand offering the kid chocolate. Jack felt his throat tighten and wondered where the boy was now, if he'd made it out of the Badlands. If he was standing, terrified, before the gates. Then he saw Teal'c carrying a scrap of a child in his arms with the rain lashing across them both.

"Help us," Faelan said, assured and calm. The voice of a leader, not the voice of a beggar. "Open the gates to your brothers and sisters. We too are Iernans, and we have been Outside too long."

Jack heard a sound at his side. Rhionna was swiping the back of her hand across her cheek. Then her chin lifted and she stepped forward. "Listen to him!" she called, but not to the soldiers this time. She spoke to the dazed people of the Ark, who stared in disbelief at the images on the screen before them while the film began to repeat. "He speaks the truth!"

A few of them turned, looking for the source of the voice. Then arms pointed, people caught between the screen and Rhionna. Jack gave her a gentle nudge. "You got their attention," he said. "Better make use of it."

With a nod, she climbed up onto the parapet and balanced there. Neither Tanner nor his soldiers made any move to stop her. "You know who I am," she shouted. "My father is Pastor here, as was my grandfather and his father too! Trust my words if you cannot trust Faelan Garret! The Elect have lied to us, they have fed us sweetmeats and entertainments and kept us in ignorance of the world beyond the Ark! But there is a way to save Ierna, to soothe the burn of the Sun so that our planet can heal and provide for all her people, as she did in the Time Before! But if we do not open our gates and our hearts to those Outside, then our last chance to save our home will be lost!"

"Heresy!" Camus shouted, shoving past the Guards toward Rhionna. "I'll see you Burn for your lies!"

She ignored him. "Open the gates!" she shouted. "Men of the Elect Guard, open the gates! In the name of mercy, open the gates!"

With a curse, Camus snatched a weapon from one of the Guardsmen and aimed it at her.

Helpless, Jack flung himself forward. "Get down!" The bullet whistled past his ear just as he slammed into the parapet.

Rhionna cried out, blood bursting forth from her right leg, her knee buckling.

Then she fell.

Teal'c placed himself between the child he carried and the wind, though he knew his feeble shelter would not save them if Daniel Jackson's plan failed.

Up on the screen images of the Badlands danced behind the rain — the Badlands as they had been before the storm. He had seen such poverty and despair on countless worlds, and it always seemed that wealth and privilege existed no more than a step away from the most desperate want.

Thus was every human world he had ever encountered.

The humans' capacity for greed and selfishness was matched only by their capacity for generosity and altruism; a conundrum of a people, unpredictable as the weather.

Safety lay within the walls of the Ark. But would the people there obey their pity or their fear? Daniel Jackson believed in the goodness of humanity, Teal'c in its capacity for evil.

Thus far, on Ierna, the two were finely balanced.

A scrawny hand clasped his arm. It was the mother of the child he held, and when he looked down he was surprised to see her smiling. Her face was wet, with rain or tears he could not tell, but her eyes were bright. "Now they will know," she shouted over the storm, her thin fingers biting into his arm. "Now they will know of us and our plight; Faelan Garret has given voice to our woes, and they will hear!"

Teal'c inclined his head, but could not share her confidence. He knew all too well the propensity of humans to misinterpret that which they did not wish to hear. By way of reply, he spoke the only truth he could find. "In Faelan Garret, you have a strong leader."

The woman nodded, another squall blowing her against him and forcing him to brace against the wind to keep his balance. "Aye, Faelan speaks for us now," she said. "And now that they know what we suffer, how could they not listen to him?"

Gentling his hand over the child's wet head, Teal'c turned his head from the storm and did not answer. The wave was nearing the shore, its towering silence more terrifying than the roar of the wind. If the people of the Ark were to listen to Faelan Garret, they must do so now or the people of the Badlands would drown. And he, along with Daniel Jackson, would drown with them.

Without thought, Jack flung himself out across the parapet and felt his hand connect with fabric and skin. He held tight though his arm was all but wrenched from its socket as Rhionna's weight tried to drag him over the edge. One arm hooked around a stanchion, he realized that it was only a matter of seconds before he lost his grip or was pulled over with her.

After a white and endless moment of muted panic — a kind

of bright space of total clarity — he felt hands on his shoulders. Pulling. Someone was beside him — Tanner, reaching down to Rhionna — and the weight eased. Jack blinked his vision clear and saw her staring at him, ashen- faced, as he and the Guardsman began to haul her back up.

His arm was almost numb by the time they dragged her to safety, her leg bleeding heavily. And it was only when he slumped against the parapet that his ears cleared enough to hear the outraged protests coming from somewhere to his left. Right arm dangling uselessly, he shifted to see Tynan Camus surrounded by an uncertain group of his own soldiers. Meanwhile, from the plaza below, another sound was beginning to rise.

"Open the gate! Open the gate!"

Bracing himself on the railing with his good hand, Jack looked down to see the once passive audience of *Sunrise* turned away from the screen that still showed Daniel's footage. They were moving toward the vast gates of the Ark. And they weren't alone. People were streaming into the plaza from the surrounding buildings, full of anger and dismay, swelling the crowd. All that stood between them and the gates was a meager line of Elect Guard. "Well, I'll be damned."

Rhionna slouched next to him while Tanner dressed the wound in her leg. She was frightened, but not paralyzed by fear. "Thank you," she said, looking up.

Jack raised an eyebrow. "It's not over yet."

Outside the thunder roared and, beneath it, he sensed the approach of something far more ominous. A vibration, without sound, rippled up through the wall and came to him through the soles of his boots. He had no idea what it was, but he knew sure as hell that it was Bad News.

It felt like what it was: the destruction of a world. Thunder came from the very ground beneath their feet, the wave so close now, an ever moving tower of black water. Sound came at last, when it hit the shore, a roar that drowned out the screams of the people who pressed against each other, seeking shelter that was not there. Only the raw sting in his throat told Daniel that he was yelling too, a fervent plea that his friends had come through.

Onward came the tsumani.

Faelan's voice was a muted rumble now as the footage played on, and Daniel could only hope that the people in the Ark had heard, that they had listened, that they had understood.

But the gates did not open.

They had minutes, if that, and terror was a sharp taste on his tongue. Around him, people tried to squeeze further back, away from what was coming, panic rising and as dangerous as the wave that rolled closer, folding on itself and swallowing land; a relentless juggernaut that left them nowhere to turn. In the press of bodies, Daniel struggled for breath, the crush threatening to suffocate him long before the water hit.

Let them listen. Please let them listen. Let the gates open now.

He flung the prayer into the void, and it seemed that some-one was indeed listening. Above the roar of the wave came another sound, an ear-splitting groan of corroded metal being forced.

The Ark was opening.

The enormous gates swung inward, slow and ponderous, and the frantic crowd surged toward safety. He went with them, caught in the riptide of panic, but when he glanced back over his shoulder all he could see was a wall of water curling over them.

Their plan had worked, but it had worked too late.

Sam felt the noise before she heard it. It rose up through the foundations of the building and shook the walls of the tower as she pelted down the stairs two at a time.

She'd seen no one, not from the moment she'd cracked open the studio door. The building was deserted, and the only voice audible was Faelan's, repeating his plea on every screen she passed. One way or another, she figured, something was happening.

At the bottom of the stairs she gave herself a slow count of five before slipping out onto the street. The noise hit her ears like a wall. A howl of screeching metal and protesting machinery. She hoped to God it was the sound of the gates opening.

Ignoring the fierce throb in her arm, she reached the street corner and stopped again to peer out into the plaza. It was swarming with people, their shouts and cries drowned by the noise that shook the bones of the city. The gates to the Ark were opening. Then, while she still watched, that noise stopped and the abrupt silence was filled with another sound — screams of terror and a terrible thundering roar of a different and much more deadly nature.

The crowd began to surge, back away from the gates, and Sam ducked sideways, sticking close to buildings of the plaza so she could fight her way forward. The gates were open, not fully but enough to admit the stumbling, mud-soaked people from the coast. But it was too late.

Skidding to a halt, Sam bit off a curse. Behind the refugees rose a barrier of water that dwarfed even the Ark's high walls. And it was going to hit, now, while the gates were still open.

As the people of the Ark stumbled back, fleeing from the tidal wave, Sam pushed and shoved her way toward it. "Daniel?" she shouted into the frenzy of noise. "Teal'c?"

She almost ran into the first clot of refugees, standing terrified and disoriented amid the towers of the Ark, clutching their ragged clothes and ragged children to them. "Move!" she yelled, prodding the first of them into motion. "Get away from the gate, let the others in!"

There were faces she half recognized, but didn't have time

to remember, as she continued to push closer to the wall.
The gate opened inward, swinging on ancient hinges, and
cracked maybe ten feet wide. Not wide enough to let all the
refugees stream in at once, but much too wide to be open
when the wave hit.

"Close the gate!" she shouted, though who could hear her
over the noise? "Close the gate!"

And then she saw Daniel. Outside. He was pushing people past him to safety even as the tsunami loomed, poised
to break above his head. "Daniel!" But her scream was swallowed by the din as the gate began to move again — too
late — and the crest of the wave hammered into the dome
of the Ark. "Teal'c!"

Water punched past the closing gates, sweeping everything
before it into the churning flood. Sam thought she glimpsed
brown skin and a flash of gold and then the water hit her, bitter cold and hard as an iron fist.

She went under, felt her weapon snatched from her grasp,
hit something solid and was carried past it. And then she
hit the ground, turning over and over like a pebble in the
surf, until she found herself beached. Water raced over her
like a river, and then like a stream. And then, with a boom-
ing clang, the air sang with startling silence and the deluge
began to ebb away.

Coughing, she hauled herself onto her hands and knees in
the freezing water. Her wounded arm screamed like the devil,
but she ignored it and pushed herself up onto her knees. Her
throat was raw from the gallon of seawater she'd swallowed,
and no amount of spitting could clear the taste from her mouth.
In front of the gates people lay scattered like driftwood on a
beach, while outside the wave kept on coming. She could see
its dark mass over the wall as it surged all around the Ark.

But the gates had closed, cutting off the full force of the
flood. The Ark held. And inside they were safe.

She got to her feet, the fear in her belly colder than the freezing water. If Daniel and Teal'c hadn't made it inside…

Carefully, she began to pick her way through the stunned people. Close to the wall she spotted a patch of olive drab and stayed focused on that. But there were too many people climbing to their feet, getting in the way and making it impossible to be certain. She didn't let herself hope until she saw that patch of color move and resolve itself into a shape. Into a man. He turned and —

"Sam?"

Relief hit her with more force than the tsunami and she broke into a run, shoving through the bewildered crowd as fast as she could. "Daniel!" He'd lost his glasses and was squinting at her past a nasty bruise that already was turning his left cheek scarlet. But he was grinning that I-can't-believe-we-just-did-that grin she knew so well. Sliding to a stop, she gave him a fierce, one armed, hug, then glanced around. "Where's Teal'c?"

"I am here," he said from behind her, his own almost-smile as telling as Daniel's grin. "It is good to see you well, Major Carter."

"You too."

"What happened to Jack?" Daniel asked, sweeping his hands through his hair and trying to squeeze out the water.

Sam shook her head. "We split up. He was going after Tynan…"

Suddenly Daniel grabbed her arm. "Look!"

"What?"

He nodded past her, over her shoulder, and she turned. All around the people of the Badlands were slowly rising. But that wasn't what he meant. Tentatively at first, the citizens of the Ark began to help. A hand here, a word there, but then a woman picked up a crying Badland child and a man offered assistance to a woman who was too injured to walk unaided.

"See that?" Daniel said. "We did that."

Sam smiled. "Yeah," she said. "I guess we did."

"Not alone." Teal'c pointed at the tall figure of Faelan Garret who walked among his people. Sam recognized the swagger in his stride, not bravado now, but confidence. Here walked a leader. He reminded her of someone else she knew.

"Daniel Jackson," Faelan said as he drew closer. For a moment he seemed lost for words, and then he raised his hands to encompass everything around them. "I never thought... Well, in my wildest dreams I never thought to be standing here and not be a prisoner." He offered a slight bow. "We owe you a debt — all of you. You've saved my people."

"Not really," Daniel said with a shiver. "All we wanted was to get home. You'll have to take the credit for leading them here yourself."

Faelan's eyes narrowed. "Will I now?"

"If you don't," Daniel said with a glint in his eye, "I think she will."

Faelan turned sharply, and then his face was split by a smile of heartfelt relief. "Rhionna."

She was already stumbling toward him, through the crowd and into his arms. "Thank the Lord," she whispered against his shoulder. "Thank the Lord you're safe, *grádhán*." Faelan clutched at her, burying his face in her neck, as if she was the only thing that would keep him afloat in the chaos.

Aiming to give them what privacy she could, Sam looked away. As she did, her eyes found another face, and her smile, she feared, probably looked much like Faelan's. "Colonel."

He strolled closer, stopping at a judicious distance from her. "Carter."

From the corner of her eye, she could still see Faelan and Rhionna holding each other tight, oblivious to the world around them. The colonel's gaze flicked in the same direction, then returned to her. For what seemed like an eternity they said nothing. There was nothing they could say. Finally he gestured toward her arm. "You're bleeding."

"Oh." She glanced down at her bloody sleeve. "Just a scratch."

He nodded, eyes fixed on her face. "Good job today, Major."

"Thanks, sir. You too."

And then Daniel was there, and Teal'c, and for a moment everything was right, everything was just as it should be. But only for a moment.

When Rhionna drew back from Faelan, her face aglow with relief and happiness, Sam knew what she had to do. Excusing herself from her team, she made her way over to the couple and touched Rhionna's arm. She felt like hers was the hand of death. "You need to come with me."

Rhionna frowned. "What do you mean?"

"I'm sorry," Sam said. "It's your father."

It was a small, if selfish, reprieve that Rhionna didn't ask for the details of her father's condition. There was no demand for reassurance that his injuries were not severe. Perhaps Sam's face said enough. At any rate, it was clear that Rhionna knew Ennis was dying.

But when they got to the studio door, Rhionna slowed to a halt.

"I can't…" Her face was pale, her jaw tight.

"Rhionna, he doesn't have much longer." Sam placed her hand on the woman's elbow, gently urging her towards the door, but Rhionna pulled back, her eyes locked on the closed door.

"You don't understand, Samantha," she said in voice that battled with tears. "There were times… He was so zealous, so blind. There were times…"

"Times you hated him."

Rhionna's eyes darted towards her, shocked. "Yes," she whispered. "I hated him."

Sam smiled, a sad acknowledgement of what felt like a shameful truth. "And yet you love him too."

Rhionna nodded, her face twisting. "How can that be?"

Sam shrugged, understanding all too well the confusion

of those conflicting emotions. "He's your father," she said simply.

Rhionna looked back at the door. "He's dying."

"Yes."

The words, said out loud, were enough to take her through the door.

The scene inside was much as Sam had left it, with Sorcha pressing the now sodden dressing onto the mortal wound she'd inflicted. Ennis's breaths were shallower now, his pallor more ashen, and Sam wondered if he was even still conscious. But his eyes fluttered open, and he saw his daughter.

"Rhionna."

"Oh God." The tears spilled over in silent sobs, and she went to her father's side, taking the dressing from Sorcha's hands.

The old woman bowed her head. "Rhionna, I –"

"Not now, Sorcha. Leave us." There was steel in Rhionna voice, a sign that recrimination would come later. Sam couldn't help but admire her restraint as Sorcha withdrew from the room, her remorse futile and redundant.

"I'll give you a moment," said Sam, and turned to leave.

"No, please stay." Perhaps it was a need for an ally that prompted Rhionna's request, perhaps the woman sensed that Sam knew what it was to face the death of a parent, but either way it was a plea that Sam couldn't ignore. After a second of hesitation she closed the door and retreated as far as the small room would allow. It wasn't far enough to keep her from overhearing the final words between father and daughter.

"Did you succeed, child?" Ennis's voice was a brittle rasp.

"Hush, father. It doesn't matter." She brushed limp hair back from his forehead, her thumb leaving a trace of red against his gray skin.

With an effort that showed on his face, Ennis reached up to grasp her wrist. "It does matter. Did you succeed?"

"Yes, we did. We brought them inside, Father. Faelan and

I. We succeeded." Her breath caught, her head dropping to his. "I'm sorry, Father. I'm sorry that I couldn't be what you wanted."

Ennis frowned and gave a sluggish blink. "You have…nothing to be sorry for. You did what I could not. What I…what I never tried to do."

"It's not what you believed in."

"A foolish old man, is what I am, child. It's just as well that my time is passing."

Rhionna shook her head. "No, no I won't…" But her words trailed off, as if she'd realized that denial would do no good. She sucked in a breath. "There's more, Father. We think we've found *Sciath Dé* — we think it's here, within the Ark. And we can make it work, we can save Ierna."

"*Sciath Dé*." The words rode on a mere wheeze. "Yes, it is here…"

Rhionna sat back, eyes wide. "You knew? You knew it was in the Ark?"

His hand reached for hers again, fumbling and blind. "Forgive me. I was… a coward, Rhionna. I was too afraid to believe that things could change."

"Where?" The steel in her voice was back, threading through her grief. "Where is it, Father?"

"The library…"

Rhionna closed her eyes. "The Elect knew, didn't they? All this time, for generations…" Tears fell again, but Sam saw as much anger as loss in them. "They let our world die just to protect their — " She let out a slow breath. With a gentle hand she touched her father's face. "Thank you," she said. "Thank you for telling me now."

He smiled. "You have always been the brave one, my child. So fierce. Like your mother. You will make a fine Pastor."

From the look on her face, it wasn't something she'd considered. "I don't know how to be Pastor. I don't *want* to be Pastor."

"Then you are more suited to the duty than anyone." His eyes looked heavier now and his voice was so weak that Sam could barely make out the words. "You will restore pride and honor to our family, Rhionna. I am so sorry that I sought to douse the courage in your heart…"

"No, Father. Please…" Her voice caught on a desperate sob. Ennis Channon was no longer alive to hear her.

Sam bit the inside of her cheek and turned away. It hurt too much to see Rhionna's raw grief as she wept over her father's body. It was a scene that dredged up to painful memories, and Rhionna would not be given the reprieve that Sam had been granted; there would be no Tok'ra symbiote to save the life of Ennis Channon.

Sam was just about to leave when the door opened and Faelan entered, his expression solemn. Clearly the death of the man who had persecuted his kind for so long was no victory to Faelan Garret. Catching Sam's eye, he nodded, a subtle dismissal. *I've got this*, it said, and she was glad to know that Rhionna would find some comfort in her grief. The last thing she saw on leaving the room was Rhionna falling into Faelan's waiting embrace.

CHAPTER TWENTY-ONE

A NEW dawn rose, two days after the storm had abated, and beyond the opalescent dome of the Ark, the sun had returned to bake the world of Ierna. Inside, however, things had started to change. Not just because the population of an almost empty city had doubled, but because minds had opened as wide as the gates of the Ark. And the omnipresent screens had fallen dark and silent.

The atmosphere in the city had acquired an edge, and Jack recognized it as it prickled the hairs on the back of his neck. A charge, an energy that just skirted the edges of danger. Hope and fear mingled in the certain knowledge that change had come and the future was unknown. He'd felt it before, on other worlds and sometimes on his own.

He'd felt it on P3R-118 when the glass ceiling had shattered and the light had blinded the people even as their eyes were opened to the truth.

His gaze wandered over to the men lined up before the open Stargate, their black robes stark in the morning sun. The Elect faced the judgment of another people whose eyes had been opened to the lies they'd been served with their morning coffee and evening entertainment. With the grim-faced stoicism of martyrs the former leaders accepted their exile, and Jack wondered if they truly believed they'd done the Lord's work. Then again he knew all too well the power of wanting something to be true, the mind's capacity to deceive itself when truth was hard and the lie so much easier to bear.

He pulled his shades from his pocket and slipped them on, aware of Teal'c hovering at his shoulder and suspicious, as always, of the Jaffa's uncanny ability to see right through him.

"The punishment is severe," Teal'c said, watching as

Rhionna Channon stepped forward to speak. "But just."

"I give them fifty-fifty odds," Jack agreed. "More, if they figure out how to dial another gate address."

"Indeed," Teal'c agreed. "*Acarsaid Dorch* is a harsh environment for men more used to luxury than labor."

Walking up the stairs that lead to the Stargate, Rhionna looked out across the crowd that had gathered on the manicured lawn outside the Chambers and beneath its cloistered walkways. Most were Badland refugees, but there were Seachráni and citizens of the Ark among them too. Then she looked down to where Faelan stood and, with a gesture, beckoned him to join her on the platform. Jack could see his hesitation, but it was momentary, and he felt a beat of satisfaction as he watched the man step up next to Rhionna. They exchanged a serious look of understanding, no smiles, before Rhionna turned back to the crowd.

"We stand before you," she said, "not as Seachráni or Elect, but as citizens of Ierna. We are two peoples united where we were once divided by the tragedy that has befallen our world. Together we can reclaim Ierna from the seas, together we can promise our children's children land as far as the eye can see, planted with grain enough to feed ten thousand mouths!" She glanced at Faelan. "The Ark was built as a place of refuge for all, a temporary shelter while *Sciath Dé* saved our world from disaster. At last, it will serve its true purpose and all those who share our desire to change our world are welcome here in peace and friendship."

On cue — Jack figured they'd rehearsed — Faelan spoke. "*An Dóchas Deireanach* is no more. The Seachráni home has gone forever, claimed by the sea. It was named the place of Last Hope by men and women who witnessed the end of their world and hoped for a better future for their children. We are their children — all of us. We are Ierna's children and in us that hope has survived. Now we stand here, together, in the Ark — in *an Dóchas a Mhaireann*."

There was a murmur of unease at the sound of the forbidden name. Tynan Camus, his robes shifting as he moved, spat on the ground and made some kind of warding gesture across his chest. But Faelan didn't hesitate, he only raised his voice. Jack smiled.

"We stand together in this, the place of *Lasting* Hope." Reaching out he took Rhionna's hand, lifting it high. "We have a saying among the Seachráni — *ni neart go cur le cheile*. There is no strength without unity. Together we are stronger, together we will rebuild our world. Together we shall live beneath a kindly sky and raise our children to love, not fear, the sunrise."

Silence fell. Absolute silence. Then the applause began, far toward the back of the crowd, and it rolled forward in a wave of enthusiasm until it became thunderous. Jack flung a look at Teal'c, who merely raised an eyebrow.

After a minute, Faelan lifted his hands to quell the crowd, and then Rhionna spoke again. "Before us stand the Elect, men whose lies have denied us, for generations, the means to heal our world. I offer them this choice; disavow your faith and join with us to rebuild Ierna, or leave through the Sungate to *Acarsaid Dorch* and live there amid the lies you have sown." She looked down at the row of men and women. "Who will join us?"

Tynan Camus stepped forward, signs of strain and fear marking his face, but defiant to the end. Jack could almost admire him for that. But not quite. "Know this," Tynan said, loud enough to be heard by half the crowd. "The Lord will punish your crimes; you have defied His Will, consorted with the damned and brought them within the Ark. Your sins will be scoured from the land and only the faithful will be spared." He turned, addressing the silent crowd. "Only damnation awaits you! Though you send us to hell it is you who will Burn beneath the Lord's wrath, it is you who — "

Something hit him. Tynan cried out, clutching his head as

blood spilled through his fingers from a gash above his eye. Then another stone was thrown. Another of the Elect was hit. The Guards didn't move, seeming nervous and unsure. And Jack saw the whole damn situation about to unravel.

"Teal'c," he said. "With me."

In two steps, he was in the thick of it and felt a stone hit his shoulder. "Tanner," he snapped at the Captain of the Guard, "get your men between the prisoners and the crowd. Faelan — give the damn order already!"

"Open the Sungate!" Faelan barked.

Jack sent a nod to Teal'c who strode over to the DHD as Jack started backing up. "Move!" he ordered the crowd as the gate began to spin. "Clear the area."

Almost tripping over their robes, the Elect stumbled backward as the last chevron locked and the event horizon surged out amid a whoosh of static and ozone. The awed crowd froze, stones dropping from limp fingers. Even Faelan looked speechless. It was Rhionna who moved first. "The Sungate is open. You have made your choice. *Acarsaid Dorch* awaits."

With the mob at their back, and hell before them, the Elect shuffled forward. Some muttered prayers, others curses. Rhionna's face remained impassive as they filed past her, she didn't even stir when Tynan Camus spat at her feet — save to put a restraining hand on Faelan's arm.

At the top of the stairs, the showman even now, Tynan lifted his arms to the sky and cried out, "I surrender myself to thy care, oh Lord!" Without looking back he vanished into the unknown.

Unknown to him, at least. Jack knew exactly what awaited him: snow, rock, and a long abandoned research station. Fifty-fifty odds, at least; men like Tynan Camus had a nasty habit of coming back and biting you in the ass.

Calmly Jack watched as the rest of the Elect followed, preferring the terrors of *Acarsaid Dorch* to the prospect of being proven wrong. When the last man had been swallowed by the event horizon, the wormhole collapsed and the gate was still once more.

It was over.

Rhionna looked shell-shocked, same as Faelan. Perhaps they'd just figured out that the whole expectant crowd was looking to them, waiting to be led. They shared a glance, then Rhionna said, "Now we wait for *Sciath Dé* — for the new world to begin."

And Jack sure as hell hoped she was right. Behind his sunglasses he squinted toward the ugly tower that housed the Ark's so-called library. If Carter didn't get the damn shield working, he doubted that the fragile coalition between the Seachráni and the Ark would last. Hope was pretty much all these people had left, and if they lost that... Well, it didn't take a genius to figure out what would happen next.

Daniel's initial reaction when Sam told him where the shield was hidden was skepticism. He'd been to the library and seen for himself the dusty, half empty shelves that hadn't held a book in almost two hundred years. It was an insult to the name 'library'; repository for knowledge it was not, much less the site for an advanced planetary shield.

"Are you sure it's here?" he said, trying not to sneeze as the dust motes swirled around him.

"Daniel..." It wasn't the first time he'd asked the question, and Sam's patience seemed to be wearing thin.

"Sorry. It's just..." He gestured at the abandoned stacks of *Sunrise* scripts and recordings. "Look at this place."

"Ennis said we'd find it here," she said, unbuckling her pack.

"Exactly. *Ennis* said we'd find it here. The man wanted us to fail from the get-go."

Sam shook her head. "You weren't there. He wouldn't have lied to her, Daniel. Believe me."

Daniel sighed, unable to do anything but trust Sam's conviction. "Then where do we start looking? What are we even looking for?"

She shrugged. "I have no idea, but I'll know when I find it."

Before they had a chance to begin their search, a noise from the other end of the library made both of them start. Sam's hand flew to her sidearm, but Daniel stayed her with a gesture. He recognized the man standing in the shadows of a stack. "Liam?"

The librarian edged out from his hiding place. "Am I to be sent with them?"

"What are you talking about?"

"The others. You've sent them to *Acarsaid Dorch*. Am I to be exiled too?"

Daniel thought for a moment, figuring it out. "You're one of the Elect too."

"I am the Archivist, as was my father and his father before him." He was on edge, wary and nervous; Daniel noticed that Sam's hand had not left her gun. Hesitating briefly, Liam added, "My family has guarded the library's secrets since the Flood."

"Its secrets?" It took a few moments for the words to make sense to Daniel.

By the time that happened, Sam had piped up. "The shield. You know where it is?"

Liam paused. "Is it true that Ennis told you the truth in the end?"

"That's what we want to find out," she said. "He said it's here in the library."

The librarian looked away with a nod and a slight smile, as if some belief had just been affirmed. Then he strode to a towering shelf, his gait purposeful now, all hesitancy gone. He slid his fingers into the gap between the shelving and the wall and, with a grunt of effort, he pulled. The shelf teetered on its edge and came crashing down in a blizzard of yellowed paper.

He moved to the next bookshelf, toppling that one too. Without another word, Daniel and Sam joined him in his task of tearing the library apart, first the shelves, then the wooden panels behind them. Once they were done they stood back, out of breath, and admired their handiwork. Behind one of the discarded wall panels they'd found a computer interface.

"It looks like the technology we found on *Acarsaid Dorch*," said Sam, approaching it with something akin to wonder. She ran her hand over one of the keyboards and turned to Liam. "Is it?"

"Yes, Major Carter," replied the librarian. "This is the Knowledge you seek. This is God's Shield."

A familiar weariness settled bone-deep into Jack as he made his way with Teal'c and Faelan to the library. The adrenaline high of the past few days over, he was braced for post-battle lethargy, a fatigue that also was evident in the heavy gait of the man who walked alongside him. Faelan Garret looked as if he wanted to sleep for an entire day at least. Shame he wouldn't get the chance.

"You've got a job ahead of you," Jack said, though he guessed Faelan already knew as much.

Garret nodded and scrubbed a hand over his face. "I don't know whether to blame you or thank you," he said with a faint smile.

"I should probably get out of here before you've had time to figure that one out." Grinning, Jack added, "You'll do just fine."

"Maybe. At least I won't be doing it alone." Faelan's smile grew broader at the mention of Rhionna.

Jack scratched his jaw and looked away. "Where'd the new Pastor get to anyway?"

"She had other business to take care of." Faelan's expression had turned serious.

Business concerning the one person who'd been conspicuously absent for the past few days, Jack surmised. Given what Carter had told him of Sorcha's part in Ennis's death, he was curious to know how exactly Rhionna intended to take care of that particular business. He had his own thoughts on the matter, but kept them to himself. And anyway, it was time to get off this planet, let these people sort their own future out.

Of course, before they did that they had one final item on their own agenda to take care of. "Do you think it's up there?" he asked, tilting back his head to take in the tall building directly in front of them.

"It could be I suppose. Though I can't see what good it'll do us now — the damage to our world is already done."

"Major Carter seems to think it could still help your people," said Teal'c, as they entered the foyer and made their way to the elevator.

"I hope she's right."

"Yeah," Jack muttered, "me too."

However, when the elevator doors slid open, it appeared that their doubts had been misplaced. The room was a wreck, shelves and paper and data cartridges strewn all around, and in the sunken central area the floor was gone entirely. In its place a huge metal disc thrummed with an energy that coursed right up through Jack's boots. Carter stood next to it, grinning with triumph.

"Just in time for the main show, sir," she said.

Jack gave a brief laugh, part amazement, part disbelief. "It works?""

"That's what we're about to find out." She turned to Faelan, who stood open-mouthed, staring. "If it does work though, Faelan, it's not a quick fix. It could take generations for you to see real benefits."

"At least there'll be future generations to see those benefits, Major Carter. I don't know if I can express my gratitude for that."

"Letting us come back and study this technology will be thanks enough."

"That goes without saying."

She gestured at the console in the wall. "Care to do the honors?"

He nodded, unable to hide his eagerness, and followed Sam to the console, where Daniel and the librarian guy, Beaker or Gonzo, or whatever his name was, were poring over the controls.

"You are not confident in this endeavor, O'Neill." Evidently, Teal'c didn't share his CO's reluctance to voice any lingering doubts.

Jack looked over to where Carter, with no small amount of enthusiasm, was explaining the workings of the console to Faelan. "Well, that'd just make me the guy who punches Santa in the mouth on Christmas morning. I'd much rather say something profound, about long journeys or small steps and huge leaps or some other cliché. Besides" — he rocked back on his heels, looking down at the vibrating floor — "it's hard to deny that something's happening here."

The next few moments were to prove, conclusively, that something was most definitely happening. With a grind of machinery, the roof itself slid open, bathing the library in filtered sunlight. The metal disc in the center of the room shone, brighter and brighter, like a coin tossed into a fire, and with a blast of energy that shook the entire building, a beam of light shot upward from its surface, piercing the dome and flooding the sky beyond.

"Well, I'll be damned," said Jack. There didn't seem to be any other way to put it.

Rhionna picked her way through what remained of the Badlands, the savage noon heat clawing at her heavy sunwear. It was a landscape transformed, scoured by the ocean and turned alien and strange. Debris from the depths of the sea — from a world long lost — lay scattered in the mud, baking hard beneath the sun. Some things she recognized — the overturned hull of the *Fánaí na Mara*, a solar sail. Others were a mystery, tantalizing hints of her people's drowned history.

But seabed treasures had not drawn her from the Ark. She had come outside in search of something else — she hardly knew what to call it. Resolution, perhaps. The closing of the past, and the opening of a future unknown.

Parched mud cracked beneath her boots, stirring dust into the stink of the air; drying seaweed and rotting fish made pungent in the noontide furnace. She should find shelter until the Burn had passed, but she did not have long and could not afford to tarry.

The familiar paths within the Badlands were gone, but she knew her direction in spite of it. How many times had she walked this way? Blind, she could have found her way to the scrap of tarp that flapped in the desiccating Badland winds.

She approached slowly, letting her presence be heard, and stopped some short distance away.

Sorcha Caratauc sat in scant shade with her bony knees drawn up to her chest and her eyes upon the glitter of the sea. Placid now, the ocean was a mere ghost of the monster that had wrought so much destruction upon the land.

Rhionna dared not remove her sunwear to meet Sorcha's gaze full on. Besides, the old woman was determinedly not looking at her.

"Why have you come?" she said at last, voice as dry and cracked as the Badlands themselves.

"In search of you."

The only sound was the distant lap of the waves on the shore, the whisper of the wind across the land. "I have spent my life collecting words," Sorcha said at last. "And yet I now find that I have none to give you this day. What words are enough to speak of my remorse?"

Rhionna crouched to Sorcha's level. The sun burned into her back, but she did not move. "You know what my father was, Sorcha Caratauc; he died a better man than he lived."

Moisture glinted on the old woman's cheek, tracing the lines of her face. "You have a right to hate me."

"No." She stretched out her hand and took Sorcha's dry fingers in her own. "What you are, Sorcha, this place has made you. You carry no blame."

"I killed your father, girl."

"He earned his own fate. But I take comfort that his last act was to share the truth."

Sorcha blinked, sharp eyes a glint beneath her brow. "The truth?"

"About *Sciath Dé*."

Like new blood flowing, hope surged through the old woman's veins. "Then you have found it?"

Rhionna smiled and rose to her feet. Above her the Ark gleamed, a giant oyster pearl offered to the sky. She held out her hand. "Come," she said. "Look."

Holding her ragged scarf tight around her head, Sorcha pushed herself upright. "Look at what?"

"Wait…"

And then it happened, as Samantha Carter had promised it would. A flare shot up from the Ark, and a rainbow flash of light danced across the deep blue sky until a dozen ghostly crescent moons shimmered far above. *Sciath Dé*, the last hope of their ancestors, spread over their world to shield them from the sun. Rhionna held her breath, not sure what to expect next. Then, though the sunlight did not dim, she felt a change in the heat.

Sorcha felt it too, pulling her hand out from within her long sleeve and turning it over in the sunlight. "It does not burn," she said, her voice a whisper of disbelief. "I had never thought to see this day. It does not burn…"

Smiling, Rhionna pulled off her sunwear. Sunlight fell on

her, a benign heat, and she raised her face to welcome it for the first time in her life. "This is only the beginning, Sorcha."

"Aye, that it is."

She looked at the old woman; the wrinkled face was as marked and damaged as ever, but her eyes were alive with renewed hope. The hope of her people, a hope she had carried almost single-handed her whole life. "I speak now for the people of the Ark," Rhionna said. "Faelan speaks for the Seachráni." Sorcha's eyes narrowed; she knew what was coming, but Rhionna forged on regardless. "Will you speak for the people of the Badlands, Sorcha Caratauc?"

"Inside the Ark?"

"We are one people now," Rhionna said, once more holding out her hand. "*Ni neart go cur le cheile.*"

Sorcha hesitated a moment, then threw back her scarf and shook out her tangled gray hair. It glinted like steel in the sunlight. "Strength in unity," she said, and took Rhionna's hand in her strong grip. "And we shall need every bit of it upon the path ahead."

Rhionna answered only with a nod, and together they began the walk, out of the Badlands and toward the bright, uncertain future.

CHAPTER TWENTY-TWO

"...AND SO," Major Carter concluded, "although the shield wasn't exactly what we'd been hoping for, I actually think it could be very valuable."

Hammond folded his hands on the desk, casting his eyes over the schematics the major had distributed. "But not against the Goa'uld."

"No, sir. But Faelan said we can return any time to study the technology and, as I'm sure you already know, geo-engineering is increasingly considered the way forward in tackling climate change."

"Yes," Jack agreed. "We already knew that."

Major Carter smiled, shifting in her seat to accommodate the sling that supported her arm. "Let's hope it never comes to that, sir, but the ability to deflect significant amounts of solar radiation might be important one day."

"So they say."

Her eyes widened. "So they *say*?"

"Come on." He cast a conspiratorial glance at Dr. Jackson. "You know what these scientists are like, Carter, it's all about the research funding."

"With all due respect, sir, that's — "

"Oh, he's right," Daniel said. "I mean, they'll come up with any crackpot theory to get money out of the government."

Teal'c lifted an eyebrow. "Such as pyramids being landing platforms for alien space craft?"

Daniel pointed a finger at him. "Exactly!"

Carter shook her head, caught between exasperation and amusement. "Okay, guys, I get it. Ha-ha, very funny."

O'Neill spread his hands. "What?"

Hammond let it ride for a moment, enjoying the camaraderie between the team, then he held up his hand for silence. "People, I'm going to consider this mission a success — on both technological and humanitarian grounds. Job well done."

Serious now, O'Neill nodded. "Thank you, sir."

"Dr. Fraiser tells me Major Carter will be fit to return to duty in one week. So, until then, consider yourselves stood down." He got to his feet, signaling the end of the debrief. While SG-1 gathered their papers and began to leave, he said, "Colonel, a word?"

With a glance at the departing team, O'Neill followed Hammond into his office. "Sir?"

Hammond perched on the corner of his desk, taking in the sunburned face and wary eyes of his second-in-command. "I think you know what I'm going to ask."

"If it's about the golf clubs — "

"Jack."

He plunged his hands into his pockets, rebellious as a schoolboy.

"I still have Dr. Fraiser's report on my desk, Colonel, and I need to know how your team is coping."

"How?" He shrugged. "The usual way. We're getting on with it, sir. That's what we do. You want me to say everything's fine now? One mission down and it's like P3R-118 never happened? I can't do that. You know I can't."

There were shadows in his eyes, and George Hammond knew better than to dig deeper into what had happened between the team in Caulder's power plant. Fraiser had her concerns, that was her job, but Hammond had commanded men for a long time, and he knew when to intervene and when to step back. With Jack O'Neill, it was almost always worth stepping back. "You helped a lot of people on Ierna," he said, getting up and moving behind his desk. "It wasn't the mission objective, son. You didn't have to do that."

O'Neill gave half a shrug. "Actually, sir, I think we did. Turns out it's kind of an SG-1 thing."

"Yes, it is." Hammond sat down, and O'Neill met his gaze with a frank stare. "It's good to have you back, Jack. All of you."

"Thanks, sir. It's good to be back."

They exchanged a look, their understanding mutual and unspoken. Then Hammond said, "Before you go, I have something you might be interested in. For your eyes only, of course; if you tell anyone you've seen it, you're on your own."

He slid a file over the desk, and O'Neill picked it up with a raised eyebrow. "Sir?"

"They're calling it the X-301 Interceptor. I thought you and Teal'c might like to check it out."

Finally, Jack O'Neill grinned. "Now *that* sounds like fun…"

AUTHOR BIOGRAPHY

J. FRANCES CRANE is the pen name of Sally Malcolm and Laura Harper.

Sally has penned three novels in the Stargate universe - STARGATE SG-1 *A Matter of Honor*, STARGATE SG-1 *The Cost of Honor*, and STARGATE ATLANTIS *Rising*, the novelization of the pilot episodes. She has also written several Stargate audio dramas for Big Finish, including STARGATE SG-1 "Gift of the Gods" and STARGATE ATLANTIS "Savarna". Her latest audio drama, STARGATE SG-1 "An Eye for an Eye", staring Michael Shanks and Claudia Black, will be available in 2011.

STARGATE SG-1 *Sunrise* is Laura's debut novel.

Writing as J. Frances Crane, Laura Harper and Sally Malcolm have recently completed their first original novel, *Sherwood*.

SNEAK PREVIEW

STARGATE SG-I: TRANSITIONS

by Sabine C. Bauer

THE DOOR stood open and George Hammond liked to think that this was a tradition he'd established. His door had always been open, to anyone. Jack sat behind the desk, looking a little unkempt for a CO — but then, what else was new? — and balefully contemplated the mountain of paperwork in his in-tray.

Biting back a smile, Hammond briskly rapped his knuckles on the doorjamb. "Permission to enter?"

The answer was a preoccupied grunt, followed by a double take, and then Jack shot from the chair and to attention. "General! That's a surprise! I didn't know you were coming."

This time there was no biting back anything. Hammond grinned. "At ease, Jack, for Pete's sake! And it's George, remember? I thought we'd discussed this."

"We have. And I've been practicing in front of the mirror every morning. Still doesn't quite sit right." Smiling, Jack swung around the desk, hand outstretched, and they shook. "Good to see you… George. Come on in. Have a seat. Have *your* seat."

"Visitor's chair'll do just fine, Jack. Don't give me any ideas." Hammond sat down, actually quite enjoying the view from the other side of the table. He missed the place, to be sure. What he didn't miss was the price you had to pay. Too many lives lost, and every one of them still haunted him.

Jack returned to his chair — *his* chair — and contrived to look like a kid who'd stolen into the headmaster's office to sit behind the man's desk for a dare. "So, what brings you here, sir... George? Routine inspection?" He was only half joking. The other half, well, that had been obvious in his emails.

"Hardly." Hammond chuckled. "I know for a fact that you're filling my — how did you put it? — very big, very shiny shoes just fine, Jack." The chuckle died. "As a matter of fact, I'm here to make you an offer you can't refuse."

"Oh?" Curiosity and suspicion just about balanced out in that little question. And the suspicion wasn't misplaced, either. Jack wouldn't like it. Much. At first.

Leaning forward, Hammond plucked the name sign off the desk and flicked his index finger at the single star on it. "You'll need a new one, Jack. That's the headliner. You'll be bumped up to major general, and I'm genuinely thrilled to be the one telling you."

Of course he'd known better than to expect a victory dance. Jack's eyes narrowed. "Where's the snag?"

"The President wants you in Washington."

"Ah." Jack settled back in the chair, found himself a pen to fiddle with. "And if I refuse this offer I can't refuse, they'll slip a horse's head into my bed one night?"

"In the immortal words of Dr. Jackson, don't be an ass, Jack."

"Sir... George... I don't want to seem ungrateful, but..." He might not seem ungrateful, but he certainly seemed to be at a loss for words. For a motor mouth Jack sure wasn't much of a talker, especially when it came to people or things he cared about. "Eight years ago you dragged me back here kicking and screaming. Turns out it was the right thing to do... I think. I belong here, which was why I agreed to run the show when you left. At least I know how you'd want this place to be run... I think." The pen sailed through the air, turned a tidy little somersault. Jack caught it, tossed it again.

"What I'm trying to say, General… what I'm trying to say, I belong *here*."

Those last three words were loaded. George Hammond sure as hell shared the sentiment. What was more, he understood it perfectly. When he'd first come here, it was a dead-end posting for surplus generals awaiting retirement. For a good long while he'd babysat a defunct piece of alien technology. Then that had changed in one big hurry, and before he rightly knew what hit him he'd had a war on his hands - and a couple hundred men and women who'd turned into a close-knit family. No wonder really, given that it was them against any number of worlds. Hammond knew what it meant to be part of that family. But still…

"Jack, the war is over. You won. Which is to say that promotion isn't a bribe. Not entirely, anyway." Hammond sighed. "You've become a member of a very select club. Your commander-in-chief has made this a request, not an order. That aside he's been shrewd enough to realize that I'd be the messenger least likely to get shot. As for me, I might not have played along, except I happen to think he's right. You're wasted here."

"As opposed to Washington? You know me, sir. It's not as if 'diplomacy' is my middle name. I'd just lower the tone."

Hammond snorted. "With all due respect, son, not even you could manage that."

"Wanna bet?"

"At the risk of repeating myself, Jack, the war is over. Which means you've become a glorified bellhop shuttling luggage to and from Atlantis."

"Tips are good." The mulish look on Jack's face brightened to something close to hopeful. "Besides, what if we've missed a couple dozen Ba'al clones?"

Oh yeah, definitely psychedelic. Hammond stifled another sigh. "The Pentagon doesn't think so. Neither does the IOA. They're married to the bellhop version. Meaning that the

SGC will be looking at massive cuts in funding. And that's not speculation, it's a promise."

"It's idiotic, that's what!"

"I couldn't agree more." Now that he'd finally grabbed Jack's full and undivided attention — not to mention indignation — Hammond allowed himself a small bout of relief. Maybe, just maybe, he could stop twisting the man's arm before he snapped a bone. "They're not looking past the obvious. Which is a) the Goa'uld are no longer a threat, and b) every time you activate the gate their electricity bill goes up by a few hundred thousand bucks. Do the math, Jack."

"What about exploration? Daniel's rocks and scrolls and anthropologically significant tea cozies? Those alien technologies everybody used to salivate over?"

"They figure the Atlantis expedition can cover all of that. With the possible exception of the tea cozies, but I very much doubt Congress will make those a budget consideration. Anyway, general consensus — however misguided — is that Atlantis can do what we're doing without damn near shorting out the North American power grid every time they're at it."

Jack's mouth had become a thin, hard line of fury, as if he were struggling to keep in an encyclopedia's worth of undoubtedly colorful invective. "And the off-world sites?" he snapped.

"Scrubbed. Ideally they want you to start pulling out personnel by the end of next month."

"Great! Just great! And I suppose I'm to nail the gate shut personally the second the last man trots down the ramp?"

"That hypothetical task would fall to your successor. Unless you manage to prevent it, of course."

"Do I look like the great and powerful Oz?"

The outburst was followed by a leaden pause Hammond knew better than to interrupt. Let the man take his time to think it through. Or let the silence get so uncomfortable that he couldn't help but say something. Anything. Of course, experience showed that in Jack's case, *anything* was more likely than *something*, simply because he knew every trick in the book, including this one.

Not for the first time, Jack surprised him. "So how would I go about preventing it?" he said at last, sounding amazingly calm.

"You do what the President's asking you to do, Jack. What they need to hear over there is the point of view of someone who's been there and done that and knows which way the galactic cookie crumbles. Even better if that someone is a bona fide hero." Hammond clocked the wince that word triggered and felt entirely unrepentant. It was true, and every now and again it needed to be said, even if the guy at the receiving end bristled at it. "In other words, you go to Washington and be undiplomatic. I think President Hayes is counting on you to make one hell of a nuisance of yourself."

"I guess I could do that," he offered cautiously. "Kinda comes natural. When would I leave?"

"Yesterday." George Hammond got within a hair of letting out a good old yell. Of all the victories he'd won throughout a long and distinguished career this one ranked right up there among the ten most improbable.

"Not gonna happen, sir. I'd like a chance to pack my toothbrush if you and the commander-in-chief don't mind. I'll also have to talk to people... Daniel's gonna be pissed, and that's just for starters. Teal'c's gonna sulk. Loudly. And Carter..." Jack dropped the pen and scrubbed his hands over his face. "You sure a nice, drawn-out root canal wouldn't do as well, sir? I'd volunteer to forego the anesthetic."

"Don't think that'll be an option, son. Sorry." Okay, Hammond wasn't sorry in the slightest. He felt relieved. And a little guilty. But only a little. At the end of the day it would be good for Jack. Not to mention the Stargate program. He rose. "You made the right choice, Jack. Even if it won't strike you that way for a while yet."

"You got that right," Jack muttered and pushed himself to his feet. "End of next week good enough?"

"End of next week will be fine." Hammond smiled and saluted briskly. "Congratulations, Major General O'Neill. Give 'em hell!"

STARGATE
SG·1

STARGATE
ATLANTIS™

SG∘U
STARGATE UNIVERSE™

Original novels based on the hit TV shows **STARGATE SG-1**, **STARGATE ATLANTIS** and **STARGATE UNIVERSE**

AVAILABLE NOW

For more information, visit

www.stargatenovels.com

STARGATE SG-1: TRANSITIONS

by Sabine C. Bauer
Price: $7.95 US | £6.99 UK
ISBN-10: 1-905586-52-3
ISBN-13: 978-1-905586-52-3
Publication date: April 2011

After her mother's death, Cassie Fraiser is moving on. So she thinks. But there are dangerous forces at work and she soon finds herself caught up in a situation far beyond her control. It's a good job Colonel Sam Carter has been keeping an eye on her...

But while Carter rallies SG-1 to Cassie's aid, events on Atlantis are going from bad to worse. Faced with a deadly plague and a computer virus that is shutting down the entire city, it looks like Colonel Sheppard's team will provide rich pickings for the in-coming Wraith hive ship.

But sometimes events galaxies apart are connected in unexpected ways — and help comes from the most surprising of places. In this action-packed story, Sabine Bauer brings together the heroes of STARGATE SG-1 and STARGATE ATLANTIS in the fight of their lives...

STARGATE SG-1: OCEANS OF DUST

by Peter J. Evans
Price: $7.95 US | £6.99 UK
ISBN-10: 1-905586-53-1
ISBN-13: 978-1-905586-53-0
Publication date: March 2011

Something lurks beneath the ancient sands of Egypt. It is the stuff of Jaffa nightmares, its name a whisper in the dark. And it is stirring…

When disaster strikes an Egyptian dig, SG1 are brought in to investigate. But nothing can prepare them for what they find among the ruins. Walking in the dust of a thousand deaths, they discover a creature of unimaginable evil – a creature the insane Goa'uld Neheb-Kau wants to use as a terrible weapon.

With Teal'c and Major Carter in the hands of the enemy, Colonel O'Neill and Daniel Jackson recruit Master Bra'tac to help track the creature across the galaxy in a desperate bid to destroy it before it turns their friends – and the whole galaxy – to dust…

STARGATE SG-1: FOUR DRAGONS

by Diana Botsford
Price: $7.95 US | £6.99 UK
ISBN-10: 1-905586-48-5
ISBN-13: 978-1-905586-48-6
Publication date: August 2010

It was meant to be a soft mission, something to ease Doctor Daniel Jackson back into things after his time among the Ancients — after all, what could possibly go wrong on a simple survey of ancient Chinese ruins? As it turns out, a whole lot.

After accidentally activating a Goa'uld transport ring, Daniel finds himself the prisoner of Lord Yu, the capricious Goa'uld System Lord. Meanwhile, SG1's efforts to rescue their friend are hampered by a representative of the Chinese government with an agenda of his own to follow - and a deep secret to hide.

But Colonel Jack O'Neill is in no mood for delay. He'll go to any lengths to get Daniel back — even if it means ignoring protocol and taking matters into his own hands.

(cover text) Jack takes matters into his own hands to save Daniel

STARGATE SG·1.

FOUR DRAGONS

Diana Botsford

Based on the hit television series developed by **Brad Wright and Jonathan Glassner**

Series number: SG1-16

Order your copy directly from the publisher today by going to www.stargatenovels.com or send a check or money order made payable to "Fandemonium" to:

<u>USA orders:</u> $10.95 ($7.95 + $3.00 P&P).

<u>Rest of world:</u> $13.95 ($7.95 + $6.00 P&P)

Send payment to: Fandemonium Books, PO Box 2178, Decatur, GA 30031-2178 USA.

Or check your local bookshop – available on special order if they are out of stock (quote the ISBN number listed above).

STARGATE SG-1: THE POWER BEHIND THE THRONE

by Steven Savile
Price: $7.95 US | £6.99 UK
ISBN-10: 1-905586-45-0
ISBN-13: 978-1-905586-45-1
Publication date: August 2010

SG-1 are asked by the Tok'ra to rescue a creature known as Mujina.

The last of its species, Mujina is devoid of face or form and draws its substance from the needs of those around it.

The creature is an archetype – a hero for all, a villain for all, depending upon whose influence it falls under.

And the Goa'uld Apophis, understanding the potential for havoc Mujina offers, has set his heart on possessing the creature…

Order your copy directly from the publisher today by going to www.stargatenovels.com or send a check or money order made payable to "Fandemonium" to:

<u>USA orders:</u> **$10.95 ($7.95 + $3.00 P&P).**

<u>Rest of world:</u> **$13.95 ($7.95 + $6.00 P&P)**

Send payment to: Fandemonium Books, PO Box 2178, Decatur, GA 30031-2178 USA.

Or check your local bookshop – available on special order if they are out of stock (quote the ISBN number listed above).

STARGATE ATLANTIS: HOMECOMING

Book one in the new LEGACY SERIES

by Jo Graham & Melissa Scott
Price: £6.99 UK | $7.95 US
ISBN-10: 1-905586-50-7
ISBN-13: 978-1-905586-50-9
Publication date: October 2010

Atlantis has returned to Earth, its team has disbursed and are beginning new lives far from the dangers of the Pegasus galaxy. They think the adventure is over.

They're wrong.

With the help of General Jack O'Neill, Atlantis rises once more—and the former members of the expedition must decide whether to return with her to Pegasus, or to remain safely on Earth in the new lives they enjoy...

Picking up where the show's final season ended, Stargate Atlantis Homecoming is the first in the exciting new Stargate Atlantis Legacy series. These all new adventures take the Atlantis team back to the Pegasus galaxy where a terrible new enemy has emerged, an enemy that threatens their lives, their friendships—and the future of Earth itself.

Series number: SGA-17

STARGATE ATLANTIS: THE LOST

Book two in the LEGACY SERIES

by Jo Graham & Amy Griswold
Price: £6.99 UK | $7.95 US
ISBN-10: 1-905586-54-X
ISBN-13: 978-1-905586-54-7
Publication date: February 2011

Reeling from the terrible events of STARGATE ATLANTIS: Homecoming, the expedition team are doing whatever it takes to find Doctor Rodney McKay—even if it means turning to their enemies for help.

While Colonel Sheppard and Teyla seek information from Ladon Radim of the Genii—and pay a high price to secure his reluctant cooperation—Ronon and Dr. Keller open tense negotiations with Todd. But are they Todd's allies—or his hostages?

Meanwhile, far away, Rodney is facing a fate more terrifying than anyone on Atlantis could possibly imagine…

STARGATE ATLANTIS: The Lost is book two of the exciting new STARGATE ATLANTIS Legacy series.

STARGATE ATLANTIS: BRIMSTONE

by **David Niall Wilson &
Patricia Macomber**

Price: £6.99 UK | $7.95 US
ISBN-10: 1-905586-20-5
ISBN-13: 978-1-905586-20-2
Publication date: September 2010

Doctor Rodney McKay can't believe his eyes when he discovers a moon leaving planetary orbit for a collision course with its own sun. Keen to investigate, he finds something astonishing on the moon's surface — an Ancient city, the mirror of Atlantis…

But the city is not as abandoned as he thinks and Colonel Sheppard's team soon encounter a strange sect of Ancients living beneath the surface, a sect devoted to decadence and debauchery, for whom novelty is the only entertainment. And in the team from Atlantis they find the ultimate novelty to enliven their bloody gladiatorial games…

Trapped on a world heading for destruction, the team must fight their way back to the Stargate or share the fate of the doomed city of Admah…